I0649907

Penumbra

A Journal of Weird Fiction and Criticism

No. 4 ☾ 2023

Edited by S. T. Joshi

". . . a voyage in the very penumbra of death."
—Sir Arthur Quiller-Couch

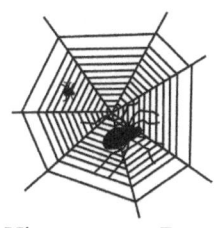

Hippocampus Press

New York

Published by Hippocampus Press
P.O. Box 641
New York, NY 10156
www.hippocampuspress.com

Cover art by George Cotronis.
Cover design by Daniel V. Sauer, dansauerdesign.com.
Hippocampus Press logo designed by Anastasia Damianakos.

PENUMBRA is published once a year, in Summer. Articles and letters should be sent to the editor, S. T. Joshi, ℅ Hippocampus Press. Literary rights for articles will reside with PENUMBRA for one year after publication, whereupon they will revert to their respective authors.

ISBN 978-1-61498-424-5 (paperback)
ISBN 978-1-61498-426-9 (ebook)

Contents

Fiction

Nonfiction

Classic Reprints

Poetry

Notes on Contributors

Adept

Geoffrey Reiter

> "And beyond them, where they stared in troubled and restless wonder, the darkness was illumed with the strange light."—Clark Ashton Smith, "A Vintage from Atlantis"

Of course, the parking lot was empty as I walked to the side entrance of the library. Most of the snow had melted, save for the remnants of plow-piles from last week. The night sky was dark and overcast, though the spangling of amber Christmas lights wrapped around campus's trees served as a substitute for the stars I couldn't see. In that strange artificial brightness, I watched my ephemeral breath emerge with each exhalation, only to be dispersed at once by the December wind. On the perimeter of the parking lot, shadows of the trees splayed out like skeletal fingers, but I stayed squarely in the light until I reached the shadow of the edifice. Reflected in the window of the entrance, all I could see were the little streaks of gray in the hair that framed my face.

I snatched the ID badge from my lanyard to scan it, then fumbled through my coat pocket until I found the key. As always, the old door yielded grudgingly; as always, I felt a brief, absurd surge of panic as I opened it, fearing the alarm, though the security light shone green. The door closed behind me, and now only the red glow of exit signs illuminated the foyer.

That glow was all I needed. What else could I need? I had walked these halls at night dozens of times, and at this time of night I could work without the interruption of coworkers, in the comfort of an oversized sweatshirt and tennis shoes rather than a blouse and heels. Besides, my Christmas gifts had been ordered online weeks ago, so I could either stay alone at the apartment listening to my neighbor and her boyfriend fighting or copulating (or both), or I could make some progress in my research at a time when I had the place all to myself. Now inside, I breathed a sigh of relief at the building's climate-controlled warmth, a breath I could not see. I walked past the check-in point, where an anachronistically sleek sign read "Welcome to the D'Ambrosio Renaissance Library" in red sans-serif lettering.

Beyond that, the DRL started to look more like the museum it truly was. The corridor was lined on either side by canvases, products from the workshops of famous artists or originals from minor painters of the fifteenth and sixteenth centuries. Once again, I couldn't help pausing at my favorite, a rendition of Prometheus by some obscure Paduan. This Prometheus was noble, his nude muscled form standing with poise while bearing a great sphere of flame in an outstretched arm, as though he were proffering it to the viewer. Around the creases of the flame one could make out wraithlike figures, like the angels in Tintoretto's *Last Supper*. But these figures were no angels; I have never known what they were meant to be. Even in the careful light of operating hours those spirits were indistinct; here in the night I could almost forget they were there. And that didn't bother me; after all, it was the great, benevolent countenance of Prometheus that excited me.

Passing through a door framed by the volutes and fluting of ionic columns, I walked across the rotunda, and the echo of my footsteps sundered the silence. In daytime, the blue of the vaulted ceiling shone like a Giotto heaven, but without the lights or the sun to shine through, the color was lost in deep night. I hastened along the marble floor to the small side door that descended into the archives. Once more flashing my badge to a machine, I pushed open the door and continued.

The stairs that led down to the archives were quite unlike the grandeur of the DRL's public sections. They were gray concrete flanked by simple metal rails against off-white walls. One day the library would have to spend the money to make the archives wheelchair accessible, but for now this nondescript staircase was the only way in. So I walked down the steps in the red-tinted deep darkness.

But I paused when I reached the archive entrance because a flickering light was shining out of the door's little windowpane. Pulsations of fear rippled from my chest through my limbs. Grades had been turned in; resident students had returned home; neither IT nor Maintenance worked in the library at these hours. Christmas was still a few days away, but break had already begun. Who could be here? And why was the light that I saw the dancing, sputtering light of flame?

Curiosity seized me, overwhelming for a moment the fear. Clutching my tablet tightly, I brought my shoes down the final steps as quietly as I could and muted my breathing until I came to the window. Tentatively, ready to flee in an instant, I peeked across the unreflecting glass and into the archive room.

The illumination came from the great yew-wood table that stood about ten feet inside the room. On it stood two simple red candles, beside which rested a plain white lighter. The dim, uneven glow of the candles created a tiny, tenuous bubble of light around the table, which was strewn with texts from the surrounding shelves. These were ancient texts, centuries old, restricted from general patrons. I recognized one with a great gilt cover, which lay open near one of the candles. Just beyond it, seated in a chair, was the person who had removed the books, his eyes cast down in concentration on the tome.

"Carson?" I said, opening the door.

His head snapped up quickly as I spoke. "Dr. Cornelius?" he responded. "I—I obviously wasn't expecting to see you here."

"I might say the same," I countered, smirking as I advanced toward the table.

Carson was my research assistant, and he looked more or less the way I always saw him, fidgeting nervously, yet oddly content when surrounded by antique books. He was sallow and slender—I might almost say gaunt—with well-coifed glossy black hair. In class and conversation he almost never met my gaze, but here his hazel eyes looked right back at mine, though the reflected candles cast an orange glaze across his pupils.

"I would guess we're here for the same reason," he suggested. "Research?"

"Sure. And of course you're welcome in the DRL whenever you need to be here. But, at the risk of stating the obvious, we do have lights in the building. You know there'll be hell to pay if the university finds you lit candles in here."

He hesitated, glanced down at the table and the books, then looked back up at me. "Yeah. I imagine it looks kind of weird. I do have a reason for them, though."

"You just really wanted the archives to smell like . . . God, what is that, sandalwood?"

He nodded, then gestured for me to join him. I shrugged and walked closer to the table where he sat. Now I saw that several texts were open on the table, and many more were stacked on the periphery. He had a laptop with him, the glow of its screen the only other light aside from the candles. On that screen, I could see what looked like strange figures, set beside a variety of words in Latin and Greek.

"What the hell . . . ?" I murmured.

"Yeah," he chuckled, "exactly."

"Carson, how did you do this? How did you figure these out?"

"Algorithms, mostly. I know you've been trying to decipher that alphabet for half your career, and I had a hunch about how those characters might be arranged, so I worked up a program to figure it out."

I knelt down beside him, still stuck in stupefied silence. He was right; I'd spent fifteen years trying to make out the lettering of those pages. Once I discovered this seemingly unremarkable yellowing book tucked away in a lonely corner of the archives, I had known right away that it could be my ticket at last to tenure. The fact that it was a detailed and hitherto uncatalogued sixteenth-century alchemical text was tantalizing enough. But then there were those six pages near the end, written in an alphabet more baffling than the scrawlings of the Voynich Manuscript.

Over the years I had been chipping away at the Latin sections, periodically presenting or publishing chapters as I completed them. I had pored over them so much that whole paragraphs or stanzas were embedded in my memory. And the allure only grew with time. The author of the book promised incantations older than historical civilization, dating back to Atlantis. He swore himself an adept from a long lineage of alchemists and sorcerers, revealing enchantments that had never been transcribed in any Indo-European tongue. It was all juicy stuff, and I had long hoped that if could make sense of those final pages, the combination of arcane subject matter and unrelenting imaginative force might be enough to pique the interest of a publisher more ambitious than any generic university press.

I knew Carson helped supplement his RA stipend with freelance coding work, and he'd been invaluable in helping me collate my materials over the past year and a half. I even knew that he came into the DRL after hours to work sometimes; I was, indeed, the one who had given him the keys and the clearance. But what I saw on that screen, if his program was accurate, went well beyond any expectations I could have envisioned. For the first time, it seemed, we could read the hidden esoterica of this five-hundred-year-old quarto.

"Damn," I whispered, peering at the screen. There they were: the invocations of an Early Modern thaumaturge, and Carson and I may have been the first humans to read them since their writing. "And what do they say?"

"I think . . . well, I think they do pretty much what you'd expect based on what you've already translated. If they're uttered the right way, they give the speaker access to realms of power that we could never imagine."

"Wow," I gasped. "This'll be huge. I'm sure we can find a mainstream publisher for this. With all the work you've put into this, you really deserve coauthor status, Carson."

I expected he'd be excited, albeit in his peculiarly reserved way. But at those words he looked over at me with a grin that was strangely bemused, almost incredulous.

"Dr. Cornelius, that's not what I mean. I'm not talking about publication or tenure. The incantations in here—you get it, right? They're real. They really did come from Atlantis."

Carson had been such a joy to teach that, with some effort, I quelled a sarcastic response. Trying not to sound condescending, I said, "Atlantis is just a myth, just Plato making up stories for moral purposes, like he always did."

". . . because there is no Atlantis, no magic, right. That's what I thought too." He looked right at me with an abrupt intensity, and his features looked all ash and flame in the light. "But then I tried them. Dr. Cornelius, I tried them, and they *work*."

For a moment I simply stared, mouth half open. Realizing how unprofessional I must look, I regained my equanimity, forcing an expression of stoic, generic interest.

"Can you tell me what you mean by that?" I inquired.

His earnest but playful Cheshire-Cat grin widened. "I'll *show* you."

He turned away from me back to the laptop. The image moved, and I could see that he was scrolling down the page. Then he came to a passage and began to recite a stanza. At first it sounded little different from any moment I might have heard in class, when he was always eager to read a section from the assigned textbook, whatever language it might be written in. But as he continued to speak, a curious thing happened. The words he was uttering sounded vaguely familiar to me, but he had imparted to his speech an uncharacteristic lilt, giving his words a lilting melodiousness I had never heard from him before. Then the candles flared unexpectedly, expanding the range of their firelight. Carson's voice sounded different now, quiet and distorted, as though I were listening to him from underwater.

The scene of the archive room began to fall away, like paint being scraped from a canvas. But beneath this scene there was another. A piece at a time, shelf and book and wall flaked off, and I found myself looking at a great vista, one that might have been a Renaissance painting itself. I stood high on a promontory, and laid out beneath me, cradled proudly in a high hillside, lay a vast city that stretched down to a bustling harbor. The sun was sinking into the sea in the west toward which the harbor faced, the sky exploding in orange along the cyan horizon, and a great commerce of ships went to and fro from the city's docks, their luxuriantly woven sails embracing the breeze like lovers. Temples rose high upon grand pillars, carved from marble of pale pink and rich red, polished to shine in the waning sun's splendor. Palaces towered higher even than the temples, wrought in a fluid dance of angle and curvature, all harmonized by a geometry that seemed invented for such beauty.

Yet there was more to the sight than grandeur and sublimity. There were houses, modest residences tucked into the threaded avenues, small yet no less elegant than the impossible symmetries of the public edifices, adorned by the weave of wine-grape trellises or little floral patterns etched minutely into window frames. Lately washed robes lay drying on cords, and the householders' green and blue fabrics were scarcely less brilliant or carefully constructed than the blood-purple vestments of priests and nobles.

And about the streets walked the people, grand and beautiful people, with flowing hair and brazen skin, sensuous and wise and imperious in their bearing, walking in stately dignity not unalloyed with tricksterish mischief. They spoke in a tongue more ancient and true than Sumerian or Sanskrit, yet I knew what they were saying and could eavesdrop upon them as they discoursed on rich philosophy and haggled over merchandise and cooed to their lightly resting infants. As the day dropped and men and women ambled purposefully but unhurriedly toward their homes, it seemed to me a picture of every national and domestic perfection I could have imagined and desired— and yes, my desire was bent toward this land and its abundances.

So when it flashed out of my view, I gasped as though I had lost my breath. The candle-lit archives looked shadowy next to the vividness of the vision I had been forced from, and the air felt cold and dry when set against the tropical lushness of the city's clime. Pale Carson was grinning at me, and the familiarity of him anchored me home, though he looked like a faded draft of the exquisite folk whose world I had just seen.

"What was that?" I asked, my voice cracking like an adolescent's.

"You saw it, right?" he said.

"I saw—"

He grabbed my arm—Carson, who had never touched me before. "You saw *Atlantis*—the civilization before there was civilization. I brought forth that vision, from the past where it had just been floating. I took it, and I put you inside it."

I squinted. "What are those candles made from, again?"

"Stop dodging the question," he insisted. "What I just did— that's *nothing*. That's like . . . a kid with the alphabet. But I can *read* this stuff."

I looked at him, then looked up around at the library, where row upon row of books were shrouded in darkness, all but the texts Carson had set upon the table before us. "What does it say, then? What can you do?"

He nodded. "Now you've got it." He clenched his fists and shook his arms, like a baby holding rattles. "It's *so exciting*. We can finally do it, Dr. Cornelius. We can put it all right."

"Put it right . . . ?" I repeated inquisitively.

"*It*. Everything. The world that's all so wrong." He paused, licked his lips as though gathering his thoughts, then resumed. "Think about all the bad stuff that's happened to you. Think about Dave and what he did to you, all his lies, all those manipulations, all those things you would tell me about on Thursday afternoons when the divorce was finalizing. All those damned old men who tried to stop you from finishing your Ph.D."

"Carson, you don't have to bring that up."

He looked at me now with the fixed intensity of a prophet. "No, I mean it. It's not just you. I think about all those years in school, all the bullies—God, with a name like Carson Bacon! Thinking in college that it would stop, that I'd be with people who *got* me, and then still getting hurt and betrayed, over and over and *over* again.

"And then multiply that a billion times and worse. The world, the injustices, the people who get hurt, the people without power." His eyes burned white hot, not from candle flame but from raw, kinetic purpose. *"We are the ones with the power now."*

I didn't reply but looked over his shoulder again at the screen. He turned it toward me so I could see more clearly. The translation he had generated with his technology and his natural aptitude—it all made sense. The words here were like flowers nourished in the soil of the text I already knew. Separately, the Latin already embedded in my mind and the deciphered text before me were dead letters, historical artifacts to be bandied about by a tiny coterie of scholars— scholars like me. Taken together, however, they erupted in vibrant, terrifying life. Even reading them this way, silently on a secondhand laptop screen, my teeth chattered as a surge of inarticulate energy seemed to writhe through my arteries. Scrolling down the page, I committed the words to memory even as I saw them, not through any great prowess of intellect but just because now they made *so much sense*.

"God damn," I breathed.

"Yeah," he affirmed. "So the question is, Dr. Cornelius . . . what do you want to do?"

"Show me more." My voice was barely audible, dry grass crackling in wind. "What can we do?"

Again he spoke words of yore, and as he did so, it sunk in to me: scrawny Carson Bacon—who ate ramen noodles for breakfast and completed smuggled crossword puzzles at student orientations, sitting here at night in a burgundy collared shirt—might be the greatest sorcerer alive. The forces he invoked didn't scorn the childishly nasal intonation of his voice; they simply gathered when he called them.

And gather they did. I have never been punched—not even by Dave at his angriest—though I imagine it feels like the weird intangible pressures that seemed to pummel my side as Carson spoke. But it was more than a sharp pressure; I felt too a squeezing, a constricting, not in my muscles but in my soul. If you had asked me an hour earlier whether I even *had* a soul, I would not have known how to respond; but the great chaotic rush that flooded my meditations gave me my answer. I knew my soul by the phalanx of unnamable entities that now stood garrisoned around it.

This was Carson's power, and he would share it with me; it might be mine as well as his. Now I pictured Dave, that ingratiating, sheepish, wolfish grin he proffered whenever I called out his deceptions, and those angular features handsome in an almost comic-book way beneath his stylized auburn beard. He was talking—God, he's *always* talking—and I could hear the tones but not the words, because how could I care about his words, knowing them all to be falsehoods? And now I realized what I might do—how, with some words of my own, I could at last silence that damned mouth of his. String together a few odd syllables, and I could rend him into a thousand thousand tiny strands of man, shredded atomies of blood and bone, yet each piece still sentient and screaming mindlessly from the agony of it all.

From Dave I worked backward, even as Carson had suggested, through all the wounds across five decades, the little casual scars that so very many people had taken the time to carve into my soul. They didn't feel like scars anymore: each hurt was fresh and raw and bleeding again, from the amassed pain of years to a word carelessly spoken. Time, I realized, had not healed them, so perhaps through these spells might succeed where time had failed, wreaking their stark justice upon my enemies.

Through the gallery of my foes' faces, I peeked out and again saw Carson here with me in the library. But now his face was nothing like the face as I had ever seen it before. Fire and shadow clouded his features, which were twisted into an ecstasy of devotion, the expression of a lover. Yet he was not looking toward anyone or anything, and I did not know what object of adoration was pictured behind his closed eyes. He mumbled the exotic phrases of the book as a mystic must mumble prayers—passionately, breathily.

So intent was he in those moments, so singularly focused on his desire, that I suppose he forgot my presence, and so he let slip free the vision he had been withholding from me. He had enticed me with the sight of Atlantis in its glory, the joyance of the wild, wise land in the aeon of its youth. Through a crack in his discipline, however, I could now behold what he hadn't dared reveal: its dying.

There was that same great port city from that same lofty precipice; yet it was changed. Cracks veined its exquisite colonnades, and chips of stone had eroded free. The panorama was dotted with some buildings taller than even those I had first seen, but they were ugly constructions, their blocky and functional gray bulks incongruous with the workmanship of the neighborhoods into which they had been inserted. Layers of mud and lichen clung to the homes of the ordinary citizens, while paint and plaster were peeling off.

And those citizens looked scarcely better than their abodes. Some in the courts and palaces and temples were still lovely—but a callow, cruel loveliness, beautiful men and women sequestered in disdain from the serpentine streets eating and drinking, then gossiping and retching, and doing it all again when the messes were cleaned. Outside in the streets, the mud and lichens were smeared blearily across the skin and robes of the folk who could not afford to be beautiful and who languished in the choking stench of fresh shit and festering death. I knew somehow that if I searched deep enough, I could have found scattered remnants somewhere, people of the same dignity and prudence as their ancestors, prophets who implored in vain their neighbors to be wary of calamity. Perhaps they had their eyes to the horizon, but no one else did.

But more than all this, I knew that beyond the welter of decay and transgression, among kings and queens and generals and natural philosophers, curious wizards held open on their tables scrolls bearing words like the ones I now could read. They were summoning forth powers from galaxies and dimensions that would have blinded their minds if they had given them a second thought. Yet why ought they to care about the sources of their strength? There were wars to be won and enemies to be subdued. At the cost of a few moments' mumblings, they held all destinies of Atlantis in their grasp.

Or so they imagined, until the day to whose dawning I now bore witness. All the forces the magicians had gathered so assiduously across the years chose this day to flash forth their freedom. The earth at the people's feet dried and ruptured, as mummy flesh, then shuddered like a wild ox shaking off a brittle yoke. Greater quakes followed, and proud towers tumbled on men and women of all rank and stature. The day passed on in my vision, wrack after wrack splintering the gates of the city until, in the evening's last red waning, following the track of twilight, a wave of salt spume that seemed to brush the clouds came racing eastward. The harbor was crowded with ships of people hoping to escape the tremors, and the wet splintered remains of those ships were cast with the limbs of their pilots upon the city's great hill, for the wave exceeded the highest heights of Atlantis. As it came, I felt a bitter bilious surge in my throat, an instant of ineluctable death as a plummeting person must know, for that horrendous tide engulfed my sight.

Then I woke from my vision, and I knew what must happen.

"Carson," I said, my voice hushed through gentleness or terror. "We can't use this. It's not right."

He looked at me, his chapped lips slightly parted, and his eyes grew glossy with restrained tears of betrayal.

"I don't understand," he responded. "I thought you'd be excited about this. All the days we talked about how bad everything was, how we needed to empower other voices. Dr. Cornelius, this is *power*."

I shook averted my gaze, shook my head. "This isn't what I meant."

His chest heaved with great, shallow breaths, and in a whisper that was also a scream he exclaimed, *"Why did you say it if you didn't mean it?"* Reining in his rage, he turned back to the book. "It's—it's okay. You weren't ready; it's wrong of me to hurry you. But *I'm* ready. I'll make things right, and then you'll see. Then they'll all see."

"Carson, please don't—" I began, but he was already chanting new spells as though I were not even beside him.

Once again I felt the coarse knotting in my soul that tracked with his words of power. Caught in that suffocation of spirit, without even knowing what I was doing, I started to speak. The words, those same words, came to me at my requirement. I had no need to read them, for year after year I had embedded them into my thoughts, my very movement, and all it had taken was Carson's transliteration to unlock their fullness. Carson had spent weeks in perfecting the technique of his incantations, but I had spent years living them.

Don't try to stop me. Carson's mouth was still uttering arcana, but he thrust these thoughts at me even as he did so. Yet I could now perceive that beneath that simple injunction was stretched out a great ocean of rage and pain, deeper perhaps than even my own anger. Who could have guessed this, passing by Magnus Hall on a typical semester weekday, that untenured Renaissance scholar Dr. Alicia Cornelius and her unassuming protégé Carson Bacon carried in their psyches such layers of wrath and spite and vile vitriol as might rend the very cosmos?

Leave the books, I implored silently back, and in the world of atoms and physics I stretched out a hand to try to touch him, like the mother I now saw he wished I could be. But he pulled his hand back as though I were a snake, clenching the fist, still speaking in ancient tongues, and so I had to do the same.

Then the powers assembled about us in the room, intelligences invoked in human language but which no vocabulary could describe. In the DRL archives, my body sat whole and well, but my soul burned in their presence with a fire that was orgasmic and agonizing, and I was in love with them and aghast at them all at once. And I wondered how Carson, or the Atlantean sages before him, could ever be so foolish as to think for a moment that these powers were theirs, for I too was aware of them, and I too desired them—oh, my blood and marrow throbbed for them—but I could never forget how casually they might crush me.

So it was, then, that I recited my own words against Carson's. I called down curses from beneath the stars—the library echoed with my screaming words—and I loved Carson, and so I hated him for bringing me to this night, this dreadful combat. I longed for him to yield and cease his speech, to become once more the meek, awkward grad student I pictured in my mind. But he did not yield, shouting words back, wrinkling his lip and he spoke into a sneer as he sought to command the forces that were congregating around us.

In panic, I cried out one last lone phrase from the text on the table. That phrase was enough. It was like kicking out the final support to a tottering scaffold, and suddenly all Carson's intricate magic collapsed, and the weight of the powers rushed upon him, like the vast Atlantic tide. A roar filled my ears, or my soul, or both, a roar like the end of an aeon, and then darkness.

I woke from the darkness into darkness, for the candles had guttered out, though their scent hung in the air. But I smelled more than sandalwood in the archives. Fumbling about, I found and grasped the little lighter, and after several unsuccessful clicks I was able to set once more a tiny sphere of flame atop one of the candles. Carson's body sat face down upon the table, blood dripping quietly from his ears and his nose and his empty eyes. His stiff left hand was clutching at the ancient book, while his right was stretched toward his tablet. Wordlessly I brought my face down and kissed the top of his head on his perfectly combed hair, which absorbed my tears. Gathering up the book and the tablet into my arms, I stared into the candle's meager fire and breathed a sigh.

Across the Wine-Dark Sea

(From Atlas to Carcosa)

DJ Tyrer

Bound to raise the sky
Atlas ossifies, becomes stone
Becoming mountains, peaking high
Across the mountainside
His son Hyas speeds by
In search of prey
Lion, Serpent, Bull, and Boar
For him to slay
Sword and bow in hand
Compassion his blow will never stay
Cornered beast turns to fight
Torn and bleeding hard
Unable to continue its flight
It turns to face him
Turns the tables with fearsome might
Fang—tusk—horn all tear
Ripping flesh and shredding skin
Burning pain too great to bear
Blood gushing forth, cry of pain
Broken bone to sight laid bare
Upon his father's stony hide
Hyas lays sprawled, unmoving
Unseeing eyes open wide
A pool of blood draining
Where he died

His sisters passing by
Stumble by chance on where he does lie

That forlorn grove where he did die
Shocked, bereaved they begin to cry
Consumed by grief they waste, sigh
Join their brother as they too die

Orion, his friend, unmoved is he
For life and death both must be
He turns his attention away
From the beasts that were his prey
To chase the sisters of his dead friend
Pursuing them without an end
As the pursuit carries them into that glen
Those sisters' hearts break again
Their brother dead, their sisters, too
Life is worthless, what left to do?
They take a shard of father's skin
Sharp stone flesh, so they begin
They slice and slit, begin to bleed
Devoted to self-sacrificial creed
And, so, they pursuit escape
Avoiding Orion's intended rape
And fall to lie upon the ground
Unmoving, dead, making no sound
Joining siblings in death
They, like them, have drawn their final breath

King of Gods roaming the sky
Happens by chance to be passing by
Perhaps attracted by their cry
Drawn near by a fading sigh
To the point where the dead do lie
Transports them star-like to the sky
The Hyades, the Pleiades
These groups of star
Attentive gazers see them

View them from afar
Within Taurus, heavenly bull
Their light shines down upon Alar
Carcosa nestles in their bosom
Circling the darkest star of all
Watching, ever watching
Mankind since their fall
Strange urges travel space
Exert their unnatural pull
Of Hyas, alas, there is no sign
The son of Atlas is gone
Does he rule and wear the mask
Listen to Cassilda's lamenting song?
Or does he hide himself away
In a place where he does not belong?
Tears from the Hyades run
Copiously they fall
Will Hastur listen there
Hear Haita's call?
And stem the flow of tears
That threaten the world with a watery pall?

Of that place Hesiod sings
To servants, phantoms and to kings:

"And if longing seizes you
For sailing the stormy seas
When the Pleiades flee mighty Orion
And plunge into the misty deep
And all the gusty winds are raging
Then do not keep your ship
On the wine-dark sea."

For Hesiod saw first what Hali did see
Misty lake Demhe and storm-tossed wine-dark sea

*   *   *

Follow the dark stars
Seek that city lost
Across the fog-foam
Of that sea storm-tossed
Cross the sea and lake and sand
Till you arrive in that Promised Land
Settle in Carcosa
City beneath moons so many
Empty, benighted
Is it home to any?
And here your journey shall conclude
Where tears your path shall occlude

Of that place Hesiod sings
Where flap those unwholesome things
Demons taken flight on leathery wings
Pay heed to what he does say
Do not leave the light of day
And sail those paths that lead away

"Then do not keep your ship
On the wine-dark sea."

He tells you true, you see
That ocean is not the place to be. . . .

An Interview with John Langan

Darrell Schweitzer

John Langan introduces himself well enough in the response to the first question here. He is a very nice guy who writes very scary stories. All I, your interviewer, can say is go, rush, run, shamble to some bookstore or the internet and find one of John Langan's books. *Mr. Gaunt and Other Uneasy Encounters* is a fine place to start. The title story is *genuinely frightening* with a relentlessness that is actually rare in what we sometimes euphemistically call the "horror field." It may also be the finest animate-skeleton story you will ever read.

DS: Give our readers some idea of who you are, where you're from, what your educational background is.

JL: I'm a resident of New York's Mid-Hudson Valley, where I've lived all my life except for two years spent in Albany in my early twenties. I have a B.A. and M.A. from SUNY New Paltz, both in English, and an M.Phil. from the CUNY Graduate Center, also in English. The vast majority of my studies has concentrated on the literature of the last two centuries or so; I've published articles on H. P. Lovecraft, Thomas Ligotti, and Sheridan Le Fanu. I teach part time at New Paltz, usually one creative writing class and one literature class a semester. Lately, I've been teaching a literature class across the river, at Marist College, too. I've been married for the last thirteen years to an amazing woman who's a full-time professor at New Paltz. I have two sons, the older of whom is a police officer in Baltimore City and the younger of whom is in the sixth grade. My older son is married to a lovely girl with whom he has two astound-

We are grateful to Jason V Brock, editor-in-chief of *Nameless Digest*, for permission to publish this interview, which he commissioned.

ing children. I've been publishing horror fiction since 2001; as of this writing, I'm author of two collections, *Mr. Gaunt and Other Uneasy Encounters* (Prime, 2008) and *The Wide, Carnivorous Sky and Other Monstrous Geographies* (Hippocampus Press, 2013), and a novel, *House of Windows* (Night Shade, 2009). With Paul Tremblay, I've coedited an anthology, *Creatures: Thirty Years of Monster Stories* (Prime, 2011). Currently, my agent is shopping around my second novel and my third collection. I also have stories forthcoming in a number of different venues.

DS: So what made you a writer, and a writer of weird fiction of all things?

JL: The short version would be my encounter with Stephen King's novel *Christine*, during the fall of my freshman year of high school. The book had a catalyzing effect on me: the moment I finished it, I knew that this was what I wanted to do.

The longer answer would be that my becoming a writer, and a writer of horror fiction, was likely overdetermined. I came from a family of storytellers: both my father and my mother were ready to drop into a story about their lives, the lives of their families, or a novel or movie they'd seen, at a moment's notice. I experienced trauma at an early age, when I had to have a piece of metal removed from my cornea at the age of about two and a half. I experienced another kind of trauma a decade or so later, when my father suffered a pair of near-fatal heart attacks in quick succession. I was raised in a devoutly Catholic household in which all manner of strange and terrible stories about the lives of the saints, in particular, were told quite often (think St. Denis being beheaded, then rising, picking up his head, and carrying it to his burial place). I was traumatized by a film adaptation of *Frankenstein* when I was maybe nine. I read tons of comic books when I was a kid, mostly the Marvel titles, and aren't they all about monstrous heroes? A lot of what I called monster movies, too, which tended to mean either Ray Harryhausen's pictures or the Godzilla films.

DS: Ah, but wasn't all that trauma (except what happened to your father) a good thing, ultimately? Look at the rich rewards you have gained from it? Did you benefit by getting the crap scared out of you by Frankenstein at age nine? But I wonder if the tendency toward the weird isn't inborn. I too was raised in a devout Catholic family, but monster movies (or even a copy of *Famous Monsters of Filmland*) were strictly banned, and the forbidden fruit. I had to rely on a friend in the sixth grade who would meet me after school and tell me the story of the latest monster movie he had seen at the matinee the preceding Saturday. And yet, here we both are, authors of scary stories.

JL: It's an interesting question: is the creative urge innate, and the trauma polarizes it in a certain direction, or does the trauma give rise to the creative urge, as a means of mediating it? I do think that pretty much every kid experiences things that are too much for them; why, then, isn't every kid a horror writer? Does it have to do with the age(s) at which the traumatic events occur? Or does it have to do with the trauma syncing in some way with a means of artistic expression? No doubt, the answer is something like, "all of the above, and more."

DS: Do I correctly discern more influence of M. R. James or Arthur Machen than Stephen King in your work? You seem to be a subtle, neo-classical sort of writer.

JL: I love both James and Arthur Machen. I've read all of James's stories, but only some of Machen's (though I keep returning to "The Great God Pan"). I am a big fan of the other James, Henry, and Peter Straub, both of whom are, of course, stylists of the highest order, as well as intensely interested in the processes of human consciousness, the means by which our individual minds apprehend and respond to their situations. What I continue to respond to in King is both the range of characters he's willing to write about, as well as the number of different kinds of narratives he's willing to explore.

DS: Of course any writer is more than the sum of what he's read. Would you agree that horror fiction, if it is any good, is intimately personal, in the sense that it must spring from the author's own dreads?

JL: I would agree that (good) horror fiction is intimately personal. I would add, though, that as far as I can see, all (good) art is intimately personal, which is to say, rooted in and nourished by the soil of the artist's particular (and maybe peculiar) self. Dread is part of that, to be sure, but so are a lot of other emotions as well, and I tend to think that, when it comes to horror fiction, the best of it tends to give you a package deal. The writer gives you a sense of her/his personal dreads, but within the context of those other emotions, so what you with up with is the expression of that singular sensibility.

DS: So how do you make a career of it, and go on scaring yourself over and over again, unless you are obsessive? As I am sure you know, the phenomenon of the professional "horror writer" is a recent one. The great majority of Poe's total wordage is not horror. E. F. Benson's ghost stories were only about 5% of his output.

JL: I'm not sure it's an absolute necessity, but it certainly seems to me a benefit for a writer to have at least a touch of obsessiveness. You might also describe it as being passionate, I suppose. In thinking about this question, I'm struck by the example of Ramsey Campbell, for whom horror seems to be a kind of lens through which to view the world, genre as a means of approaching and (maybe) apprehending existence. There's something similar at work in Peter Straub's fiction; indeed, after the publication of his most recent novel, Straub wrote a defense of the horror narrative as a means of engaging the darker side of human experience. If there's an answer to how you continue to work in horror without becoming a parody of yourself, I think it lies in that inclination and ability to use horror to dig into the human condition.

DS: So do you have any idea what you're particularly obsessed with? Or is that for critics to work out after you're dead?

JL: Was it Jim Thompson who said something to the effect of, there are thirty-two different plots, but only one real story: things are not as they seem? That's a dramatic oversimplification, of course, but there's something to it. I think my particular take on that ur-story tends to skew in directions that are central to the horror/Gothic tradition, i.e., the world we think we know is not the world as it is; the self we think we know is not the self as it is. The abyss underlies what's outside and inside us. The sins of the past reach down into the present. I think my work shows a concern with ways of (not) knowing that manifests in a lot of its academic trappings and themes; it's also fascinated with the traditions and history of the horror field. I love monsters.

Having said all this, however, I'm fully aware that there may be a great deal going on in my work of which I'm unaware; indeed, I rather hope that that's the case.

DS: Yes, it can be tricky not to slip over into parody. But there is a matter of dark humor, examples of which we can find as far back as Poe. I read "A Cask of Amontillado" over and over again to writing classes before I began to notice how funny it actually was, while still being horrifying. What is the nature of this balance?

JL: I'm not sure; although I suspect it's of the old "it's humor when it happens to you and horror when it happens to me" distinction that Mel Brooks has observed. At its worst, it has to do with a lack of empathy on the part of the audience for whomever the horrible event is happening to. This is always the risk in working in horror, that it becomes an extended exercise in sadism, a kind of ultra-violent Three Stooges. It's the problem, as I see it, with so much slasher film and fiction, the substitution of ever-more-elaborate means-of-death for any substantial character development, so that what you wind up with is a lethal Rube Goldberg device, whose ingenuity is as likely to produce laughter as anything.

In the case of the Poe story, there's a fascinating manipulation of our empathy for old Montressor, isn't there? How deftly Poe draws us into his point-of-view! (Nor does it hurt that Fortunato comes off as a bit of a buffoon.) I think your question actually contains its own answer: it's a matter of balance.

DS: Maybe the difference between horror and humor is one of realism? Does the pain really hurt or not? The Three Stooges would not be funny if someone was blinded by the eyepokes, or Moe's hammer blow split open Larry's skull and blood and brains went flying.

JL: I think it has to do with the way in which both the perpetrator and the victim of the violence contextualize it through their responses to it, i.e., when Moe strikes Larry with the hammer, he treats the act as both appropriate and not fatal—not even all that harmful, really—and while Larry shows pain, it's not debilitating. The audience cues its response to the context they provide, and laughs. In a horror narrative, in contrast, when Leatherface chainsaws his latest hapless victim, he clearly intends to injure them to the point of death, and the victim responds in a way that shows s/he is being grievously, even mortally, hurt, and the audience adjusts its response accordingly. I suppose this is another way of conceiving what you're talking about when you speak of the realism of the horrific elements.

DS: Let's talk about how you construct a story. I read in the story notes to your collection *Mr. Gaunt* that the title story was rather cursorily rejected, and the language of that rejection sure sounds to me like a *Weird Tales* brush-off of the sort that happened when somebody was rejecting 100 manuscripts a day. (I can assure you I didn't see the story. I tended to write more personalized letters.) Anyway, I gather that afterwards you held the story off the market for a while and then rewrote it considerably. How different is the published version from the original? Do you normally do that much revision, or do some stories just pop out fully formed like Athena from the head of Zeus?

JL: The published version of "Mr. Gaunt" includes an introductory and a concluding section that were not present in the first draft of the story. When I was starting out, I tended to work slowly—indeed, that was almost a mantra for me, work slowly. As long as I could have one story published a year, I told myself I could be satisfied. To be fair, the generous reception my early stories received made it easier to maintain this attitude. But it allowed me to labor over those stories until I was sick of looking at them, whereupon I sent them off to Gordon Van Gelder at *The Magazine of Fantasy & Science Fiction*. At the same time, I thought that it would be nice to be able to complete more than one piece a year. That came with time; once I'd finished my first novel, *House of Windows,* I started to increase the number of stories I was completing each year. I suppose I was becoming more confident in what I was doing. Today, I tend to work on a piece steadily until it's done; although I like to have a month or two to do so. Part of that time, I set the story aside for a few days every so often so that I can return to it with fresh eyes. There are stories that I've been working on, on and off, for a few years, now—"Mother of Stone," the original novella in my most recent collection, took me a number of years to complete. It started off as something I was going to write for an anthology of regional horror stories, and then it kept growing well past the word limit (and well past the deadline for the book). Every now and again, I would return to it between other stories, but it continued to expand. Finally, when I needed an original piece for my last collection, I decided to complete it. I think the last story I substantially revised was published under the title "Bloom," in S. T. Joshi's second *Black Wings* anthology. I had written it a couple of years earlier for another volume of Lovecraftian stories, but the editor rejected it for being "too tentacular." So I completely rewrote the second half of the story. I think the second version is probably a better story; certainly it's more complex than the original.

DS: Too tentacular? What exactly does that mean, in a Lovecraftian context?

JL: Well, I think it meant that the editor was concerned I had aped the external qualities of a Lovecraftian tale without evoking the deeper thematic concerns you find in Lovecraft's work. That said, I do have a story I hope to get around to some day whose title is "Five Million Bullets and Five Million Tentacles."

DS: You seem to be such a slow and deliberate writer. How did you make the transition from shorter stories to novels? How did your first novel come about?

JL: Actually, the first draft of the novel took me about ten months from start to finish, and came in at about 130,000 words. I find that, once I'm engaged in a longer project, it's easier for me to write more—to expand on what I have. As for the genesis of the novel: *House of Windows* was supposed to be a short(er) story that I interrupted what I thought was going to be my first novel in order to dash off. Needless to say, that did not happen. Once it had gone beyond novella length, I decided to go ahead and finish it. I conceived it as my take on the haunted house narrative, and while some of that remains, it seems to me now much more the story of a curse.

DS: Do you see yourself as a classical or neo-classical author, a practitioner of the traditional ghostly tale? "Mr. Gaunt," for instance, deliberately references both of the Jameses, Henry and M. R. So how do you deal with the balance of influence and your own voice or viewpoint? What is the relationship between literary classicism and growth?

JL: I definitely see myself as working within the larger horror tradition, and am happy to identify myself to anyone who asks as a writer of horror stories. That said, I think that the horror field is composed of any number of sub-fields, from the traditional ghostly tale, to the psychological ghostly tale, to the classic vampire story, to the conte cruel—you get the idea. The danger, as I see it, in identifying as a traditionalist comes when your conception of your literary inheritance is overly narrow and rigid. It seems to happen when people decide that only a couple of stories represent what a given writer is actually about, and thus settle for a limited understanding of what that writer was doing. As an example, a couple of years ago I sat down and read through M. R. James's complete ghost stories for a review I thought I was going to be writing. I was astonished at the range of James's achievements. Yes, there were the familiar pieces such as "Count Magnus" and "Casting the Runes," but there were also things like "The Story of a Disappearance and an Appearance," which is just a knock-out of a story. There have been any number of stories inspired by "Count Magnus," but I'm not sure how many there have been that have engaged "The Story etc." So I think that if your understanding of the tradition in which you're working is a more expansive one, then you've already helped yourself not to be straitjacketed and suffocated by it. Not to mention, an appreciation of the way that a writer such as James continued to try new things with the ghost story over the course of his career can help you to undertake your own experiments. Rather than a hindrance to individual growth, an ongoing engagement with a tradition can be a prompt to it.

DS: So can you think of other writers on whose shoulders you stand?

JL: Absolutely—in fact, the more I think about the question, the more writers I can name. To keep the list reasonably manageable: Robert E. Howard, Stephen King, Peter Straub, Flannery O'Connor, William Faulkner, Henry James, and Charles Dickens. I loved Howard's stories when I was in grade school; though it was reading King's *Christine* my freshman year of high school that made me decide this was what I had to do with my life. Straub's fiction offered an immediate and compelling example of how complex horror narratives could be. I think the remaining writers, O'Connor, Faulkner, James, and Dickens, each expanded my sense of how character could be portrayed and how style could be experimented with. At the same time, none of that quartet lost sight of the importance of narrative to a successful fiction.

There are also a number of writers who are my contemporaries or just slightly older whose work I've benefited from reading: Laird Barron, Jeff Ford, Glen Hirshberg, Stephen Graham Jones, Sarah Langan, Lucius Shepard, Paul Tremblay.

DS: What is your relationship with Lovecraft? A major interest? Have you been reading him all your life? Someone you got to later?

JL: I knew about Lovecraft early on, in part because I'd heard his name in connection with Howard's work. Then, when I read King and became interested in contemporary horror, Lovecraft's name popped up again, as an influence on many of those writers. The first work of his I read, however, was *The Dream-Quest of Unknown Kadath,* which left my adolescent self pretty cold, and it wasn't until my late teens/early twenties that I read any of what I guess would be considered his central stories, things like "The Colour out of Space," "The Call of Cthulhu," and "The Shadow out of Time." At that point I was very impressed with Lovecraft, in part because I'd been studying a lot of Modernism, and despite his confessed disdain for much of that literary movement, his fiction struck me as a kind of bizarre version of it. In the years since, I've continued to read and study Lovecraft's fiction. I admire him a great deal as a writer and as a stylist, but the cosmicism that informs much of his work doesn't do much for me—strange as it seems to me to say so, I suppose I still find the viewpoint of many of Howard's stories more congenial.

DS: So what are you up to these days?

JL: Currently, my agent is shopping around my second novel, whose working title is *The Fisherman.* I also have a third collection, *Sefira and Other Betrayals,* that I think we're drawing very near to placing with a publisher. I have stories forthcoming in Ellen Datlow's *Doll Collection* and your own *That Is Not Dead.* I'm trying to complete a half-dozen different stories for various anthologies, and also continue work on my next novel.

DS: Can you imagine yourself moving outside of the horror field, or are you a ghostly guy for life?

JL: I'm pretty happy to be where I am, writing-wise. I love crime fiction, and while I can imagine writing a James M. Cain-esque narrative of murder and revenge, I'm pretty sure it would wind up being a horror story under another name. Horror seems to me the biggest of big tents, and if I live a very long time, I suspect I'll still not be done with it.

Addendum

JL: In the years since last we talked, I published my second novel, *The Fisherman,* which was received much better than I had any right to expect. It won the Bram Stoker Award and the This Is Horror Award, and has been a steady seller in the years since. I followed it with three collections: *Sefira and Other Betrayals, Children of the Fang and Other Genealogies,* and *Corpsemouth and Other Autobiographies. Sefira* and *Children of the Fang* were both nominated for Stoker Awards, and both won This Is Horror Awards. I've continued to publish regularly, usually several stories a year. At this point, I have enough stories for another two collections, but I'm holding off on any more collections until I can complete another novel (which I have started and am hoping to have finished next year). In the mid-to-late 2010's, I reviewed horror and dark fantasy for *Locus* magazine; it was great fun, but it took away too much from my own writing and so I stepped away from it. In the middle of the decade, together with my younger son, I earned my black belt in the Korean martial art of Tang Soo Do. In 2018, I left behind my job as an adjunct instructor in the English department at SUNY New Paltz for a position as a high school English teacher at the New York Military Academy. (Donald Trump's old boarding school, for those interested.) The switch helped my family's financial situation considerably, but it was a difficult transition for me. Teaching in a military boarding school is not for the faint of heart. I wound up as interim dean of academics for most of a year, which I am glad I did, but which I am also glad to be done with. My younger son started college, and is now about to enter his junior year. I joined the adult program at the rock academy he had attended, and just took part in my fifth end of season performances with them. I am ever more aware of the passing of time. In October of 2022, I was on a panel discussion with Grady Hendrix, Stephen Graham Jones, Bracken MacLeod, and Paul Tremblay, at the beginning of which, it occurred to me that we were no longer the new guys. We weren't quite the old guys, either; we were just the guys. Where Stephen King and Peter Straub had been when we started publishing, now we were. (Less the millions of dollars, of course.) I remain ambitious for my work, and gratified to see my friends pushing ahead with theirs, even as such newer figures as Rachel Harrison, Hailey Piper, and Premee Mohammed are making themselves known. I miss Peter Straub, and try to keep his example in mind.

I'm sure there's more to say, but this at least gives some idea of what's been going on in the intervening years.

Come Home, My Children, the Sun Is Gone Down

Arthur Staaz

The whole congregation had noticed a change. A chill unrelated to the outside temperature had begun to infiltrate the church's doors and windows. Night fell suddenly, earlier than usual even for mid-autumn. Everywhere was the smell of mildew and the feel of a pervasive dampness on the skin. We traded stories of nights restless with bizarre dreams and unearthly voices. Those among us who had always slumbered soundly were now induced to wander in their sleep. Then in a vacant lot bordering on the grounds of the church appeared a circus tent, seemingly out of nowhere, abandoned by its proprietors.

Bathed in the crimson glow of an almost full moon, the tent was encircled by rusty steel barricades carelessly arranged around the tract's perimeter. Its three poles were topped with tattered pennants that hung limply above the tent's peaks. In the dim light they appeared to form a claw that clutched at the night sky, as if demanding recognition. Some claimed to hear a rhythmic beating coming from the big top, as if the tent harbored some ritualist drumming monotonously. And though the night was strangely windless, we could nonetheless hear the billowing of the canvas, even as all around was still. The leaves and litter lay dead and undisturbed on the ground, the naked limbs of the nearby trees motionless.

The morning after its discovery, scores of parishioners assembled at the site of the spectacle, as if compelled. All acknowledged that the previous night had been riddled with sinister dreams of the tent. In the shimmer of the morning light, the tent's lurid colors molested our eyes and aroused feelings of obscenity. Gathered in small groups, we tried to recall where the tent had come from, what circus had come to town, and whom we should contact to arrange for its removal. Not one of us could recall having visited the circus. For hours we circled the structure like devotees at a vulgar canvas temple, scanning the grounds for ticket stubs, advertising flyers, and other clues. But the vacant lot disclosed nothing to us.

Left without answers, we soon turned to gossip and rumors. Some told of a traveling show that appeared late one night at the stockyard and marched in silent procession to the lot behind the church. Others passed on rumors of obscene midnight revels on the vacant lot. Whatever occurred, we all agreed that the proprietors and performers had made a quick and quiet exit, leaving us with this scandalous structure.

Among our congregation was one, a traveling salesman, to whom we turned to make sense of this occurrence. For many years we had looked on him with suspicion due to several incidents, long past, involving some unfortunate contacts with children. At the time, we had all thought it wiser not to trouble the authorities with the matter. These things were best handled internally. But there was also another reason. He had always had a strange way of knowing things. Confidences no one had ever shared with him. Affairs we were certain he could not have witnessed. Rumors spread that he had knowledge of matters that could put several leading parishioners in a compromising position.

Nonetheless, when the time came we were glad to have him at our disposal. For the salesman had a deeper relationship with corruption, one that seemed to give him a more profound understanding of the abnormalities that were popping up around us. It was the salesman, after all, who first pointed out the unfamiliar stars that had suddenly appeared in the night sky. And during the barren light of day in the strange journey through this ominous season, he was the one who had called our attention to the thickening darkness that accumulated in places where shadows ought not to be.

Now, in the wake of the circus tent's senseless appearance, many of us looked into his eyes, hoping to make sense of the anomaly that had taken up residence next to our church. *You know,* so many of us thought to ourselves. *You're always the first to know.* And as we wandered around the vacant lot like bewitched sleepwalkers, it appeared to us that potent visions were bodying forth inside him. For there was an unusual effect in his eyes. Of course, it may have just been the excessive brightness of the morning sky or the reflection of the tent's garish colors. But all agreed there seemed to be a ghostly flickering to his eyes, as if a magic lantern were projecting odd images from inside his head.

The salesman's mysterious knowledge, the secrets we believed he concealed, had concerned us for some time. But it was the discovery of the circus tent that fully exposed a greater anxiety that had been lurking for as long as anyone in the parish could remember—an anxiety without reason or focus in the spectacle now on display. Each aspect of the scene—the brilliant colors and glaring sky, the leaves and litter lying still and lifeless on the ground, the defoliated trees pointing with gaunt fingers in every direction—seemed to be the manifestation of an inward turmoil that we all felt. As we stood in quiet vigil around the tent, many swore they heard something like a heartbeat coming from inside.

By dusk most of the assembly had sought shelter, leaving only a few of us, the more devoted observers. Among these was our pastor, who cited several passages of scripture condemning the erection of such a blasphemous structure so near to a house of worship. We instinctually began to dismantle it, tearing at the poles and canvas, ripping the shoddy fabric to pieces, and snapping the fragile wooden supports. Only then was it revealed to us what lay underneath, for a strange uneasiness had dissuaded us from entering the tent.

There should have been nothing there. There were bleachers, of course, made of rough-hewn wooden planks and corroded steel. But there was also a burbling pool of black liquid. Bubbles of a strange consistency mushroomed up from it, forming spheres whose regularity and perfection of form seemed to be the handiwork of some otherworldly master craftsman. As we watched mesmerized, the minister grabbed a longer piece of shattered pole from the surrounding debris and thrust it into the pool. The beam was snatched out of his hands and absorbed almost instantaneously by the pitchy reservoir. The mysterious liquid was otherwise unaffected. Its boiling went on uninterrupted, its percolating black spheres continued rising flawless, geometric, oneiric, levitated by some unfathomable force.

We all gathered around, entranced by the unholy well and its seething gloom. Some few dared to touch the scandalous fountain but had little to report, finding neither the sensation of liquid nor air but something else, something almost impossible to describe. It had the properties not of tangible matter but of some kind of corrupt ether, something that exists in a strange intermediate state between the physical and the phantasmal. And no matter how we attempted to churn the liquid, the procession of perfect spheres continued, rising like flawless specimens of black crystal balls.

"Let's fill it in," the minister said. We all agreed and quickly set about our task. A nearby sand-and-gravel operation provided shovels and fill, and we went to work trying to bury the corrupt font under mounds of gravel and dirt. Yet each shovelful promptly disappeared into the obscurity of the pool. No matter how much we attempted to apply, the fill was swallowed.

For more than half an hour we desperately pitched shovelfuls of dirt into the black liquid, while an assortment of camping lanterns and flashlights cast our dancing shadows across the vacant lot. But the infernal spring was unaffected. Recognizing the futility of our exertions, we stopped and watched as the hideous orbs continued in their eccentric and delirious orbits. Then the full and reddish moon crept above the horizon to mock our useless efforts, its stingy light chilling us as we huddled close together. Helpless, without answers, we engaged in ever more useless deliberations. Eventually discussion failed us and we dispersed quietly, seeking refuge in our various homes.

*　　*　　*

Upon waking the next day, we were once again summoned back to the empty lot from the shadows of our dreams and dark reveries. It was clear that some parishioners had been called from their beds during the night, victims of the sleepwalking that had started to afflict some of us. These were found slowly waking, seated on the bleachers surrounding the effervescent darkness where the main ring should have been, an awakening congregation in search of a nocturnal liturgy.

As we gathered around the bubbling pool, we began to share remarkably similar stories of our overnight experiences. Our beds had provided no sanctuary from the seething cauldron that inhabited that empty landscape. It seemed to demand offerings throughout the night. For some the sacrifice was sleep. The insomniacs among us had approached sleeplessness with the formality of mourners at a wake, sitting quietly or pacing slowly, pensively. For many others it was our troubled dreams that constituted the offering. And we who dreamed shared a common dream. A dream of a church that was not a church but an endless expanse of vacant lot under a black liquid sky circulating with infinite currents of swirling putrescence. An enormous wasteland dimly illuminated by a blood-soaked moon and inhabited by circuses, jugglers, endless rivers of filth, lecherous laughter, and strange transfigurations of the parish landscape. All around there were hawkers and peddlers selling hearts, small fresh ones, still beating and dripping with blood. We all woke up with a feeling of overwhelming foulness, of being no more than a speck of dirt caught up in a black torrent.

One by one we took turns staring into the balls of impurest night rising from the dark liquid. Last of all was the traveling salesman. It soon became clear to us that he had seen what we had seen. For when we turned to him, eyes questioning and imploring, he said, "No. It's not true . . . Well, not completely . . . You wouldn't understand . . . And besides, I have moved on, I assure you."

Our eyes were insistent, vile, fully aware. But he would not give us the satisfaction, certainly not of any further admissions. Nor of now using his particular skills to come to our aid. He walked away, leaving behind a throng that continued throughout the day to occupy that empty space, entranced by the dancing globes of rot and the images they were broadcasting to a wretched congregation.

Again that night, the congregation was molested by fits of sleeplessness and diseased dreams. We who dreamed felt something of our very substance feeding that terrible fountain, as if what circulated in it flowed also through our own veins, thick and contaminated. But we knew not whether we dreamed it or it dreamed us. And once again that night an even larger collection of sleepwalkers paraded to the vacant lot, stray disciples answering the silent invocation of the black pool.

The crowd of sleepwalkers found stirring in the bleachers the following morning was only one example of the mysterious presence that had overtaken our congregation. In retrospect, this presence had always been with us, nameless and just beyond the realm of the senses. But now it was actively haunting our parish, taking up residence in the growing darkness left by the declining sun and providing a poisonous sting to the seasonal cold snap. It seeped through our skin into our very bones. And deeper still. This deviant force had always been there, constantly churning and slowly rising. But now it had erupted from its dwelling place, blossoming from a teeming, dank abyss. Its dark globes boiled up from the poisoned spring like a spurt of black seed, a climax that yearned toward the bloodshot moon and the eccentric movement of the stars. We foolishly continued to look to that very sky for some sense of hope, of deliverance from a higher power. But already we sensed hope was gone, entombed in the darkness beyond the reconfigured constellations.

As we grew more desperate, the salesman began to win a degree of approval. His errant wanderings in years past had undoubtedly been troubling for many of us. And though he had acknowledged to us certain of his transgressions, we had still held our brother at a distance, lest his stain touch us. But now we understood the unique perspective he had on the congregation's predicament. We were sure he could provide invaluable assistance in mitigating the problem. Forgiveness for previous trespasses was abundant, the few he had disclosed to us and the many we suspected he continued to hide. Any suspicions we still harbored were outweighed by our awareness of the seemingly prophetic nature of his past sins. After all, what we had seen in the dark, syrupy burbling of the fountain could not be denied.

Even as the congregation showed its newfound approval of him, the salesman sought to avoid us, at least to the extent he could. But he, like each one of us, was subject to the strange visions that now appeared everywhere and daily called us back to the dark font. He too could not avoid noticing the intertwined vines that ran up the brick walls of the church. How they resembled human limbs, young and old, entwined lasciviously. Hidden in wisps of smoke rising from the censer during our services, lewd faces looked down on him, as they did on every one of us, prompting impure thoughts. By night his darkened bedroom walls, like those of each congregant, lighted up with freakish picture shows—displays of sinister subconscious worlds and regions of absolute chaos. His psyche drank from the same foul stream that surged through the core of each one of us and threatened to sweep us back to an unhuman era. And of us all, he was most affected by it.

Finally, when the black pool started to overflow, when it began to send a tendril of liquid down toward the fence in the direction of the church, things became clear to us. Action was required. We confronted the traveling salesman and insisted that he once again take up his deviant practices. What we required of him was barbarous, true, but only he had the unique expertise for this. And neither refusal nor avoidance were offered as options. Oddly, he seemed quite accepting, relieved even.

Without delay, he began his journey to old familiar haunts in rundown districts of the surrounding city. The salesman traveled alone, isolated all the more by our fear of what his return would confirm to us about ourselves. For he represented our future, a future we had consistently, hopelessly denied. But our fates were inescapably intertwined. We existed now as symbionts, like lichen overspreading a dead stump. His nature slimy and algoid. Ours like fungus, inhabiting and feeding from the dark substratum.

He scoured dingy neighborhoods and disreputable quarters of the city, searching among trashy motels that lined sordid avenues. There one might encounter youngsters more likely to be victims of prior abduction than to be safe within the refuge of a stable family. There one could rely on a ready-made shroud of enforced silence, a silence in which lesser crimes served to conceal greater crimes.

That night, each one of us, the sleepwalkers and the waking sleepers, waited in the bleachers. Our eyes glowed with the lightless radiance of the onyx liquid bleeding across the dirt of the vacant lot, oozing ever closer to our sanctuary. Entranced, we watched the stream, which at times glimmered with putrescent blues and purples, reds and greens, before deepening to black. Its swirling currents reflected the stars of the sky above, generating bedimmed new galaxies on the ground before us.

The traveling salesman returned to us amidst a tension so great in the parish it felt as if the church and statuary, the well-maintained greenery and the cars crowding the parking lot might suddenly shatter into a million pieces. With eyes focused so intently on the moving liquid, we were all suspended in a strange space between complete horror and spiritual ecstasy.

At first we did not see him making his way toward the main ring. Accompanied by the subject of his quest, who was clad in a shabby red-and-white pinafore, he drew near to the dark fountainhead. The congregation descended from the bleachers to surround them and to gaze more deeply into the bubbling corruption that now aimed itself at our darkened church. The fountain's dark orbs exposed many secrets to our enraptured senses. Through some fiendish glamour, a rapid-fire assault of sickening images, sounds, sensations, and fantasies was displayed to us—all the hidden, perverted things each of us had ever thought or done was revealed. Yet somehow they appeared to us as visions of beauty.

He motioned her to come closer. Shy and uncertain, her eyes wandered among the parishioners that surrounded her, a glint of hope in them. "Look," he said. "Look at the bubbles." Obedient girl, she did as she was told.

What happened next is not clear to us. We like to believe she saw what she needed to see. We like to imagine her with a smile on her face, sensing her vital importance to the life of our parish. But perhaps an impulse long suppressed by the salesman produced in him a sudden, fervid episode of frottage. Or perhaps it was mere clumsiness, a thoughtless brushing against her hip. Maybe it happened as many of us swore it did, that the fountain reached some kind of climax, sending out viscous tendrils. Whatever the case, she was absorbed, taken by the dark wellspring all in an instant.

It soon became apparent that the fountain had been placated. The overflow was stopped and the dark liquid withdrew, once again contained within the borders of the pool as we had originally found it. Slowly we began to scatter to our various homes. We found them suffused with a sour smell, as of vermin rotting behind the walls. Despite this, we all reported falling into a deep sleep. That night no one dreamed and no one roamed.

What crime occurred? None, we told one another. We tried to look on the event as a sort of exchange, a payment-in-lieu for the sins made visible in those black orbs. Mostly sins committed through our thoughts and words rather than our deeds, we assured ourselves. And after all, we had an obligation to save the church. In that sense, we were just as helpless as the little ragamuffin, each one of us answering the demands of a non-conscious and non-rational force.

Yet not one of us could deny what we wanted to happen had happened. In the end, something in each of us had demanded that the sludge-dark stream of our communal sickness boil up in a perverse ritual of desecration to submerge an innocent. What could be seen in that fountain was merely the projection of our most secret memories and desires. And certainly once the child had witnessed this, she could not have been allowed to leave.

Since then, we have built a new church over the fountain. Where once only a vulgar circus tent had provided shelter now stands a basilica of the finest granite and most exquisite ebony woodwork. Led by our new minister, the traveling salesman, the new faith has been a success. Not one member of the growing parish misses the nightly worship services. The old church now lies shuttered and empty on the other side of the parking lot.

Day and night, one can hear our prayers rising over the dark orbs, black seeds of decay drenched in the slurry of our corruption and fed by the city's unwanted innocents. We pray without hope, but still we pray. We give thanks to our submerged god for every offering it accepts, for each additional day we are preserved from our fate. We pray for delirious visions from the bubbling shadows, for rapturous nightmares of the crimes we cannot escape.

Mostly, though, we pray for the time that is coming. The time when our destiny is fulfilled, when our being will be dissolved in the endless rivers of our own contamination. We cry out to a god without ears, we plead to a god without mercy, that when our time comes we will be spared from the curse of consciousness.

The Weirding of Climate Change in China Miéville's "Polynia" and "Covehithe"

Deborah Bridle

The two short stories "Polynia" and "Covehithe" were published in China Miéville's 2015 collection *Three Moments of an Explosion*. Although they are set at an unspecified time, the reality that is represented could very well be part of our own present. In "Polynia," icebergs inexplicably materialize in the London sky, while "Covehithe" imagines the return of collapsed oil rigs, emerging from the depths of the oceans like so many awoken Cthulhus. Those two stories are characterized by their resolute belonging to the weird, with their radical alien presences invading our reality, their straddling of various genres without clearly committing to one, and the absence of epistemological closure (Edwards and Venezia 14).

While climate change is never clearly mentioned by the two narrators, it is not difficult to see the apparition of icebergs as a possible consequence of climate imbalance, while the return of collapsed oil rigs is necessarily conjuring up visions of our capitalist petroleum-based economy and its influence on global warming.

One might wonder how the weird's radical alterity, its "beyond-meaning-ness" (Miéville, "On Monsters" 382), and its unrepresent-ability can describe and give any kind of comment on climate change, in all its actuality and its urgency. I contend that the weird and its fundamental slippery nature can attest to the immeasurable scale of climate change today and in the future, and to its somewhat alien nature. By favoring the weird in those two stories, Miéville suggests modes of thinking that engage with our reality differently and may shift our anthropocentric position entirely.

This paper will purposefully focus on a conception of the weird founded on the tenets of the Old Weird rather than those of the

New Weird. Notwithstanding the fact that Miéville is often herald-ed as one of the figureheads of the so-called New Weird genre, the author himself has disavowed the New Weird label (Venezia, "Weird Fiction" 3); more importantly, I believe that the very format chosen by the author—the short story—is a clear tip of the hat to the old masters of the weird. Furthermore, "Polynia" and "Covehithe" create fictional spaces that are less resolutely fantastic than, for instance, those conjured in the Bas-Lag trilogy, considered to be a pinnacle of New Weird. The distinctive features of the weird as proposed by Miéville—the weird as sensation, as irruption of the unfamiliar and the alien in a comforting environment, and the awe and fascination it produces (Miéville, "Afterweird")—are shared by Old and New Weird works alike, hence my choice not to use the New Weird category.

"Polynia" and "Covehithe" are clear representatives of the weird. First of all, they hover over that intersection of genres between super-natural horror, fantasy, and science fiction which Miéville takes as a defining feature of the weird (Miéville, "Interview" by Morgan). Fur-thermore, the weird forms the third point of the triangle of "canni-ness," along with the canny and the uncanny—the abcanny (Miéville, "On Monsters" 381). The abcanny differs from the uncanny in that it does not signal a return of the repressed, therefore the known, but an invasion of the utterly unknown and incomprehensible. As Mark Fisher explains in *The Weird and the Eerie,* the weird is associated with wrongness because it should not be here (Fisher 9). One might disagree and counter that, in both "Polynia" and "Covehithe," the invading presences—or monsters, to tie in with Miéville's love for teratology—are akin to hauntological ghosts, since the readers learn that the floating icebergs are the same as those that had detached themselves and melted in the Antarctic years before the diegesis; and the oil rigs in "Covehithe" are those that had sunk to the bot-tom of the ocean after various accidents. However, the conditions of those returns are so abnormal and unexpected, and more important-ly incomprehensible, that it is not difficult to see those monsters as abcanny occurrences rather than ghostly ones.

In both stories, the narrator toys with his readers by delaying the revelation of what the monsters are: the reader knows that something unusual and shocking is taking place, but the actual labeling of those forces as icebergs and oil rigs is not immediate, therefore reinforcing their outlandish nature. The characteristics and functions that the invading elements showcase also contribute to their categorization as weird objects: not only are the icebergs floating in the London sky, but whenever a fragment breaks apart from the main mass, it seems to levitate there for a moment, defying gravity, before reattaching itself. The icebergs' movements seem haphazard, some of them moving quite briskly while others are almost immobile, never following the movement of the wind. In a clever twist that mirrors the abcanny nature of the weird, Miéville notes that the unknown part of those icebergs is now the tip, which nobody can see from the ground, therefore reversing the famous trope. Finally, the most striking and weird characteristic of those icebergs is that anyone who tries to climb to the top of one of them inexplicably vanishes. In "Covehithe," the oil rigs emerge from the water like huge marine creatures; when they manage to get to land before the army attacks, what first looks like autonomous drilling, then like some sort of feeding, actually turns out to be the laying of eggs in the ground, confirmed by the later apparition of baby oil rigs returning to the sea like baby turtles.

While the weird is the home of the abcanny monster—the Lovecraftian entities are meant to be impossible to describe, impossible to comprehend (Miéville, "On Monsters" 379)—it is also, paradoxically, the perfect environment for characters to express their doomed-to-fail urge to understand, explain, rationalize. In "Polynia" and "Covehithe," this impulse is shown by the need to analyze, identify, and ultimately control the entities, expressed by organs of power and authority like the scientific community, the army, the government, and even the clergy (or other forms of religious faith): "scientists, professional explorers, a few international observers, and escort of Royal Marine commandos" ("Polynia" 8), "while the scientists investigated, a small, powerful cross-party group of MPs demanded that the government blow up the icebergs with incendiaries" ("Polynia" 13), "National governments subcontracted strategy to the UN Platform Event Repulsion Unit: scientists, engineers, theologians and exorcists, soldiers" ("Covehithe" 346). In "Polynia," the icebergs are numbered, identified, and taxonomized, while the oil rigs in "Covehithe" are all found to be previously fallen structures, their names registered as well as the dates and locations of their original demise. Teams are then sent on the ruins of the rigs that the army was able to stop, and a human justification is even sought after as the authorities wonder what they are being punished for. But of course, those efforts are vain, and the monsters remain unattainable in their epistemological alienness.

Miéville's stroke of genius in these stories is that, instead of choosing the point of view of a scientist, an expert, a politician, a general, or any custodian of knowledge and/or power, he prefers to focalize on the other people: in "Polynia", the first-person narrator is an eleven-year-old boy, while "Covehithe" uses the viewpoint of Dughan, a soldier who was among those sent to fight the first oil rig. Even though he is part of the team sent for investigation on the carcass of the Rowan Gorilla I, Dughan is not privy to the discussions and the decisions of those in charge. The purpose of this focalization is twofold. First, it highlights the utter impossibility of grasping the meaning of the monsters' presence. Secondly, it also shows how those presences have invaded our horizon and hijacked our daily conversations and beliefs, just as climate change has. In "Polynia," "social media went mad with theories. The things were dismissed as mirages, advertising gimmicks for a TV show. They were heralded as angels, abominated as an alien attack or a new superweapon" (5), mirroring our own divide between climate skeptics and believers in global warming, with a dash of conspiracy theories, political manipulation, and plain old apocalypticism.

The new entities also correspond to textbook weird creatures, characterized by their inhuman proportions and/or their composite and aberrant nature, displaying a certain grotesquerie that is known to tread the same paths as the weird (Fisher 15; Gunderson 13–14). The icebergs are "glowing things the size of cathedrals" ("Polynia" 5), and the oil rigs are akin to exabyssal[2] gigantic structures part machine, part animal, part plant: "the pylon barnacled, shaggy with benthic growth now lank gelatinous bunting" ("Covehithe" 343), a "quadruped skiing" (343), "their cables and pipes are flailing like ill-trained snakes, like too-heavy feeding tentacles" (345), leaving behind a "mashed-up trail, [a] rainbow-filmed liquid spoor," "struts still thick with coraline outgrowths" (346), "shaft-legs like some impossible dreaming pachyderm" (347), full of "abyssal rot and chemical cracking" (348), the portrait of alien hybridity and weirdness culminating in the imagination of oil rig sex, and the vision of one of the rigs' "drill ovipositor injecting slippy black rig eggs into England" (352).

However, one might wonder whether the weird short story is an adequate and even desirable way of representing climate change. Ecocritics such as Adam Trexler and Astrid Bracke have noted the novel's difficulty in tackling something like climate change because of the immeasurable scale of the phenomenon and the novel's fundamental anthropocentric position, with its traditional focus on human affects (Trexler, "Mediating Climate Change" 205; Bracke 424). Others, such as Schneider-Mayerson, believe that the novel's possible complexity and scope is the least that is needed in the fic-

---

2. Exabyssalism: "The cultural weight of many horror-inflected denizens of earth or water is not derived only from their subsurface existence, but has its vanishing point in that submergedness's momentary cessation at the point of predation—the breach. The bad numinous of sandworms and ant-lions, great whites and the trout that tries to eat Jeremy Fisher culminates in those brief hungry emergences-into-light. Thus describing the former two as 'telluric' or 'chthonic', the latter as 'aquatic' or 'submarine' is, while true, inadequate. Such dryland breachers would better be described as eruchthonous; the wet as exabyssal" (Miéville, "An A–Z of China Miéville": E is for Eruchthonousness & Exabyssalism).

tional format to represent climate change adequately (312). For both those standpoints, the short story would seem to be far too limited to be a suitable vector for the representation of climate change. It is also a form that is known to cultivate a unity of effect and a focus on sensation that would appear to offer only a partial view to the matter at hand. In the case of Miéville's short stories, this is heightened by the fact that the author deliberately obscures the events of the plot, gives a limited number of details, and never explains the reason behind the weird phenomena described.

So how can the weird short story succeed where the science fiction novel (or saga) is known to excel? Indeed, science fiction is the choice literary genre to describe climate change because of its necessarily futuristic outlook and the importance of scientific knowledge in the description of climate phenomena (Canavan and Robinson x). What the weird manages to achieve particularly well is the major step that needs to be taken away from anthropocentrism. Marianne Gunderson states that we are facing today "the limits of anthropocentric perspectives, the subjectivity and agency of the fundamentally non-human, and the otherness of the natural world" (13), what Miéville calls the weird's "anthropoperipheral universe" ("Quantum Vampire" 112). Even though humanity has a large role to play in the advent of climate change, a weird approach serves to shift the focus on the never-before-seen scale of its phenomena, from extreme weather manifestations to the new forms of diaspora they cause. Consequently, the absence of explanation serves the same purpose. As Phoenix Scholz writes in a review of *Three Moments of an Explosion*, "like all the best Weird short fiction, the stories often start with something very mundane, followed by the realisation that the world just doesn't work in the way their characters had always assumed, and that there's no coming to terms with that."

As Miéville himself explains in an interview conducted by Jeff VanderMeer, "given the somatic impossibility of monsters—without which they are nothing—their simple there-ness and specificity is indeed part of what makes them what they are, a self-contained, if highly and, one hopes, effectively hermetic, narrative, an implied 'There was a thing that was, impossibly, like this'" ("China Miéville and Monsters" 4). Because the monsters he describes are a totality in and of themselves, they can work as a way to represent climate change in all its alienness, because that is the way it can make us feel in the way it disrupts our lives and our future. Because climate change is protean, hard to circumscribe, overwhelming, and never seen before, it can admirably be represented by the weird, which, for Miéville, is "a placeholder for the unrepresentable" (Edwards and Venezia 4), while its monsters are the "narrative actualisation of the Weird-as-novum, unprecedented, Event" (Miéville, "Quantum Vampire" 110). The absence of any given meaning does not signify that there is no meaning, that it is all absurd, but that the meaning is beyond anything we can grasp: "That is the axis on which [the abcanny] works, and by the deployment of which it (inevitably) means. These monsters mean, while they meta un mean" (Miéville, "On Monsters" 382).

As a result, not being given a meaning does not preclude our trying to find one, and the alterity and the scale of the weird phenomena described in the two stories can be seen as a way to describe climate change as a weird global invasion of our reality. In "Polynia," there are passing references to other inexplicable manifestations in the world that may be linked to the London icebergs: in Brussels, coral has started to grow over the surfaces of buildings all over the city, while factories of electronic components in Japan have been invaded by rainforest undergrowth. The global impact is shown in "Covehithe" by the fact that eight oil rigs that collapsed in different parts of the planet are now resurfacing in various locations over the planet. As far as time is concerned, the stories convey the idea that the phenomena described are not going to stop anytime soon, and that they are the consequences of actions in the past (icebergs having disappeared in the Antarctic, which can be linked to the melting of the ice caps, and the collapse of the oil rigs decades earlier). The new weather conditions that are induced in London—microclimates of intense cold directly below the icebergs—brings climate change and its unnaturalness to our doorstep, something that the following image brilliantly shows: "the iconic shot of the team crossing an ice bridge between two forbidding white crags, with the slates and aerials of Wandsworth far below" ("Polynia" 9). In "Covehithe," the apocalyptic dimension of climate change is crystallized in the pithy expression "Hydrocarbon Ragnarok" (346).

Interestingly, it can be said that, as the weird offers a new vision of climate change, climate change in turn infuses literature with a new impulse and encourages the exploration of new modes of writing. As Adam Trexler notes, "the narrative difficulties of the Anthropocene threaten to rupture the defining features of genre [. . .] Novels about the Anthropocene cannot be easily placed into discrete generic pigeonholes" (*Anthropocene Fictions* 14), and therefore converge toward a blending of genres. For Pieter Vermeulen, climate change is a hyperobject "that eschews representation, and that is intimated precisely in the *breakdown* of literary form. Planetary change remains fundamentally unrepresentable, and [. . .] literature must first of all register the insufficiency of traditional modes of expression and representation. Form, in Timothy Clark's words, is merely 'something to be interrupted, broken or questioned'" (9).

As a genre that is difficult to pin down and that is at the crossroads between different categories, the weird encourages this "breakdown of literary form" and prompts authors to think of our world differently. This is why the weird is, for Miéville, something to take at face value. Many critics have underlined the lack of ironic distance that distinguishes the weird from postmodernism (Murphy and Noys 128; VanderMeer). Miéville himself frequently mentions the need for a "literalism of fantastic" ("China Miéville and Monsters" 3), in the sense that genre fiction literalizes its metaphors rather than function as allegory only:

> to literalise your metaphor does not mean that it stops being a metaphor, but it invigorates the metaphor because it embeds its referent within the totality of the text, with its own integrity and

realism. [. . .] The point of course, is not only that you could have both: the paradox is that genre *by its very literalism* invigorates both its metaphor and its 'internal' reality. ("Gothic Politics" 65)

In another interview, Miéville describes this interplay between literalism and metaphor as the surrealist and the rationalist facets of the weird ("Reveling in Genre" 366).

Taking the weird manifestations seriously within the fabric of the story also means accepting the awe it is inseparable from, and the surrender to the weird that the author advocates on an everyday basis. Indeed, the weird

> is to do with the sense of the numinous, [. . .] as being completely embedded in the everyday, rather than an intrusion. To that extent the Weird to me is about the sense that reality is always Weird. [. . .] I think what the Weird can do is question the arbitrary distinction between the Beautiful and the Sublime, and operate as a kind of Sublime Backwash, so that the numinous incomparable awesome slips back from "mountains" and "forests," into the everyday. So . . . the Weird as radicalised quotidian Sublime. ("China Miéville and Monsters" 2)

In "Polynia," this surrender to the weird as an acceptance of our reality is best seen through the behavior of the narrator and his friends, all pre-teenagers who embrace the weird event as part and parcel of their world, who play games mimicking the explorers' ascension of the icebergs, and who collect information on them and sometimes exchange them as they would Pokémon cards. It takes longer for the adults to follow, but little by little the weird is accepted as part of their daily lives: new items of clothing, named "bergcoats," are designed to allow their wearers to switch effortlessly to warm winter clothing when an iceberg flies over their location, Stansted Airport reopens, followed by the other London airports, the BBC commissions a drama series on iceberg investigators, and the City sets up telescopes at various points to turn the icebergs into tourist attractions. Far from being considered normal, the icebergs still elicit awe in humans, but they have been accepted in their quotidian life.

The point of this acceptance is to engage metaphorically with our present reality and potential future. The fantastic, and in particular the weird, has the ability to speak about real-life issues. For Timothy Murphy and Benjamin Noys, "rather than the ontological creation of an alternate reality, Weird fiction probes this 'absolute reality'" (128), and Miéville has frequently commented on his belief that the fantastic is no less sincere and insightful about reality than so-called realistic books ("Editorial Introduction" 42; "An A-Z of China Miéville": Z is for Zone), and on the idea that "changing the not-real allows one to think differently about the real, its potentialities and actualities" ("Editorial Introduction" 46). Therefore, genre literature can also include a reflection on the future, based on how it makes us think about our present. This is why Miéville is absolutely opposed to the consolatory trend in Tolkienesque fantasy and refuses "to posit societies as internally coherent, consistent, bounded, and essentially safe. They are fractured and dangerous" ("Reveling in Genre" 373). Because reality is absurd and grotesque, the weird can be used as a tool to reflect on it and to explore the instabilities that pervade it. And because the weird is a subtle and protean manifestation of the fantastic existing in its "interstices" (VanderMeer), this definitional uncertainty makes it the perfect medium to look through the holes in our ripped worldweave (Miéville "Afterweird" 1146).

One of the most important things that the weird therefore reveals to us is the profound alterity of our reality. Alterity is what constitutes the main focus of genre literature for Miéville ("Gothic Politics" 64), which explains why he proposes to revisit Suvin's definition of science fiction by focusing on an estrangement based on alterity rather than a cognitive one, which will in turn allow the erasure of the hierarchy between SF and the other modes of the fantastic. The weird becomes a metafictional tool to observe and analyze issues of alterity, hybridity, and liminality, and therefore to "wedge open a space in which to consider radically Other subjectivities and wholly alien ways of thinking" (Edwards and Venezia 5).

In "Polynia" and "Covehithe," we are made to acknowledge that the weird has invaded our reality and made it even weirder than it was before. We need to accept the phenomena depicted, in all their awesome weird alterity. In the two stories, the experience of the weird manifests itself in the new experience of climate change. By refusing consolation but also a vision of doom and gloom, Miéville makes us wonder about what our future with climate change will be and encourages us to find new modes of thinking to accommodate the weird. For Zak Bronson, "by constructing fantastical worlds that continually thwart established rules and expectations, Miéville [. . .] unmasks the limitations of social imagination and holds open the utopian possibilities of imagining the world otherwise—of conceptualizing 'the not-this-ness of this' (as he puts it in *Iron Council*)." This is also what Gary K. Wolfe calls "the post-genre fantastic," which Miéville uses to think through different political alternatives (Edwards and Venezia 7). Even though the author does not use his fiction as a propagandist tool, he allows some of his political concerns to seep in his stories (Miéville, "Reveling in Genre" 363), which goes hand in hand with the fact that, as Adam Trexler notes, "nearly all climate change fiction is political, in one sense or another" (*Anthropocene Fictions* 119). In an article, Miéville tackles the problem of climate and its political dimension by claiming that the Anthropocene should rather be called the Capitalocene ("The Limits of Utopia"), but his novels, and even more so his stories, will not spell it out so clearly. As Mark Williams explains, the reader has to "pick up the threads which lead out into the wider world of the story; and thence into a new perspective on their own location within the complex webs of actually existing globalised interrelationships, previously unseen or unconsidered, in their own lives" (31).

The two stories invite this mental process of analysis of our current world—the global scale of weird natural phenomena in "Polynia" questions our globalized economy and the potential repercussions of our actions at the other end of the planet, while the last paragraph of "Covehithe" allows us to see the oil rig return as part of a wider and human-sanctioned network of cause and effect rather than just a weird kaiju scenario: "Dughan turned and took in the length of Covehithe Beach. They were out of sight, but he looked in the direction of the graveyard, and of St Andrew's stubby hall where services continued within the medieval carapace, remains of a grander church fallen apart to time and the civil war and to economics, fallen ultimately with permission" (353).

Because the stories are neither consolatory nor hopeful nor pessimistic, they also reflect Gerry Canavan and Kim Stanley Robinson's comment on the necessary dialectics between utopia and apocalypse: "they are each disguised versions of a single imaginative leap into futurity" (16). It all starts in the present and very much depends on how we decide to take action today. Miéville even goes further by stating that "we live in utopia; it just isn't ours. So we live in apocalypse too" ("The Limits of Utopia"). The current political, economic, social, and ecological situation is both utopian and apocalyptic, depending on which side you stand. There is undeniable futurity to climate change genre fiction, but for Miéville the urgency is in the present, and the fantastic can be politically relevant without being future-oriented: "no matter how commodified and domesticated the fantastic in its various forms might be, we need fantasy to think the world, and to change it" ("Editorial Introduction" 47–48), and that change is an urgent matter.

"Earth: to be determined. Utopia? Apocalypse? Is it worse to hope or to despair? To that question there can only be one answer: yes. It is worse to hope or to despair." In a capitalist world precipitating the climate catastrophe, there is such a thing as bad hope and bad despair, so "we must learn to hope with teeth" (Miéville, "The Limits of Utopia"), which means sustaining a hope tempered with constructive pessimism, keeping on dreaming our impossible utopias, and fighting for social change—the only way that environmental change can really happen.

Works Cited

Bracke, Astrid. "The Contemporary English Novel and Its Challenges to Ecocriticsm." In Greg Garrard, ed. *The Oxford Handbook of Ecocriticism.* Oxford: Oxford University Press, 2014. 423–39.

Bronson, Zak. "Thinking Weirdly with China Miéville." *Los Angeles Review of Books* (13 January 2018), lareviewofbooks.org/article/thinking-weirdly-with-china-mieville/. Accessed 5 March 2023.

Canavan, Gerry, and Kim Stanley Robinson, ed. *Green Planets: Ecology and Science Fiction.* Middletown, CT: Wesleyan University Press, 2014.

Edwards, Caroline, and Tony Venezia. "UnIntroduction." In Caroline Edwards and Tony Venezia, ed. *China Miéville: Critical Essays.* Canterbury, UK; Gylphi, 2015. 1–38.

Fisher, Mark. *The Weird and the Eerie.* London: Repeater Books, 2016.

Gunderson, Marianne. "Decentering the Human in Weird Horror." *Women, Gender & Research* Nos. 2–3 (2017): 12–24.

Miéville, China. "Afterweird." In Ann and Jeff VanderMeer, ed. *The Weird.* New York: Tor Books, 2011, ebook format.

Miéville, China. "An A-Z of China Miéville." 26 January 2012, www.panmacmillan.com/blogs/science-fiction-and-fantasy/an-a-z-of-china-mieville. Accessed 31 March 2022.

———. "China Miéville and Monsters: 'Unsatisfy Me, Frustrate me, I Beg You.'" Interview by Jeff VanderMeer. *Weird Fiction Review* (20 March 2012), weirdfictionreview.com/ 2012/03/china-mieville-and-monsters-unsatisfy-me-frustrate-me-i-beg-you/. Accessed 5 March 2023.

——— "Covehithe." In *Three Moments of an Explosion.* London: Macmillan, 2015. 5–25.

———. "Editorial Introduction to the Symposium: Marxism and Fantasy." *Historical Materialism* 10, No. 4 (2002): 39–49.

———. "Gothic Politics: A Discussion with China Miéville." Interview by Stephen Shapiro. *Gothic Studies* 10, No. 1 (May 2008): 61–70.

———. "Interview: China Miéville." Interview by Cheryl Morgan. *Strange Horizons* (1 October 2001), strangehorizons.com/nonfiction/articles/ interview-china-miville/. Accessed 15 March 2023.

———. "The Limits of Utopia." *Salvage.* salvage.zone/mieville_all. html. Accessed 20 March 2023.

———. "M. R. James and the Quantum Vampire: Weird; Hauntological: Versus and/or and and/or or?" *Collapse* 4 (May 2008): 105–28.

———. "On Monsters: Or, Nine or More (Monstrous) Not Cannies." *Journal of the Fantastic in the Arts* 23, No. 3 (2012): 377–92.

———. "Polynia." In *Three Moments of an Explosion*. London: Macmillan, 2015. 339–53.

———. "Reveling in Genre: An Interview with China Miéville." Interview by Joan Gordon. *Science-Fiction Studies* 30, No. 3 (November 2003): 355–73.

Noys, Benjamin, and Timothy S. Murphy. "Introduction: Old and New Weird." *Genre* 49, No. 2 (July 2016): 117–34.

Scholz, Phoenix. "Three Moments of an Explosion by China Miéville." *Strange Horizons* (26 October 2015), strangehorizons.com/nonfiction/reviews/three-moments-of-an-explosion-by-china-mieville/. Accessed 20 March 2023.

Schneider-Mayerson, Matthew. "Climate Change Fiction." In Rachel Greenwald Smith, ed. *American Literature in Transition, 2000–2010.* Cambridge: Cambridge University Press, 2017. 309–21.

Trexler, Adam. *Anthropocene Fictions.* Charlottesville: University of Virginia Press, 2015.

———. "Mediating Climate Change: Ecocriticism, Science Studies, and *The Hungry Tide*." In Greg Garrard, ed. *The Oxford Handbook of Ecocriticism*. Oxford: Oxford University Press, 2014. 205–24.

VanderMeer, Ann, and Jeff VanderMeer. "Introduction." In Ann and Jeff VanderMeer, ed. *The Weird.* New York: Tor Books, 2011, ebook format.

Venezia, Tony. "Weird Fiction: Dandelion Meets China Miéville." *Dandelion* 1, No. 1 (Spring 2010): 1–9.

Vermeulen, Pieter. "Beauty That Must Die: *Station Eleven*, Climate Change Fiction, and the Life of Form." *Studies in the Novel* 50, No. 1 (Spring 2018): 9–25.

Williams, Mark. "The Weird of Globalization: Esemplastic Power in the Short Fiction of China Miéville." *Irish Journal of Gothic and Horror Studies* No. 8 (2010): 30–40.

Through Enchantment

Geoffrey Reiter

The journey passes through the darkened wood
The well-worn path a slice of gathered green
Shard-shadowed at the margins, thick as blood
And bark. Here goblins grow in stones, unseen,
As dryads dance to please a fairy queen,
Who reigns in rage and revelry, while elves
Flit feyly from their firelit haunts between
The boles and knolls and deeper diamond delves.
The people passing on the path themselves
Thread through the thicket where the sunrays slant.
Perhaps they see past shadows to the shelves
Where fair-folk flock and spirit-sprites enchant.
They crowd in crowing wrath and languid laughter—
Then, past this path, we find our ever after.

Just Like Them

Norbert Góra

Since I came to the city, I immediately realized that I wouldn't fit in there. This place was nothing more than a round-the-clock mirage of lights with colors that change depending on the time of day and noises of various intensity that resembled thickening, devilishly black clouds of smoke, pushing aggressively into the mouth.

I was slowly dying mentally. I felt like a visitor from distant stars. Dead inside, though the body was young. I woke up in the morning to the sounds of a community that never seemed to sleep. Night brawls mixed with dawn screams, afternoon meetings, then hustle and bustle of conversations in crowded venues, reeking of sweat and alcohol.

This city was like a blend of a thief and a serial killer. First it stole time; then savings and health; finally it took your whole life. Knowing what I was losing while staying here was definitely killing me.

I've tried everything to neutralize the despair rising in my heart. I started with wine. Well, on TV they kept repeating it could heal us, so one glass of this drink a day was highly recommended. I didn't even notice when one turned into three, then six. It was easy to guess that, after all, I couldn't get through twenty-four hours without at least a bottle of wine.

I switched to drinks, but they quickly wore off as well. After four glasses, I cried more than when I was sober. The passage of time was pushing me more and more against the wall, separating me from finding a remedy for depression.

The feeling of overwhelming senselessness, which had already reached the size of a black hole in my mind, sucking all the life energy into itself, led me to this final thought. I chose a specific day from the calendar and acknowledged it for the end of evil. I even wrote a script, step by step. To realize it, I had to go to a pharmacy.

Leaving this place filled with shelves full of medicines, after walking less than a kilometer, I stopped for a moment at a clothing store that was located next to my block of flats. I gazed at the glass case. Something stirred in me. I knew my plan would fail.

Behind the glass separating the shop from the street stood a dainty mannequin. It was wearing clothes that meant nothing to me. I admitted it without a shame: as a young woman I had absolutely no sense of fashion and current trends.

I stopped believing in the normality of fashion designers long ago, but now I stood and admired. No, not clothes. The mannequin was the reason.

Big eyes looked somewhere to the left. Watching them, I wasn't aware I was getting closer and closer to the glass. I wasted my time staring at the static, human-like figure. There was something hypnotic, magical about those eyes.

It took me a few blinks to realize that I was standing almost glued to the glass, and two women behind me whispering. I glanced in their direction. They looked at me with a mix of surprise and disgust. I took a step away from the storefront and quickly reached for my cell phone. I wasn't going to call anyone. I just wanted to give them a reason to go away. When they finally left, I looked back at the mannequin. For a moment I had the irresistible impression that those artificial, factory-printed eyes blinked. I flinched. No, it's not possible. I must have been imagining something, but . . . damn it, I could have sworn it was real.

Without thinking, I turned toward the front door to my stairwell and headed in that direction. However, before I crossed the threshold of the apartment, a feeling came over me that I hadn't dealt with in a long time. It couldn't be described in words. A sense of gradual loss of particles from a huge collection called the soul. Most importantly, it had nothing to do with depression.

I wasn't sad. Rather, I was terrified that the remnant of my normality that still held me together in this strange, incomprehensible world was about to leave. I tried to sleep, but every time I closed my eyelids I saw the mannequin behind the window, blinking again and again like some kind of wind-up toy.

I decided to find another way to work and back, so there were no longer nightmares. One day I was returning in an extreme rush and completely forgot about my resolution. I took the old route past the store. I stopped, wondering why I was going this way.

It was too late. The dummy behind the glass was turned toward me. I wanted to leave, but whatever was with those fake eyes was preventing me from doing so.

With great resistance, I glanced at the street. Then something happened that I never expected.

"Be one of us."

I heard this voice in my head. Subtle, warm, and soothing. Finally, after a long time, the overwhelming feeling of life's emptiness disappeared. I looked back at the figure.

"How?" I asked after making sure no one was around.

"Take me with you."

Another voice in my head, responsible for self-control, growled: "Idiot! The mannequin can't talk. Don't take it serious, girl! You're tired, it's true, so relax."

Anyway, I took a step toward the front door of the store with a ready scenario of what would happen. Nothing could stop me. Not now, when the blessed feeling of silence was pouring into my soul.

I made up the craziest story about an uncle opening a tailor's shop, who needed the dummy urgently. I told it to the manager of the store, swearing I would surely give it back.

My words, filled with pleas for help, seemed to soften the heart of this girl. When I left the store and came to the apartment, I felt relief. I put the figure on a large couch, upholstered in a ruby-colored leatherette that didn't quite match the rest of this room.

"It's time to begin the initiation," said the same voice in my head. I sat next to the mannequin and looked at it.

"What should I do?"

"Let the static win in your body."

"What does it mean?" I asked, knitting my eyebrows together.

"Let the silence flow through you as if you were a river. Don't think about anything that worries you. Reunite with your inner calm."

Not knowing how exactly I was supposed to reunite with my inner calm, I slid off the couch, sat on the mahogany parquet floor, and began to meditate. Previously I considered such practices to be an absolute waste of time. Now it was different.

A sound in the endless darkness. At first it was weak, as if coming from behind a thick wall. It reminded me of the blow of a fly-swatter. I don't know where it was coming from, but I heard it. Then it gradually gained in intensity. It brought back to my mind the sound of a drop hitting wood. Later it transformed into the pouring rain. I even felt it dripping onto my face.

Drip. Drip. Drip-drip-drip. Damn it!

I woke up screaming. My eyes slowly regained focus. I was lying on the floor. The sounds of rain came from my cell phone. I swallowed and looked at the screen. It was seven o'clock in the morning. The alarm went off. It always did that from Monday to Friday, bringing me from the dreamland to this vale of tears. I narrowed my eyes. I don't know when I fell asleep, but I knew I wasn't going to work.

I dialed my manager's number and informed him that I needed a week off. He didn't even ask. Only confirmed and hung up, laconically saying, "See you then."

Sweet God. It was another proof that my presence in this company didn't change anything. I might as well bleed to death within these walls. They would replace me faster than a chair. Sighing, I looked over to the couch. The mannequin was still there.

"Don't stop."

Even though I was sore, I had no intention of doing so. I haven't felt as happy as I do now in a long time.

* * *

After a week, I was close to perfection. I could stand still for ten hours. I didn't eat and drink. I managed to turn off the consciousness. I was immersed in the vastness of inner silence. On Sunday evening, at the end of my week off, I heard this voice once again.

"You're ready."

I smiled, but it quickly faded from my face as the sound of the doorbell pierced my ears. I felt a shiver of anxiety. When I peeked through the peephole, I went pale. It was the landlord. A gruff old man with almost platinum hair. He burst into the hall like a locomotive.

"God, what a stench!" he roared, waving his hands. "What were you smoking here? This suffocating smell can be felt from the entrance to the staircase!"

I glanced over to the couch and sniffled. I didn't feel anything, though I didn't remember much from that week. The landlord finally entered the living room and stood frozen, staring at the mannequin laying on his couch.

"Please, I will explain everything," I stammered with difficulty, taking a step back. The man turned to me and narrowed his eyes.

"Enough! I didn't intervene when a neighbor reported to me that you throw two or three bottles of wine into the waste bin every night. I didn't say anything when you were late paying your rent. Now you've overdone it. I won't let you ruin my flat!"

I put my head down. Not to show remorse. I had no interest in fulfilling the expectations of him or any other man. People have always wanted something. They kept demanding, but as soon as I made a request I was disregarded. No one has ever understood what I feel. Loneliness in a crowded city took the air out of my lungs.

"Tomorrow, at eight P.M., you have to give me back the keys. The lease agreement is over," the man said dryly and left the apartment. Under any other circumstances I probably would have collapsed. I might even run after him, begging him to change his mind. But now I just closed the door and went back into the living room.

"Don't worry. You're ready," I heard a whisper in my head. Then I started practicing for the last time. I concentrated as hard as I could and I did it. Finally. I turned off my consciousness. Forever. I was just like them.

The Dead Have Left a Wake-up Call

John Shirley

Grandmother Musquette lifted her head
You hearin' things again, her husband said
"'Twas a chiming in the empty hall
"For the dead have left a wake-up call!"

Half-mad Lindy couldn't hold his hounds
It seemed they heard an unhearable sound
They ran through the brush to the graveyard wall
"For the dead have left a wake-up call!"

The priest was fearful to be discovered
He prayed his crimes were not uncovered
Then he heard a bell where there was none at all
"For the dead have left a wake-up call!"

Wild-haired Wendy was reading my palm
When her cockatoo sang an unknown psalm
She said, what cannot walk can always crawl
"For the dead have left a wake-up call!"

A troubadour heard a voiceless choir
And a fingerless strumming on his lyre
His horse was shrieking in its stall
"For the dead have left a wake-up call!"

The Day of Domino: Capitalist Monstrosity in Thomas Ligotti's *My Work Is Not Yet Done*

Christopher Brawley

> "I would say and do only that which I was supposed to say and do" (15).

> "I keep my head in the sand. It feels good down there" (34).

In her work *Pretend We're Dead: Capitalist Monsters in American Pop Culture*, an analysis of capitalist monstrosity, Annalee Newitz points out that "nothing is more dangerous than a monster whose story is ignored" (2). Postmodern critical theory has done much to show readers the need to listen to monster stories; they contain warnings (*monstre*, from the Latin *monere*, "to warn"), and the "otherness" of monsters often conceals deeper issues related to class, politics, nationality, race, sex, and gender. By no means are these issues exhaustive, however. As David McNally shows in his *Monsters of the Market*, monsters are not equal; simple dichotomies such as human/monster, us/them, good/evil, or even inside/outside are mere reference points and do not always reflect the complexity of the monsters in a given text. In order to understand the "warnings" of the monster, what is needed is a multi-accentual approach to monsters themselves, since, as Judith Haberstam claims, monsters are a "mobile, permeable, and infinitely interpretable body" (21). Looking more deeply into the complexity of what specific monsters "mean" allows readers insight into just what warnings monster stories provide.

McNally argues that one critical area that has been totally ignored is the "horror of the workplace" or what he identifies as a "Capitalist Monsterology," the study of capitalism itself as a monstrous system, "one that systematically threatens the integrity of human personhood" (3). He argues that one of the main reasons why this critical area has been ignored is because capitalism is so normalized and ingrained in day-to-day life for so many people that it goes unnoticed and unquestioned. In fact, this normalization is so pervasive that scholar Mark Fisher argues it seems as if any other system that offers a challenge to capitalism cannot even be imagined. Without questioning the capitalist system, the commodification of human labor leads to exploitation and the disintegration of the human subject and results in a malignant, self-annihilating world system whose effects are seen in such social ills as depression, drug abuse, and violence.

According to McNally, what is needed in dealing with capitalism is a "dialectical optics," a way of uncovering the unseen. Instead of only examining the disintegration of the human laborer, critics must go beneath to see the system itself, and how that system is, in fact, the real monster story that should not be ignored. And it is in relation to dialectical optics that McNally points to an effective tool in challenging the capitalist system: the fantastic. By this, McNally means literature that positions monsters at the center, such as fantasy, science fiction, and especially horror. As a genre that deals with monsters and their power to uncover invisible dangers, horror is one of the most powerful ways to address commodified existence. Powerful capitalist images such as the vampire or the zombie evoke a sense of estrangement and de-familiarization that, upon deeper reflection, allows readers to see everyday reality as something that is in fact quite strange itself. Here, McNally offers two powerful points. First, "fantastic genres, be they literary or folkloric, can occasionally carry a disruptively critical charge, offering a kind of grotesque realism that mimics the absurdity of capitalist modernity the better to expose it." Second, "only images of explosive power can break the web of mystification" (6–7).

In his fiction and in his nonfiction, Thomas Ligotti is certainly an author whose work contains "images of explosive power." One of the greatest living authors of supernatural fiction, Ligotti writes dark and surreal stories filled with puppets, dolls, sideshows, and foreign towns that are often a foreground for a bleak vision of existence. In addition to these supernatural stories, however, Ligotti also wrote what he termed his "corporate horror stories," perhaps the most autobiographical works in his oeuvre due to their basis in his own experience working in a large corporation for more than twenty years. These stories address the "horror of the workplace," or as Darrell Schweitzer says, "the dehumanizing effects of large, cubicle-filled offices where vast numbers of anonymous, white-collar drones waste their lives on meaningless tasks" (127). Ligotti's stories of this type are contained in (but not limited to) his collection *My Work Is Not Yet Done: Three Tales of Corporate Horror*.

Ligotti's most exhaustive and explosive corporate horror story is the title story, *My Work Is Not Yet Done*. Frank Dominio is a worker in a corporation. Feeling slighted by the company's lack of acknowledgment of his "New Product," combined with false accusations of theft, sexual harassment, and being "dead weight" to the company, Dominio is forced to resign his position. He secures firearms, proper clothing, and a Buck Skinner hunting knife, but before he can enact his plan of revenge toward his co-workers (referred to as the Seven), he gets hit by a bus, which leads him to a comatose state in a hospital bed. He then becomes a disembodied self, and he exacts his revenge on his co-workers in increasingly violent and surreal ways. The story ends with his wish to end his own life.

What is interesting is that Ligotti wanted both to portray his fantasies of vengeance and at the same time to show a very human side to the frustration within real corporate systems. Frank Dominio was meant to be a symbol for real psychological torment within the corporate system, but was also meant to be a "sympathetic character" (Ligotti). In fact, Ligotti has stated on multiple occasions that he was both "surprised" and "disappointed" at critics who failed to see Dominio as a sympathetic character, calling Dominio simply a "psycho." The failure to see the disastrous effects of commodification through capitalism is thus a failure to see the impact of Ligotti's critique of system itself.

David McNally argues that a genuine critical theory of capitalism must operate through "estrangement effects," making ordinary reality seem strange and monstrous itself; again, what this involves is an engagement with the fantastic, in which a monster can offer a "disruptively critical charge" that comments on the threat not only to personhood under a capitalist system but to the system itself. By means of a thesis, I would like to suggest that by employing a fantastic genre (the weird), Ligotti's novella *My Work Is Not Yet Done* offers readers a genuine critical theory of capitalism by 1) offering "explosive images" that expose the negative effects of capitalism and allow readers "to see the monstrous dislocations at the heart of commodified existence"; and 2) employing subtle hints and episodes with Lillian Hayes (a friend of Dominio) that reposition the main character, Dominio, not as the "psycho" who is to blame for the violence, but as a "sympathetic character" against the real monster, the capitalist system itself.

Monstrous Capitalism

In an interview with Tina Hall, Ligotti has stated that he is a self-proclaimed socialist, and he refers to capitalists as "unadulterated savages" (177). It is no surprise that these are his leanings, as he has seen the dehumanizing effects of malignant corporatism himself for more than two decades. In a capitalist system, even though we act as if we don't believe it, everything has a monetary value, and the constant drive for money detaches the laborer from the labor, producing a system that vacillates between highs and lows. It is this vacillation that takes a tragic toll in the form of mental illness, often creating monsters. As Annalee Newitz states, "Mutated by backbreaking labor, driven insane by corporate conformity, or gorged on too many products of a money-hungry media industry, capitalism's monsters cannot tell the difference between commodities and people. They confuse living beings with inanimate objects" (2).

It comes as perhaps no surprise that according to a World Health Organization study, the United States is at the top of the list of countries in terms of emotional distress, and that a major cause of this distress is the overemphasis on materialism, the hallmark of capitalism. In his book *The Selfish Capitalist*, Oliver James shows through countless studies that materialism, the heart of selfish capitalism, increases depression, anxiety, substance abuse, narcissism, and an overall lack of joy. The emotional distress brought about by selfish capitalism has been on the rise since the 1970s, when there was a massive concentration of wealth. According to James, this "Selfish Capitalism" has four defining features: success is defined by a "share price" and not the good of the company; the privatization of collective good such as gas, water, and electricity; minimal regulations that benefit the employers and not the employees; and finally, the conviction that "the market" can meet every need.

And, of course, the market cannot meet every need, which drives the consumer to keep consuming in a never-ending cycle of constant seeking. Mark Fisher suggests that affective disorders should not be personalized but seen as the end result of social causation. The whole therapeutic industry is based on capitalism's monstrosity: the more we can individualize mental disorders, the more the pharmaceutical companies can continue to pump out new medicines and fight over prices. According to Fisher, a change can only occur when blame is directed at the real cause, capitalism.

Capitalist Monsters

In director Victor Halperin's 1932 classic film *White Zombie*, zombies are employed in the production of sugar in "Murder" Legendre's (Bela Lugosi's) mills. In one shocking scene, the zombies carry baskets of sugar cane on their heads, walking in single file to dump the sugar cane into the millstones. One zombie falls over the edge, only to be ground up in the millstones below. The rest of the zombies are unaffected by the tragedy and business returns to usual without the slightest delay.

Monsieur Beaumont enters the sugar mill, and Legendre apologizes for being late to the meeting, stating that he has been looking for "men" to help in the sugar mills. Beaumont questions the use of the word "men," since what he has seen appear to be zombies. Legendre responds: "They work faithfully, and are not worried about long hours." Being zombies, they don't seem to be worried about much of anything.

The zombie is certainly one of the most widely used monsters to expose the brutality of the capitalist system. Not possessing individual agency, zombies are subjected to the powers that possess them. As a capitalist image, of course, these zombies are used as a means of producing goods for the satisfaction of the market; in turn, however, because these zombies possess no agency of their own, they require nothing in return for their labors. The zombie image was successfully employed by Karl Marx in his works, representing "dead labor," where the time the worker puts in is not his or her own time, but time solely for the employer's use. In a sense, the zombie laborer "belongs" to the employer, and the time spent is "dead time"; instead of the time being used to generate any enjoyment in life, the individual laborer becomes a commodity. Annalee Newitz summarizes the zombie predicament quite well: "the longer you stay dead, the more you'll get paid. And, as a corollary: the more death you make, the more you'll be paid as well" (34).

The other monster that most effectively speaks for the capitalist system is the vampire. Again, Marx favored the vampire as an apt symbol for capitalism: "Capital is dead labour which, vampire-like, lives only by sucking living labour"; "The vampire will not let go while there remains a single muscle, sinew or drop of blood to be exploited" (342, 416). David McNally sees the vampire image as extremely powerful in exploding the capitalist system due to three key similarities: first, the vampire is exploitative, needing the blood of its victims to keep itself alive, just as capital feeds of labor; second, vampires must move at night to conceal themselves, similar to the "invisibility" of capital where you can't really "see" what it's doing; and third, vampires represent alienation, which involves an inversion, the living into the dead, and, in capitalism, material objects taking the place of actual, living workers.

The postmodern trend of emphasizing monsters such as the vampire or zombie within capitalistic structures, often referring to them as "Zombie-Systems" or "Vampire-Systems," is effective but, perhaps, not effective enough. If McNally is correct in pointing out the need for "images of explosive power" to demystify and put into focus the dangers of capitalism, then what better explosive image is there but the individual, the one who struggles against the system itself? This is in accord with what scholar Judith Haberstam argues is the locus of the Postmodern Gothic: "It is the human, the façade of the normal, that tends to become the place of terror with Postmodern Gothic" (162). In his semi-autobiographical character Dominio, Ligotti does just that, giving readers a Jekyll-and-Hyde character, a divided self that is the result of the capitalist system. Dominio is a divided self, a "place of terror," but that does not necessarily mean he is a "psycho." To employ McNally's dialectical optics, readers may look beyond Dominio to the corporate system itself, the real monster that threatens the integrity of the individual working within it.

The Company

Dominio says that "the company that employed me strived only to serve up the cheapest fare that its customers would tolerate, churn it out as fast as possible, and charge as much as they could get away with" (43). The "market strategy" the Company seems to follow is to sell the ultimate product, which is Nothing, for the ultimate price, which is Everything. This corporate model will go on until one day there will only be a shining, windowless structure with machines calculating profit, a structure that savages will worship as a god.

This description of the corporate atmosphere in the novella has its origin in Ligotti's own workforce experience. According to Ligotti, after having experienced the slow decline of the company he worked for, Gale Research, he says he retreated further and further into his cubicle, and what started as a somewhat interesting and rewarding career turned into a nightmarish hell in which the corporate system consumed his identity. He says his "real hell" began in the last two years of his career, when half a dozen coworkers were trying to run him out of the company, and he started having fantasies about what he could do to them if he had them in one room. He realized that what he had previously managed as a panic-disorder suddenly became "a real time of moral and psychological torment" (Ligotti). He says that even though he didn't want to go on a random killing spree, he was "obsessed with fantasies of mayhem and terrified of facing work each day" (Ligotti). Ligotti dealt with this torment by transferring his very real fantasies of vengeance into what he termed his "corporate horror tales."

According to a personal email, during the 1990s Ligotti witnessed the decline of his company through many typical corporate changes: outsourcing of work, the mania for reorganizing companies, the collective obsession with working long hours to meet promotional needs, and most importantly, the advance of the computer. In a personal correspondence, Ligotti stated, "The day they put a computer on your desk will be the beginning of the end around here." This disdain for the computer is referenced throughout *My Work Is Not Yet Done,* when Dominio refers to it as the "lousy computer," when the word "software" gets stuck in his throat, or when, adjusting his tinted glasses to see, he says, "Boy, do I even hate to use the word: Computer—there, I said it" (20). Of course, the most obvious reference to Ligotti's hatred of the computer is when Dominio destroys his computer with a bat before the detectives get to his place. After he has a few whacks at it, he drops the bat and gets to work on the "beast's entrails," tying up the transistors and "melting wiring boards and decimating the soul of that thing—those diabolical chips—on an atomic level" (82). Given Ligotti's admission of the computer as the beginning of the end, I would argue that the violence with which Dominio destroys the computer is an "explosive image" and that it is a statement not only about the computer itself, but the whole corporate system that is behind it, led by the Company itself.

The Company that Dominio works for is comprised of seven main characters, referred to throughout the novella as "Swine," and also the "Seven Dwarfs"; they are also seen as a Machiavellian mob with Richard as the Prince, or a beast with Richard as the head, and six other snakelike protrusions from this head. As Dominio acts out his supernatural revenge on the Company for rejecting his "Idea," readers become aware of just why these characters are Swine; furthermore, they are disposed of in ways that often reflect their underlying obsessions. Perry, who is a drug addict and a "Jazzy" kind of guy with amber-tinted sunglasses, is left for dead in an abandoned warehouse with two left-handed mannikin hands sown on his cut-off hands; Sherry, who is an alcoholic, attractive but possessed of some alien quality that makes her a "Sherry-thing," is sucked up by a small door with little faces on it; Chipman gets lost in a labyrinth of doors leading to infinity while he looks for Sherry; Harry, who is an "enigma" on the whole but has done time in prison for home invasion and molestation, is caught up in a Cream of Mucous Membrane soup when he tries to rob and attack Lillian Hayes; Barry, whose body betrays a love of hamburgers, tacos, fried chicken, and ribs, and whose OCD leads him to constantly reorganize, is turned into a pig at a fair and is fixed and sold to a slaughterhouse; Mary, whose love of cosmetics makes her resemble a mannikin, is turned into a mannikin herself and is raped and beaten by derelicts at the Mechanic Street Museum; and, finally there is Kerrie, who is anorexic, who accuses Dominio of stealing her stamps, and who goes to an S and M establishment, only to be consumed into the body of a person named "The Can," who is a human garbage can and also a cannibal.

Another explosive image that Ligotti gives readers relates to the head of the Company, Richard, who is an athletic type and a "team player." All the workers at the Company are "chosen" by him, and he refers to them as a "family." At one point he even says, "We are the only family that any of us have" (80). But exactly what kind of family is Richard the head of? When Perry is left for dead, with two left-handed mannikin hands sewn onto his arms and his amber-colored glasses broken and injected into his bloodstream, Richard does not seem too concerned. In fact, he says of Perry, "He wasn't fully focused on the one important thing in all of our lives—the Job" (81). The image of Perry with two mannikin hands sewn on his hands is disturbing enough; to know that Richard blames Perry's lack of focus on his job as the cause of his slow death is a result of the dehumanizing effects of a capitalist structure.

Dominio and Domino: The Divided Self

At one point Dominio says of the Company, "I had been railroaded into the status of a non-person in an organization I had served so long and so well" (65). The reference to a "non-person" relates to the malignant, dehumanizing effects of the capitalist system, in this case one that results in the narrator starting to refer to himself as a dual personality, both Dominio (his real name) and Domino (the name Richard uses). For instance, Dominio is referred to as "a man of hyper-charged and off-kilter imagination," although ruled by his own inner fears, while Domino is "completely warped" and "belonged to a class of demon himself" (86). What begins to emerge in the narrative is a Jekyll-and-Hyde duality within the narrator himself, one that is the result not of a natural psychosis within a unified self, but of the commodification of the corporate system, where human agency does not exist. In *Pretend We're Dead*, Annalee Newitz uses the Jekyll-and-Hyde duality in her chapter on "Mad Doctors."

Although Dominio doesn't exactly fit the trope of the "mad doctor," he does represent the struggle for identity in the corporate system and the horror of discovering that at the end of the work day you are nothing but a product yourself. As Newitz points out, the horror of *Dr. Jekyll and Mr. Hyde* is not just the darker, more bestial Hyde, but the fact that both Jekyll and Hyde are in one person; this represents the contradiction of corporate life, "the split of those who own the means of production and those who work for them to produce commodities" (60).

Newitz states that "Jekyll and Hyde is quite literally about how one professional is so riddled by internal contradictions that he literally self-destructs" (66). This is exactly what is represented by the split in Dominio/Domino. On the one hand there is Dominio, who is consumed by his fears of everything, trying to fit into the corporate system by "aching" to show his plans for a "New Product" that will increase the prosperity of the company; and then there is Domino, who, after killing Perry, the first murder in his monstrous spree, says, "I was insane, a monster, an inhuman malefactor with no good excuse for its abominable actions" (74).

Again, the locus of postmodern horror, according to Haberstam, is the self; it is the monstrous condition that comes not from vampires or zombies as creatures from "without"; rather, it comes from "within." In desiring to add his new idea to the Company, Dominio is trying to walk with his "cloven feet" in the same swinish direction as the other employees, but he is at the same time only a worker, a small cog in a big machine. This contradiction is such that the only logical conclusion is to self-destruct. The split for the worker happens when he or she is confronted with this contradiction: how do we sell our ideas but still remain ourselves? This leads to what Newitz claims is the ultimate horror: "The horror of mental productivity and the horror of discovering you have become a product" (56)

Darkness, Pigs and Cockroaches

Employing McNally's dialectical optics allows readers to look beyond the internal conflict within Dominio, seeing him as merely a "psycho," to a wider understanding of what is behind Dominio's split. At one point Dominio senses a dark force when he traps a cockroach under his boot, first feeling a sense of communion with it, then a "deeper communion" allowing him to sense the "buzz of swinish agitation and turbulent blackness" that is underneath the cockroach. Similarly, when Dominio protects Lillian Hayes by entering her body, he senses this same blackness, the only difference being that Lillian has self-consciousness while the cockroach does not. What is sensed by Dominio, and what acts as the nightmarish backdrop to the malignant Company (and in fact all existence), is the Great Black Swine Which Wallows in the Great River of Blackness, a malignant force that resembles Schopenhauer's Will-to-Live. It is described as "a grunting bestial force that animated, that *used* our bodies to frolic in whatever mucky thing came its way, lasciviously agitating itself in that black river in which the human species only bobbed about like hunks of excrement" (109). When Dominio struggles to write his Ultimate Statement, he finally reaches the poetic conclusion that what people see as skyscrapers, funerals, birthdays, cellphones, in fact literally everything that exists, is a mere particle that has its being within the Great Black Swine.

What makes Dominio a sympathetic character and not just a "psycho" is that although he is a victim of the Great Black Swine, he is a rare individual who has an awareness that the Great Black Swine is the foundation of all reality. This awareness of the Great Black Swine leads him to the conclusion that "after all, the planet that I inhabited, the reality in which I was captured, was brimming with all kinds of potential victims, all of whom, to some degree, were swine that I dearly wanted to lead into my house of slaughter," and, further, that "all of them must be done away with . . . everyone must go!" (109–10). However, the important detail is that Dominio does not do this. He limits his killing to only the seven swine, and he feels his plan is not anything more than what they deserve. As Ligotti states, "These are not his ways; they are the ways of the Great Black Swine" (Ligotti). Dominio is being manipulated by the Great Black Swine; he has tried medications and therapy, and he says if there had been any other option, he would have taken it. Instead, Dominio says, "I was still being manipulated, I was still being crowded and conspired against by something beyond my control and frustrating to my Will" (110).

Up until the end, Dominio is fighting against the Great Black Swine. He not only wants to limit his killing to the seven, but he wants to finish his plan before the day ends. Every time he kills one of his co-workers, the world gets darker, and the Great Black Swine consumes him. The references to Daylight Saving Time, when Dominio is "scrambling against the clock (darn that lost hour!)," again show that he is trying to limit his destruction to the seven (for what they deserve) and not be overtaken by the Great Black Swine's insistence that the whole world has to go. In the end, the only solution for Dominio is to take his own life by running into a bus, trying to kill himself. While it is not a glamorous solution, readers can understand his attempt, especially given what he's up against, the Great Black Swine that underpins the malignant corporate system, a system that makes swine of us all and an imprisoning system of which most are unaware. Dominio is a sympathetic character because he is aware of this force and fights against it as nobly as he can.

"For Lillian Hayes. Thank you"

This subchapter takes its heading from a scene where Dominio depletes his life savings, places it in a taped-up box, and writes "For Lillian Hayes. Thank you." Lillian is described as the closest person to a family Dominio has. Frank says of her, "Now here was a woman who, I believed, was as decent as anyone could be, as close to being a non-swine as any human could get" (109).

According to Ligotti, Lillian Hayes acts as "a counter to the corrupt and toxic world in which Frank Dominio slaves" and that he "intended his casual friendship with her to make him sympathetic" (Ligotti). The character of Lillian is based on fond memories of Ligotti's black housekeeper, who would provide lunches for him and his brother while their mother was caring for their father in an institution. In many of the scenes in *My Work Is Not Yet Done*, the interactions between Frank and Lillian, and by association the setting of the Metro Diner, portray a counter to the corrupt and toxic workplace environment. The fact that Frank lives above Lillian in the Metro Diner, and that the diner is an escape from the "ritualized behavior" of the marketplace, offers readers a glimpse of the humanity of two characters who are at odds with the malignancy of the corporate world.

One notices this humanity as soon as Frank enters the diner. Frank smiles at Lillian and she waves to him. When Dominio reflects on how good the coffee is at the diner, he wonders if Lillian might just be another cog in the corporate machine, much like his boss Richard, but then he thinks, did the coffee have to be so "carefully prepared" or "reasonably priced"? Dominio seems to know that Lillian (and the diner) exist outside of the malignant corporate system. And, just as he did when he entered, Dominio waves at Lillian upon leaving.

Lillian Hayes is also protective of Dominio. When detectives White and Black are interrogating Lillian as to the whereabouts of Dominio, she says, "I feel I must respect the privacy of my tenant," and she is later described as "soft-spoken" and "flawlessly evasive" in her responses to the detectives. In fact, Frank even says he was almost "moved to tears" over the way Lillian evaded the detectives in favor of protecting him. This mutual love and understanding between the two offers "explosive images" of the humanity existing in contradistinction with the destructive effects of corporate structures.

Perhaps the most powerful display of humanity between Dominio and Lillian is when Harry, one of the swine who has been incarcerated for home invasion and molestation, approaches Lillian at the Metro Diner to rape and rob her. Dominio says, "I had no special plan except to keep Lillian safe" (95). In a liminal state, Frank is able to enter Lillian's body, while at the same time rendering her somewhat unconscious. Now, Frank can deal with Harry. Entering a back room where a safe is located, he locks the door, turns Harry's bullets into globs that fall to the floor, and then Harry is served in the soup called "Cream of Mucus Membrane." While he is dying Harry asks, "Who is this?" and although Frank is still operating Lillian's body, he allows Lillian to look directly in Harry's face with "a lurid rainbow of glowing colors playing across her face, her mouth grinning wide" (98).

These episodes between Dominio and Lillian in the diner combine to make an overall statement of humanity over and against the capitalist sociopathy evident in the Company and the Seven Dwarves that slave under it. Lillian and the Metro Diner aid in bolstering the reader's sympathy for Dominio. If everything in existence is a mere particle of the Great Black Swine, Dominio should be lauded as a noble character, one who, in the midst of the darkness he is a victim of, fights against it as best he can.

Conclusion

After killing Perry, Dominio says of himself, "I was insane, a monster, an inhuman malefactor with no good excuse for its abominable actions" (74). My purpose has been to question this. Is Dominio really a monster? Or is capitalism, the mechanism that reduces humans to commodities, really the monster? As Rachid M'Rabty argues in his article, "Occupational Hazards: Nihilism and Negation in Thomas Ligotti's 'Corporate Horror,'" whether *My Work Is Not Yet Done* is a parable of the dehumanizing effects of corporatism or a manifesto for self-destruction, there is value in the subversive ideas of nihilism. Those familiar with Ligotti's nonfiction work *The Conspiracy against the Human Race* know that, for Ligotti, the malignant force that appears in the novella as the Great Black Swine is very real; it is no fictional device. So, given the metaphysical reality of an overwhelming darkness that manipulates everything in its wake, what are we to do? Can we rebel in any way? Or is it "pigs all the way down," as Jonathan Newell argues, and the only escape is our degree of participation?

Ligotti has stated that he was surprised and disappointed in critics who viewed Frank Dominio as a "psycho" and not the sympathetic character he wished to portray. In a personal email, Ligotti is clear on this point: "Frank is not a monster. And the prospect of becoming one is the basis of a conflict within him" (Ligotti). In *My Work Is Not Yet Done*, the conflict is the result of a monstrous capitalist system that threatens the integrity of the person. As David McNally argues, "Capitalist Monsterology" allows readers to look beyond the surface conflicts in a story to see the underlying systems of domination, a dialectical optics that can challenge the normalization and day-to-day ignorance of a system that takes away humanity. And specifically weird fiction, with its deliberate displays of monstrosity, is, as Oliver Rendle says, "uniquely positioned" to expose the dangers of this system, "offering an alternative frame of ontological reference that renders a set of presumed values obsolete" (5). Although Dominio's conflict leads him to the darkest of solutions, when he runs in front of a bus, Ligotti is showing readers that we do not need to be resources. We can always forfeit our part:

> To whom it may concern—I hereby refuse to be a swine living in a world of swine that was built by swine and belongs only to swine. This swine has been fed full of his swinish ambitions, his swinish schemes, and, over and above all, his swinish fears and obsessions. Therefore I forfeit my part of this estate to my heirs in the kingdom of the swine. (136)

Works Cited

Fisher, Mark. *Capitalist Realism: Is There No Alternative?* Winchester, UK: Zero Books, 2009.

Halberstam, Judith. *Skin Shows: Gothic Horror and the Technology of Monsters.* Durham, NC: Duke University Press, 1995.

Hall, Tina. "The Damned Interviews: Thomas Ligotti." In Matt Cardin, ed. *Born to Fear: Interviews with Thomas Ligotti.* Burton, MI: Subterranean Press, 2014, 175–81.

James, Oliver. *The Selfish Capitalist: Origins of AFFLUNZA.* London: Vermilion, 2008.

Ligotti, Thomas. *My Work Is Not Yet Done: Three Tales of Corporate Horror.* London: Virgin Books, 2009.

———. "Paper:" 19 April 2022. Email.

———. "Paper:" 19 July 2022. Email.

———. "Re: Possible Help?" 5 January 2021. Email.

McNally, David. *Monsters of the Market: Zombies, Vampires and Global Capitalism.* Chicago: Haymarket Books, 2012.

M'Rabty, Rachid. "Occupational Hazards: Nihilism and Negation in Thomas Ligotti's 'Corporate Horror.'" *Dark Arts Journal* 2, No. 1 (Spring 2016): 43–67.

Marx, Karl. *Capital.* Volume 1. Tr. Ben Fowkes. New York: Vintage Books, 1976.

Newell, Jonathan. "Pigs All the Way Down: Capitalist Realism and Neo-Reaction in Thomas Ligotti's *My Work is Not Yet Done.*" *Studies in the Fantastic* No. 11 (Summer 2021): 1–21.

Newitz, Annalee. *Pretend We're Dead: Capitalist Monsters in American Pop Culture.* Durham, NC: Duke University Press, 2006.

Rendle, Oliver. "'We Are All Human Resources': The Weird as Neoliberal Critique in Thomas Ligotti's *My Work Is Not Yet Done.*" *Pulse: The Journal of Science and Culture* 7, No. 1 (Summer 2020): 1–18.

Schweitzer, Darrell. "Ligotti's Corporate Horror." In Darrell Schweitzer, ed. *The Thomas Ligotti Reader: Essays and Explorations.* Holicong, PA: Wildside Press, 2003. 127–34.

White Zombie. Directed by Victor Halperin. Halperin Productions, 1932.

In Stone

Livia E. De Souza

There was something unsettling in the placid faces, the human forms bound in stone: every inch restrained, yet struggling. It was a conflict to which Cather had never grown accustomed, even as he made the production of these cold likenesses his life's work.

Cather could confess only a passing familiarity with the purported miracles of the woman whose likeness he carved, and he had no desire to learn more. After all, he would make the work entirely his own and create a masterpiece of devotion, if not to a saint than to perfect artistic form.

Perhaps the haste of this most recent assignment had been to bolster the cathedral's promise of divine invincibility, perhaps to gently ease from the congregants' minds the image of the young man whose body had lain shattered beneath the crushing stone.

Regardless, the idea to salvage material from the fallen ledge had been entirely Cather's.

Cather drew the riffle file firmly over the stone, his strong hands applying a firm pressure to the implement.

Rather than smoothly shaping the features, the file tore a ragged slash across the cheek. The saint now sported a deep abrasion beneath the left eye: an impossible mistake to make, if only by nature of the material.

Hesitantly, Cather picked up his point chisel and gently ran the end over the surface. A slight mark resulted, like a cut, and he brushed his fingertips over the cold stone, still half unbelieving.

It was as though in a trance that Cather continued his work. Proceeding with tremendous care, he shaped the visage as if from soft clay, bringing forward forgiving lips and searching eyes, knowing that a moment's heavy hand could destroy the blessed corpus in whose service he was now enslaved.

The inexplicable malleability of the saint's stone body allowed a level of delicacy Cather could ordinarily only imagine. Every fold of the heavenly garments, every small line gracing the features, was as though carved into living flesh.

The saint stared back at him, willing itself into existence, using the sculptor's hands as an unorthodox channel to the mortal plane.

Entranced by the impossible acquiescence of the stone figure, Cather worked long into night. Shadows flickered along the wall as the lamps sputtered against their lagging fuel. With this rising of light, the warmth of pride surrounding Cather's heart corrupted and decayed within his chest.

His pulse quickened, muscles tightening with unprovoked rage against the world and against himself. The longing to strike out at another, to draw blood to his fist, pervaded his being. Yet, more than this, he desired to see his own body bound and trampled.

Traces of darkness danced along the baseboard, sightless and soundless in their indulgence. A knocking came through the walls, and deep, frantic cries reverberated through the closed door.

The strength was sapped from his legs and he fell, his knees cracking with a sickening sound against the floor. Pain radiated through him, crushing the rage, drawing him into a deadened disquiet.

Cather crawled to the statue of the saint, its sacred patience an exercise in cruelty. Though the stone's coloring was dark gray, the material was soft and warm, seeming to carry its own unnaturally slow pulse.

The face dominated his vision. Everything besides the haunting thing had become a steadily growing haze, succumbing either to obscurity or unimportance.

He seized a chisel from the table and struck forward, but the tool slipped from his grasp, clattering on the floor, and rolling away in a taunting arc.

The saint's demure smile had morphed into a grin, exposing inches of teeth Cather knew his hands had never formed. He felt blindly on the floor for the chisel, unable or unwilling to turn his eyes from the deftly crafted face, but his hands remained empty.

Yet the saint's façade was still soft.

Cather struck out with bare hands. He felt his fingernails tear from his flesh, watched as, with each assault against the damned figure, crimson streaked the dead-gray stone.

When the ends of his fingers were nothing but blood-wet stumps, he began his next attack with a fresh frenzy. Possessed by an animalistic desire to survive at any cost, he bit at the face, intending to maul the complexion of the saint. Yet it was his own blood and fragmented teeth that were spat out over the impervious surface.

His skin was coated in a cold sweat, and he could smell only the metallic tang of his own blood. His senses were swamped in the wet, red haze, until he could see nothing beyond the unebbing flow of his own life's essence: the crimson, rising sap of a felled man.

Cather stumbled away. He could feel its gaze, how his every movement was joyfully drunken in. Outside the workshop, in the cold night, he found his footing and fled. The grit of the street coated his torn hands, and he sputtered blood with every faltering step.

Although only one year would pass before Cather could bring himself to return to the city, the streets had already become foreign to him. Above the hallowed grounds by the northeastern side of the cathedral, he saw his saint.

The figure appeared exactly as he had first envisioned it: passive hands folded, soft shoulders, and yielding eyes.

As Cather stared against the sun, he saw the lips widen into a smile.

Fixed in Cather's mind was the dwindling number of his days. A fatal fragility disrupted his every breath, invited into his body by the pain of unnatural wounds. For every hour he held fast, he lost another shred of himself to the void.

He sat down on a low wall beside the cemetery and waited. It seemed only right that the master sculptor should spend those fading hours beneath the watchful gaze of his final creation.

Mantic Moon

Leigh Blackmore

I dream a swelling, mantic moon
That sails above the sundered ships
Of scattered navies, drowned too soon;
The yellow tallow-candle drips.

I hear a siren serenade
That floats afar above the sea
And sings of lethal crimson blade
Wielded in war; oh, piracy!

I see a cohort grim and grey,
Stark silhouetted on the hill—
The Crown's dull troops stand in array
In serried ranks—frustrated, still.

I touch the flintlock, old and worn,
Beside me on the cabinet;
Would snatch it up, had I not sworn
To bide in peace so passionate.

I smell the ozone on the air
That drifts from shore to reach me here,
Beckons me back, like phantom prayer,
To seas where I did buccaneer.

I taste the spume and see the flag,
Its skull-and-crossbones fluttering there!
The troops, well-armed, on yonder crag
Will never catch us! Come, let's dare!

I dream a sinking, mantic moon
That sets below the land and sea.

Awake, but all alone too soon,
I dread that lunar prophecy!

McNaughton's Witches

David Rose

> "The world that McNaughton has created in this book is the world of the ghoul; and who knows but that *The Throne of Bones* will become the standard textbook for the care and feeding of ghouls just as *Dracula* has become that for vampires?"
>
> —S. T. Joshi, Afterword to *The Throne of Bones* (338)

> "If one had to name a single book that represents the finest literary depiction of ghoulery in the same manner that *Dracula* represents the definitive vampire novel, that book would have to be the late Brian McNaughton's collection *The Throne of Bones…*"
>
> —Scott Connors, "The Ghoul,"
> in *Icons of Horror and the Supernatural* (263)

No doubt, Brian McNaughton (1935–2004) is known primarily for his writing on ghouls. A careful study, however, shows he also wrote about a classic horror figure with true mastery: the witch. McNaughton linked witches—differentiated from necromancers and warlocks—to gender and socioeconomic roles, as they are commonly understood, and in so doing created characters who are distinctly feminine. It is through this exact, distinct femininity that evils unique to their makeup are born.

What follows are four examples, ranging in setting from contemporary to period piece to secondary world. We shall examine McNaughton's use of stereotypes, patriarchal structures, and how McNaughton's witches are thrust into action almost exclusively by a perception, gross or slight, of being slighted. These four examples should provide a convincing case that the melding of depravity with the writer's evocation of pathos and his characteristic tone results in potent anti-heroes and truly formidable antagonists.

First we have Phitithia Glocque, who appears in the story "The Art of Tiphystorn Glocque," set in Seelura (the world where *The Throne of Bones* occurs). She is the daughter of a wealthy fish merchant who recently died eating the poisonous ovaries of a blowfish. She is also the younger sister of Tiphystorn, a now-rich artist who, after watching her stand on a beach casting her spells, says: "You have a special knowledge of the sea. You know certain secret properties of its plants and creatures—to cite one example purely at random, the poisonous nature of blowfish ovaries" (*The Throne of Bones* 252). To which she replies: "Whom do you want poisoned now?" (252).

We have Alison Strange, the crazy-old-lady-next-door who, in "Congratulations!" (*Nasty Stories*), confounds her neighbor (and the story's narrator) by connecting them with a box-and-string telephone that works way too well. Next: the horrendously unattractive Friedegunde. Living in the Germanic territories at the end of the tenth century, the daughter of Graf Heinrich von der Hiedlerheim "hoarded slights and could sob bitterly over any one of them" (*Nasty Stories* 8). A deadly trait, because to the misfortune of several warriors in her father's court already, "the wise woman of the woods had taught her [witchcraft]" (8).

And we have Lady Lereela. The most cunning and evil of McNaughton's Seeluran characters, she is the great-granddaughter of Vendriel the Insidiator, the most ruthless of the island's rulers. Said to possess his white-hot will, she aims to merge what could be referred to as "church and state" by becoming the capital's Grand Enchantress *and* First Lady: a feat unseen and referenced in "Vendriel and Vendreela," a tale that takes place after the Lady's inevitable reign, as a cataclysmic disaster:

> It was this Vendriel [the Insidiator] who built the New Palace, shunned since the ultimate metamorphosis of his great-

granddaughter, Lady Lereela . . . So black is the shadow cast by that Lady, last of the Vendren rulers, that it has leeched the blackness from the names of her ancestors. (*The Throne of Bones* 284)

For McNaughton, witches are prompted by wiles and desires commonly understood to be of the female point of view. Strongly connected, therefore, are the obstacles in front of them. Phitithia was forbidden to marry the man she loves. Alison Strange lives alone, offering (in vain) her help to those who view her as something akin to a crazy cat lady. She is painfully naïve, gullible to the cons and frauds who especially prey on the elderly. Friedegunde is not only a subjugated wench but a collector of injustices predicated on her ugliness. She is also driven by lust, her ideas of love unattained, and where the two meet.

These positions, the unwanted stances of the put-upon, are directly tied to their socioeconomic/gender roles and the subsequent underestimation such roles can carry. Though Phitithia conspired with her brother in the murder of their parents, her brother wouldn't dream the girl with the "weak chin" who "wobbled perilously close to ethnic caricature" would use her magic or knowledge of poisons against *him*. He is too busy gloating over new wealth and his newfound artistic freedom to notice the strategist slinking in the shadows. Alison Strange uses the box-and-string telephone because she wants her neighbor to watch for the arrival of the Prize Platoon (a satire of the Publishers Clearing House) while she takes a nap. She has fallen prey to a classic scam of the 1990s, and her distracted neighbor doesn't at first have the heart to tell her. Friedegunde is underestimated simply by no one knowing she is a witch, and although Lady Lereela is remarkably different in this regard, she is fawned over by the city's denizens in such a way that they never grasp the extent of her wickedness: certainly an underestimation in its own right.

From these women's perspectives, they merely want what they feel they deserve. Phitithia helped her brother and now she wishes to marry her lowly sponge-diver. Miss Strange won a huge prize, fair and square! Friedegunde just knows deep down she's a good woman, destined to be bad, and just wants to experience life as Jezebel and Salome did, since "they'd gotten some fun out of their sins" (*Nasty Stories* 9). Lady Lereela is the rightful heir to the rings, the Insidiator reborn, and becoming the wife of the First Lord is simply her destiny.

But let us examine what happens when these women's destinies are impeded.

Though they are put upon by sociological forces (domineering men, beauty standards, etc.), the reader is never goaded to sympathize fully with them or to view them as victims. With what we could call gender pejoratives, McNaughton often displays characters at their stereotypical worst. Politicians: corrupt. Poets: self-absorbed and drinking on credit. Witches: women, some of whom are obsessed with appearance, others with men. Unforgiving. Conniving. Women who are as spiteful as they are petty. And though they may be underestimated, they are powerful as hell!

Perhaps driven by a modicum of guilt, to honor his father, Tiphystorn will not allow Phitithia to marry the sponge-diver she loves. When she rebels he tries to have the diver killed. In classic McNaughton moral irony, when Tiphystorn's newest murder is foiled and Phitithia finds out, we see a bewitched sort of emperor's new clothes. Though she had used her magic to assist his artistic endeavors in the past, what is set to be his greatest unveiling ends up with him deluded and soon thrown in an asylum; seeing fantastic colors in what are really just streaks of sludge.

In another moral irony, Alison Strange, though exhibiting a bizarre twist in Gilligan's "ethics of care"[3] by offering her powers to help with her neighbor's thankless job and kid's disability, once the old woman learns she's been duped we soon see Ted McGoohan, leader of the Prize Platoon, being tortured by imps on the very television he'd duped her on, and Alison Strange standing in her living room, demanding of him her ten million dollars. Then, a short time after:

---

3. Psychologist Carol Gilligan, in her book *In a Different Voice* (1982), proposed that, whereas men prioritize a rigid sense of justice, women's moral priorities orbit a sense of care for themselves and for others.

In the special announcement on all the networks, McGoohan looked ghastly, especially when his cheery smile degenerated into tics. His famous chuckle might have come from the grave when he tried to explain the error that necessitated a special award of ten million dollars to Alison Strange. (*Nasty Stories* 62)

Friedegunde executed a whole host of foul deeds on those who had insulted her:

> "Poor Siegfried, for instance, later fallen from her father's banquet-table to die in the grip of a long fit that had hammered his heels against the back of his head, had been overheard to say she had less a nose than an old corpse, and that it sickened him to stare into nostrils like gaping grave-pits. And Gunther, tragically cut down in the prime of his vaunting heroism by some unknown coward who had waylaid him and stamped his spine to the consistency of fingernail-pairings, had unfavorably compared her generous mouth to an old sow's pudendum, bristles and all" (*Nasty Stories* 8).

Most sinister of course is Lereela. The Lady suffers none of the subservient, castaway burdens her sisters in magic do. Though a wielder of dark arts, she is beautiful, adored, and a rising power, but, due to McNaughton's unfortunate death and the subsequent incompletion of "The Deposition of Leodiel Fand" (the novella in which we officially meet Lereela), we too will never know her wickedness's full extent. But, wonderfully, we have been left clues. There is her striking beauty:

> Although she was only sixteen then, her lean face showed the ageless serenity of funerary sculpture; her imperial posture and gait made the most elegant ladies in her train look clumsy. Her hair, worn extraordinarily long in defiance of fashion, was so black that it adopted the alternate shades of the shafts from the high windows as she glided through them, now yellow, now blue, now red . . . ("Deposition" 138–39)

An examination of the text suggests that there may be a type of dark metamorphosis occurring during Leodiel Fand's actual deposition. To the magistrate he says:

> To describe Lady Lereela is pointless . . . because everyone sees her differently. Every day she looks a little different to me, as if, recreating herself from the dream-stuff each morning, she forgets the specific tilt of her eyes, the precise line of her nose, her height to the inch or weight to the ounce. (138)

If ever was there a writer who alchemized all nouns to have a specific meaning, that writer was surely Brian McNaughton. Nothing was arbitrary. His recycling and escalation of objects were of the highest quality. Lady Lereela wore on her cheek the tattoo of a butterfly; it is bright blue and is mentioned several times. Taking the previous quotation from "Vendriel and Vendreela" about metamorphosis into full consideration, the tattoo is likely her own dark joke; a being involved with drastic changes to become their true self.

There is another clue, albeit vague, though it does conjure up a disturbing image as to the Lady's ultimate nature. Referring to giant humanoid rats that live under the palace and are, by magical means, connected to the Lady's family, Squandriel Vogg, a Seeluran historian, states: "It was said that Lady Lereela, when she came to the capital from Fandragord some threescore years later, trafficked with these creatures of the abyss: who might have been her rather distant cousins" (*The Throne of Bones* 292). Yet in the timespan of "The Deposition of Leodiel Fand," the darling of the mob is in full beauty—ever changing in the eye of her beholders—perceived almost exclusively by Leodiel, the embroiled narrator, as dripping with the corruptions that may come with power and rapturous praise. Politically correct or not, her pettiness resonates with the common consciousness. The Lady, her memory sharp and her spite so venomous, recognizes Leodiel, who threw a stick at her when they were children. When he had bent down to pick up another, the twig had turned into a viper, biting his hand and almost killing him. Now that they are young adults, she skips over and embraces the very hand that had thrown the stick all those years ago; soon Leodiel is showing again horrid symptoms of a snakebite.

But displays of her pettiness serve only as baselines to witness the escalation of her wrath when want she wants is impeded. The First Lord was apparently the only other person who agreed with Leodiel when he said: "The prospect of a First Lady of the Frothoin who would also be chief cleric of a deity known to most as Goddess of Evil boggles the mind" ("Deposition" 143). As a result, the aging leader aims to marry off his son to a series of women who all end up suffering cruel fates. First there is Lady Marmorilla, who chased a preternaturally blue butterfly and slipped into a canal, never to be seen again. Second is Frissa Fand, a distant kinswoman of Leodiel's, who publicly insults Lady Lereela and instantly goes up in flames. A nearby torch and new perfume take the blame, but the "stench of witchcraft" is smelt. And finally there is Ailillia Fronn. Due to the aforementioned passing of the author, we never get to learn what fate befell her when the angered Lady learns the First Lord defied her warnings and announced Ailillia would soon become First Lady. Again, there are clues, but not enough for one to bring forth a confident hypothesis. The best we are left with is a groan from Leodiel. Suspected of harming Ailillia, he proclaims his innocence, and, referring to Ailillia's refusal to heed his warnings about Lereela's power, says: "In her arrogance of intellect, she would reason herself all the way to hell" ("Deposition" 159).

McNaughton did two things. He crafted women so that their place in the world and the times in which they lived were distinctly female. He also ensured that they were in possession of, and afflicted by, troubling forces. In so doing, McNaughton left us with witches of the master grade.

We may wonder if the strapping young diver was only interested in Phithia's inheritance, and what vile deed she may have done if she learned this was so. We may wonder what new care millionaire Alison Strange has given and thank the heavens we never ran into

Friedegunde von der Hiedlerheim; and as far as the bewitchment of Lady Lereela goes, as Sean O'Leary, editor of *Lore*, states with regard to McNaughton's final, unfinished tale: "the fact that it is unfinished will, perhaps, encourage us to linger a bit longer in Seelura, conjuring the final scenes in our mind. There are those of us who might never leave" (122).

Indeed.

Works Cited

Connors, Scott. "The Ghoul." In S. T. Joshi, ed. *Icons of Horror and the Supernatural*. Westport, CT: Greenwood Icons, 2007. 1.243–66.

Joshi, S. T. Afterword to *The Throne of Bones* by Brian McNaughton. Black River, NY: Terminal Fright, 1997. 338–41.

McNaughton, Brian. "The Deposition of Leodiel Fand." *Lore* 2, No. 1 (April 2012): 123–68.

———. *Nasty Stories*. Berkeley Heights, NJ: Wildside Press, 2000.

———. *The Throne of Bones*. Black River, NY: Terminal Fright, 1997.

O'Leary, Sean. "A Note on 'The Deposition of Leodiel Fand.'" *Lore* 2, No. 1 (April 2012): 122.

Ancient Teeth

Maxwell I. Gold

Wrapped beneath cloaks of death and sin, I saw harbingers wrought with calamitous hunger, where the jaws of a thousand starving nightmares were plunged into the flesh of my dank, rotting dreams. No one understood my horror, but I walked in fear of the cape of night which descended from stony castles nestled in black mountains; the horrid music of leathery wings flapped through cold streets where soon, the sounds of their feed smacked into my ears.

Ancient teeth, dogmatic and primal, gnawed under the glint of a yellow moon whose lust for flesh was so great, not even twelve million years could stay their yearning. One bite after another with bloody smiles stretched across pallid faces, illuminated the night with a sinister recompense. These winged children were the bastards of Death and Entropy, flying across lidless nights with appetites unmatched, where not even the deepest abysms of space were enough to chasm their woeful depths. Their black stomachs filled with dust and shadow never knew the sweet protrusions of satisfaction, only the deathful urges covered in blood and ruin; and despite it all, I found myself awash in uncontrollable hunger wrapped beneath cloaks of death and sin, embraced by ancient teeth.

Malevolence

Harris Coverley

The wind crashed through her veil of sleep. Katie's meek dreams had been chilly, and her subconscious had known there was something wrong, but the grand *boom* was in the end what awoke her.

She opened her eyes into a deep blue grimness, devoid of electric light, the pain of the cold on her face.

She put her hands over her eyes and groggily swung her legs to the floor, putting herself on the edge of the couch.

Her naked feet burned as they touched the carpet. She removed her hands and saw the streaks of ice crystal weaving their way across the old Persian pattern.

The wind blew sharply again, this time with the groan of wood. She turned to her left and saw its source: the patio doors were wide open, broken and buckling, grinding back and forth, their glass cracked in some panels and outright shattered in others. Sleet was spread across the floor. The gas fire beneath the mantelpiece was out.

"Nana!" Katie cried, fully roused. "Grandad! Nana!"

There was no answer.

"What?" answered Ben, who had been asleep on the opposing couch, protected from the worst of the wind by its backrest.

The boy, aged seven, four years Katie's junior, sat up fast, his legs not long enough to reach the icy floor.

Braving the bitterness, Katie leaned under the coffee table and pulled out her slippers, shaking off any frost. They were damp, but they were better than nothing at all.

By the time she had got them on Ben was crying.

"Where are Nana and Grandad?" she shouted at him over the ever angrier gale.

He shook his head, closed his eyes, and lay down, pulling his blanket back over him.

"Ben, this is not a dream!" she called, but he did not remove the blanket.

She stood up and pulled it off him.

"Leave me alone!" he wept, his tears freezing his face. "This is just a nightmare! Mummy always says to close your eyes and let it pass!"

"It's not a nightmare!" Katie shouted, and grabbed him by the shoulders. "We need to shut those doors!"

"No!"

"Come with me!"

Katie dragged him off the couch. He fought her, but she was bigger and stronger. She shoved his own slippers on his feet and almost carried him from the living area, across the open space where the Christmas tree now lay on its side, its crowning star splintered, its baubles crunched under the weight of their formerly supportive branches, all the way to the patio doors, the loose glass shards crackling underfoot, indistinguishable from the ice.

Standing against the squall, Katie put Ben down and said once more, "We need to shut the doors!"

Ben was too terrified to respond, but he understood all too well that this was no nocturnal delirium, and something had to be done.

To give it one more go, Katie screamed into the house for her grandparents, to no avail. Beyond the reach of the wind, the rest of the house was dead and quiet.

Pulling back the thin left side curtain to get it out of the way, Katie took the end of the left patio door, Ben beneath her, and they began to force it back.

It shuddered against them, glass shards still stuck in the frame swinging about like lethal icicles.

As the children finally got the door back against the doorframe, Katie fitted the bolt down into its hole. They released the door and it hung awkwardly in the gale, trembling to mimic Katie and Ben. It was almost like the door had been mismatched to its frame, as though it were at war with itself. Still, Katie pulled the curtain back over it and wrapped its tie around the handle.

"Look!" shouted Ben, pointing into the darkness in the open gap next to it.

Katie looked and saw in the distance, within the woodland beyond their grandparents' garden, a faint yellow glow. This was odd, she knew—there was nothing in the woods that could or would make such a light, for she had walked down there with her grandmother many times.

"Forget it!" she said to Ben. "We have to shut the other one!"

They did the same with the right-hand door, but halfway closed Ben's hand slipped on the frame's melting frost and it fell against a shard, cutting his palm.

He shrieked and held his hand to his chest.

Katie took him and looked at the injury: the damage was not too bad, although it would need stiches.

"Keep it against you!" she said, trying to adapt what she had learned in a first aid lesson at school. "But you've *still* got to help me!"

Weeping, Ben nodded his head, and using his good hand assisted Katie in at last closing the right-hand door. She bolted it and pulled the curtain over to its counterpart, tying them together.

The doors groaned, and bits of glass still tingled to the floor, but at least the curtains, despite being decades old and due for replacement, protected them. The onslaught of wind in the front room had been greatly eased.

Katie and Ben stood there looking at their work, her arm over his shoulder, his around her back.

"Katie, what's going on?" he asked, still holding his bloodied palm against his chest.

"I don't know," she admitted. "But we need to find Nana and Grandad."

They went back across the open space, passing the tree.

"There are no presents!" cried Ben. *"They're gone!"*

Katie would have been lying if she had said that her heart had *not sunk even more* at Ben's realization, but she was mature enough to know that there were more important things at hand, and so she pulled him on, telling him that they could look for them after they had found their grandparents.

The door into the main hallway was almost frozen shut and had to be virtually pried open. The rest of the house was as cold as the front room, but no more windows or doors were smashed or cracked.

The children searched every room, even crawling under each bed and opening each cupboard. They even went down to the garage and looked under the car, which was undisturbed. Their grandparents were nowhere to be found, nor were there any written notes posted or other signs of them leaving. There were no burglars or ghosts or ghoulies or goblins to be found either—the children, it seemed, were utterly alone.

They had to undertake this search in near-darkness, as there was no power.

Katie picked up the telephone, an old-fashioned ring dial, and was met with a completely dead line, not a fuzz of signal. The radiators, usually burningly hot at this time of the year, were stone cold.

It was as though the entire house had been abandoned for years, never mind less than a night.

Katie and Ben made their way back into the front room to check the patio doors.

Even though the wind outside had lessened, and they had remained steady enough, the frame itself was beginning to warp.

"What are we going to do?" Ben asked.

Katie saw that he was very pale and ignored his question to check his palm. The bleeding had stopped, but it was an ugly wound.

She took him into the kitchen, where she got the medical kit and using an old bandage wrapped him up.

"It's ticklish," he said, sniffling as much in pain as for the cold.

"We'll get somebody to look at it," she said.

"When? What's going on?"

"I don't know! Don't be a brat!"

"You can't call me that! I'm gonna tell . . ." Ben shouted, but lost his thread, and broke down again.

Katie was annoyed with him but decided to embrace him, and then she took him back to the front room.

They surveyed the tree, and indeed all the presents had been taken.

"Was I on the naughty list?" asked Ben.

"I don't know," Katie repeated. "Maybe we both were."

"Has Father Christmas . . . betrayed us?"

"I——" started Katie, but she paused and did not resume. She had long ceased to believe in Father Christmas, but with what had happened *anything* seemed possible now.

They stood there, trying to make sense out of any of it.

It had been the mid-evening, about nine . . . Christmas Eve . . . they were staying with their grandparents . . . their parents would be here in the morning for Christmas Day . . . the gas fire had been on full, blazing away . . . Grandad had been telling one of his silly, heavily embellished wartime Christmas stories . . . Nana had been knitting . . . they had drifted off on the couches in their pyjamas . . .

Through their escape into memory something caught Katie's eye.

She turned to the patio doors. The yellow curtains were so thin as to be translucent, and had never guarded against the sunlight much.

There was now a small glow, like the one they had seen in the woods, against where the left-hand door was, seeping through the curtain.

Was this some rescuer?

Katie told Ben to stay where he was while she walked over to see what it was.

Her hopes rose—maybe this was her grandparents with a perfectly logical explanation. Maybe some madman had broken into the house, stolen the presents, and had been chased into the woods by Nana and Grandad. Was that glow torchlight? What about the power, and the radiators, and the telephone? Had the madman ruined all that *too?*

As she got closer to the glow at the patio door, her hopes dropped. The glow was small, at the height of her face, but a dread began to grow within her, an unreasoning fear worse than any other she had experienced in her childhood.

She halted a couple of feet from the door, the chill nipping at her pallid, exposed skin.

The glow stayed in the same place yet grew more intense, flaring like a firework in slow motion.

"What's that?" asked Ben, suddenly behind her.

She was too scared to be upset with him for following her, and yet, against the terror, she *had to know* what was behind the curtain.

A whistling sound swelling from beyond, she slid her hand into the gap and briskly pulled it back.

With a flat-topped head, a pointed chin, and bottomless eyes and mouth was a white-hot face, smirking at them, floating without a body before the broken glass.

As the two children screamed the face matched them, the whistling rising to a roar, the whiteness of its form growing brighter still into an explosion of suns.

Katie fled, grabbing Ben, and they ran howling out of the front room and into the hall, slamming the door shut behind them.

Thinking fast, Katie found the key for the door in the drawer of the hall table and locked it.

Although they had their own separate rooms in the house, that night they slept together in the grandparental bed, largely because it was on the ground floor—away from the front room, but not *too far*, so that they could hear what was happening in there—but also for the extra blankets their grandmother kept at the end, fresh and dry, on a wide velvet stool. They cocooned themselves in, locking the bedroom door in spite of its stiffness.

Ben cuddled into Katie, and, the digital alarm clock blank and useless, she checked a wristwatch of her Grandad's, left on the side cabinet: it was just past three in the morning.

"Mum and Dad are coming at nine," she told him. "They said they would . . . they *have to* . . ."

When she knew Ben was asleep, with all her adrenaline spent, she took the opportunity to cry, softly, for the first time that night.

When Katie awoke, Ben had climbed out of the bed and was looking out of the window into a whitened realm.

"It's snowed," he said to her, without any boyish wonder.

Katie checked the time on her grandad's watch: it was nearly nine o'clock.

They inspected the front room and found it as they had left it, the damaged doors having held against the weather. Furthermore, whatever that *thing* had been it had not attempted to break into (or *back into*) the house.

The winds had gone, and it was calm and cool.

They went to their respective rooms, dressed for snowfall, and went to the kitchen, where Katie poured them both a glass of milk (the fridge had been more than cold enough to keep everything in there fresh, regardless of the loss of electricity).

After they had drunk up, they put on their wellington boots and gloves, Ben forcing his granddad's much larger glove over his bandaged hand, and they went outside into the back garden, bathed in an ugly light.

The snow that had covered the grass and the plants was thin but dense, crystalline and hard. They went up to the end of the garden and looked into the woods, which had become a truly wholesome seasonal landscape, daubed in silvered powder.

"Nana!" Katie cried in vain into the trees, just to try it one last time. "NANA! GRANDAD! It's me, Katie, and Ben!"

"Nana!" Ben joined in. "Grandad! Help us!"

Their voices bounced into the timbers and echoed weakly back, as though the woods had returned them with sullen regret: *Sorry, kids, nothing to see here.*

Going back to the house, Ben stopped by a plant pot that had earlier that year contained freesias, and asked Katie to come and have a look at something.

In a pile of snow, poking out, was a strange object, cast in white.

Katie picked it up and turned it over in her hands.

"What is it?" Ben asked, shivering, nearly rubbing his uninjured hand against his wounded one and then thinking better of it.

"It's a mask," said Katie, as indeed it was: little bigger than a real adult's face, flat-topped with two sides, joined at the cheeks, one smiling, one frowning. It was made of something that Katie thought was either plastic or wood, or perhaps neither.

"It's Sock and Buskin," she said.

"What?"

"You know? The theatre masks . . . like when our school did *Bugsy Malone:* tragedy and comedy, make you laugh, make you cry."

Ben stared at the artefact, as Katie turned it back to its smiling face. Both children's eyes locked onto that grimace.

Fear flooding back through them, Katie instinctively tossed it long and hard into the woods. It spun in the air and disappeared amongst the trees. They heard it clatter and rattle, and then registered no more.

Katie looked up at the neighbor's house, a semi-detached in the neo-Tudor style: tranquil, lifeless, with no signs of Christmas celebration.

She took out her grandad's watch again: it was ten past nine, and they were *still* alone.

They stood on the pavement at the front of the house.

No cars went by, the snow in the road itself unmarked by any tires.

There was no distant grumble of engines, honking of horns, or rattle of the train on the bridge opposite the hill.

There were no TVs nattering, no carols, no music, no dogs whining or barking, no stomping of boots, and definitely no festive greetings from anyone to anybody. There were, Katie realized, not even birds sat on the branches or pecking in the snow. Human or animal, the *whole world* was as frozen as the puddles in the gutter.

Katie had made Ben eat a banana, almost too solid in the atmosphere of the house, and then wrapped a scarf around him.

She made to take his good hand, but he was resistant.

"They said they would come, Katie!" he asserted, pulling away. "They said they would! *You* said they would! They have to!"

"Look," Katie said channeling her mother. "They're *not* here. It's nine-thirty now. We *have* to walk home. It's the only way Ben. We'll *die here* otherwise."

Katie immediately regretted that last phrase as Ben teared up.

"Ben," she said as tenderly as she could, bending down to him. "You have to *trust me* . . . we have to get home and see what's happened."

"But—" said Ben, struggling. "But what if we get home . . . and they're not there?"

Katie considered this, but could only give what had become her standard answer: "I don't know, but you *have* to trust me."

She held her hand back out. He looked intently and then took it.

They started up the hill in the direction of their house, with the occasional slip.

They passed empty house after empty house, cars parked neatly and unperturbed. Their feet alone broke the virgin snow. Sound itself seemed to fall flat without reverberation, and the children said nothing to each other so as not to realize this barrenness.

As they walked, hand in hand, Katie began to sense something behind them. Continuing on, she looked back to see, in the far distance, a gray shadow trailing them.

Instinctively she sped up, not saying anything to Ben. But, as the journey up the hill dragged on, as though she and he were on a long white treadmill, tilted at an upward angle, the two children slowed down, and the shadow, gradually blending into a figure, caught up with them, pulling up at their left side and keeping their pace.

Katie appreciated that she did not feel any fear, and saw plainly that neither did Ben. They carried on.

The figure was human, a woman, trim and pale, clad in a gray-white cloak, adorned with a close-fitting skull-cap of the same color, her feet and legs securely wrapped up as though they were bandaged.

They walked on for some time until the woman, unsmiling but without threat, spoke to them: "Where are you going?"

"We're going to find our parents," replied Katie, glancing briefly at the woman before facing forward again.

"Yes," Ben said after her, quietly and without feeling.

"You will not find them," said the woman. "You are trapped. You must come with me."

Katie stopped and pulled Ben still with her.

She looked into eyes of the woman. Cool but not vacant, they conveyed the serene truth of their situation.

"What was that face, the two-faced thing?" Katie asked, genuinely curious.

"The very position of death can be both tragic and humorous," the woman replied. "What you saw was the paradox trying to right itself within this loose fragment of the living world you two formerly inhabited."

The language was complex and confusing, but Katie and even Ben understood implicitly, nodding along.

Considering this, Katie then, with much inner bravery, asked her, "Who are *you* then?"

"I," began the woman, but she finally faltered and struggled to find the correct word. "I—*I* am . . ."

Ben broke his silence and beamed, *"An angel?"*

The woman at last smiled, revealing clean if narrow teeth, and cocked her head.

"If that helps, then yes, an *angel*."

She held her hand out for Katie.

"You *must* come with me."

Katie looked at the hand as Ben had looked at hers not so long ago, but then remembered her own words to her brother, and she grasped it tight.

The chain of three people walked unhurriedly on up the hill into a growing white mist. It would be a long, long walk.

Cassilda, November

Ann K. Schwader

Carcosa autumn, ominous with leaves,
Sends jaundiced tatters fit to gild a king
In premonition. As each cloud-wave grieves
Carcosa, autumn, ominous with leaves,
Goes masked beneath black stars no one believes
Until they fall. Amid this reckoning,
Carcosa autumn, ominous with leaves,
Sends jaundiced tatters fit to gild a king.

Night of Pan

Scott J. Couturier

I ran, heedless and weeping, down the sidewalk, colliding occasionally with some passerby or the blunt side of a building. The unfathomed metropolis loomed to all quarters, an endless labyrinth in which I scuttled like a brain-mad rat. My heart throbbed with such force that I expected, at any moment, to feel it explode or, worse, burst the jail cell of my ribs, crawling from my chest cavity on arterial limbs. Such were the moribund visions flooding my brain, itself squirming and throbbing with unwholesome and absolute revelation. Senses undone, mind and soul flayed, body broken on the wheel of hysteric comprehension, I careened blindly I knew not where until finally my legs failed me, collapsing in front of a small, dimly lit café on a street corner I did not recognize. Hardly unusual, given The City's mammoth size, yet somehow I felt I had stepped free for a moment from the inescapable clutches of madness.

I couldn't make out the name on the sign. In my flight, words had wriggled and writhed in my vision, slithering snakelike from signposts or storefronts to nip at my heels. Static *hissssses* suffused my brain: a blank channel, a canceled program. Now I blinked, and my eyes began to focus. The revelations I had lately received would never cease to torment me, not while I lived—and quite possibly even beyond the grave. Yet here on this quiet corner, the streetlamps shedding a diffuse golden glow, I caught a few momentary seconds of peace. My disordered vision corrected itself, lurking patches of gloom skittering off to the recesses of back alleys, shadows of bloody and evil deeds done throughout the centuries still stalking, yearning ever to recur.

I rose and staggered across the street, pushing my way into the café. Inside was all soft glow and cool shadow, fat-bladed fans lazily rotating above, a dozen small, unoccupied tables set in sloppy rows.

Gritting my teeth, I slid quietly past the front counter, which stood unattended; I could hear voices murmuring in a back room. No bell announced my arrival. I went and sat at the table furthest in the shadows, hoping to go unnoticed. There I crossed my arms, bent my head, and wept in silence, only an occasional wheezing gasp marring the quiet.

It all returned to me, over and over again, as if some past version of myself were more real than my present self, ever projecting into my current mind its impressions and experiences. A slide-show cast against my inner eye, from which I could never again turn except in the briefest moments of distraction or sleep. . . . Not that I had slept since the revelation, nor even tried to. Malingering on through five restless days and nights, trembling and sweat-coated, stinking with fear so intensely my neighboring boarder called the police, thinking I might have died and been rotting. But no—I live, and am rotting! A far more terrible fate!

The fan directly over me clicked out a steady rhythm with its motor. The conversation in the back had turned into something more intimate. I heard short, sharp gasps of pleasure and looked up, wondering why my entrance hadn't triggered the bell. There it hung, silver and motionless, waiting to be rung. A frown of perplexity rather than misery creased my brow, but just as I rose to investigate the door flew open, a man in a long dark cloak and tall hat, as of another era, stepping inside with a swish of ostentatious garments. The bell chimed loudly at his entrance.

"I say!" he declared, as if speaking to a companion though he stood manifestly alone. "Such a bitter night out. Grateful I dressed for the occasion."

His declaration, to me, seemed nonsensical. It was mid-August, and certainly not chilly outside. But, as the man made the declaration to himself, I saw no reason to interject. Perhaps—was my reason so far gone? *Was* it winter, and I thought it summer? *Had* the bell chimed when I entered, but I could not hear? Paranoia erupted pustule-like in my brain, and I clutched at my face, rocking back and forth and moaning as the man stepped up to the counter, hand promptly falling to strike the service bell: *Ding ding ding!*

Cursing from the back room, two male voices. A young man rushed out to greet the customer, shirt disheveled, hand fumbling to buckle up his belt. "Yes, sir?" he asked as he reached the counter, breathless and flushed, reeking of sex.

The man in the long cloak and tall hat seemed not to notice. "A coffee, and quickly, my good man!" He paused, squinting, then leaned back from the counter. "You look a bit peaked, if you don't mind my saying so. Hopefully not that fever going around?"

My good man? Peaked? That 'fever' going around? I stared at the oddly dressed customer, my lips curled into a quivering grin. I understood, then, the extent of my reason's undoing. The pulses of horror in my head, the frighted and despairing palpitations of my heart were merely the interior symptoms of an external disease. I refrained from laughing as the hallucinatory scene played itself out, the young man assuring his customer he was fever-free before filling up a cardboard cup with some feel-good logo printed on the side. I tried to read it, but the words started to squiggle, so I looked away.

I only raised my head when the man in the cloak and tall hat settled in a chair across from me. He smiled when he saw my face, though I must have looked ghoulish and terrified, my eyes wide as dinner plates. "I say, is this seat taken? I should think not, on such a dreary night." Spoken in a sharp, educated English accent. He chuckled, lifting the coffee cup to his lips as I continued to stare at him in dumbfounded perplexity. Could he not see the mark of terrible happenings on me? Or was he drawn to me *because* of that mark? His clothing, air, and accent, from another century and continent . . .

"You're not from around here," I managed to stammer, every word a croak.

He raised his dark eyebrows. "You could say that everyone is from everywhere, if you stop to think about it. Especially in The City. But come, this is no way to start our talk. I felt drawn to you as soon as I entered—noting, if I may, certain signs that led me to deduce you have lately borne witness to marvels."

My lips parted in a rictus, through which ugly laughter burbled. "Marvels? No. I have stared into the bottomless pit, whilst gazing into the utmost heaven. You have no idea what I've seen!"

The man's smile widened: he still had not introduced himself. He raised his cuppa again, and I spied a few tiny tufts of black, goat-like hair sprouting between his fingers. "It is confirmed, then. Tell me, to what society do you belong? I noted this mark"—here he reached forward suddenly, tapping a faint triangular scar on the inside of my left wrist. "It confirmed what I only suspected by your aspect. A man sundered by fresh apprehension of the utmost truth! Here, see," he said, pulling down the left sleeve of his gray flannel suit to reveal a similar triangular burn on his wrist, made recently enough that it still showed red at the edges. "My own lodge—The Universal Divinities of Our Brother Set—have a temple over on Eastside, though I daren't say where exactly. I am to undergo the trials next week, that is, the Rites of Pan. I take it you have already seen the Great God for yourself?"

As he spoke, a stifling animal taint invaded my nostrils, stench of barnyard rutting and offal, the ammonia of pooled urine. The black hair, originally limited to patches between his fingers, spread rapidly to overtake both of his hands. His fingers, the bones grinding faintly, melded together into hooves that yet had the facility of hands. His hat fell off as horns crept from beneath his curlicue tousle of blue-black hair, peeping up like obscene nestlings before their true nature became apparent. His snout elongated, and a fire as of witches' oils burned restlessly in each unblinking eye. I watched his transformation in horrified silence, mouth agape, drool pattering on the tabletop—yet my unwelcome guest only smiled and raised his cup, now clumsily clutched between the cleft of a cloven hoof.

"That expression! I take it the generative void looked back into you? Give in, my friend. Surrender. It is your fate to know what most do not, what most could not without slaying themselves in dumb horror. Revel in it, man! As I say, I am soon to undergo the rite myself. Though I have some ken of what lies beyond that veil, never have I offered up my own ego for the slaughter. Should I come out of it broken, as you, still will I shriek blessings to the firmament that something akin to absolute truth is attainable by us fool mortals, terrible and final though it may be."

Something bumped our table to one side, sending his remaining coffee spilling to the ground. I gulped and jumped up from my chair, seeing my guest's fast-swelling phallus was to blame. His body bloated and churned as I watched, until he towered over me, horns digging into the plaster ceiling overhead, fan blades breaking free and clattering floorward. The barista stood calmly behind the counter, disheveled hair now combed back into place, shirt tucked in and apron reapplied. His paramour came out from the back—a sandy-haired boy with mischievous blue eyes. Together they shared a covert kiss, all somewhat visible from the remote corner of my eyes. I strained to focus on them as the thing across from me distended and stank, its words now sounding more like a beast's guttural bray than human speech.

"I—" I said, and gulped, slowly turning to regard this looming nightmare. "They took me to a house. I didn't know what they wanted of me. A Sabbat celebration . . . I watched them kill a goat and drink its blood. Then, worse profanities, and worse, until— What it was I don't know, but they made me drink it out of a human skull. Then through the curtains, locked in with a goat's carcass!" I convulsed then, for no words could convey what followed. The inconceivable, the impossible, the inevitable, the insatiable—I moaned in torment, beating my forehead with my fists as the goat-thing chortled from on high. "This scar . . ." I stretched my left hand out, revealing what the man in the cloak and tall hat had mistaken for an occultic brand. "I burned myself as a child on a hot poker. Before that night I knew nothing. Now, I know *everything*."

Speaking such finality aloud sent me into a sort of shock. The animal stink was overpowering now. The fiend's erection rose from a mat of coarse black pubic hair to the height of a man, white burbles of semen erupting in geyser-like spurts from its tip. I felt hands on me, touching me, reaching down to caress my groin—but they were cold hands, spectral hands, the hands of the dead. I heard a vast, gulf-spanning chuckle, and looked up one final time into the eyes of what was once the man in the cloak and tall hat.

Eternity seethed in those abyss-black pits. Whirling of atoms, whirling of suns and planets, squirm of sperm in the birth canal. Growth and degeneration, protoplasm and polymorphous evolution, germ of seed and cell, bacterium and virus. Parthenogenesis, wild copulation—birth, sex, slaughter, death, swift decay. My mouth worked a silent litany of insane fear and anguish as the great black goat's engorged testicles ruptured, spilling out a tide of maggots.

Matter striving against itself, order arising solely to feed the hunger of chaotic degeneration. I screamed and screamed, maggots flooding into my mouth. The black goat tottered, still laughing, a torrent of blood dripping from the triangular blazon on its left wrist. "Give in to the Night—for it is endless, endless!" it roared.

Slipping on the tide of pestilence, I reeled toward the door, the barista noticing me for the first time and crying out "Hey!" I threw open the door—the bell rang. I seem to still hear that note, chiming in my mind like a star ever more distant.

Then I fled out, forevermore, into the Night of Pan.

Peter Straub and the Magic Taxi

John C. Tibbetts

> "What do you feel? What do you see? Wonderful things, right? Extraordinary shows? Isn't this very beautiful? And terrible? And very dangerous?"—Charles Baudelaire, *Théâtre de Séraphim*

> "Beyond my walls and windows is a world toward which I reach with outstretched arms and an ambitious and divided heart."—Peter Straub

> "You start to grow up when you understand that the stuff that scares you is part of the air you breathe."—*Porkpie Hat* (89)

Clasped within the pages of Peter Straub's estimable short story collection *Houses without Doors* is a peculiar little story—little more than a sketch—called "Something about a Death, Something about a Fire." A scant four pages long, it was written long before the more extreme visceral horrors and Byzantine narrative convolutions of Straub's more famous, at times controversial novels, such as *Ghost Story, Floating Dragon,* and the "Blue Rose" trilogy. I've never forgotten my first encounter with it. Even if more than twenty years later, and in light of Straub's subsequent work, it no longer baffles and excites me in the same way—aren't we all different persons when we revisit our first loves?—I honor the *frisson* of that first encounter and respect the story's subsequent influence on his later stories, particularly in its early grappling with what might be described as the "transcendence" of horror.

But look now: the curtains are parting and a circus clown known only as Bobo drives his Magic Taxi—or is it driving him?—into the circus ring. "At this moment," reports the story's narrator, "the audience falls silent, as if hypnotized. You feel uncertain, slightly on edge, as if you have forgotten something you particularly wished to remember." Bobo wears a funny suit and blats a little horn. No sooner does the performance begin then it is over. What has happened? Children see "great exploding patterns" shooting off from the Taxi. Adults see only Darkness, at first, and "we remember our sins, our meagerness, our miseries." Later a beam of light like "a transparent wire" projects from the Taxi into our eyes, and we find ourselves in "a country that has been calling to us all our lives," where we sense "something about a death, something about a fire." We cry out in happiness as we review the "littleness" and the "foolishness" of scenes from our lives. Finally, as Bobo leaves, blatting his horn and regretfully waving his three-fingered gloved hand, "we awake as if from a trance, drawn up out of unhappiness by our love for this tinted waif." Scholars argue over the meanings of it all and seek analogies to Darwin, Mondrian, and Beckett. "I skimmed the books," reports the narrator, but did not feel "that they had touched the real Bobo, the real Taxi."

It is speculated that before he was famous Bobo may once have been an "ordinary man with an ordinary job," a man like any of us, strapped in his own blank reality. His adventures began when one day he left his house, "going to work in the ordinary way," stepped to the curb, and found the Taxi waiting for him. No one knew just how the Taxi was magic—there was "no special apparatus or mechanism enabling it to astonish, delight, and terrify." But it was his destiny, "entirely unforeseen, black and purring softly, pregnant with miracle" (215–19).

There is something rather mysterious about the circumstances behind this seemingly modest but fascinating little story. While writing my book, *The Gothic Worlds of Peter Straub*, I pressed Peter Straub on several occasions for more information about it. All he could remember was that it was probably written in Milwaukee around 1967–68—or was it Dublin in 1970? "That was a long time ago, when I was writing mostly poetry and couldn't publish anything. 'Bobo' must have been one of those sketches." I pursued the question: How did it come to be published in *Houses without Doors*? "I had thrown everything away," he confessed, "but I must have kept it. There was a terror and splendor there that seemed to fit in *Houses without Doors*" (interview, 1991).

My subsequent search through Straub's papers at the Fales Archives at New York University yielded no notes or typescripts—nothing whatever, in short, about the story.

Peter Straub is customarily lauded—and sometimes criticized—for the convoluted tangles of his narrative structures. The "Blue Rose" trilogy, for example—*Koko, Mystery, The Throat* (1988–93)—is essentially a detective story that involves multiple (frequently unreliable) narrators, serial killers, and shifting locations in time and space, from Milwaukee to Vietnam. Considered together, they constitute one of the most complex bodies of work in all Straub's oeuvre—or, I submit, in that of anybody else. "Whodunit?" Darned if I know. Moreover, as the artistic and spiritual heir of the American Gothic tradition, Straub evokes in other novels, such as *Ghost Story, Shadowland,* and *Mr. X,* the buried guilts, ancestral transgressions, ghostly doubles, and monstrous progenies in the works of Nathaniel Hawthorne, Henry James, and H. P. Lovecraft.

Underlying it all is something central to Straub's oeuvre. The Magic Taxi that awaited Bobo at the curb transformed his humdrum life into a "destiny entirely unforeseen," a condition or "terror and splendor." Here in a nutshell is an example of Straub's paradoxical relationship between horror and the transcendent. Is Bobo *escaping* reality or, in a transformative moment, is he plunging *deeper* into it? "The works of Peter Straub . . . seek to find room for something like the sacred," writes Gary K. Wolfe, Straub's most insightful critic. "This revisionist approach to horror breaks through both horror and fantasy tropes to arrive at a kind of transcendence: a heightened sense of reality laced with deeper, more difficult, and more powerful meanings than are available through traditional genre protocols" (153). "At moments of terrible terror and extremity," Straub explains, "one can experience a sort of clarity that nobody would want to go through . . . But at those moments, one sometimes can really *see*" (interview, 2011). For Bobo, the earliest of so many of Straub's protagonists, the world is washed clean of habit, and it suddenly *blazes, sizzles,* and *gleams* (to use some of Straub's oft-cited adjectives) into a carnivalesque pageant which we, unable to share in the revelation, can only sense as something once experienced but mostly forgotten.

Straub finds precedents in these transformative, epiphanic encounters in works by his favorite writers, particularly Nathaniel Hawthorne and Dashiell Hammett. "Amid the seeming confusion of our mysterious world," observes Hawthorne in words that perfectly describe Straub's stories, "individuals are so nicely adjusted to a system, and systems to one another and to a whole, that, by stepping aside for a moment, a man exposes himself to a fearful risk of losing his place forever" ("Wakefield" 75). Consider a key scene in Hawthorne's *The Marble Faun:* Donatello and Miriam in a moment of desperate impulse have thrown the body of her mysterious offending pursuer off a precipice to his death. At that moment they turn to each other in a "conspiratorial embrace" and in their shared guilt they achieve a "moment of rapture," a "dark sympathy" that is "a bliss, or an insanity, which the unhappy pair imagined to be well worth the sleepy innocence that was forever lost to them" (690–91). Turning to another work Straub frequently cites, Dashiell Hammett's *The Maltese Falcon,* a family man one day finds his life transformed by a single moment. After narrowly missing death from a falling beam on a construction site, spared only by blind chance, "Flitcraft felt like somebody had taken the lid off life and let him look at the works," and the "clean, orderly, and sensible affair" of life was now "fundamentally none of those things." He walks away from his wife and family into a new reality where, through a haphazard and blind chance he meets another woman and begins a new life and family. "He wasn't sorry for what he had done," writes Hammett; "He adjusted himself to beams falling, and then no more of them fell, and he adjusted himself to them not falling" (54).

Likewise, moments of trauma and extremity—that fateful "step to the curb"—induct Straub's characters into their destinies. In "The Buffalo Hunter" Bobby Bunting observes:

Let's say you're just walking down the street . . . and you're not thinking about anything in particular . . . you're absolutely, completely, inside the normal world. And then something happens—a car backfires, or a woman with a gorgeous voice starts to sing behind you—and suddenly you see what's really there—that everything, absolutely everything is alive . . . like you don't really exist anymore in the old way at all. (175)

Several of Straub's ghost stories strike a reverse angle, as it were, wherein ghosts, shorn of their materiality, hunger for the starkly physical world. In *The Throat* we are told that ghosts "still want things. They look at us all the time, and they miss being alive. We have taste and color and smells and feelings, and they don't have any of those things. They stare at us, they don't miss *anything*. They really see what's going on, and we hardly ever really see that" (175). And in "The Hunger," a personal favorite, the newly executed murderer, Frank Wardwell, returns to gaze raptly through a window at "this little miracle" of a five-year-old child, ravenously drinking in the details of the child's "inward-looking little face," her every emotion "written in subtle but powerful runes on the blank page that is her face" (247–48).

Like a modern-day John Ruskin, Straub and his characters recover the surfaces of reality in all their texture and detail: "You must *attend* to things," he says, "as one is asked to do with those Andy Warhol movies in the '60s. You experience almost a supernatural payoff . . . And you have these images that are very important, like the glass of water shining on the tabletop. It's an image of immense mystery: you can see through it, it's pure and nourishing, it gives life, it's inert, yet somehow magical, laden with inexpressible yearnings and meanings" (interview, 2011). "I've tried to notice things," says Professor Alan Brookner in *The Throat*, "to pay *attention* . . . There is another world, and it's *this* world" (235–37). "Every leaf, every pine needle, every path through the woods, every bird call," says detective Von Heilitz in *Mystery*, "had come alive, was vibrant, full of meaning. Everything *promised*. Everything *chimed*. I knew more than I knew. There was a secret beating away beneath the surface of everything I saw" (98).

Even the tortures that characters such as Harry Beevers in "The Juniper Tree" inflict on his younger brother and the atrocities the eponymous Mr. Clubb and Mr. Cuff subject upon their victim in that masterpiece of comic guignol are, well, *instructional:* "'We do not assault,' Clubb and Cuff say. 'We induce, we instruct, we instill. These cannot be crimes, and those who do them cannot be criminals'" (*Magic Terror* 323). "Think about Clubb and Cuff," Straub observes,

> they come out of nowhere. They give you what you really want, even though you didn't know what you wanted! It's their business and it's a sick, bloody business. It's an art form for them. They understand themselves to be artists, and who's to say they're not! They certainly get to where they're going, unlike most of us. When they get their hands on you, they're going to get the results they want. (Interview, 2011)

Perhaps too casually, I have employed the term "carnivalesque" in a foolish attempt to capture the "something about a death, something about a fire" of Bobo's circus performance. Typically, the term, as derived from Rabelais by way of Mikhail Bakhtin, refers to the unbridled collapse of all hierarchical rank, privileges, norms, prohibitions, wherein differences between the cruel and the merciful, faith and doubt, the divine and the human are suspended. Straub himself prefers the term "revel," as derived from critic John Clute's book *The Darkening Garden:* "This is the penultimate movement in a classic horror fiction," Straub explains, "when the bonds have burst, demonic things, unbalanced things have been set free. And they really 'play' with ordinary life, distort it, kill; and you can hear the background music of the circus band" (interview, 2014).

Bobo's revels remind us of the phantasmagorias that abound in later, more well-known stories. In *Ghost Story* the malevolent black jazz musician, Dr. Rabbitfoot brings his evil carnival to town while, at the same time, the local Milburn Rialto movie theater screens a riot of comic-book horror and conflagration. In *Floating Dragon* the mirror of the ghostly Gideon Winter discloses a burning picture of "the damned town of [Hampstead] turning into a funhouse" (367). And there are the deranged vaudeville acts in Coleman Collins's *Théâtre des illusions* in *Shadowland* and the family of Ned Dunstan in *Mr. X* with their wild talents deteriorating over generations. In *The Talisman* and *Black House* the Territories "contain a kind of sacred magic: "In the abyss below the steps, they see circling birds like vultures with the white screaming of lost babies. In a long, narrow room like a Pullman car, living cartoons—two rabbits, a fox, a stoned-looking frog wearing white gloves—sit around a table catching and eating what appear to be fleas. They are *cartoons*, 1940s-era black-and-white *cartoons*" (*Black House* 779).

And yet, amid the horrors and confusions brutal and comic by turns are moments that prove definitively that Straub, like Hawthorne—and we recall the aforementioned scene in *The Marble Faun*—in the final analysis, is very much the humanist. Not the hack writer of spooks and madmen, but an artist with profound existential concerns. "You know," said Straub, in our 1986 interview, "John Keats said something in a letter to the effect that in the creation of a soul, things that injure us affect the way our soul is written upon, the way our soul is able to expand. This is a guy speaking on the verge of death. He knew what was in store for him. He could understand what suffering had given him, which was a depth of understanding you don't get unless you are profoundly beaten up by the world. We are *all* maimed" (interview, 1986). Thus Bobo's "painted figure" is so akin to us: "We are drawn up out of unhappiness . . . We remember our sins, our meagerness, our miseries. Some of us weep. Bobo invariably sobs, the tears crusting on his white makeup, and blats and blats his little horn." At the end of *Ghost Story*, released from the horrors and trauma that had engulfed him, Don Wanderley experiences "a wave of love for everything mortal . . . For everything with a brief definite life span—a tenderness for all that could give birth and would die, everything that could live . . . He knew it was only relief and adrenalin, but it was all the same a mystical, perhaps a sacred emotion." He silently salutes his friends, living and dead: "Dear brothers, dear humankind" (483). In the horrors disclosed in "A Short Guide to the City" it is concluded that "Violence is the physical form of sensitivity" (105) . . . And in *Black House* Jack Sawyer suffers an apotheosis mingling "Beauty and terror, beauty and pain—there is no way out of the conundrum. Exhausted, strung out, Jack cannot hold off his awareness of the world's essential fragility, its constant, unstoppable movement toward death, or the deeper awareness that in that movement lies the source of all its meaning" (679).

It is clear to me that the Magic Taxi is Straub's metaphor for coping with the trauma and pain of his own damaged childhood, including the terrible accident that resulted, he claims, in a near-death experience. "Most writers have had sketchy childhoods," he confessed guardedly,

> in which something went awry, something went amiss, or they became aware of sexual dysfunctions which had to be concealed. Nothing is safe. Terror and pain are beneath everything. When I was a kid, I was a fictional character, but the fictional character was *myself*, the self my parents wanted me to be, the self I would have been perhaps had I not been injured and abused as a small boy. I didn't want to be the person who was injured and abused. It didn't fit my *idea* of myself. I always experienced myself as a person of some integrity and wholeness; and also of a certain mental or spiritual force of some kind. I didn't see myself as being victimized. It was a horrible insult; it made me angry and humiliated and ashamed. So I had to pretend it wasn't true. (Interview, 2011)

How, then, to reconcile Straub's horrors, atrocities, and serial killers with the blessings and transfigurations that illumine his stories? It seems he has done just that—not by denying so much, or privileging one over the other, as by *accommodating* their conjoined realities. It is the "sort of accommodation" that Gary K. Wolfe declares underlies Straub's finest work: "A novel such as Straub's *lost boy lost girl* begins with the emotional devastation of serial murders and a suicide, but seeks to move its central character beyond this toward some sort of accommodation, possibly even toward some version of grace" (153).

In our last interview, in 2015, just after his move from Manhattan to Brooklyn, we turned again to "Something about a Death, Something about a Fire." I couldn't let go of Bobo and his Magic Taxi. The little story had come up in our first interview in 1986 and here it was, again, like the Magic Taxi, ever purring at the curb. "I guess you could say that story was my own Magic Taxi," he admitted, opening up at last about it, "or that it indicated the existence of a good-sized Magic Taxi somewhere within my own mind and imagination. It's about wonder and close attention and the way close attention can widen out into a sense of mystery, of unknowingness; there's a sense that glory may not always end that way. Everything has its own twin that trails along after it."

He paused then, and I can still see him leaning back in his chair at the kitchen table, half-empty coffee cup beside him. "To think there really is no meaning in life," he continued, "is to live in an empty, dead world, I think. Is the everyday a kind of blank, or does it reveal a transfiguration? Is there a hidden radiance or a hidden nothing?" He paused again, then suddenly smiled broadly with his customary good humor. "There's no question which side of the duality I have chosen as the truth. I like the drawing by Chris Van Allsburg in his book, *The Mysteries of Harris Burdick*. It could have been an illustration for *The Talisman:* It shows some children pedaling a machine through a desert; and there before them is a huge palace. The caption says: 'If it was anywhere, it was there.' Although I don't really think there is a theological or supernatural motif that breathes through the world, what I really believe is that the world is its own meaning."

Peter Straub and me at our last interview,
19 October 2015, Brooklyn, New York

Works Cited

John C. Tibbetts interviews with Peter Straub:

Providence, R.I., Halloween weekend, 1986. World Fantasy Convention

New York City, 5 May 1991

New York City, May 2011

New York City, 13 November 2014

Brooklyn, New York, 19 October, 2015

Bakhtin, Mikhail. *Rabelais and His World.* Tr. Helene Iswolsky. Cambridge, MA: M.I.T. Press, 1965.

Clute, John. *The Darkening Garden.* Cauheegan, WI: Payseur & Schmidt, 2006.

Hammett, Dashiell. *The Maltese Falcon.* 1929. New York: Alfred A. Knopf, 1957.

Hawthorne, Nathaniel. *The Marble Faun.* In *The Novels and Tales of Nathaniel Hawthorne.* New York: Modern Library, 1937.

———. "Wakefield." In *The Celestial Railroad and Other Stories.* New York: Signet, 1963.

Straub, Peter. *Ghost Story.* New York: Coward, McCann & Geoghegan, 1979.

———. *Houses without Doors.* New York: Dutton, 1990. [Stories cited: "Something about a Death, Something about a Fire," "The Juniper Tree," "In the Realm of Dreams," "The Buffalo Hunter," "A Short Guide to the City."]

———. *Magic Terror.* New York: Random House, 2000. [Stories cited: "Hunger, an Introduction" and "Mr. Clubb and Mr. Cuff."]

———. *Mystery.* Dutton, New York, 1990.

———. *The Throat.* New York: Dutton, 1993.

———, and Stephen King. *Black House.* New York: Pocket Books, 2001.

Tibbetts, John C. *The Gothic Worlds of Peter Straub.* Jefferson, NC: McFarland, 2016.

Van Allsburg, Chris. *The Mysteries of Harris Burdick.* Boston: Houghton Mifflin, 1984.

Wolfe, Gary K. *Evaporating Genres.* Middleton, CT: Wesleyan University Press, 2011.

Ronin: The Combat Journal of Mark Bullet

Carl E. Reed

05-05-20—

If only Uncle Charlie could see me now! Dressed in black from head-to-toe: T-shirt, jeans, combat boots. His old Ka-Bar fighting knife snugged into a sheath in my right boot, .45 auto tucked into the waistband of my jeans. Hatchet, Louisville slugger, and hammer near to hand. Shotgun and machete cleaned, oiled, and ready for action in the gun cabinet. He wouldn't dare lay a hand on me now. Not if he knew what was good for him. Oh, no! He wouldn't dare suggest we go down into the basement now.

"Now"—it's such a vital, imprisoning, monosyllabic utterance, isn't it? The only time frame we can ever be said to inhabit fully; the only time we can truly call our own. Let me wax florid on you for a moment in the manner of the Masters. What is the past but a conclave of ghosts? The future but a conjectured congeries of phantoms? But now—ah, that's where the action is! Right *now*. Say it with me—tongue positioned behind your upper central incisors preparatory to sounding that insectile-whine consonant, breath expelling a near-diphthongish elongated vowel bookended by a fuzz-pedal wah-wah "w"—jaw clenched, lips in a tight circle like plains Indians circling Custer's 5th Cavalry, vocal cords vibrating: *now*.

Hell of a word, ain't it?

Well, dear ole Uncle Creepflesh and Aunt Can't-Hear-So-Good aren't here *now*. No indeed. They is no here, no more. Yowza! Mark 'em down in the Book of Rotters as the first gibbering, wild-eyed victims of the ZA. Cue violins, weeping angels, and all that sap-happy horseshit. (If that's your cup of tea. It ain't mine, sister.)

All Whitmanesque posing—literary and colloquial ("I am large; I contain multitudes") aside, you must understand: I'm righteous now. Death-spitting pistol in one hand, blood-drenched combat knife in the other. A locked-&-cocked, lean-&-mean, black-clad motherfucking badass killing *machine*. Yee-hah! Hacking down zombs left and right. Four kills under my belt so far. Geronimo! Last man standing in Darton, Ohio, battling alone against the zombie hordes. You wouldn't recognize me all grown up, folks.

05-06-20—

You never get used to the gore. That part still gets to me. The horror of body disintegration: blood, brains, guts, shotgun-spattered chunks of oily hair and rotting flesh, flying through the air like a Tom Savini special effect in a George Romero film.

Uncle Charlie and I talked about violence while he still was alive. Given that he was a retired homicide detective and all. And one of Uncle Sam's Misguided Children before that. Caught the tail end of Vietnam just before Saigon was overrun. Gooks in the wire, heh! Served in the infantry. Military occupational specialty oh-three-hundred eleven: grunt. Ooh-rah! Then forty-some years on the Darton PD as deputy chief. He was the real deal. Then he ran out of good years and they forced him to retire. So I know he saw some shit.

Not that he ever wanted to talk about it. Dear warrior uncle was an accomplished rapist but surprisingly reticent about discussing the wet work. He really was. When I asked him about all the fighting and killing he'd done he'd go stone-faced and change the subject fast. Hell, that was the only reason I let him touch me in the first place. Got it? I respected him as a warrior. Figured he'd earned it. Like the Spartans in ancient Greece, pairing off with one another. The Theban Band. Knights Templar. Samurai in feudal Japan.

Not that I liked it. I didn't. Most of the time. That kind of stuff wasn't me. It's confusing. It's all twisted up: pain and pleasure. Sometimes I thought about doing it to others. Which I never did, because I'm not like that. As I just said.

Let me be very clear: if you swing a certain way it isn't any concern of mine. To each his own. *Vive la différence,* right? Just don't force me, motherfucker! Rape is downright rude.

Wandered off-topic there for a second. Apologies to all concerned.

I was talking about killing.

The name is Bullet. Mark Bullet. I honed my skills on the job. I kill zombies. Ghouls, walking cadavers, parasites. Skeletal horrors and all manner of undead, creepy-crawly things that refuse to lie down and die.

Until they meet me.

Going out on another combat patrol tonight.

05-08-20—

That was close. Too close. Got cornered in a cul-de-sac and had to hack my way out. Wish I had a wicked-cool samurai sword for close-in wet work instead of this damn clumsy machete. But to paraphrase a late-great Secretary of Defense of the good ole USA: You fight a ZA with the tools you've been given, not the tools you wish you had. And what a pussy-ass, bullshit title "Secretary of Defense" is anyway! Sounds like the nickname of a talented hockey goalie, or a defensive coach for an NFL football team. Or some cunt typing up reports in the basement of the Pentagon. War Czar—now that's a title fit for a supreme warlord! Death Commander. Lord God of Battle.

The point is: three more zombs terminated. Which brings my total kill count to seven. Lucky number, right? Seven down and a horde to go. Still, that's three less undead to deal with now at a cost of zero bullets fired. No small thing, since bullets aren't easily replaced nowadays.

05-12-20—

I'm keeping this journal as an act of faith. That's a self-consciously ironic sentence because I don't believe in God. I believe in Ayn Rand. Nietzsche. The code of Bushido. Will-to-power, the superman, rational egoism. Looking backward at the present from the moment of your own death. Living as if you were, in fact, already dead. Which you are, in the future. Yes? Which keeps on turning into *now*. All that stuff. I'm an immovable-mover, beyond mere good and evil. Like the Spartans or the samurai. Choosing death in all things I become the Slayer of Death: master of myself.

This journal is my last will and testament. I keep it for the benefit of other warriors, in other cities and towns, who might be fighting back against the zombs and ghouls.

I refuse to believe that I'm the last man alive on Earth. I'm sure it just feels like it. I can't be the only one left with the brains to fathom the problem and the balls to do something about it.

So. A little background on Yours Truly:

I was born Eric Pulvermacher. I went to Westfield High over on Stonewall and Addison. Of course, that life is over and done with now. That all ended last year when I was expelled from school and ordered to talk to Dr. Hartmann as a condition of my probation after I choked out Dick face Perez, my history teacher. The prick wouldn't accept my paper. I could see knocking points off for being late, but punk-ass Perez wouldn't accept my paper *at all,* you understand? He just flat-out refused to accept it. We argued and things got a little crazy. The next thing you know I'm choking this guy out in the classroom and he's going all bug-eyed red-face and my fellow students are shouting, "Get off him! Stop it, Eric! Let him go!" Stuff like that. A couple of jocks got up from their seats and advanced on me, so I let Perez go. No big deal. Nobody died. Or was even hospitalized, for that matter. My reward for showing restraint here? I got expelled. Remember this, friends and neighbors: no good deed goes unpunished.

As for the rest of the teachers—they liked me well enough, I guess. I was good with words. That may sound like bragging, but I assure you it isn't. Wasn't. Isn't. That is to say: I could wax prolix when the spirit moved me and lay down as lapidary and/or purple a line of polysyllabic nested subordinate clauses as you'd ever hope to encounter. I was by turns: a scrivener of ye-olde terror tales working by flickering candlelight; red-eyed Jack stalking Victorian alleys through London fog; a slick-haired, gum-popping '50s juvenile delinquent eager to flick out his switchblade and bury it some hopeless square's gut, Daddy-O! I read hundreds of books on every subject under the sun. You see, I believed—believe—in expanding the mind. I wrote stories and poems and drew cartoons and performed in plays. I played Kreon and Tybalt and The Boy (in Luigi Pirandello's *Six Characters in Search of an Author*) and my favorite role of all time: a ronin in some kind of Japanese chop-socky production put on by pretentious, goggle-eyed Mr. Tiernin.

A ronin—now there's a killing machine for you! A renegade, masterless samurai. Implacable, remorseless, unstoppable. The role that was assigned me by fate—twice. Once in play; once for real.

Diagnosed hostile personality disorder or no (what bullshit—I don't suffer fools gladly, that's all. Who does?), the future looked fairly bright. If things had turned out differently I would have graduated and then enlisted. Become a Navy Seal, Marine Corps Force Recon commando, Army ranger, or paratrooper. And gone to college on Uncle Sam's dime. Or if that wasn't possible (due to Dr. Hartmann's blackening of my good name), I would have enlisted in the French Foreign Legion. *Marche ou crève* (march or die), you sons-of-bitches! That would have given me some street cred. Then again, if things had continued as they should I could have picked up freelance security work advertised in the back of *Soldier of Fortune* magazine: strung together a bunch of one-off assignments and traveled around the world wasting fools and writing books about it. People pay big money for that kind of stuff. A little of the old "ultraviolence," as Anthony Burgess termed it in his exhilarating novel *A Clockwork Orange.* The reading public can't get enough of it. So give the people what they want, I say: violence and death spiced with a little torture. I would have been good at it.

But life is funny. Not "funny ha-ha" but hold-you-down-in-the-dark-and-cornhole-you-while-you-scream-for-help-and-no-one-comes kind of funny. Yeah. While someone else pretends not to hear. It's enough to make one philosophical.

Well, enough writing for now. I've got to keep a balance between intellectual pursuits and action. Like the samurai. Hacking off heads one moment, then sipping tea, writing haiku, and painting ethereal scenes of smoke-wreathed mountains the next.

Did I mention that I'm up to seventy knuckle push-ups and two hundred sit-ups a day?

And oh yeah—I turned seventeen today.

05-19-20—

Haven't written in this journal for a week. Guess that's obvious from the dates on the last two entries. I didn't go out on patrol, either. No stomach for it. I hunkered down to conserve my strength. I read, worked out, slept a lot. Lucid dreams at night. Especially the one where I kill Uncle Charlie and Aunt Can't-Hear-So-Good over and over again, taking control in the dream when I realize it's a dream. That's what makes it a lucid dream, see? Control. Manifesting all manner of weapons in my hands with which to do them in. Cartoon insanity: chainsaws, bazookas, giant battle axes and halberds; bundles of red-stick dynamite.

I barricaded the front door of the house. Broke up the furniture. Found some sheets of plywood down in the basement and hammered them into place over the first-floor windows. Left the curtains up, though. From the outside things still look fairly normal.

Uncle Charlie is still down in the basement here with his pretend hard-of-hearing wife. Both of them dead for over a month. Despite the plastic bags I wrapped them in they're beginning to smell. I used up all the spray cans of room deodorizer long ago. Ain't that a bitch?

05-21-20—

Got careless on this last raid and paid the price. Battled two zombs up-close-and-personal in one of their lairs. I tried to get cute by going in fast and quiet with the hammer, and this wild-eyed harridan turned just as I was raising the weapon and raked my face with her claws. Now I've got blood-red furrows running forehead to chin. Damn near lost an eye! I unslung my shotgun and gunned her down along with her undead consort, a haggard-faced ghoul whose liver-spotted hands closed around my throat during the attack. All that screaming—some of it mine. Stomped matchstick arms into kindling. Caved in the ghoul's bony chest with the hardwood butt of the shotgun. Gave both of them a couple of point-blank double-ought blasts. That did the trick; yessiree Bob!

(Tactical note: Saw the barrel off the shotgun for better maneuvering in close-quarters combat.)

05-25-20—

I oftentimes wonder who it is I'm talking to in this journal, myself or posterity? Both. Neither. Someone else. It really doesn't matter. Ultimately, the point is to write yourself sane. Isn't that what Bradbury advised? You face the blank sheet of paper in order to be able to face the world out there, for the blank sheet of paper contains/implies/organizes the world out there—and the boundless depths within. Macrocosm/microcosm.

Free-writing. Defeat the internal censor and keep the pen moving across the paper. Tokyo is burning. Stalingrad. The five-and-dime on the corner. Nietzsche was a demigod who died too soon to fuck Ayn Rand and leave behind a glowering panzer-bellied Buddha who could have launched a redemptive Age of the Selfish Superman. Then we would have seen the rise of the best and the brightest, the boldest and the bravest to their rightful places as warrior-poet/philosopher-kings of the new society. Bushido! Leaving the cringing herd animals mewling in terror and crying out for the extinction their nasty, brutish lives so richly deserve. Them and the zombs who parasitically cling to life long after any self-respecting people would have offed themselves as their intellectual and physical strength began to fail.

You see? Stream-of-consciousness: a great technique for breaking down barriers and getting to the heart of things. Like cutting your stomach open to feel your intestines spill onto your lap to redeem your honor. Those fuckers weren't kidding around; the word "honor" meant something in feudal Japan, by god! I'm not going to go back and clean any of that up. You should see how the truth-sausage is made—fragments, grammatical errors, awkward phrasing and all. Learn from it. Delve deep into the mind to bring forth monsters and the weapons to slay them. What was it the Gnostics and Philip K. Dick used to say? "If you bring forth what is within you, what you bring forth will save you. If you do not bring forth what is within you, what you do not bring forth will destroy you" (*Gospel of Thomas*).

All important thoughts are set down in writing.

I'm ready to talk about my parents now.

Mr. and Mrs. Pulvermacher died in a car crash when I was five. Dad was drunk-driving home from some beer-fart honky-tonk while my mother was jacking him off in the front seat. I guess that's redundant to state because they couldn't be in the back seat, right? In a moving car? But a handjob, though. I mean, how lame is that? Kid stuff. They smashed into the back of another car parked on the shoulder of the road with its lights off. Some doddering geriatric spoozle had pulled over when she ran out of gas and just sat there until she got rammed from behind. Of course she lived, fractured spine and all. The old lady, not my mother.

Good ole Uncle Creepflesh gave me the gory details when I was ten. Why tell me this shit? Hell, is the story even true? Sometimes I wonder. The accident happened, sure enough; and the old lady lived on with a broken spine. But that bit about the handjob? Uncle Charlie said all the details were in the police report; a trucker who'd passed my parents just before the crash reported that detail to the police. Still, I have my doubts. Uncle Charlie told some tall tales every once in a while. So I dunno.

Ultimately, though, does it matter? I mean would it make any difference if my parents had died in a terrorist attack in a Paris café? Crashed their private jet into the Caribbean on the way to a resort in

Jamaica? Got run over in the street by a bus? Died in their sleep from carbon monoxide poisoning due to a leaky furnace?

The salient fact is that they left me when I was five.

I was then sent to live with my dad's older brother and his ancient white-haired wife: Uncle Creepflesh and Aunt Don't-Hear-So-Good. That concludes the story of me and my parents.

Boring, tedious irrelevancy. I merely state it for the record.

05-27-20—

A good night's hunting. Tracked a checkered-overcoat-wearing zomb back to her basement lair in the red-bricked, three-story apartment building at Chattam and Wentworth behind the burnt-out ruins of the Cloverleaf Mall. The doddering zomb was using a walker. A frickin' walker! Came in behind the thing as she pushed open the door to her lair. A couple of blows with the hatchet and she crashed into a wall, slid down to the floor, and curled into a fetal position, moaning. It took a couple dozen more whacks to finish her off. That old bird was stringy but tough. While I was terminating the zomb a black Lab came crawling down the hallway on its belly, keening and whining. Eyes rolling white in its head. Absolutely terrified.

I left it alone, of course. It wasn't a zombie dog. It was just a dog dog. I think that animals are pure, unfettered Dionysian spirits.

I let the poor dumb animal out of the apartment after I whacked its undead masters. It's all alone now in the world. Did you know Hitler liked dogs? The man who said "life doesn't forgive weakness" loved dogs and vegetables while hating on tobacco and strong drink. He really did! I wonder what Ayn Rand thought of him . . .

05-29-20—

Tomorrow's the big one. I've located a large nest of zombs—at least a hundred of them—and will go in hard (shotgun, pistol, combat knife) after nightfall to wipe them out.

Like Marcus Aurelius writing in camp before closing with German hordes across the Rhine on the morrow, or King Henry V mingling in disguise amongst his soldiers to gauge their morale on the eve of the Battle of Agincourt, I feel the need to scribe a few meaningful (last?) words and take the measure of my own fortitude.

"He who fights with monsters must take care lest he become a monster," warned Nietzsche. Profound words. I have not become a monster, though I battle with monsters. I continue to write, think, self-reflect. I *feel*.

There really is only one question remaining. It "isn't who is going to let me; it's who is going to stop me." Right you are, Ms. Rand! Your books opened my eyes to the slave mentality and sick herd morality that seeks to bind the great and the powerful in chains of the *Untermenschen's* devising. Your writings turned me from victim to conqueror: from an angry, lonely boy to a gimlet-eyed warrior bringing cold steel and hot gunfire to the matter of a final solution to "the zombie question." God, how I wish I could fuck you! Hard cock pistoning in and out of your tight Russian cunt, those unblinking black materialist eyes of yours squinting at me through a haze of burnt nicotine, cigarette holder clenched in your teeth while you bark out savage pillow talk: "Don't make me pity you! I'll hate you if you make me pity you."

I feel the ghosts of dead ronin and Spartans and Templars about me now, legion upon legion of hard-bitten warriors who feared neither man nor cutting-edged steel while alive—only dishonor. As that ancient noble tome *Hagakure* instructs (paraphrased from memory): "The way of the warrior is death. If given a choice between two actions—one leading to life, the other death—always choose death. In this way you will never hesitate or flinch at the moment of truth."

I jump up and scream, body locked and rigid, clenched fist punching at the storm-clouded sky: *"Tenno Heika Banzai! Banzai! Banzai!"*

I am a nihilist-objectivist ronin zombie-slayer, readying myself for final battle. And I fear absolutely nothing.

05-30-20—

I'm alive! The biggest combat mission of my war against the undead to date and I'm still alive! Unbelievable. Killed so many zombs I lost count. My hands are shaking as I pen these lines. (I packed this journal in with my gear so as to be able to write in it immediately after battle.)

Here's how it went down. I broke into their two-story lair through an unguarded back window. Damn near vomited from the stench of piss, shit, rotting flesh, and cleaning chemicals. Found three zombs in torpor and dispatched them with point-blank shotgun blasts, whirled and gunned down two more shuffling into the room.

The rest is a blur. Running down corridors. *Blam-blam-blam!* Aged faces appearing in doorways only to disintegrate in clouds of spattering brain and bone-chipped red mist. Duck into a room and terminate the skeletal fucks cringing there, reload—eight 12-gauge rounds in the shotgun—then back out into the hallway for another helter-skelter dash past walls festooned with the most godawful and banal of oil-painted subjects: flowers in vases, bowls of fruit on kitchen tables, seascapes, sad clowns, rearing horses. In the midst of this hideousness I rendered the very air electric—all was booming gunfire and acrid gun smoke. Burned through an entire box of shells: fifty rounds.

I came upon a nurse in a common room with a cell phone clamped to her ear. When she spotted me, she attempted to duck under a table. I dispatched her with another blast of the shotgun— irritated at having to waste a shell on a person instead of a zomb— but then those who aid the undead in defiance of natural law and Ayn Randian principles must be prepared to die alongside their monsters. So be it.

A second later I found myself confronted by an orderly who rose up from behind an upholstered chair wielding a length of pipe. I raised ole Boomstick, pumped the slide-action and fired—click! Out of ammo.

Okay then—hand-to-hand. Get some!

Mr. Pudgy—a ghostly-pale middle-ager with a bowl haircut and a propensity to sweat like—well, a guy fighting for his life—and I did a little jig in the common room. The paint on the wall? Puke green. Honest to god. He's swinging at my head while I jab at his jiggling stomach with the empty shotgun. Got him off balance and he fell. Yank the Ka-Bar from my boot, pounce, stab him in the face and throat. Now *that* was a kill I earned! Fucker thrashed and fountained blood everywhere, but I rode him like a cowboy a bucking bronco (sorry for the cliché, Mrs. Henrietta: Freshman English) and I kept stabbing him in the face and throat until he stopped fighting and lay there gurgling. I stood up and dispatched him with a two-shot double-tap to the chest from the .45. He earned that mercy, fallen warrior that he was. Even though he served the zombs. You gotta respect a fighter.

I left the premises when I heard the wail of approaching sirens. Back out the window. Retrieved my duffle bag from the concealing bushes beneath the window, shoved the shotgun in it, and slung the duffle bag over my shoulder and hot-footed it away from Green Acres nursing home. Ran almost two miles through Foster Woods forest preserve until I came out on Eddington Avenue and caught the bus.

The burnt-out Cloverleaf Mall is passing on my left as I write this. The place burns to the ground every three to five years; they must be torching it for the insurance money. Not a bad scam if you can pull it off.

Almost home.

Steady, deep breaths. Center and focus. There'll be time to deconstruct this raid in more detail later, incorporate lessons learned into future mission planning. The important thing is that I survived. Survived unwounded and—

Fuck! Flashing red-and-blue lights behind me. The bus is pulling over. Fuck fuck *fuck!*

Three magazines of .45-caliber ammo left. I'm not going down without a fight. No way; no how. You've cornered a fighter. A survivor! A fearless ronin.

Mark Bullet, over and out.

Azraelle, the Lich-Queen

Manuel Arenas

I. *Good Morrow, Azraelle Undercroft*

Scud clouds darken the griseous skies and hover like a headsman's axe over the vicarage. Seated at his oaken desk, the Vicar Rhodes removes his spectacles and kneads his temples as he slowly exhales a breath infused with the whisky shot he shared earlier with the sexton to calm their nerves after the man burst into his office in a tizzy, ranting and dragging the vicar to witness the ghoulish tableau he had discovered in the churchyard while making his morning rounds. It appears that someone dressed up a couple of old cadavers to look like satanic headbangers and left them strewn amongst the headstones. The perpetrators also left behind a ghetto blaster under the lychgate that the already shaken sexton had backed into during his initial retreat from the scene which prompted it to blare a blasphemous clamor that sounded to him like "the devil's own choir." Now the vicar must prepare himself to answer the many queries of the constable waiting for an audience in the vestibule.

Returning his spectacles to the bridge of his aquiline nose, he rises from his chair and walks across the room to a small mirror that he often times refers to when fastening the many buttons on his sarum. Examining his haggard reflection in the glass, he feels alternately drawn to and repelled by the mirror. Fixated on the reflective surface, his pupils begin to widen and his eyesight becomes murky. However, a staccato knocking on his door breaks the thrall and he blinks his eyes, shakes his head, and turns to open the door to receive the constable.

On the other side of the mirror, in a macabre dimension of benighted spirits and pernicious entities, Azraelle looks back from her vanity mirror, smiling, and says *"Proximo tempore, sacerdos."* She chose to learn Latin, which is not native to her, because she saw it as being the language of the churchyards. *Requiescat in pace, memento mori,* every legend on a plaque, every epitaph on a tombstone seemed to bear an inscription in the *lingua Latina.* At least in the Western world, it was her key to the city of the dead. Hiding in the lower berths of churches, known as undercrofts (hence the sobriquet), where the sarcophagi of the church elders may be found, Azraelle would linger in the darkness, listening through vents and peeping through keyholes as she snuffed the tiny lights of crypt vermin while listening to the novices learning what was once the language of the Roman Empire; the days of which are long gone, yet Azraelle remains.

Worshipped by a misguided few and often mistaken for Death itself, Azraelle is a soul-eater, which feeds off of the anima of her victims. Looking into her maw is like looking into a walking Hell-mouth from which there is no hope of salvation, a sort of death for the dead. Like the Lord of Hell, she is known by many names; but the one that has stuck with her, and with which she is most often identified nowadays, is Azraelle Undercroft, an appellation given her by Emanuel Sands, a two-bit English Gothicist and armchair occultist, in his specious treatise on the monstrous lineage of Eve's seldom-mentioned predecessor, entitled *Children of Lilith* (1914).

In said tome, Sands cites an account that he claims to have translated from an eighteenth-century German manuscript relating the horror that befell a group of Wallachian vigilantes who had assembled in their local churchyard to dig up and dispatch an alleged vampire that had been terrorizing their village. Sands claims that when they exhumed the narrow house of their late neighbor, they found that the original tenant had been deposed and lying in wait for them was a hellish revenant that grabbed the group captain as he opened the lid of the coffin and drew him in quickly, like a trapdoor spider. Momentarily stunned by the dreadful sounds emanating from within the coffin, the remaining mob members were brought back to the moment when the husk of their comrade was ejected from the pine box as a rawboned claw seized the wrist of another of their mates, causing the others to flee, screaming.

At this point Sands claims the lid, and then the lifeless shell of the second vigilante were cast aside and the revenant leapt from its hiding place to assail the fleeing men. "One by one she picked them off (for the author of the manuscript claims the revenant—our dear Azraelle—bore the semblance of a female form, though hominid woman it was not) with alarming alacrity, the only survivor being a young man who made it past the threshold of the churchyard gates, which Ms. Undercroft did not seem to be able to cross. When he turned back to look for his compeers he saw their withered skins strewn across the headstones and clinging to the fencing with shriveled hands, their bones jutting like tent poles in their desiccated corpses. And looming haughtily over the slaughter like a grim subjugator was Azraelle Undercroft, leering with her overlarge grin and blackened brow. Lifting her bony claw to wave farewell, she then vaulted the overturned coffin which she effortlessly pulled from the plot and vanished into the open grave below." [*Children of Lilith* (1914), page 13.]

Many scholars denounce this tale as spurious sensationalism and question Sands's sources, since no other record of this event appears to be extant in any form other than his purported retelling. Sands never produced a copy of the original manuscript but persisted in averring its authenticity until his disappearance in 1917. Authentic or not, its delineation of her *modus operandi* rings true enough, although the vigilantes either had to be foolish enough to visit the churchyard by night or Azraelle was above ground during daylight hours, which does seem unlikely, for she is nocturnal, being a daughter of Lilith, after all.

No matter what Sands or the classical mythologists might have believed of her, she is her own woman, after a fashion, and does not trouble herself with their fantasies, nor the scribblings of some fey, laudanum-addled scribe. She existed millennia before them, and she shall continue to do so aeons after they have gone to their just rewards. She ekes out her noxious existence in her world between worlds and pays them no mind at all . . . rather like the zombie sluggishly lugging the lacerated and withered carcass of her latest inamorato from her chamber of horrors where she entertains her hapless guests.

Although she exists in a world far removed from the sun's inimical rays, she must still find time to process the energies she has consumed during her heinous repast. So, as she prepares for her moment of quiescence (peeling off her bloodied dress, returning to her bath to wash the mess of her gruesome pastime from her face and figure; rinsing blood-spatter from her long black hair and scraping the gore from under her long red nails), her zombie minions refresh her bedclothes and pump the bellows to fan the fire in the grate as the temperature in the wasteland tends towards the gelid.

Rising from her bath, she is approached by a minion whose clumsy attempt to pat her down ventures on the inappropriate. Annoyed, she places her rawboned hand on its scalp and pushes it away (almost removing its moldered scalp in the process) and heads toward her sarcophagus, which she uses to remind her whence comes her bounty. Once inspirited, however, she is up and off again to find more souls to swallow.

Good morrow Azraelle Undercroft—sleep tight—and remember, whenever you awaken, somewhere out there, it will always be night.

II. The Toilette of Azraelle

Azraelle rises with the sunset and performs her nightly ablutions, employing a lachrymal vase, brimming with tears culled from the doleful eyes of children she has orphaned. Steeping in her sitz-bath, she moons over abattoirs and scaffolds as she drifts off to the cacophony of pain and horror wafting through the vents from the dungeons below.

A tugging at her ebon mane breaks her reverie as an undead minion haltingly drags a comb, fashioned from the phalanges of a minikin hand, through her tousled locks with a forcefulness that belies her cadaverous appearance. The rawboned lummox grips and pulls the grisly comb, tearing through knots, much to the displeasure of her minacious mistress.

The minion's cloudy undead eyes peer into the inky luster of Azraelle's tresses while her ghastly noggin slowly bobs as if hovering at the drawing vortex of the black hole that is the quintessence of Azraelle's edacious anima. Otherwise catatonic, she does not even register a wince as she is buffeted with an oath and dismissed by her grim mistress for her unhandiness.

As the lich lumbers back to her cell, Azraelle saunters over to her vanity to "put her face on." The maintenance of her awesome visage is of the utmost concern for our vainglorious Lich-Queen. Her routine involves a poultice of mixt martyr's blood and ashes to blanch her pallid face, the latter of which she oftimes uses like kohl around her large black eyes to give her that hollow, haunted look. The former she mixes with a tallow rendered from the offal of her evening's slaughter to color her livid lips; the remainder she then has her minions employ in the fabrication of the candles that illuminate her tenebrous chamber.

Seated in her velvet cushioned bench, she reaches for a vial with long bloodless fingers, her rubicund talons clinking on the adjacent mirror glass as her bony digits close around the tiny bottle. Scooping a few droplets within her thorny ruby nails, she dabs four thieves' vinegar, as a masking fragrance, onto her long pale throat, suggestive less of a swan than the stretched gullet of a hanged man.

Catching a glimpse of herself in the reflective surface, she pauses to smile, large red lips retracting to reveal what the philosopher Seneca called her "eager teeth." For she whom the poet Horace once referred to as *pallida Mors* is the reason your grandsires covered mirrors in the death room. Woe betide the unwary soul which flew to the uncovered looking glass, for it is *she* whom they would find looking back from the other side, hungry Azraelle and her gaping maw of eternity.

Painted and perfumed, she moves on to her armoire to select the evening's cerement. Thumbing past the garments in her closet, she muses, "Black for dark deeds? Red for bloody? Nay, let it be white, for I shall turn it red by the end of this night!"

Thus ends the toilette of Azraelle the Lich-Queen, and so begins her nightly hunt for a hapless soul to swallow.

Transcendence

Ngo Binh Anh Khoa

The wise monk, having reached enlightenment,
Transcended and unlocked the Sight to see
Beyond the Veil that shrouds Reality,
The goal for which he'd lived at last was done.
But minutes after that Sight had been gained,
He gouged his eyes out, screaming all the while
About old, eldritch Powers—vast and vile—
Whose presences left him insane and pained.
His students tried to write down what he said,
But most were senseless and inhuman noises
Made by distorted, overlapping voices
Before he stilled, not living, but not dead.
Those blood-soaked eyes, sealed in his mummy's clasp,
Gaze still at things beyond frail mortals' grasp.

Bunyips in the Mulga

Anthony M. Rud

[First published in *Golden Fleece* 1, No. 2 (November 1938): 2–35.]

All of a sudden, as they passed through a ten-foot thicket of wattle, hideous yells sounded and a shower of spears flew.

Chapter I. Two Yanks

Across the dry beds of the Salt Lakes, thirty miles northeast of Kalgoorlie, the bearded, dust-grayed driver of a spring wagon halted his weary pair of horses. He unhitched and made desert camp.

Through binoculars he carefully scanned the desert sunset horizon. Not even a dust puff raised by some lolloping, lone kangaroo, showed above the sand and stunted mulga scrub.

The bearded messenger nodded silent satisfaction. He had been careful to keep his starting time a secret. That was the chief reason why he had made so many safe trips between the bank at Kalgoorlie, and the new dry placer camp of Kargie. The last two weeks, however, there had been rumors. The giant, black-bearded inhuman monster, Paxton Trenholm, had been glimpsed not far away, leading his camel-riding Malay murderers from the North.

This bushranger, Paxton Trenholm, for all his awesome fits of madness and violence, had uncanny sources of information regarding mine bullion, payrolls, and even the occasional lucky finds made far north on the pearl beaches. He had a way of turning up and looting, where the honeypot of wealth was stickiest.

There were thirty-one separate rewards on Trenholm's head.

The dusty messenger. Tom Varney, took two water cans, a galvanized pail and a sack of oats from the back of the wagon, now he believed it safe to stay here. He cared for the horses. Then he brought out a Primus stove, and prepared a frugal meal of tea and damper for himself.

Packing away everything, since he intended to start at first streaks of dawn, and breakfast in Kargie, he put both hands reassuringly upon a small, oblong chest hidden under the seat. It was made of teak, brassbound and held closed by three Yale padlocks. The duplicate keys to these locks were at Kalgoorlie and Kargie. The messenger never carried them on his person.

Ten minutes later he made a blanket bed which would have looked familiar to an American cowboy—which Tom Varney had been, years back. In a few minutes more, he slept.

His camp-making hail been watched. From the crest of a low sand dune more than a mile away, a black-bearded man wriggled back into the hollow where the camels were lying and men crouching. The bushranger, Paxton Trenholm, closed his folding brass telescope and put it away in its leather case.

"All top-hole," he said with satisfaction. "We'll give him an hour to be snoring. It will be pitch dark then. Keep those camels lying down, and don't let them grunt and groan too loudly."

The sleeping messenger, Tom Varney, never had a chance. He awoke suddenly to find the weight of a squat, muscled Malay on his chest, and the sharp blade of a kris at his throat. At a distance of three yards stood a tall, black-bearded, well proportioned white man who held a dark lantern now unhooded. In his other hand a revolver slanted, aimed at Tom's head.

"We have no particular need to kill you, Varney," said Trenholm, sounding negligent and rather haughty with his English public school accent. "So turn over obediently like a good lad, and let us bind your wrists."

Gritting his teeth in savage, hopeless anger, the messenger was forced to comply. He knew it was a mere whim on this madman's part, that he still breathed. Trenholm was like that—a paranoiac whose fits of murderous insanity came in cycles. In between rampages he was known to be quiet, cultured of manner, almost sane.

Varney said nothing at all, as he was trussed with skill—albeit loosely enough so he could work free in the course of an hour or two.

They paid him no more attention then. While the Malays and the seven-foot, skinny blackfellow servant got their camels, Paxton Trenholm harnessed the horses and drove away into the night. Helpless, writhing against his bonds, Tom Varney had to let them get away with the treasure entrusted to his keeping.

Tom took a deep breath, and then started to work free. But even when he succeeded, what then? In the brassbound teak box had been the money of other men, slightly more than nine thousand dollars, brought back in payment for the pokes of new gold sent in his care to Kalgoorlie by the dry-placer miners of Kargie.

Was there any chance at all that these rough miners would believe his story, and forgive the loss?

Their curt, angry answer was given at nightfall, when Tom arrived. Growling a beginning frenzy of disbelief, threatening a rope, they threw the unlucky messenger into his own corrugated iron shack, and padlocked the door.

At the rude barrel house which served Kargie as a pub, an angry meeting started. Tom had a few friends, but only a few—due to the fact that he was a Yank. The friends did not have much to say. They had known him as taciturn, and a good shot with revolver and rifle. They knew he had come from a far-off place called Texas, and that he was thirty-two years old. Not much in that on which to build a defense. Except the one noted and peculiar fact that Yanks did not seem to lie. Not the way Chinks or Cockneys did, anyhow. Tom Varney, of course, had sworn harshly that his tale was true, The police might have been ready to believe. Not these men.

When the crowd had drunk itself into a lynching fury, and had come surging to the iron shack after Tom Varney, they found a hole burrowed under one wall, and the prisoner gone. That tore it.

"We have no particular need to kill you, Varney, so turn over obediently like a good lad."

5

He had left one scribbled letter, with the plea that it be mailed to his kid brother back in Texas. The letter read:

> Dear Sam:
> I'm damn glad you stayed on the ranch. I'm in bad trouble. They say I stole about nine thousand dollars. Acourse its a lie, but I cant prove it, lessen I can bring in the head of Paxton Trenholm in a sack. Likely I'll lose out, but anyhow I aint being taken alive by police or anybody. And I aim to get Trenholm.
> Goodbye, kid. Love,
> Tom.

The police took charge of the letter. After a time it occurred to someone that it might be a good idea, after all, to keep other Yank Varneys out of Australia. So the police did mail the letter to Sam Houston Varney, at Sweetwater, Texas, with a grimly explanatory enclosure—stating their case against Tom.

But if their intention was to keep young Sam out of the Antipodes, they had adopted exactly the wrong tactics. Within a week after receiving that horrible message, Sam had sold the paternal ranch and small herd, and was on the Pacific Ocean bound for Melbourne—and more trouble than he ever dreamt existed.

Two months had passed. The hunt for Tom Varney had subsided. Then it was a tall, bronzed, gray-eyed young man in a broad-brimmed black hat, presented himself at the headquarters of the West Australian Provincial Police, at Kalgoorlie. Sam Varney had reached there by railroad, but had found it practically impossible to go one step further toward the mine town of Kargie. Larrikins, indigent prospectors, and men hauling liquor, made the trip. But Sam Varney was not accompanying any of these—not until the money in his belt had been put down on the line for a certain purpose.

"I'm Tom Varney's brother—you'll remember, I reckon, a man named Tom Varney?" he said quietly to the policeman.

"Hm. Yes, we remember Torn Varney. Why?"

"He's accused of stealing $9,200," was the reply. "That's a lie.

However, till I can prove it ain't true, here's all of the money I c'd raise. You'll find $8,500 there. Also there's my I. O. U. for $700. I'll take that up soon's I can. G'bye."

And dropping the money belt before the astonished officer, Sam Houston Varney strode out of the office, paying no heed to the voices which called after him.

"Well—I'm an emu's uncle!" gasped the desk policeman. Or words to that effect. "Perhaps we don't need to worry about keeping Varneys from Texas out of Australia, after all?"

"There's lots worse than Yanks," admitted a brother officer with extreme tolerance. "Wonder what he's going to do to raise that extra seven hundred? Rob a bank?"

Like many plainsmen, young Sam Varney had been impressed and thrilled by his crossing of the ocean. He decided to try a job on a coaster for a while, till he got his bearings. One thing was sure. He did not want any of the dry goldfields—which were said to be petering out, anyhow.

He had met a sea captain, and the latter, glad indeed to get a hand in these days when men were scarce, had told him to come along and meet the Narwhal at Freemantle. Sam, of course, had not the slightest idea of the reputation along the coast of the tramp freighter Narwhal, or of the even less savory things said about Captain Moebus and the tow-headed Axel Larssen, his mate.

There is no use going into a log of his experience. First he was robbed of his few possessions. Then he was beaten in three plucky but hopeless fights with the captain and mate. Bruised, sore, sometimes unconscious, he was tied up every time the Narwhal made a regular port. Not until they put in, several weeks later, at a small island near shore in the Bight, did Sam have any chance to escape.

They did not tie him this time. What use? The Bight swarmed with sharks. Even if a man made shore, there was nothing at all in front of him but waterless desert. On the tiny island, of course, there was no chance to escape. There was only a beachcomber's hut or two—and with these Captain Moebus had a little nefarious business with contraband.

When the captain and mate had gone ashore to transact it, Sam looked longingly at the mainland shore. Less than a mile away. He thought he could make it—and did not think at all about what he might find, if he proved successful. Taking his chance when other members of the crew were below, he dove from the side, and swam hand over hand for the desert shore.

An hour later the captain and mate, returning, made sure he was not on board. There was no small boat missing. The answer seemed plain.

"Good riddance!" snarled Captain Moebus. "The white-pointers 'ave 'ad a meal!"

He was wrong. Just twenty minutes earlier Sam Varney had hauled himself to the sandy, barren shore of the Bight. He was near the point of complete exhaustion from his long swim, and the physical batterings received before. But no shark had noticed him.

Chapter II. Monsters in the Mulga

The first thing the Yank saw, when the smart of salt was out of his eyes, was a fence. It was a good strong fence, built of close mesh—not barbed wire. It came right down and ended at a stout pile driven in below tide marks.

Sam grinned at it, and sat down beside it to rest. Time had been, back on the Panhandle range, when he had cursed fences. Now one looked like a friendly and familiar thing. Prob'ly a ranch or sheep station right near, he said to himself drowsily. He slid slowly over on one side and slept.

Two hours later from the west came six swift camels—racing maharis, not the undersized, slow creatures used by Afghans here. One camel carried packs. It was led by a tall, skinny blackfellow on another camel. This was a Kimberley Lake aborigine, Paxton Trenholm's bodyservant.

The big white man, the notorious bushranger-madman, rode another camel.

The big white man, the notorious bushranger-madman, rode another camel. Likewise mounted, three squat, high-cheekboned Malays followed him.

They came right down to the end of the fence, and there discovered the sleeping Yank. By this time Sam had an arm over his eyes, and was snoring—the way very tired men always do when they lie on their backs.

Pistol in hand, Trenholm frowned down. Then he shrugged, and threw a shot down into the ground, so sand sprayed over Sam's face.

The sleeper grunted, His arm fell away, and his eyes came partway open. Then he snored again. He had not really awakened, though Trenholm thought so. A queer inspiration had come to the bushranger. He shouted something to his riders, and rode down around the end of the fence, and on out of sight to the east.

An hour later he returned. The sleeper was still there. Trenholm motioned silence. Like ghosts the camels circled the fence, getting wet to their knees. Then they disappeared in the dusk, bound northwest.

Trenholm chuckled in his beard. The madness was coming on him gradually again, and he would have slain the lazy white man sleeping there—except for one thing. The police had been a little too close lately. It would help a lot to have this lazybones report that Trenholm had crossed the fence line, and gone east. If they started looking for him over in South Australia, he would have time to seek refuge with the giant blackfellows—the Aruntas, Parrabarras, or Kimberleys, among whom he was regarded as a demi-god, or more. He had riches enough for this year. He wanted a chance to lie low and foment trouble for the police and for other white men. He hated all of his own color skin.

In early dawn Sam awoke, shivering, to blink in wonder at a strange world. The first object he beheld was the fence. He got to his feet, swung his arms to start circulation, and looked along the wire in hope of seeing a building, a ranch-house. None was in sight. He shrugged philosophically, in spite of hunger and a degree of thirst from the salt water, and started to tramp northward along the friendly fence.

Funny, he had a dream about men riding camels, going around the end of the fence. Just nightmare, of course. He'd been dead tired, and still ached. The sun would be up soon, though, and it would warm up his bones. If he stuck to the fence he'd have to get somewhere sometime, wouldn't he?

Not necessarily—not within walking distance, Sam. This was like no fence you ever saw in Texas. One of the longest barriers ever built by man for any purpose, it had cost the Australian Government $1,000 a mile. There were 1,500 unbroken miles of it. It stretched from Starvation Boat Harbor in the Bight, where Sam had swam ashore, straight north across the whole continent, to Condon, on the muggy, crocodile-infested Ninety-Mile Beach!

There was not a single ranch or sheep station on its entire length. Just jungles, deserts, wastes of mulga scrub, gidgie bush, beefwood and wattle. The fence was built, and watchfully patrolled by men, for a strange but deadly serious purpose. It was meant to keep the plague of rabbits out of West Australia.

As he trudged, his garments clinging after their sea-water shrinkage, Sam thought grimly of his double task—triple task, really, for it entailed getting hold of his brother. Torn Varney had vanished so successfully that the police of all Australia had not been able to arrest him. Sam realized that nearly broke, with that $700 note to meet, he could not hope to find Tom except in one way. Get on the track of Paxton Trenholm. Somewhere, following the bushranger, trying to capture or kill him, would be that stern man of single purpose, Tom Varney.

Sam had to have a job of work, or starve. Getting something would be easy, he thought. But it would just be something temporary, to let him get oriented. Once he had a good idea of the bushranger's trail, and a stake sufficient to provide him with rifle and a mount, Sam would break loose for the manhunt. The rewards accumulated on Paxton Trenholm would repay the sum of Sam's note fifty times over.

Now he grew increasingly thirsty. In ignorance of this part of Australia, and hoping it was not like the gold deserts, he still scanned the horizon for sign of a ranch. There was none. But now in the mulga there was wild life on every hand.

Doglike creatures, dingoes, howled at him and slunk away. They haunted the fence—for a reason Sam discovered. He came upon a built-in rabbit trap. Two of the stringy, long-eared creatures were prisoners, and the dingoes had been trying to dig in to get at them.

Sam became thoughtful. He studied the unending fence, straight to the northern horizon like a railway track on the Texas plains. Then, wishing he had a drink, he unlatched the trap, took out one of the stringy jacks, killed and skinned it. His waterproof match safe held a few matches. He gathered branches of mulga, lit a fire, and spitted the tough rabbit.

"They sure go in for ranches as are ranches, out here," he muttered. "I haven't seen hide or hair of any critters, though. Doggone, but I c'd use a drink!"

Ironically the branches of thorny acacia crackled and snapped on his fire. Ironically—for unknown to Sam, the heavier stems of this mulga held pure water. Like the barrel cacti of southwestern American deserts, it was there to save the life of man or beast. It was the sole reason wallabies and other creatures could live in many thousands of square miles of this continent.

He ate the rabbit. Thumpings in the sand, and whistles of breath made him turn. There, galumphing away toward the dreary sameness of horizon, were five big kangaroos and two small joeys.

"Bunyips in the mulga!" grinned Sam dryly, recalling crew yarns of the fearsome interior. Bunyips really were imaginary monsters of lesser degree in the lodge of devils believed in by the blackfellow aborigines.

Old Mooldarbie (chief devil according to many tribes) kept him a ferocious pack of bunyips. Unless propitiated, sometimes by human sacrifice, Mooldarbie loosed these hungry scourges. Then lone blackboys, even whole (nomadic) villages disappeared.

The word nomadic really explained the disappearances; but the tall, half-starved black aborigines are Stone Age children in their minds as well as in their weapons and manner of life.

Five minutes later Sam looked up, stopped and stared. Two dots were moving slowly and dustily down upon him from the north, riders on the west side of the fence. Sam gave a dry shout of gladness, and waved one arm like a semaphore. Maybe a drink!

The dots grew in size, and now Sam saw that here were two men actually mounted on camels! Then perhaps his odd nightmare might have been reality, after all!

Chapter III. Fence-riding Cameleer

These mounts were the undersized Sudanese camels, brought via Kenya. They were necessities in a land where the only water for hundreds of miles was brought to the surface by artesian bores. The brutes, mean and complaining as they always were, still could go five days at a stretch in hot weather without drinking. And they could subsist when they had to on spinifex, the prickly, coarse grass of the plains.

The two bronzed riders came. They looked down wonderingly and somewhat suspiciously at a man on foot in this mulga waste-land. But Sam was too thirsty to stand on ceremony.

"Howdy, strangers," he greeted, his voice little more than a croak. "Where can I get a drink of water?"

The elder of the pair, a man with lined, leathery face but clear, sun-squinted eyes, unbent a trifle. "Here's the nearest supply, friend," he answered, unbuckling a canteen and unstoppering it. "You're a long way from a well."

There was a hint of inquiry in the last, but Sam waited to gurgle down a full pint of the tepid water, which tasted better to him than champagne right then.

It would take Sam a little while to learn, but the elder of these two men was Fence Inspector Goelitz, in charge of the three southern "lengths" of the rabbit fence. The younger was Bart Jolley, a recruit fence-rider.

After the drink, Goelitz offered a cheroot from a long, narrow case. Sam accepted with a grin. "Now, I'll tell you all," he said, puffing with satisfaction, though choking momentarily on an inhalation of the strong smoke. "I s'pose you're police?"

No, not police. Goelitz explained a little, and learned Sam's name. Then Sam told briefly of his six weeks nautical experience, and mentioned the Narwhal, Captain Moebus commanding.

He probably could not have given himself any better break. The reek and stench of the Narwhal's unsavory reputation had reached both men. Anybody who could not stand Moebus and Axel Larssen, probably was a decent sort. The Inspector's manner became more cordial.

"So now I'm looking for a job. Any job at all," concluded Sam, saying nothing about his brother, or the quest of vindication.

"What can do you?" asked Goelitz. This was a form inquiry. Right then expansion in Australia was at its height, and the fence was starved for men. The Government wage was not as large as that any able-bodied man could earn with shovel and pick working for other men in the goldfields, and almost every man who could raise a grubstake was prospecting on his own anyway.

Sam told of Texas and his ranch ex-  perience. He was modest about a real ability as a rider. Also he said nothing about the accomplishment which had been his chief pride—his shooting. Yet Goelitz, looking critically at six feet of lean, bronzed American manhood, was grimly satisfied.

The Villain

"I'll take you on," he said, "if you're not shy of a fight now and then. We ride heavily armed—for good reason. The blackfellows have been troublesome of late. They're always cutting the fence to get wire frameworks for their wurleys; but lately it's worse than that. Someone or something is making bloody trouble."

"Better try me," suggested Sam, smiling. This sounded better than he had dared hope. "I'll hold up my end."

"Very good!" snapped Goelitz. "Then, this is the job!" He explained tersely.

Sixty years earlier a misguided Queensland larrikin brought ashore four mated pairs of rabbits. They promptly escaped into the mallee of the eastern coast. Now the descendants of those eight bunnies numbered millions, perhaps billions. They had overrun and practically ruined all the agricultural and grazing lands of the eastern half of the continent, despite the several kinds of deadly warfare carried on against them.

There was a reward of $150,000 and five square miles of any unoccupied land in Australia waiting for the man who suggested a plan for controlling the rabbit plague. The great scientist, Louis Pasteur, had been employed in the hope of working out a bacterial method of extermination. Even he had been forced to surrender.

Meanwhile, this fence was to shut out rabbits from the rich agricultural areas of the southwest, where the plague had not yet appeared.

Sam caught his breath at thought of such a reward. There was a fugitive thought of importing American coyotes to prey on the rabbits, but it vanished. Coyotes could be worse than rabbits, especially in a land where valuable Merino sheep were raised in enormous herds. And then Sam caught himself sharply. No matter what else happened, he had to find his brother Tom, and help the elder snare Paxton Trenholm and vindicate self-respect before the world.

"You'll work hard, and live for the fence!" concluded the inspector. "You'll fight for it—and I may as well warn you right now that ten or more riders in the north sections have been killed by blackfellows in the past six months!"

"Fine!" said Sam. "When do I start north?"

"You'll stay right here with me in the south for now," said Goelitz. "There are troubles enough here without hunting new ones."

He clasped hands with Sam, as did Bart Jolley—the latter smiling genuine welcome to a personable companion of his own age.

The three of them, however, little suspected that trouble brewed by a madman, even at that moment, was gathering for them—at a spot in the gidgie bush less than thirty miles away.

Chapter IV. Death in the Gidgie

The first day, clinging to the bony rump of the inspector's camel, Sam was broken in to the work. With Bart Jolley, they headed south for the few miles Sam had trudged, examining each post, each yard of wire, killing and skinning the rabbits found in the traps, making sure that repair materials were in the hidden caches away from the fence.

(When the blackfellows found these caches they stole everything.)

"I s'pose," observed Sam, "all east and west travellers have trouble getting through. Prob'ly have to go clear down and around the end of the fence, eh?"

"Hm. Traffic isn't what you'd call heavy."

"I saw five-six jiggers on camels last night, headin' east."

"Eh? What's that?" Goelitz suddenly tensed, looking backward over his shoulder. "You saw—what?"

Sam explained that he might have dreamed it, but he thought he had seen a tall white man with a black beard, a skinny blackfellow, and some squatty brown men, all on camels, ride eastward around the end of the fence.

"Paxton Trenholm!" burst out Bart Jolley. "Going east!"

"That means that maybe West Australia is rid of him at last!" breathed Goelitz, not noticing that Sam's hands suddenly had clenched till the knuckles came white. "Also it means we hump it to Murriguddury, where I can get on the end of a telephone wire!"

But despite this excited phoning which Goelitz did, as soon as they reached the supply point of Murriguddury three miles west of the fence end, they never found Paxton Trenholm in South Australia. Scores of police hunted him, but he lay back in a village of the Parrabarras, west of the wire. He was planning, with cold fury, greater trouble for the white men than he ever had caused.

Goelitz also called up the provincial police, asking as a matter of routine if they had anything against a young man named Sam Houston Varney, his new rider.

When he came back there was a peculiar light, almost of respect, in his eyes. But he said nothing. He outfitted Sam with clothes, rifle, revolver, ammunition, canteens and a swag (saddle roll of blankets, cooking utensils, with salt, sugar, pepper, tea and two cans of condensed milk). Then they picked him out a mangy camel, and a saddle, both decidedly shopworn in appearance.

The more permanent parts of his outfit would go north by the next bullockie train (supply wagons, drawn by six yoke of oxen apiece, each driven by a bullockie). A railroad had started northeast from Adelaide, but it had not got far as yet. The greater part of the fence was supplied from the north and south by these ox-wagons.

Sam himself was rather white under the bronze of his cheeks. His eyes were grave. If this had been Paxton Trenholm, indeed, then should not he, Sam, try for another job in South Australia? It was fortunate for him that the stark need of eating and living forced him to shelve that idea for the time being.

Lyre Bird

He finally told the story briefly and passionately to Goelitz, warning the latter that probably he would have to quit him some day when he had a fair stake, to take up the long hunt for Trenholm and Tom Varney.

"I 'spect Tom's dead by now, or he'd have got Trenholm," said Sam. "Just the same, we Varneys stick to what we start. That's why I'm warning you, Goelitz."

"I'm glad to have you, Sam, as long as you can stay," said the Inspector, and meant it. A young man, Yank or otherwise, who would sell all his possessions to help square up an unjust debt of an elder brother was a new experience. Goelitz warmed to his recruit rider, and privately hoped that the police would catch or kill the bushranger shortly, so Sam could stay on indefinitely.

There was a contract-sameness about the great fence, as Sam learned in the days that followed. Each one hundred miles was called a "length." It was supposed to be patrolled by two riders. In the middle of each length was an artesian well, and a corrugated iron shack which the riders used as headquarters.

The inspectors, of whom there were five, each had charge of three fence lengths. Each inspector had a fairly comfortable cabin placed near the artesian well on the middle length of his division. It was possible for an inspector to marry. Two of them had done so.

Men were short now. Bart Jolley had the southernmost length to himself. Goelitz and Sam left him at the northern boundary. A ratty, mean-eyed fellow was met now, Koken by name. Goelitz passed him with only a few inquiries, evidently not caring much for his company. But after they had got further along, expecting to meet the second rider of this length, Goelitz began to worry.

"Don't like it," he frowned, scanning the northern horizon. "Morrison's a good man. He ought to've met us this noon—five hours ago. I think we'll wait tucker an hour, and see if he doesn't show up. There's a dust storm coming," he added, peering through his binoculars. "Not a real hell-roarer like we get sometimes, though."

The coming of the wind, with its load of stinging, suffocating particles, made them seek shelter in a thick growth of golden wattle. An hour passed, then the wind died, and they could light a fire for tea and damper. It was too late to go further. They camped right there, and the missing cameleer did not arrive.

Next morning they had breakfasted early, and gone two miles on their way when they came upon a saddled camel. The beast was grazing, untethered.

"This is bad," worried Goelitz. "I hope it's only an accident. But we have to find Morrison right away." His eyes were searching the almost impenetrable scrub to his left. He lifted his rifle from the boot, and levered a cartridge into the chamber.

Sam Varney did the same. He also unbuttoned the dust flap of his revolver holster, and buttoned it back out of the way of a quick draw. Easing the heavy revolver up and down in leather, he tested the feel of the grip, and the balance. Not as good as his old Colt, but a serviceable weapon with smashing power.

A sudden cry burst from the inspector's throat. They had come to a glade-like pocket which stretched back some eighty feet into the wall of scrub. There were the evidences of a one-man camp. A dead cooking fire. A scattering of effects mauled through by blacks. And on his face, one arm outstretched forward, lay what was left of Morrison, the cameleer!

Dismounting hurriedly, the two men ran to the body. Goelitz cursed savagely, going down to one knee. The body had been mutilated in horrible fashion.

"Look out!" suddenly shouted Sam, who had been fidgeting uneasily. He had glimpsed a tell-tale movement in the scrub.

That second spears whizzed!

With his split-second of warning, Sam was able to plunge sidewise, slapping down his palm in a fast draw almost as good as he had been capable of in Texas days.

His revolver crashed—once, twice, thrice—and then as he ducked a spear, a fourth time. He had the hot satisfaction of seeing two contorted and hideously painted black faces, suddenly disappear. A third leapt upward with a howl, then fell back at Sam's last shot.

The scrub shook frenziedly as one survivor—possibly wounded—left the scene as fast as his legs would carry him. The attack was over.

Restraining the impulse to dash in pursuit, Sam turned to his companion. Goelitz was down on hands and knees, half-fainting from pain. An obsidian lance had transfixed his right thigh from the rear.

"Just let me alone—one minute. Then—help!" gasped Goelitz.

Sam nodded, understanding. Swiftly reloading his revolver, he went cautiously into the scrub. Nothing seemed to move there now.

But at that moment something whizzed up from the ground, aimed at his head! A stone-weighted waddy!

It was thonged to the wrist of a black-fellow who lay there, frothing blood from a chest wound, but malignant to the last.

Sam dodged, managing to throw up his left arm and deflect the blow which otherwise might have brained him. Leaping back, he aimed the revolver—but did not fire. That one effort had been the last for the aborigine. Now he shuffled his skinny legs in the leaves, shuddered all over twice, and lay still.

There was a second white-striped body spread-eagled across a bush, which bent under the weight. And two yards further a third blackfellow with yellow circles painted on his cheeks sat with head slumped forward to his chest, and both arms clasped about his mid-section.

Varney went back to his wounded chief. "Three of 'em accounted for," he reported, "and I think I tagged a fourth. Ready for me to cut off that spearhead and pull it out of the hole?" He opened his keen-bladed jackknife.

"Go ahead. It can't hurt worse 'n it does!" bade Goelitz, white-lipped. He gripped his thigh with both hands to squeeze the nerves. "Wish to hell I had a spot of wheat whiskey!"

Sam, knowing a little of range surgery, was careful and deft. Just the same, Goelitz fainted when the spear was pulled out. By the time he returned to consciousness, Sam had the wounds bound tightly, and was riding the rump of the inspector's camel, leading two more, and holding Goelitz in the saddle before him.

Thus they reached Goelitz's own comfortable cabin, and that night the inspector told Sam that he was to take over this length of mulga and gidgie in place of the dead Morrison.

Chapter V. Molango Corroborree

The recruit cameleer had cooked himself ten kettles of soup from the tails of young kangaroos, and was well on his way to becoming a seasoned rider before he had another encounter with the blackfellows. Aruntas and Parrabarras roamed this region, and until this year they had been friendly enough—if troublesome as thieves.

Sam did his job. It was absorbingly interesting to him. But every man he met—the bullockies who came with supplies, the Afghan camel couriers, the railway engineers who came over from the new line on the east for gossip or occasional supplies—was besieged with questions regarding Paxton Trenholm, the twentieth century bush-ranger.

From the men, and then from a file of old papers kept by the sour, fox-faced rider, Koken, Sam learned practically all that was known about his quarry. Trenholm was a remittance man of proud English family—one who had not deigned to change his name the way most banished men did. The scandal back home probably had been caused by one of his first maniacal rages, then unsuspected. He had been attacked by a palpably drunken man whom he did not know, and had retaliated with such fury and such giant strength that the unfortunate drunk died of a broken skull and broken jaw. The English jury had deliberated long, but finally acquitted Trenholm. His family possibly sensed the truth. They shipped him to the An-tipodes.

Trenholm, with some capital to start, turned up on the north-western pearl beaches, as a buyer. He went seasonally from Broome to Anchor, to Vesey Beach, over to Perak, and back to the Burdetts in his own power schooner.

Then one day at Highgate Mibs his recurrent insanity betrayed him. For reason unknown, possibly attempted thievery, he strangled and broke to a pulp a half-caste pearler.

That was when he went wild. He took to the scrub, murdered two provincial policemen sent after him, and got himself a roving band of Kimberley Lake blackfellows. For periods he would be qui-et, and no man would see him or hear of him. Then he would start on red foray. He was out-and-out bushranger now, pearl pirate, and a sort of inhuman demi-god to the blacks and Malays.

"When his fit of madness is on him," Goelitz told Sam, "he will kill anyone of white skin he meets."

"I hope he's mad when I meet him again," said the young rider grimly, "because I'm going to shoot on sight!"

Hot weather came, bringing an oily reek of tarweed. Pests of flies made life miserable for camels and men. Inspector Goelitz was hobbling about again, taking up his duties by graduated stages.

Sam had been having his troubles. A village of Parrabarras lay about three miles west of the fence. These tall, emaciated blacks raided the fence and broke through every time Sam's back was turned. And strangely enough, they invariably attacked a certain spot just east of their village. Sam had got to the point where he hurried through every other duty in order to get back to this spot. And then usually he found a disheartening job of fence repair awaiting.

This was serious. As yet few rabbits had reached this part. Yet any day the vanguard might arrive, and enough bunnies seep through to start the plague in the west, and make the fence of no more avail.

Sam got an interpreter to help him out—he had learned a little of the aborigine dialects, but too little for extended conversation—and tried to talk to the gaunt villagers. No dice. They simply refused to say anything at all. And then immediately he returned, they picked up their whole portable array of wurleys (cone-shaped huts), and moved to within less than a mile of the sore spot in the wire!

Sam told Goelitz, and brought him to the scene. "I'm going to fix 'em next time!" the recruit announced. "Come back here and have a look at my own devil-devil. I only wish they'd start their damned bull-roarers now! I'd like you to be with me."

Goelitz frowned and followed. Like most Australians, he felt that the sooner the aborigines were exterminated, the better. But it was impossible to carry war to them.

Behind a covert of dwarf screw-pines Sam Varney had concealed a ten-foot contraption of wood, canvas and paint. It was a toothy, menacing face outlined in red paint, a scarecrow whose outstretched arms could be made to flap the canvas sleeves up and down when a cord was pulled by the man carrying the whole thing. Childish, of course, but then these blacks were nothing but superstitious children.

"It might work—but then there probably would be fifty spears sticking through the middle of that nightgown," said Goelitz. "Better not risk it when you're alone, Sam. I need you."

They had no more than started back to the fence and their tethered camels, however, when a nasal, whining shriek brought them up standing. The first of the bull-roarers, the whirring hand-sirens which always signalled the banishment of the gins from the ceremonial circle of corroborree. Instantly a dozen more bull-roarers joined. The air quivered with that whining, nerve-jangling nastiness of sound.

Koala

"Reckon you got to see!" said Sam with grim satisfaction. "We've got an hour before the bucks come, but the gins 'll be down cutting wire in half that time. Le's hide the camels first."

When the sound died, the two fence men crouched down back of the screw pines. Already they could hear the far-off chattering voices of the gins. These women would come down and do the first work. Then they would scatter when their lords and masters came.

The chattering grew to an ululating clamor of weird cries. The gins came running, scampering, leaping high in the air, turning, kicking their toothpick stilts of legs, brandishing whatever weapons or tools they had been able to gather.

They did not immediately attack the wire, but went through a seemingly endless and meaningless ceremonial capering on the far side. Sam watched intently. The conviction was growing in his mind that these raids were not for the purpose of securing wire, but for some superstitious or religious notion. Perhaps this particular spot where the wire always was cut was thought to be a special highway of the devils of the scrub.

The time grew short. Sam was impatient, wiping cold perspiration from his forehead. There was no use doing anything until the bucks came, but they were due any second. Why didn't the gins begin? They had to do most of the heavy work, anyhow.

But now high-pitched screams sounded, and as if these meant acknowledgment of permission for their work, the gins turned and charged the wire. With clubs, pick-axes stolen from caches, obsidian knives, old waddies and other implements, they went at it with an intense fervor. In a surprisingly short time the posts went down. Then the wire was hacked, bent, broken, torn away.

The white men, though cursing below their breath, did not interfere. The warriors had not come.

But then the women cried out in fear, and scattered back into hiding. When their men were painted in the vertical white stripes of Molongo corroborree, it was death for any gin to get in their way.

Naked, white-striped so they uncannily resembled skeletons, the warriors—about thirty-five in the band—converged upon the twenty-foot fence gap. They hurled spears into the ground ahead of them, yelling fiercely. Wrenched them out, hurled them again. A few brained imaginary enemies with waddles. Others sent the heavy, non-returning (though curving) war boomerangs sailing through the fence gap.

"I tell you, they're driving bunyips *through the fence!*" whispered Sam with sudden conviction. "Getting rid of vermin! Now my number is up!"

With that he produced a short reed horn of cardboard, clasped it in his teeth. It was the sort of horn children blow on holiday celebrations, and it gave a moaning snort intense and arresting.

Now up from the screw-pine covert flip-flapped the ludicrous scarecrow of red-painted canvas, and a hoarse, awesome sound seemed to come from its throat!

Slowly, swoopingly it appeared to fly along the ground . . . With each flap it gave its haunting, terrible cry . . .

19

Slowly, swoopingly it appeared to fly along the ground, straight for the defiant warriors and the gap in the fence. With each flap it gave its haunting, terrible cry—

For six seconds the painted warriors stood petrified, gaping at a materialization of the most dreaded spirit of the mulga. Then shrieks and screams rent the air. Stumbling, falling in their frenzy to escape, the entire band of painted Parrabarras turned and fled. Their diminishing yells of terror floated back as they sprinted for the safety of their wurleys, a mile distant.

Sam kept going. This was going to cure the blacks, he swore. Despite a cautionary shout from Goelitz back there, he flip-flapped straight into the scrub, and kept on for about half a mile.

There the scrub thinned, and a glade opened. He stopped, planted the pole which held up the scarecrow, fixing it so it appeared to be lurking behind a low bush, ready to leap out upon any black fellow crazy enough to come near.

Satisfied, Sam started back. At the end of the glade he turned for one last glance at his handiwork—just in time to see an erect, black-bearded man on a camel, accompanied by a blackfellow likewise mounted, yank the scarecrow pole out of the ground!

Paxton Trenholm!

His eyes starting from their sockets, Sam yanked out his revolver. But he did not get time to circle for a shot at decent range. The two there at the other end of the glade started up their camels, and headed away in the direction of the Parrabarra village, dragging the scarecrow behind them!

On foot Sam was at a complete disadvantage. Cursing, half-praying, he turned and sprinted back to the wire. He had to have his own beast, and warn Inspector Goelitz so the latter could send police. He knew the elder man would forbid, thinking only of the fence. But even the loss of a job he thoroughly liked would not stop Sam now. Here was the insane bushranger-murderer who had ruined his brother!

Chapter VI. Wanted Men

Unexpectedly, Goelitz offered no objection. There was a queer light in his eyes, and he clasped Sam's hand strongly in farewell, saying gruffly that he would send word to the police that Trenholm had doubled back, and was not in South Australia after all.

Sam was glad. He did not know, but that phone conversation Goelitz had had with the police, at the time Sam was recruited, was the reason. The inspector realized clearly that Sam would go—hell and high water notwithstanding. He was a good man, anxious to face almost certain death. Might as well be cheered on his way.

Sam whipped his camel into a shambling run, straight for the Parrabarra village. As he went he levered a cartridge into the rifle chamber. All he asked for was a chance to face Trenholm. If the other man got him, at least Sam would fling one shot—and there would be the rightful vengeance of all white men in Australia, wrapped around the nose of that bullet!

The scarecrow had worked too well. When Sam came to the native village, he found that only about one-third of the wurleys had been carried away by their blackfellow owners. The rest stood empty, deserted. In the middle of the cooking square lay the effigy of Mooldarbie, flat on his back. Trenholm probably had meant to point out to the blacks how easily they had been fooled. Finding the aborigines vanished, the bushranger had dropped the contraption in disgust.

Now the cameleer had to think. He had visited this village only a few days earlier, and was certain it had not then been used by Trenholm as a base. The bushranger, too, was reputed to surround himself with creature comforts when he deigned to pass any time in a native village. Here the wurleys were all small and poor, mere aboveground burrows.

Nothing to do but dismount and hunt camel tracks leading away. For some time, circling, Sam had no luck. If only he had a blacktracker, one of those trained natives said to be able to follow a trail too cold even for bloodhounds.

But at some distance from the village he came upon plain prints in soft sand. Five or six beasts being ridden away at a good gait.

Well, Sam followed at a walk. Twice when he tried to speed up matters, whipping his camel, he lost the spoor, and had to go back and start over. It was slow going. He ground his teeth, knowing that Trenholm and his men, up on meharis, could be putting tremendous distance between themselves and the slow pursuer, supposing they had glimpsed Sam back there in the glade.

"I'm saying they didn't!" he gritted, and kept on. Half an hour later, topping a dune like a small hill, Sam suddenly whirled his camel, made the beast kneel, then lie down as he leapt off to take cover. Just beyond, in a shallow valley, stretched the huts of a large native village. And Sam's first glance had caught one triple-sized, high-roofed wurley, surely more commodious than any Parrabarra or Arunta aborigine ever built.

Headquarters of the bushranger, Paxton Trenholm!

Taking his rifle, making sure that his revolver was loaded with six cartridges and the hammer lowered, he tossed aside his bat and bellied a way toward the crest of the dune. Just one good bead on Trenholm, and—

"Stick 'em in front of yuh, palms down!" came a low, savage voice from the rear.

Out of the scrub unseen by Sam Varney, had stalked a grotesque apparition. A white man whose graying beard was eight inches in length and blowing in all directions. A white man clad in horrible rags of indescribable filthiness.

Varney swore and sat up, instead of obeying literally. He was prodded by the barrel of the rifle in the newcomer's hands, so lifted his own thumbs ear-high.

"One of Trenholm's gang, are you?" Sam snarled, infuriated at his failure. He would die now, of course, and Trenholm probably would escape again. "Well, take it from me, I——"

The words died in his throat. Something strange and awesome had happened to the bearded brigand. A choked cry came from his throat. The bloodshot eyes fairly started from their sockets. The rifle drooped.

"My God A'mighty!" he said in a gasping whisper, clawing at his eyes with his left hand. "You, Sam! Oh, damn your hide, Sam, why did you come to Australia?"

With a gulping cry of horrified recognition, Sam was on his feet.

"Tom!" he choked, and flung arms around the wasted frame of his elder brother.

Goelitz had reached his own cabin, bathed, and was resting his wounded leg—after sending a courier with news of Trenholm to the nearest police—when a strangely clad youth tramped wearily up and got himself several dippers of water at the artesian well.

Sam still had a Winchester rifle, but no bandoleer of cartridges. No revolver or holster. On his feet were broken, worn-out relics of boots through which his toes projected. He wore the lower half of a suit of underwear, and beside that—nothing. Gone were his canteens, swag, camel and everything else!

"I s'pose I'm fired," he said when Goelitz came to him, frowning. "I ran into a desp'rate man, and this is all he left me—oh, hell, Chief, I got about $180 coming. Let me go ahead and work out what I owe for the rest of the outfit—camel and all.

"That was my brother, you see. He was almost up with Trenholm. I—I had to stake him, because there wasn't enough for two. So I—I reckon I owe the Government a lot."

"For sending Nemesis on the trail of Trenholm the bushranger?" asked Goelitz in a peculiar tone. "No, Sam. Australia has spent

$50,000 and more trying to catch Paxton Trenholm. I don't believe another four hundred, more or less, will break the treasury!

"I just hope, Sam Varney, your brother is as good a man as you are!"

"Tom? Huh! Tom's the goods. You wait. Trenholm's as good as dead and buried, right now! Tom doesn't ever quit—anything."

Chapter VII. Duster Girls

A trans-continental railway was being resurveyed. On the original survey, north and south, a few miles of steel had been laid from Adelaide to Oodnadatta. From Palmerston, far north on Clarence Strait, a few miles of road had crept southward. The middle 1300 miles, however, were being changed by surveyors, bringing the line quite near the great fence.

Heavy freight and occasional passengers came by rail to Oodnadatta, thence to the bullockie lines at the fence. Sometimes the fence ox-wagons were sent over for stuff shipped up from Adelaide.

The riders knew when the bullockies were coming. This meant mail, candy, newspapers, tobacco. Each division point and post which marked the end of each length of fence was a meeting place and post-office.

A spruce but taciturn, rather gloomy young man named Farrand from the next northern length, met Sam one day at the dividing post. One of the fence teams was due to return, bringing papers and mail. A hearty, red-faced Irishman named McManus, was the bullockie. He was usually half-snorted on wheat whiskey, but belligerently jovial. Sam liked him for his zest, and for the tall yarns he told around evening camp-fires.

Sam rather liked Farrand and wanted to be friends, but the other rider was reserved—not unfriendly, but simply aloof. He was the son of an English general, but had not inherited his father's abilities in Math. Farrand had been sent down from Sandhurst as a Hunker, and had banished himself. He felt that his world had come to an end.

It was to be interesting enough to see how quickly the coming of this bullockie was to change the Englishman's viewpoint!

They saw the dust of the ox-wagon long before it arrived; and had a blazing fire, with tucker ready when McManus came. This time, however, they saw to their amazement that the Irishman was walking.

He had two blackboys with him, and six led camels followed the covered wagon. But the reason for walking was that three dustered female figures occupied the whole of the seat. Passengers—and women, in a land where white-skinned girls or women were almost non-existent!

In the flurry of greeting, camp-making, and hurried toilettes, Sam met a middle-aged, gloomy woman named Sara Peabody. She was the widow of a celebrated bushranger, who had been hanged with appropriate ceremony eighteen years before. Since that time she had been housekeeper for a rancher, Randall Smith. When his ranch failed, Smith took a place as fence-inspector, and Sara Peabody came with him to care for his motherless daughter, Claire.

Claire, now returning from three years of school at Perth, was a laughing, tomboyish sort, with freckles on her small nose, and ready comradeship in her clear blue eyes. Sam liked her at first sight, but found that there was always a queer constriction in his throat when he tried to talk to her. She accepted him without constraint, and soon was jollying him—exactly as she talked with Farrand, or Mc-Manus, or Sara Peabody, for that matter.

The third duster girl was a young widow, just discarding mourning for an elderly husband. Her name was Elinor Mathes, and she was a coquettish brunette, friend of Claire, and ready for any new sensation she could find. This trip was an adventure, and on it she secretly meant to turn as many masculine heads as she was able.

Oddly enough, Farrand was entranced by her, and followed her around as though hypnotized. On the other hand, Elinor Mathes immediately showed a partiality for Sam Varney—and he could talk spiritedly to her because he knew much more about girls of her sort than he did about the Claire Smiths of the world. Sam never would be a victim of Elinor Mathes. She sensed the difficulty, and it put her on her mettle. Before that first meal was over, she had decided to add Sam to her string. But the man queerly enough showed only a sort of exasperation when she gave him all the opportunity in the world to fall in love.

Kangaroos

After tucker there was the job for the men of raising the fence— the posts having been uprooted and the wire laid flat to allow the ox-wagon to reach the west side. The two younger women came out and talked, while Sara Peabody went about preparations for the night in the tent McManus pitched for them.

Then early goodnights, for the travellers were tired. McManus sat up smoking and talking to Farrand and Sam for an hour after this. But the bullockie was not his jovial self. He had a bunion that ached, and be had heard tales about trouble all along the fence line. It seemed to be spreading further and further north, steadily.

"I'm told it's that divvil Trenholm that's behind most of it," the Irishman said. "It worries me, with these colleens along. Lave the blackfellows alone, an' they're peaceful entirely. Poke 'em up an' they may do anything a-tall!"

Sam learned that Elinor Mathes would visit Claire Smith and her father, Sara Peabody now returning from her luxurious three years as chaperon, to take up the duties of housekeeper again. Their place was far in the north, however. Sam Varney realized with a peculiar pang that in the ordinary nature of things he never would see Claire Smith again. She was the sort he genuinely liked. But, of course, with Trenholm still on the loose and his brother Tom still unsuccessful in the chase, Sam could not think of girls. That debt of

$700 would take him a full year to clear, even if he spent nothing save odd silver for his own wants.

Next morning breakfast was early, then dust and swearing from McManus as the oxen were yoked, and the northward journey begun.

Claire came to Sam, waiting until Elinor's last dark-eyed coquetry had wasted itself. Then they shook hands. It was Claire who held to that clasp a second longer than necessary.

"Goodbye, Sam Varney," she said. "Come and see us when you're up our way."

"I'll come to see *you!*" he replied, since Elinor was getting into her seat in the wagon.

"That's what I meant, Sam Varney!" she smiled—and then a moment later leaned out from her side seat to blow a kiss in his direction. Claire perhaps had her own style of coquetry, a little slower but far more effective with men like Sam.

Farrand did not say goodbye to Sam. The Englishman was riding north one hundred miles with the ox-wagon, to the end of this fence length. And for this stretch Farrand meant to improve every minute, which meant ceaseless attention to Elinor Mathes.

Chapter VIII. War Drums Thunder

While Sam went about the routine of his work, his mind was filled with a desire to get transferred north. He liked Goelitz, and the inspector certainly had given Sam more than one unusual break.

Paxton Trenholm and presumably Tom Varney were up north somewhere now, however. And so was Claire Smith. McManus had intimated to the men alone that he thought Randall Smith a complete fool to bring women in to the lonely well cabin at a time like this. There would be days and nights when Smith himself could not get back to his headquarters, and the three women would be completely alone.

In past times this had been all right, but now with Trenholm fomenting raids, there was no guessing what might happen.

Oddly enough, Claire Smith thought a number of times, as she rode the slow ox-wagon north, that she would suggest Sam Varney's name to her father. It might be that Inspector Randall Smith could arrange unobtrusively to have the young rider transferred.

After saying farewell to Farrand, the ox-wagon entered the jurisdiction of Inspector Harris, and remained there for the next three hundred miles. After that dreary nine-day part of the journey was finished, traveling from dawn to dark of the summer days, they entered the three-length demesne of Inspector Burke. Claire's father was the next inspector to the north.

At the midway point of Burke's lengths, McManus the bullockie would turn back from the center of Australia and make his slow way back down the fence, gathering rabbit skins in bales and taking outgoing mail. One of the returning ox-wagons from the north would take Claire and the other two women the rest of the way home.

That was the plan, but it did not work out that way. Occasionally at sunset they heard a far-away whispering murmur of sound. It made the camels uneasy. Claire looked a little frightened, but said nothing to Elinor. These were the war drums of the aborigines.

The day before they reached the central well of Burke's sections—three hundred miles from home—the drums came nearer, and could not be blinked. McManus swore softly to himself, and Elinor asked wondering questions.

Up here the cameleers rode in pairs for protection. Several of them had been killed. There had been trouble three months earlier, but now it had returned with much greater seriousness. Afghan couriers came on swift meharis, but they spoke in gutturals only to the bullockie. Sara Peabody knew the signs, but she spent her time sitting straight and stiff. Her lips moved as she muttered prayers. Her refuge from everything was religion.

McManus went to Claire finally. "I'm worried, Ma'am," he said in a gruff undertone. "I wish you'd turn right about an' come back with me. Thim black Kimberley divvils from the northwest have been raidin'. The Parrabarras an' Aruntas ain't so bad, but the sivinfut Kimberleys! Tch! Then 'tis said the Parrabarras took a couple Kimberleys captive, an' ate 'em. That don't help none to speak of."

"Oh!" cried Claire, paling. Cannibalism, she knew, was impossible to suppress completely, but here it probably meant a long drawn out war between these two nomadic tribes, with white men suffering from the violence of both.

Something happened, however, to relieve McManus of responsibility, and make the remainder of the journey seem perfectly safe for the three women. A big stagecoach loaded with Government surveyors, and bristling with the barrels of ready rifles, caught up with McManus.

In the palaver that ensued, it developed that the surveyors would be only too glad to crowd together, some climbing to the top, in order to make room for three women—two of them young and pretty. Thus several days would be cut from the journey, and there would be plenty of defenders in case of attack. So it seemed.

Claire, Elinor and Sara Peabody made the change gladly. They learned the disturbing fact that the Government, valuing the line of protective fence more just at this time than it valued the completion of railway survey, had ordered every available man over to help defend the Smith and Doremus sections—Doremus being inspector of the northernmost division. It was thought that Paxton Trenholm had been stirring up the black nomads to war between themselves, and also to make attacks upon the fence and its defenders—

The horse-drawn stagecoach made much faster time—and necessarily, since cans of water had to be crowded on to supply man and beast for the full hundred miles between each two artesian bores. The coach was so crowded that everyone was uncomfortable, yet it seemed safe. They heard the drums fitfully, but there was nothing like a continuous booming of them. The aborigines really were few in number, though they traveled over vast distances, and might be a menace anywhere at any time.

It was the next to last day of the journey for Claire, when the attack came without warning. All of a sudden, as they passed through a ten-foot thicket of wattle, hideous yells sounded and a shower of spears flew. Two of the horses went down badly wounded, and the others, transfixed less seriously, snorted. squealed and thrashed about in a frenzy of fear.

The driver of the coach leaned sidewise, and fell off to the ground. The blade of a darrah-wood boomerang had crunched into his skull like a hatchet-blade into a pumpkin. The crazed horses, trying to bolt from the dying bodies of their companions, tipped over the stage. Terror-stricken men spilled out, clutching weapons but unable to get clear of the wreckage in time to use them speedily enough.

A dozen ochre-painted blacks sprinted forward to the massacre, shrieking their blood-madness. They swung stone waddies, stabbed with knives of volcanic glass. And so swiftly did it all happen that three of the surveying party went down with riven skulls before any one of the defenders could get clear of the debris and fire a single aimed shot.

But then came sudden change. Three men hacked, crouching, pumping lead from hot rifles. Then came the flatter thunder of short-arms. It was a fury of extermination! Six, eight, ten of the blackfellows went down almost at once. The remaining ones saw and tried to flee, but too late. The revolver slugs cut them down without mercy. In less than fifteen seconds the entire fight was finished, and the scrub was a shambles.

Claire Smith had been flung out through the open door. Sara Peabody fell on top of her—and that saved Claire's life. A waddy stroke killed the elder woman, who had not even seen the black murderer making for her.

Inside the smashed coach they found the senseless Elinor Mathes. Outside of bruises—and a hair-raising adventure—she had not suffered seriously. But it would take several days before she would get over shivering.

They fixed up a rude drag, out of parts of the stagecoach. On it rode Claire and Elinor, while the surviving men walked alongside.

Thus they came north, and were met unexpectedly by Inspector Randall Smith himself, and two of his cameleers.

Then they were safe enough, though no one felt like wasting time in getting back to the well cabin.

From two miles distant on a small, wooded knoll, a black-bearded giant white man had watched the destruction of the coach, and the final defeat of the black raiders. Now a snarl burst from Paxton Trenholm. He snapped together the brass telescope, and thrust it back into leather case.

"We ride another fifty miles north!" he rasped. "Bring the camels! They're not through with me yet!"

His black bodyservant and the three squat Malays ran immediately for the meharis.

Chapter IX. Black Fires

Inspector Goelitz had refused Sam Varney's first overtures toward a transfer north, but ten days later news broke which changed everything. Sam did not hear until the end of the week, when Goelitz, with Farrand and a bearded jackaroo named Corbie, rode into his lonely camp to tell the ominous tale of what had happened in the north. Goelitz was to go with his experienced men. The supply base at Murriguddury would send men to take over temporarily. Corbie, a loose-witted drifter, was the first of these.

"Trenholm's blacks have stormed the wire! Attacked a stagecoach with three white women in it! Killed surveyors!" bellowed Corbie, who seemingly could not wait for the recital of his superior. "Blue-blazin' hell's to pay!"

"Claire Smith!" ejaculated Sam. "Was she—"

"Not hurt," said Goelitz. "Now you shut up, Corbie. He's going to take your place for now, Sam. The whole upper third of the wire is threatened. You, I and Farrand are going to ride night and day till we get there! Get your guns, ammunition and swag. Hurry!"

Five minutes later they left without ceremony. Riding all day, resting only a brief hour of the night to keep their camels going, they pressed north. Four days passed. On the northernmost section of Harris's part of the fence they found this inspector and all his cam-deers working hard on an immense repair. Blackfellows had cut and carried away over two hundred yards of the posts and wire!

"You can't tell me my Parraharras ever did this on their own!" snorted Harris, a belligerent, stocky man of middle height, with bushy reddish mustaches. "That black-whiskered fiend Trenholm is behind it. He sent a whole damn village to tear down this fence while I was thirty miles north. They killed Hank Jasper, and then put a spear through Ballinger's leg. Ballinger has the pack of rabbit hounds up here, you know."

Emu

The danger from rabbits was great, with so long a stretch of wire down. Goelitz, Farrand and Sam lent a hand in stretching the new wire. And while they were at it, back in the scrub sounded the whirring whine of many bull-roarers!

"I only hope Trenholm's with 'em when they come!" said Sam Varney grimly.

"No hope. He just eggs 'em on to raid, then sits back and watches the trouble. Crazy as a bedbug, of course."

This time there was no thought of allowing any work of destruction. The armed men met the gins, when they came from corroborree, and fired a volley over their heads. Disappointed in their hope of lifting another great length of wire, they fled with wailing cries.

But the skeleton-striped blackfellows, when they came, evidently had been fired with Trenholm's frenzy to a point where the threat of guns and determined white men could not scare. Howling, flourishing their waddies, spears, and hurling boomerangs, they swarmed to attack the whites between them and the wire.

The latter, just finished with the arduous fence repair, were merciless. The repeating rifles and small arms kept thundering, and fully twenty-five of the attackers died without ever getting close enough to kill a single white. Several of the fence men had minor spear wounds, and one had been knocked senseless by a glancing boomerang. But that was all. The black survivors finally realized that it was no use. and fled.

"That's all!" cried Inspector Harris. "Lord, aren't they gluttons for punishment!"

"Well, we'll press right along then," said Goelitz. "I think you've got this situation under control now."

As Sam rode his camel northward, however, a word of Harris's had started a train of speculations in his mind—golden speculations, tied up with dim, wondering thoughts of a girl who had freckles on her nose.

Gluttons! The reward for a suggestion which would end the rabbit plague in Australia! Claire Smith!

Sam had recalled with a thrill, tales told by one of his uncles who had been in the Klondike from '98 to 1901. The uncle had brought back little gold, but one of the stories he told now seemed to Sam extremely pertinent. It concerned a little animal of the north country which went around killing rabbits for the sheer fun of it!

This was the Canadian glutton—or wolverene, as some named it! Why should not Australia import a number of these small but ferocious killers, and let them loose to murder rabbits?

The very first chance he got, some days later, Sam put this idea in form of a letter, and sent it south by Afghan courier. Like all contestants for prizes the world over, then he dreamed of what he meant to do with $150,000 and five square miles of land. Naturally enough, most of those dreams had something to do with a girl who had blue eyes and freckles on her nose.

*   *   *

The next day saw a distinct change in the vegetation, as they pressed on toward the sections of Smith and Doremus. The mulga scrub thinned out and vanished. Its place was taken by beefwood, baobabs and kashew trees, and over the rolling plain small bolsons of kangaroo grass made the feeding of the camels easier.

Three more days, and they entered the section of Inspector Randall Smith. Goelitz kept scanning the northward horizon, and a frown corrugated his brows.

"Don't like it!" he said half to himself. "We haven't met a courier or a fence-rider—anybody!"

"There's a war on," Sam said, concealing his inward apprehension for Claire Smith and the girl, Elinor, who had gone north with her. "Prob'ly there're all up helping Doremus with the top section."

"The loot would look better here. Smith has the best house on the fence. Then—there's the women," said Goelitz grimly. Without more words the three men urged their camels to a shambling run. The beasts were nearing the point of complete exhaustion from their grueling trip, and the riders themselves were not much better off.

Nothing appeared that day. Next afternoon they reached the artesian well on the lowest length of Smith's section. Here stood the corrugated iron shack, iron water tank, windmill and pumphouse, and nothing else. The door of the shack sagged open, half-broken from its hinges. They knew the story before they reached the shack.

"Looted!" cried Farrand, who was first to dismount and take a look inside. The shack had been stripped of everything. Even the iron cots were gone.

"There were two riders here," said Goelitz, sadness in his eyes. "Let's shove along. It may be still worse up above."

Sam's face was drawn and stern. If Paxton Trenholm really was behind all these outrages, where could Tom Varney have gone? On a good camel, with the bushranger only a short way ahead, he must have caught up with the outlaw band long since.

The answer seemed plain. Tom had met Trenholm, and failed. It was all up to Sam now to uphold the honor of his family.

Progress now had diminished in heartbreaking fashion. The camels were ready to drop. Food had run out. There was no chance to hunt, except now and then to take snapshots with rifles at the small but edible "Nor'west parrots," which were a screeching nuisance everywhere. There were few rabbits in the traps of the fence, and in this hot climate the flesh of these stringy jacks was too strong-flavored to stomach.

Then on the second morning, as they were trying to flog Farrand's camel into rising to its feet—instead of lying there and moaning until it starved to death—all of them heard faint thunder of rifle firing ahead of them in the north. They mounted somehow, and forced the staggering, exhausted beasts onward.

Unshaven, hungry, in need of sleep, all three men were in a savagely worried frame of mind. And now appeared a terrifying discovery. Far ahead against the horizon, a column of thick, black smoke arose. At the height of perhaps one hundred fifty feet it mushroomed in a threatening club like the head of a waddy!

"Smith's house!" cried Goelitz bitterly. "Those poor women! It can't be anything but the house. That's built of darrah wood—pitchy. That's why the smoke is so black."

"Claire Smith!" whispered Sam to himself. His face had blanched beneath the dirt and tan. This was what they had feared. Yet the arrogant optimism of youth had said all along to the rider that this thing might happen to others, but not to him. Not to the girl he loved! Oh yes, it might not be love. He didn't really know. But that would be something to figure when and if——

The inspector's guess was proved certainty as they drove the gasping, tottering camels to the limit—and beyond. Farrand's mount suddenly collapsed under him, but he sprang free.

"Keep going!" he cried sharply, tugging at the rifle in the boot. "I'll be with you!"

Sam and Goelitz nodded, taut-lipped. They now could see the rolling billows of black smoke rising from the burning house. And now appeared an evil eye of red in the midst of the black.

Then the inspector shouted, reining up and holding one hand aloft. His camel immediately went to its knees with a stifled groan, then fell over. Goelitz leapt clear, running to where a dead body lay half-slumped, half-hung on the fence.

The dead man was undersized, stocky, brown of skin. His flat countenance and high cheekbones bespoke the Malay. He had been shot between the narrow eyes.

"Looks like one of Trenholm's gang!" shouted Sam. "Come on!"

He and Goelitz dashed through the aisles of a compact grape arbor, then across a small, irrigated truck garden near the artesian well. But both men knew at heart they were too late.

"No use at the house. Roof's fallen in!" shouted Sam. He shielded his face from the heat and circled.

Suffocating fumes swept at them from the blood-red, pitchy fire, blotting out their sight of one another. And then came a shout of discovery in Farrand's voice. He had dog-trotted after them. Reaching the far edge of the vineyard he had stumbled upon two headless corpses, and with them the body of a third man, unconscious but still breathing. It was patent, however, that the poor fellow could not live.

"Three cameleers!" gulped Goelitz, and swore savagely. "There's the pile of blackfellows they got before they cashed in! This chap—I don't know him—well, he's gone."

"Where are the women? The three girls?" cried Sam, beside himself with horror.

No present answer to that. In another angle of the grape arbor the searchers came upon all that was left of Inspector Randall Smith. Like the cameleers, he had fired every cartridge he carried, then died in hand-to-hand conflict, taking no less than six blacks with him—not counting those who doubtless fell at longer range.

One of Smith's arms had been chopped off just below the shoulder, and a waddy had smashed his skull to the bridge of his nose. They had stripped the body of clothing.

Later the bodies of two more men would he discovered in the cooling ashes of the house. But for now one thought and one only gripped Sam Varney.

"I'm going after her—then!" he told Goelitz. "I've tracked cows that were lost. Mebbe I can do something here. You—well, you get in touch with the police if you can."

"All right, Sam," said Goelitz soberly, taking no offense at being ordered about by his agonized subordinate. "God go with you!"

"I'll need a thousand devils if I find Trenholm!" grated Sam.

Chapter X. Answer to a Widow's Prayer

Sam went on foot, travelling out west into the scrub, then circling, He came upon traces of two parties of blacks. No camel tracks. No sign of white woman's shoes.

"Mebbe only blacks were there—and they took her away!" breathed Sam. "Trenholm 'd be sitting back somewheres—like a big, black spider—"

Forced to choose, he took the second trail, which seemed to have been made by a party of fifteen or more blackfellows. The distances between footprints were enormous. Sam shuddered. He had glimpsed one of these Kimberley Lake blacks on two occasions—the times he had seen Paxton Trenholm with his bodyservant. The tracks made it almost certain these were not Parrabarras or Aruntas, who were of lesser stature. Many of the gaunt, somber-visaged Kimberleys were said to be seven feet tall—the tallest men of any race on the face of the earth.

In half an hour, though, he reached heavy thickets, where twigs and heavier branches lay springy in the leaf mould underfoot. Here the trail petered out, though evidently still bound in the same general direction.

Sam plugged on, going now in long, slanting zigzags first to left, then to right. He had the luck to cut the trail again, but now darkness was coming. He resolved to keep going, trusting in the coming of an early full moon. Chances were slender indeed, but he felt he had to give every one to the women caught by these primitive devils.

Moonrise found him still going. He stopped a few seconds every now and then, listening, hoping to hear the sounds of a native camp or village. If that were ahead of him, and the women captives there, Sam knew he would have the only advantage a lone white man could have. These superstitious aborigines never ventured out at night, peopling the dark with blood-thirsty bunyips and all other manner of man-eating devils.

Two more hours, three, passed slowly by—with fatigue gradually dulling the senses of the plodding man. Then suddenly he came to himself, falling! He had gone sound asleep on his feet!

Duck-billed platypus

He was forced to give up for the time being, make the best of it. He lay down, and instantly was gripped by the dreamless sleep of exhaustion. While he slept forces he did not suspect fought to give him a chance. The indefatigable police had been warned the previous day, and four detachments had closed in, hoping against hope to trap the wily bushranger Trenholm, who had caused this uprising, as well as punish the murderous blackfellows.

And the police had succeeded in one thing, at least. They had turned back two forces of blacks, kept them moving through the night. Even now one of them was approaching the sleeping Sam Varney.

The jar of distant shots awoke Sam with a start. It was still bright moonlight, and he leapt up, dazed for a moment to find himself in the jungle thickets.

He came to his senses not a second too soon. Coming toward him through the thicket, hurrying like gaunt black specters of silence, came a scattered line of blackfellows spaced from one another like skirmishers.

With a yell of surprise, Sam dodged a spear as one of the black phantoms rushed at him and hurled a death shaft. A second later that aborigine sprawled on his face, one of Sam's rifle bullets through his bony chest.

Sam found himself facing three more—one of whom carried a limp, unconscious bundle in his arms. A white woman! Of course it had to be Claire. Sam forgot completely that there had been two others in that moment of flying spear and spouting lead.

Down went two of the blacks. And on both sides others yelled, probably thinking they had been trapped by more police. They fled at top speed, paying no attention to Sam, fortunately.

The gaunt Kimberley now flung aside the girl's body, and came for Sam with waddy swinging. Sam's rifle clicked—a dud cartridge, or else it had gone empty before he realized!

The stone waddy whished sidewise at his knees—the cunning stroke which cripples and fells an enemy, leaving him an easy victim for further attack.

Sam shouted, as he snatched desperately at his revolver. He leapt high, as a schoolgirl leaps over a skipping rope. And the waddy knocked away one of his heels, but did not touch flesh or bone!

As he alighted, and before the terrible club could be swung a second time, Sam shot once, twice, pointblank into the torso of the black. The aborigine bellowed, folded up and sprawled, twitching. It ceased. He was dead. Crouching, expecting more enemies, Sam stared about in the thicket. Nothing.

He was alone save for the girl he had rescued, there on the ground. She moved as he ran to her side, and lifted her face.

It was the coquette, the widow Elinor Mathes!

"Sam! *Sam!*" she cried, her voice breaking with incredulity and gladness. "Oh, are you *real?* That—that black man—"

She reached up both arms, sobbing as she clasped them tightly about the neck of the astounded Sam Varney, who ejaculated something suspiciously like a bitter curse.

"Where is Claire? Have these men got her?" He gestured in the direction the blacks had vanished.

"Oh no. Another bunch, I think," she sobbed. "Oh, carry me, Sam. I—I don't think I could possibly walk!"

Cursing inwardly, unable to desert this girl in distress as he wanted with all his heart to do, Sam picked her up roughly in his arms and began stalking back toward the fence.

Chapter XI. The Last Bushranger

A few minutes ended that. Sam still was tired, and ferocious at the turn of fortune which had thrown this woman into his arms—instead of Claire Smith. There came a distant sound of firing, at right angles from his course back to the fence! That could mean only one thing—a rescue party of police or surveyors!

Instantly Sam put down his burden. In spite of Elinor's wailing protest, he made her use her own feet. His own strength and ability might be needed any second. He set a pace through the thickets which had her stumbling and gasping, afraid to be left behind.

More scattered shots, nearer! Armed white men were harrying a party of blacks—or possibly chasing Paxton Trenholm himself! For weeks the police had been closing in on the bushranger, at last nearing the moment when he would have to stand at bay. This might be the last battle!

With the breathless young woman stumbling after him, Sam kept on toward the spot from which the sounds had come. Then the sudden crackling of branches ahead caught his attention. Here was a sort of glade in the gidgie and beefwood, lighted by first gray of dawn and last wan moonlight. As Sam stopped, rifle loaded again and ready, large animals crashed through the scrub in his direction. Camels!

A hoarse shout burst from Sam's throat. These were not police or fence men! The first two riders were squat-bodied, brown men, naked above the waist. The third was a skinny, coal-black giant, a

Sam saw a horrible thing. The limp figure held against Trenholm's chest was the unconscious body of Claire Smith!

Kimberley blackfellow. Then came a huge white man, black spade bearded——

Paxton Trenholm had ridden to his reckoning!

They came fast, straight at him. Seeing this was to be close action, Sam dropped his rifle and yanked the revolver. At the same instant the foremost Malay screamed a warning, and fired a rifle from his hip—and unaimed.

Sam shot from a crouch. The slug struck the Malay in the chest, sending him sprawling. With a yowl the tall black leapt down and fled back on the camel trail. He went straight into the hands of police, who would have use for him later. He would lead them to Trenholm's caches of loot.

The camels came right up to him. Sam shot a second time, winging the second Malay, but feeling the hot crease of a bullet across his own shoulder-blades. Trenholm had shot!

* * *

Sam saw a horrible thing. The bearded bushranger had lifted a limp bundle, using it as a shield as he maneuvered for a better aimed shot down at Sam. The latter dodged as the shot blazed.

The limp figure there, held against Trenholm's chest, was the unconscious body of Claire Smith!

For a precious second the American could not fire; and with a maniacal snarl of triumph Trenholm threw down a third time.

Sam's left leg went out from under him. By the agonizing pain he suspected his kneecap was shattered. On the way to the ground, however, he loosed his own delayed bullet, pumping it straight into the chest of the camel, just inside the left foreleg.

The beast gasped piteously and slumped to his knees. Two human bodies went plunging from the saddle—the second of these the mad bushranger, Paxton Trenholm.

He landed heavily on his side, with an explosive grunt. Disregarding the agony in his leg, Sam crawled across the two yards that separated them, and threw himself upon the giant quarry, striking savagely down with his revolver barrel, half-stunning Trenholm who roared with rage and pain and turned to grapple.

The huge arms clutched Sam Varney, who realized the folly of holding his fire and grappling with this madman while disabled. Now Sam strove for just one thing, a chance to shoot. He still had the revolver, but his arms were pinioned, and the great black-beard was crushing his ribs inward—

Having no other weapon now, Sam butted with his head. Trenholm cursed savagely, crazily—but for a split second his hugging arms loosened a trifle as he spat forth a tooth.

Sam's chance! With a wrenching jerk he tore loose his right arm. Slam! Slam! Two heavy slugs tore into the bushranger's torso.

A shuddering shriek cleft his throat. He jerked backward, thrashing, flinging Sam from him as if the Yank had been a straw man. Incredulity and terror suddenly cleared the brain of Trenholm.

"You've—murdered me!" he shrieked. Then bloody froth came to choke his words.

"Not murder—vengeance!" said Varney, from between taut lips set against his own overbearing pain.

That was the moment when the sobbing Elinor Mathes ran to him. Sam thrust her away.

"See to Claire," he bade in a croaking voice. He lifted the revolver and fired, as a half-dozen fleeing blackfellows came toward them.

But these aborigines sought only to escape. They divided, and passed him and the two girls. That moment Trenholm's back arched, and the death rattle sounded in his throat. He slumped— and the man who may have been the last of Australia's bushrangers was dead.

Now came a lone figure on a worn and shambling camel. It was a gray-bearded man who stopped dead at the sight of Sam and the revolver. Then the newcomer slid off, making a choked sound, and ran forward to the motionless body of Trenholm.

"Tom!" cried Sam. "Take care of these girls. I—"

But for several long seconds the elder brother paid no heed.

"An' you wouldn't save him for me, kid!" he said then. "He was mine. I—" The words died in a mutter.

"I couldn't,' said Sam. "It's all in the Varney family, though."

That was when the force of Territorial police reached them, to exclaim and stare in fascinated triumph down at the corpse of the most dreaded raider of the mulga.

Chapter XII. Little Texas

The Yank Varneys were exonerated. Not much more remains to be told—or can be told, since these lives are far from ended.

Sam's leg took a long time to mend. Tom stayed right with him. So did Elinor and Claire. In the end Sam was forced to desperate measures of plain speaking with the widow, who after her rescue did her best to earmark the Texan as her own property.

Sam finally blurted out to her that he loved Claire. And that was a good fortnight before he got up courage enough to say so to the right person. It was just possible that the girl with blue eyes and freckles had a faint idea, though, since she just smiled happily and sat down upon his knee saying something obscure about being relieved that her husband-to-be wasn't tongue-tied.

The rewards for Trenholm were paid promptly, and that meant capital for the Varneys. Sam insisted that Tom was a full partner, over the latter's protests. But when they got down to the details of starting a cow ranch in the kangaroo grass country, Tom forgot all about his scruples in enthusiasm for another sight of some Texas whiteface breeding stock.

Real luck perched on the Varney banner, though it did not come until after their tiny ranch was started. Sam did not win the grand prize for his idea regarding the rabbit plague. But down in New South Wales, one year later, the Commission solemnly voted him $10,000 as a special award. Gluttons had been tried out, and certainly killed rabbits wholesale in the cooler parts of Australia.

Because too few of the Canadian killers could be secured, and because gluttons did not thrive where tropical temperatures were the rule, they were not the final answer to the problem, though they certainly helped.

The only unhappy man of all the contingent, perhaps, was Inspector Goelitz. He offered Sam the inspectorship on the division of the dead Randall Smith. But Sam shook his head. Claire positively refused to have anything more to do with the fence.

"Sorry," the ex-cameleer smiled. "I'm going to be busy down at Three Flags. I want you to come and see us, though."

"Three flags?"

"Yeah, the ranch. We're going to fly the Australian flag, the Lone Star banner, and the American flag!"

"Well," shrugged Goelitz ruefully, shaking hands in farewell, "that surely ought to scare away the bunyips!"

Anthony M. Rud:
Consummate Professional

S. T. Joshi

The emergence of the "pulp writer" dates to the early twentieth century, when the pulp magazines became both a commercial and cultural phenomenon. While some scholars believe the pulp era began so early as the establishment of the *Golden Argosy* in 1882—one of the flagship publications of Frank A. Munsey's variegated chain of popular magazines—it is safe to say that the movement gained momentum soon after the turn of the century, with the establishment of such periodicals as the *Popular Magazine* (1903), the *Black Cat* (1904), and Munsey's *All-Story* (1905), among many others. Indeed, H. L. Mencken and George Jean Nathan, the editors of the highbrow but poorly selling *Smart Set* (1914–23), founded *Black Mask* in 1920 in a calculated attempt to appeal to what Mencken derisively termed the "booboisie." Mencken could hardly have imagined that, in a few short years, it would become the venue for the distinctively American subgenre of the hard-boiled detective story. The celebrated *Weird Tales* (1923) was established with the express goal of presenting readers with "different" stories—i.e., stories of terror and the supernatural that were not appearing either in other pulp magazines or in the mainstream markets of the day, whether it be popular journals such as *Saturday Evening Post* or loftier serials such as the *Atlantic Monthly*. *Amazing Stories* was inaugurated in 1926 in the wake of the burgeoning interest in "scientifiction."

In spite of the poor pay of most of these magazines (usually a penny a word), their proliferation created ready markets for those writers capable of generating material to suit each periodical's quite specific requirements. It is difficult to regard these authors as anything but technicians or businessmen; few of them possessed literary gifts beyond the ability to keep a certain kind of reader engaged by means of fast-moving plots, readily identifiable characters, a conventional love interest (exclusively heterosexual, and frequently involving a woman-in-peril scenario whereby this damsel in distress is conveniently rescued by the valiant hero at the end), and other elements of popular fiction that had already been featured in best-selling novels of the day.

And yet, some pulp writers did manage to infuse their work with a modicum of distinctiveness and originality even in the midst of an otherwise mechanical formula. One of these was Anthony Melville Rud (1893–1942).

Rud was born in Chicago. After graduating from Dartmouth in 1914, he studied medicine for two years at Rush Medical College in Chicago. He himself was the son of two physicians. But he never completed his medical degree. By the end of 1916 he had published his first work in a magazine—not a story, but an article, "'Love at First Sight' Analyzed" (*Illustrated World*, December 1916). In early 1918 his output of fiction commenced, and from that time until his early death he published an enormous quantity of fiction in pulp and popular magazines. His tales ran the gamut from detective fiction (he created his own detective, Jigger Masters) to Westerns[4] to adventure fiction to tales of horror and the supernatural to stories of the sea and much else besides. Rud also published seven novels, several of which had previously appeared in magazines.

Whether Rud had any particular interest in weird fiction is unclear. His early tale, "The Specter at Macey's" (*Green Book Magazine*, September 1918), merely suggests the supernatural before explaining it away. It is true that Rud had three stories (one published under a pseudonym)[5] in the first two issues of *Weird Tales*,

---

4. Some of these appeared under the pseudonym "Anson Piper."
5. "The Forty Jars," as by "Ray McGillivray." It should be noted that the widely held belief that Rud was the author of four stories published in Weird Tales as by "R. Anthony" is likely to be false. The stories were

but after that he did not publish any weird fiction until the 1930s, when he returned to *Weird Tales* with two stories; in that decade he also published weird and science fiction stories in *Blue Book* (one of the best-paying pulps) and *Thrilling Wonder Stories.*

It is arguable that Rud's best work is his earliest—and perhaps his single best weird tale is the celebrated "Ooze," which appeared in the first issue of *Weird Tales* (March 1923). One would like to think that, in this early period, Rud was not quite as addicted to formula writing as he was in his later career. "Ooze" is the compelling story of strange occurrences in a remote area of Alabama, where the protagonist—a "scribbler of general fact articles"—investigates a "pet" owned by the father of the author's roommate. This creature appears to consume enormous amounts of meat and eventually bursts out of the house and goes on a rampage. In the end we discover that the entity is an amoeba grown to enormous size.

The pseudo-scientific rationale of "Ooze" is worth noting, as is its probable influence (along with several other literary works) on H. P. Lovecraft's "The Dunwich Horror" (1928). Lovecraft read *Weird Tales* from its first issue onward; and although he does not specifically comment on "Ooze" anywhere in his correspondence, there is little doubt that some of the details in the story are duplicated in Lovecraft's tale, which similarly features the bursting out of an immense, invisible, and extraterrestrial entity from its confinement in a farmhouse, going on to cause mayhem in the rustic Massachusetts town of Dunwich.

Lovecraft does comment glancingly on "A Square of Canvas," Rud's second *Weird Tales* story (April 1923), noting in a letter published in the magazine that "'A Square of Canvas', by Anthony M. Rud, would be a close second [to Paul Suter's 'Beyond the Door'] if not so reminiscent in denouement of Balzac's 'Le Chef d'Ouevre In-

---

probably written by R[ichard] A[nthony] Muttkowski (1887–1943), a professor of biology at the University of Detroit who specialized in entomology. Several of his stories deal with strange properties of insects.

connu'—as I recall it across a lapse of years, without a copy at hand."[6] In fact, the two stories bear little resemblance to each other, and it is unlikely that Rud was influenced by Balzac's story, which appeared in English as "The Unknown Masterpiece." Rud's tale, like Balzac's, does depict an obsessed artist—in this case, one who is fascinated by "the struggle against *death*." But the somewhat predictable outcome of the narrative does not give it a high place in Rud's work.

In that same issue of *Weird Tales* Rud published his pseudonymous tale "The Forty Jars"—no doubt because he or the editor, Edwin Baird, did not wish to have two stories by the same author in the issue. This is one of several Rud stories that deal with exotic locales, and this penchant eventually led Rud to venture into the subgenre of the "lost race" narrative. The first of his 1930s *Weird Tales* stories, "The Place of Hairy Death" (February 1934), is emphatically of this sort—a gripping tale set in the Quintana Roo district of the Yucatán peninsula, where young Americans trying to find lost treasure are beset by huge white spiders. The tale is non-supernatural, as is Rud's next venture, "Bellowing Bamboo" (*Weird Tales,* May 1934), set in British Guiana.

By this time Rud was thoroughly comfortable working in a variety of modes in his pulp fiction. His penchant for detective stories re-emerges in "Choctaw Rose" (*Phantom Detective,* September 1935), reprinted here chiefly because of the rarity of the magazine in which it appeared. *Phantom Detective* was published by Standard Magazines as a rival to Street & Smith's *Shadow Magazine,* running for 170 issues (1933–53); but although it was chiefly devoted to stories featuring an enigmatic detective nicknamed the Phantom, it occasionally contained stories of other sorts. Rud's tale is set in the Cajun country of Louisiana, and it effectively depicts the topography and inhabitants of that remote area, in a story that conjoins detection with an action-adventure narrative.

---

6. Lovecraft to Edwin Baird; published in *Weird Tales* (September 1923); rpt. in *Miscellaneous Letters* (New York: Hippocampus Press, 2022), p. 39.

The novella "Waters under the Earth" (*Short Stories*, 10 October 1936) is again set in Quintana Roo, and again involves the quest for hidden treasure—this time a cache of gold hidden away by the Mayans. Rud is clearly intent on keeping the reader turning the pages in this thrilling narrative, although it gets bogged down with the unnecessarily lengthy account of a boxing match; and it is unsurprising that at a climactic moment we are faced with the probable sacrifice of one of the central figures and a nubile female, only to have the protagonist come to the rescue in the nick of time. Once again, there is nothing supernatural in the tale, but elements of the quasi-weird are scattered throughout. (No one, however, need think that Rud's frequent references to the "Old Ones" is a nod to Lovecraft.)

Other tales of the 1930s utilize pseudo-scientific premises if they do not venture entirely into the realm of science fiction. "Sinister Hollow" (*Blue Book*, April 1937) presents us with the mystery of a small town in Vermont where all the inhabitants have apparently fallen asleep as the result of some newly invented gas or other cause. "The Molten Bullet" (*Thrilling Wonder Stories*, June 1937) deals with two astronomers engaging in acts of mutual vengeance; the reason for the tale's narration from the point of view of a Martian becomes evident at the end. Finally, "Visitors from Venus" (*Blue Book*, October 1937) begins with a meteor falling in the Berkshires, a highland region in central Massachusetts. It is possible to see here the influence of Lovecraft's "The Colour out of Space" (1927), which similarly deals with a meteorite falling on a farm in central Massachusetts, but the development of Rud's tale is very different from Lovecraft's. We learn that a scientist has been in touch with the Venusians for years, and this meteor contains a "gift" that they have sent him. But the creatures released by the meteor are designed to overrun the Earth, and it requires heroic efforts by the protagonists to obliterate them.

"Bunyips in the Mulga" (*Golden Fleece*, November 1938) could be considered another "lost race" narrative, but its chief virtue is that it features an extraordinarily rich and detailed evocation of the topography and culture of Australia, which Rud must have visited in order to become so familiar with its language, flora, fauna, and other details. The framework of the story merely involves the hunting down of a vicious murderer, but the vivid portrayal of the landscape demonstrates once again that Rud (in another parallel to Lovecraft) might have been more taken with places than with people in his tales.

Reading these stories by a veteran pulpsmith is instructive in numerous ways, as they provide a window into the popular culture of the period. From our vantage point, what strikes us most forcibly is the blandly unquestioned prejudice found in the depiction of non-Western peoples and cultures. Rud is by no means an open racist, and in "Waters under the Earth" the main protagonist criticizes his colleague for prejudice against Mexicans; but the depiction of the Indian tribe (the Sublevados) in that tale, as well as the "blackfellows" in "Bunyips in the Mulga," is laced with an axiomatic assumption of their intellectual and social inferiority to the "white man." To some degree this prejudice extends to the white or mixed-race inhabitants of Alabama, Louisiana, and other American locales in other tales. This phenomenon should allow us to gauge the more open prejudice exhibited by Lovecraft, Robert E. Howard, Jack London, and other hallowed figures in a broader historical context.

Anthony M. Rud was a resolutely professional pulp writer, and for all the stereotypices and formulas found throughout his work, some of it retains a vitality and effectiveness born of his sensitivity to exotic landscapes and his assured mastery of short story technique. No one is likely to think of his tales as high literature designed to endure through the ages; but a surprising number of them have qualities that make them memorable and enjoyable a full century after they were written.

"Bunyips in the Mulga": A Distant Appraisal

Duncan Norris

One of the great paradoxes of the American pulp magazines was that they were habitually interested in tales set in exotic locales, yet such tales were frequent written by authors with not only no experience of them, but little interest in finding such out. Exceptions to both exist. More than one pulp writer was a world traveler with exciting adventures to embroider further as fiction, and authors who were dedicated researchers after authenticity. As an adjunct business there were even those who made an income selling local color details to pulp writers to add verisimilitude to their stories. But in the main there is a reason why the bulk of pulp authors have vanished with the yellowed pages of their publications. The tendency not just to ravage popular nonfiction sources for material—pulpsters drawing from William Seabrook's seminal *The Magic Island* (1929) created a legion of zombie and voodoo tales that continues into the present day—but to imitate other pulp stories created a relatively closed circle of feedback and information, and results in a great deal of misinformation, caricatures, stereotypes, stock situations and locations, recycled plots, and endemic racism.

With the forgoing in mind, let us examine Anthony M. Rud's pulp tale of robbery, adventure, and revenge set in Australia, "Bunyips in the Mulga," which appeared in the November 1938 issue of *Golden Fleece*. Whether Rud ever set foot in Australia is unknown, but it is from the Australian perspective that we will examine the story, and see the view of the distant, mysterious, and exotic land Down Under as offered via the lens of an American pulp author.

From the very title there can be no doubt as to the geographic location of the tale. Bunyips are a mythological creature, of a vague and ill-defined nature, in the tales of a number of Australian Aboriginal communities. The mulga tree, more formally the *Acacia aneura*, is a native Australian species of extremely wide distribution and hugely variable size, but which is most often thought of in the context of the Australian Outback, where its extremely effective roots allow it to flourish in the arid conditions that predominate away from the coastal regions of the country. Immediately we have a contradiction. Mulgas are, as noted, more frequent within arid regions—unlike the more famous eucalypts, they do poorly in the fires that habitually ravage the more coastal forests—and Rud's story takes place specifically in the dry lands of Western Australia. Bunyips are much associated with water—creeks, billabongs, swamps—and the name itself derives from communities in the more well-watered southeast of the country, where the Indigenous peoples speak very different languages. This usage of language provides us a first means by which to begin examine the tale.

The title of the story is uttered early in the tale by the main character of Sam Houston Varney. This name is itself a clue that we are dealing with the broad unimaginative style of the pulp. "Bunyips in the Mulga" is stated out loud by Varney to himself, as if perhaps in repetition of something heard earlier. Although the phrase was not an expression I am at all familiar with, and with literally the only reference to it on the internet being to this story, I mentioned it to a friend, who immediately recognized it as something her grandparents were much wont to say. Further investigation amongst various friends and acquaintances revealed that most had never heard the expression, but those who had all noted it was something older people had said when the listeners were themselves young.

The initial chapter heading is given as "Two Yanks." With the characters in question soon revealed to be from Texas—and there is no more Texan name than Sam Houston—it seems thus to be a glaring and obvious error, and perhaps even fighin' words to some. Yet this actually is a factor that subtly adds to the authenticity of the tale. In Australia, both then and now, it is common to refer to all Americans simply as Yanks. The subtitles of difference concerning the widely differentiated geographic origins of Americans are often lost, or more commonly ignored, often in a rough good humor or gentle mockery.

To more specific usages of language "Bunyips in the Mulga" has a decent sprinkling of both idiomatic Australian terms, more formal local terms, and some words from Aboriginal languages, although this will later be dealt with more specifically in the section on the portrayal of the Indigenous peoples in the story. Before commencing, it is worth noting that the seeming simplicity of the Aussie argot is frequently misused or mangled by those not intimately familiar with it, especially in small ways. As exemplar, consider the term flog, a versatile word that, depending on usage and context, can mean to steal, sell, assault physically, be beaten in an endeavor by a wide margin, to be physically tired, to treat roughly with excessive use, or a crude term for masturbation.

The first significant term mentioned is that of the figure who will be the antagonist of the tale, Paxton Trenholm, who is described as bushranger. The iconic folkloric robber of Australia, the bushranger remains indelibly a part of the country's modern mythology, bush lore, and self-perception. The most famous of them, Ned Kelly with his legendary and distinctive helmet, is culturally ubiquitous and holds the status of national hero, still common on everything from high art to mailboxes, bronze figurines and beer labels, T-shirts, postage stamps, and in every tattoo shop and souvenir stall. Kelly was hanged in 1880, and this is also generally considered the end, or at least the beginning of the end, of the bushranger era. To have one active in the 1930s is wildly anachronistic.

The having of "a frugal tea and damper"—a traditional bush sourdough bread made of flour, salt, and water, then commonly cooked in the ashes of a campfire—on the same first page rings true. However, later on Sam is given a swag—a bundle of possessions for traveling—which does not contain flour, and thus one could not make damper out of it. The travelers also eat tucker—which simply means food. This is another especially typical usage for the time, and still in the popular vernacular. Food sellers inside schools are still called tuck shops in many areas, and the very Australian (and notoriously profanity-filled) YouTube cooking show *Nat's What I Reckon* refers to the microwave as the Tucka Fuck. That characters cook on a primus, which while not exclusively Australian by any means is well used in the tale, although most bushmen would probably use a wood fire. Oddly absent is the iconic term billy, which is the can in which one boils water for making tea, and that is a widely used metonym for it.

Other small uses also feel authentic. The pub—short for public bar and still universal in Australian usage—at Kargie, and white-pointers for the great white shark—then a dread enemy, now a protected species—ring very true. Galumphing for the movement of kangaroos is an interesting choice, but the word of course is far from exclusively Australian, deriving as it does from the famous work of Lewis Carroll. Bullockies is another typically informal Australian language usage—biscuits into bikkies, poker machines into pokies, postal deliver worker into postie, etc.—as is jackaroo, the former being a bullock driver and the latter a young male worker on a sheep or cattle station—jillaroo is the modern female equivalent. The former is a cognate with the American bullwacker and the latter (far more loosely) an "apprentice" cowboy: a full-trained and experienced jackaroo would be called a stockman.

Finally of note is larrikin, a curious word that pops up in several places. In modern usage it means a bit of a wild and often funny person, boisterous and prone to mischievous but rarely malign acts, frequently rough about the edges culturally: the aforementioned Nat was literally labeled as one as the first descriptor in his introduction to an extended television interview on the national broadcasting network ABC. However, larrikin originally—beginning in the 1860s—had a harder meaning, more closely associated as an equivalent to hooligan. Again the usage here by Rud feels largely anachronistic, with much of the transition in meaning having evolved out of World War I, the notoriously anti-authority attitude of the otherwise highly regarded Australian troops softening the edges of the term: *Backs to the Wall: A Larrikin on the Western Front* (1937) by George Deane Mitchell neatly illustrates the transition.

As a parochial obligation, I feel obliged to mention for the record that, despite the story claiming that a "Queensland larrikin [who] brought ashore four mated pairs of rabbits" caused the plague that their unchecked mating would result in, it was actually an English colonist, Thomas Austin, who deliberated released twenty-four wild rabbits for sport hunting in 1859 at his property in Victoria. This was proved genetically in 2022, as government scientists in Australia apparently have no better tasks than definitely assigning blame to people dead two centuries ago. Incidentally, rabbits remain illegal to possess as pets in Queensland, and as Rud's story states there was a reward offered to eradicate rabbits—£25,000 in 1887 by the government of New South Wales, not $150,000 and land as the tale inflates—as well as an attempt by Louis Pasteur to create a bio-weapon to exterminate them.

Upon the subject of flora and fauna, in one of the better pieces of writing in the tale Rud notes of the fire and the protagonist's thirst: "ironically the branches of thorny acacia crackled and snapped on his fire. Ironically—for unknown to Sam, the heavier stems of this mulga held pure water." While the mulga is a highly effective drawer of water—it tends to have few plants around its base as it effectively monopolizes all moisture in the soil about it for several meters—it does not contain free water available to drink in the classic manner of the jungle vine, so often portrayed as such in fiction but stemming from actual practice. Also noteworthy is that Australian acacias are almost all thornless, unlike the famously thorny acacias of Africa. Mulga, gidgie bush, beefwood, wattle, mallee, dwarf screwpines, baobabs, and kangaroo grass are all genuine native plants to Australia and largely appropriate to the areas under description, although the kashew tree—presumably the native cashew *Semecarpus australiensis*—has as its habitat is the tropical rainforest of the northern coasts.

Rud's mention of jungles on the rabbit-proof fence also seems very out of place and reinforces my feeling that he is sourcing his information from texts rather than experience. There is a constant mention of certain flora, but little description, which as just noted is occasionally incorrect. This broadly true but slightly askew feel is reinforced by the original illustrations that accompany the tale initial publication in the *Golden Fleece*. Therein shown in individual black-and-white sketches between scenes from the text are Australian native animals the kangaroo, emu, lyre bird, platypus, and koala. Only the first named makes any appearance in the tale, with an emu being tangentially referenced. The lyre bird and platypus both live on the opposite side of the continent from the events in the story, while the image of the koala is so questionable that without a description a reader could be forgiven for not recognizing it. To the same wider point is the clinical way the camels—an introduced species, now constituting the largest feral population in the world—are depicted in the tale. There is a distinct mention made of some being the racing Maharis, not the slow Afghan camels and "the undersized Sudanese camels from Kenya." But again this feels like a product of research rather than observation. We the reader are simply told this, and not instead given a genuine description of difference.

To the same point the central linkage of the tale, the rabbit-proof fence, has all its details essentially correct, as if copied from an article or survey. They are in fact so correct that if one investigates the fence today all the key facts mentioned in the tale will swiftly come up in an extremely similar manner, although the importance of the fence itself largely diminished after the introduction of the engineered disease myxomatosis designed to wipe out the rabbit populations in the 1950s. Initially extremely successful, the mutation of the viral strain and resistance of the rabbits necessitated a second engineered plague, the calicivirus, to be created in the 1990s, but this escaped testing grounds and the measure failed in effectiveness as a result of the uncontrolled distribution. A second variant was released more successfully in 2017. Ultimately it too has failed to eradicate the feral rabbit population, which numbers some 200 million and occupies nearly three-quarters of the continent, although myxomatosis in particular helped cull the population down from a previous high of 600 million.

In addition to the obvious editorial news value inherent in building the mammoth rabbit-proof fence, the locale was in the news in the early 1930s for what became known as the Murchison murders. Stockman Snowy Rowles—a.k.a. John Thomas Smith—robbed and killed three companions along the rabbit-proof fence, but was caught in part because of a discussion he had with fence rider and would-be novelist Arthur Upfield. Upfield was trying to find a resolution to a self-created conundrum in his detective novel in which he had the killer dispose of the body via burning with a large animal's remains and various other additions including sifting, acid, and pounding the remaining bone to dust to scatter to the wind to eliminate all traces of the crime. He found this too efficient, and needed a way for a clue to be left, and would ask people on his travels for ideas. Rowles was one such individual, and he later used Upfield's methods with grim success, but failing to procure acid a ring with an identifiable solder mark upon it ultimately sealed his fate, and he was hanged in Fremantle Prison on 13 June 1932. Upfield went on to a successful career as a novelist, in no small part because of the publicity surrounding the case, having as his heroic protagonist Aboriginal Australian Detective Inspector Napoleon "Bony" Bonaparte—such a seemingly surreal name being in truth commonly given to children of mixed racial heritage who were taken away from their communities and raised in various missions and government institutions.

Germane to the same issue, no mention of the fence would be complete without reference to *Rabbit-Proof Fence*, a 2002 film based upon *Follow the Rabbit-Proof Fence* (1996), which loosely tells the true tale of three Aboriginal girls in 1931 who escaped their interment after being forcibly taken from their community—as per standing government orders for any Aboriginal children having what was then called mixed blood—and used the fence as a guide to head back to their homeland and families. It is not a film with a happy Hollywood ending.

With the forgoing in mind as the backdrop to the era in which Rud's story was written, before discussing the portrayal of the Aboriginal peoples of the story I wish to note that he is not in any way a scholar of Indigenous Australian culture, which encompasses tens of thousands of years of history and hundreds of different language groups. Furthermore, I am very much a city mouse, as it were—like the overwhelming majority (90%) of Australians, who live on a mere 0.22% of the landmass: 40% of the entire population live in just two cities, Sydney and Melbourne. That being said, even I can note the lack of fidelity that permeates the tale in this regard. To a degree this can be lain at the feet of it being a pulp tale rather than an anthropological work. Yet it is more than this blanket "othering" to create a faceless enemy for the heroic Sam Varney to battle against, which is itself typical of the racist narratives that fill the pulps. No Aboriginal is given so much as a name in the tale, and their characterization as being that "half-starved black aborigines are Stone Age children" and "superstitious children" is sadly typical of the times. Equally true to life is their constant portrayal as thieves, a common clash with cyclical nomadic peoples who have a very different conception of possessions and ownership from the legislative and proscriptive societies commonly involved in colonizing activities. Even without this, the dark irony of the colonists who have stolen the land from its immemorial inhabitants calling them thieves over taking small pieces of wire or food animals is distinct.

The various attacks on the travelers in the tale feel very much lifted from an American western, simply with a very generic substitution of native peoples. Likewise with the war drums, which seemingly come straight from an African adventure and do not reflect local practice. In a similar manner the idea of the bushranger stirring up local tribes to war feels grafted on from such a setting. Most Indigenous-versus-colonialist attacks across the period seem to occur, not as planned hostilities, but more often as a reactive result of specific actions, frequently the sexual assault of Aboriginal women by outsiders. The inverse fear is of course a driving factor in the drama of Rud's story. For comparison there was a noted insurrection in the Kimberley region in the 1890s led by Jandamarra of the Bunuba, but it was far more the actions of a solitary band of guerrillas than a multi-tribal uprising, although Jandamarra did enjoy a popular support and esteem across the Indigenous communities of the region. The bushranger Trenholm can be seen, perhaps, as a distorted version of this type of action, but I feel this is a misreading, given that Trenholm in the tale is explicitly stated to be at least partially acting on insanity. Thus while the notes in the tale about the men on the fence traveling in pairs because of problems in the north reflect real practice, the portrayal of hordes of Aboriginals on the (culturally transposed) warpath is not, although there were numerous killings rising at times to large-scale massacres of Aboriginal peoples by a combination of settlers and police, with the infamous Oombulgurri (or Forest River) Massacre in the very far north of Western Australia having occurred in 1926. The aforementioned Jandamarra was himself killed in 1897 after another Aboriginal tracker was brought in to find the elusive rebel. Jandamarra's head was removed and sent to England as a trophy for the gun manufacturer William Greener as proof of the efficacy of his weapons, and it still remains unrepatriated in a foreign land against the custom of his people.

Of the three main names of Indigenous Australian communities cited in the tale, Kimberleys is not a true ethnic designation but a geographic region—Oombulgurri is located there—which has in it a number of different communities noted for their linguistic diversity. Aruntas—now more frequently transliterated as Arrente—are a well-known community, and many of the common conventional images outside of Australia of Aboriginal peoples commonly derive from their culture, whose traditional lands include the largest inland desert city in Australia, Alice Springs. To the contrary, the name Parrabarras does not appear on any listing of modern Australian indigenous communities or linguistic groups, and whether this reflects an older term or a simple invention is unclear. Given the specificity of the repeated descriptions as an extremely tall people, which has the cadence of regurgitated information, it is possible that the word is a misunderstanding or misspelling by Rud—a conflation with the Pitjantjatjara of Central Australia, or with the Dharug-derived word Parramatta, the location of the first inland colonial settlement by Europeans, now a city in its own right inside Sydney—seems possible.

An interesting case in point is the English writer Violet M. Methley, another occasional author of weird fiction—she had two stories in *Weird Tales* in the 1920s—but who was far better known for her popular children's novels. These too are frequently set in Australia and feature many sound local details. Yet at times her the usage includes place names like Worrabanda, which sounds Australian—akin to Worrabinda, Wollahra, and the Warrumbungles—but is actually nonsensical, or at least nonexistent. Parrabarras are also mentioned in two other of Rud's Australian tales, "The Red Scorpion" (*Argosy*, 26 October 1935) and "Byng of Ballarat" (*Argosy*, 30 November 1935), with almost the same descriptions as in "Bunyips in the Mulga." The pairing of Parrabarras in "The Red Scorpion" with Aruntas walking the ports of Melbourne, the latter thousands of kilometers away from their traditional lands in the desert of Central Australia and with their unrealistic depiction in ceremonial costume outside of the ritual times, along with Rud's brief mention of a character being "escorted out to the foothills near where now is Parramatta" in "Byng of Ballarat"—the story is set in 1813, but Parramatta was founded in 1788—show that, at the least, Rud's understanding is limited.

A particularly odious note to the tale is the repeated usage for the term *gin* for Indigenous females in the story. The term is highly offensive—a rough cognate may be understood by the Native American term squaw as it was arrogated into English usage—and has a number of equally horrible related terms that I will not revive here. It should be noted that in modern urban Australia the term has been long ejected from polite society: a number of people I questioned about it—especially younger people—had never even heard the term. By contrast, Rud's usage of blackfellows is not an insulting term intrinsically, and the word—most commonly as blackfellas, following the Australian linguistic trend for abbreviating and limiting enunciation—is still in common usage in many areas today. Despite the odd name, bull-roarers are a traditional Aboriginal instrument for numerous communities—obviously under different names—and the idea of women being banned from ceremonies wherein it is used reflects genuine practice. The *corroboree* is a well-known umbrella term for an array of community meetings that may be sacred, festive, warlike, or a number of other things in combination, and the description of the white-striped painted bodies common to a number of Aboriginal communities does in fact have a resemblance to a rather artistically licensed skeleton. The scene with the attacking of the rabbit-proof fence in order to allow spirits to pass had a distinct specificity, although it was not familiar to me. Whether it is based on some real event, something transposed from another cultural setting, or made up from whole cloth is beyond my ability to reconcile with any definiteness.

Wurleys (a native hut), *waddies* (clubs or sticks), and boomerangs are all reasonably well-known and well-attested terms, although speaking of the racism that undergirds so much of the tale, and the times, wurley is also a term for the nest of the house-building rat of Australia, while the people for whose language it derives—the Karuna—were driven to extinction by colonization. The mythical devil figure of Old Mooldarbie, who is featured briefly, was not specifically a familiar figure to me, as I am admittedly not deeply versed in the numerous traditional legends of the many communities of First Peoples in Australia, but the name had a resonance, and there are a number of other variants that fill a similar role. The exact name does appear in an account of a young Aboriginal boy who was taken as a slave and whose story was written in early twentieth-century newspaper accounts as "An Australian Huckleberry Finn."

Rud also uses Mooldarbie in the aforementioned "The Red Scorpion," another heavily fictionalized historical account of bush exploits set in Australia whose genuine and slightly altered names would have been familiar to any local primary school child of the time. There are other, more nebulous connections as well, namely that there are two separate spearing incidents that both take their victim in the leg. Spearing through the leg is a well known and still practiced punishment meted out in some Aboriginal communities.

To other relevant notes in the tale, neither the Malays or Afghans in the story gain the dignity of names or real personalities. The villainous Malays with their distinctive kris are very much a pulp device, but not without a semblance of connection. Malay merchants and divers were common enough visitors due to the still active pearling industry assonated with the northern coast of Western Australia, and which is referenced in the story itself. The Afghan cameleers—typically for the time, they weren't all Afghani, but merely uncaringly labeled so as a basic designation for brown foreigners (other points of origin included Egypt, Turkey, and the wider British colonial possession in India)—who helped open up the interior of Australia were likewise a reality, and the train that runs north/south across the desert the width of Australia from Adelaide to Darwin is still named The Ghan for its connection with these desert travelers, although the exact reason remains disputed.

The Australian bush characters of the tale by contrast feel remarkably true to life. The laconic but friendly manner in which some alternating with highly taciturn individuals turn up in any old accounts with an almost mechanical frequency is notable, the bush life having a tendency to attract a certain type of individual. The importance and scarcity of women was a key factor in early modern Australian life and culture, with the population always disproportionately male until World War I, and this remained true in rural areas long after: the much idealized tradition of mateship in Australia is another side effect of this demographic. Thus the view of the women in the tale by those inside, however paternalistic, chauvinistic, and idealized it might seem to the modern reader, is decidedly reflective of the times.

Equally true to the times is the universal racism of all the named characters in the tale. This was mentioned previously, but the most egregious usage is the statement of the Fence Inspector Goelitz that "like most Australians, he felt the sooner the aborigines were exterminated, the better." The word exterminated in unambiguous and resonates with the plan mentioned earlier by Pasteur, who envisioned the "bacterial method of extermination" for the rabbits. The writer, perhaps unconsciously, sees the rabbits and the human inhabitants as equal menaces, and equally without value. What is even worse is that this was in fact the opinion of a great many Australians at the time. Perhaps the politest version of this genocidal sentiment can be seen in G. V. Portus's *Australia Since 1606: A History for Young Australians* (1932), a school text from Oxford University Press that was reprinted numerous times and was still in use after World War II. After describing the eventual securing of the land from the native inhabitants, Portus casually and chillingly notes, with an air of piety, "the killing-off policy was abandoned, and the last days of the dying race are being passed in a better atmosphere of mercy and succor from their white brethren."

Nor was this opinion simply the product of Australians; it was reflective of the scientific racism of the times, which placed Indigenous Australians as the nadir of human beings on a false and entirely imaginary perceived scale of humanity. Such insidious notions were promulgated, on the one hand, by numerous (then) respectable anthropologists and ethnologists and, on the other hand, by more esoteric variants of such unsound thinking, with Theosophist William Scott-Elliot's much reprinted *The Story of Atlantis* (1896) stating:

> The degraded remnants of the Third Root Race who still inhabit the earth may be recognised in the aborigines of Australia . . . The entities now inhabiting these bodies must have belonged to the animal kingdom in the early part of this Manvantara [a cyclical time period arrogated from Hindu cosmology]. It was probably

during the evolution of the Lemurian race and before the "door was shut" on the entities thronging up from below, that these attained the human kingdom.

With such abhorrent sentiments coming from both extremes, it is unsurprising that such beliefs made their way easily into the pulps. Walter H. Munn's "The City of Spiders" (*Weird Tales,* November 1926) posts the narrator's thoughts in which "I had the impression that these were intelligent, reasoning beings hunting together for the good of the many, and as far above the ordinary spider as the Anglo-Saxon is above the Australian Bushman." Frank Belknap Long's "The Dog-Eared God" in the same issue offers "even your barbarous black fellow in Africa and Australia would be incapable of worshiping anything so vile," while Edmund Hamilton in "Evolution Island" (*Weird Tales,* March 1927) openly states that "the native Australian, the bushman, is without doubt the lowest form of human being on earth."

Rud's story is an interesting exercise in the view of the exotic land of Australia from the vantage of the American pulps. It is perhaps something of an idea of a cosmic view of justice that its most important lessons, of the evils of racism laid bare, is something Rud, with his basic action-adventure story, never intended. It is a salutary reminder that the past, and our perception of it, echoes into our future, and George Santayana's famous quotation proves its value still: "those who cannot remember their past are condemned to repeat it."

Frontiers and Fences: An Australian's Rumination on Stereotype and Authenticity in Anthony M. Rud's "Bunyips in the Mulga"

Ellen J. Greenham

When Anthony M. Rud wrote "Bunyips in the Mulga," he was not simply telling a rollicking good story of bushrangers and bogeymen, frontier gold and damsels in distress; he was writing a narrative that nearly a century later resonates with me as a decently authentic representation of the West Australian landscape in the early years of the twentieth century. Undoubtedly, the reader can indulge a thirst for adventure in the somewhat formulaic story of a man's unintended misfortune and a brother's quest to redeem him, but woven into this is a more subtle narrative concerning the landscape itself. For a twenty-first-century reader, Rud's story tends to encapsulate some of the best and some of the more problematic elements of early twentieth century "pulp" literature, as noted by S. T. Joshi (in his essay on Rud elsewhere in this issue) regarding "an axiomatic assumption" about matters of race that nonetheless reflects a more broadly situated historical and cultural perspective in the West at the time.

Rather than offer a generic and somewhat eastern seaboard kind of Australia, Rud demonstrates a capacity overall to present an Australia that is identifiably West Australian. With Rud making good use of Australian slang, I find the landscape and people in "Bunyips in the Mulga" flow from the pen of an America writer tapping into a sense of authenticity better than some Australian-born writers have done for me. Did Rud ever visit Australia? We do not know. Speculation aside, there is no real reason to suppose that an American writer is incapable of believably rendering Australia, and Rud delivers a sense of understanding some part of this vast land with such nuance as to suggest a knowledge gleaned, or ability to translate knowledge into written text, that stems from more than simply absorbing encyclopedic entries from a library shelf elsewhere.

The narrative style is engaging, with a pace referred to by Joshi as "fast-moving" and possessed of "readily identifiable characters" and "a woman in peril scenario." Within this structure, Rud offers the figuration of bunyips that manifest themselves in the story as creatures of Aboriginal Australians' lore, kept as "a ferocious pack" and "loosed" by "[o]ld Mooldarbie" (10),[1] or used as devices of terror in action against them with the ruse of the scarecrow (17–18).

From the first to the last word, while the narrative pace befits the adventure, the landscape in which the action takes place seeps through with its characteristic sense of deep time and vast distance across which little seems to change. Settlers, adventurers, and the authorities alike are connected across this landscape via ponderously slow modes of transport and communications, exemplified by "the bullockies who came with supplies" (16). As I read, I feel an Australian's uneasy understanding that anything could happen in this land and by the time help arrives, it may already be too late. Even today, nearly one hundred years later, the remote areas of Western Australia throw up an unrelenting challenge to outsiders, Australians and tourists alike. People still die here simply through underestimating conditions and overestimating their ability to survive. "Bunyips in the Mulga" is not a weird tale by any means, but Rud's scribing of the Australian landscape resonates with a certain kind of foreboding that, more broadly, continues to stamp its presence in the Australian imagination.

This is a frontier narrative similar to that of the American wild west, and Rud takes the familiar tropes of gold rush, fortune and adventure, villains and heroes, and drops it all into a wholly familiar-unfamiliar landscape. Undeniably, the hot, parched conditions of

---

1. Rud, Anthony M. "Bunyips in the Mulga," *Golden Fleece* 1, No. 2 (November 1938): 2–35. All page numbers refer to this edition of Rud's story.

remote Western Australia where history records its own gold rush, the legacy of which continues today in the city of Kalgoorlie-Boulder, has its parallels to inject just the right level of authenticity into the canvas.

Necessarily, characterization tends toward the formulaic and relies on the reader's ability to understand the requisite stereotypes. From the protagonist and antagonist, right through to the most inconsequential of individuals, Rud populates this story with stereotypes and then puts flesh on those bones with characteristics and actions that draw upon State history. Tom Varney, an American and former cowboy now responsible for transporting money and gold between Kalgoorlie and Kargie, plays opposite in the opening scenes to the principal human villain, Paxton Trenholm, "the bushranger," who, like a pirate "black-bearded" (3) and with his "folding brass telescope" (3–4), is English, insane, and sent out of sight from civilized society by his own family (16). As the story progresses, Trenholm becomes the vehicle through which the reader understands something of the dark vein that runs through the cultural mythology of Australia; that this is a place where the insane and the dangerous can thrive.

Characters are like familiar hooks on which to hang the garments of the landscape, and it is here that Rud presents that landscape as something known and unknown—a land at the metaphoric ends of the Earth. Australia is the Antipodes of everywhere; of the United States from which the Varney brothers come, of Britain from which Paxton Trenholm and indeed the overall majority of colonizers and settlers in Australia have come. To immigrant villain and hero alike, outside its relatively civilized settlements, Australia seems diametrically opposed to what is considered familiar with its strange creatures, strange land, and strange people with whom, as Rud offers, the powers of language are rendered close to useless as "[t]hey simply refused to say anything at all" (16).

When first ashore from the *Narwhal*, Sam Varney lands at the southern end of Western Australia's rabbit-proof fence.[2] In depositing him here, Rud signals to the reader a real location near the port settlement of Esperance in the Great Australian Bight that, combined with other named locations such as Perth, Fremantle, Kalgoorlie, Ninety Mile Beach—actually called Eighty Mile Beach—and Broome, cumulatively map the action across the landscape in a manner that enhances a sense of the known world as it collides with the unknown Antipodean interior. Australian-born and living for most of my adult life in Western Australia, I find that Rud draws a convincing landscape resonant with the danger and mystery of the Outback and framing my Anglo-cultural heritage.

While not a story about the fence in and of itself, the rabbit-proof fence pervades the landscape as a barrier to intruders; it is a point from which Paxton Trenholm can stage a sleight-of-hand regarding his location and direction of travel in order to deceive the authorities; and it determines the line in the landscape along which Sam Varney is compelled to travel in search of work and his brother. The fence dominates the landscape and haunts Rud's title, as timber from the mulga tree was used in its construction. The fence as a historic fact of some marvel in itself, becomes a potent plot device for regulating human movement and directing the storyline. The fence keeps the intruding rabbits out, the civilized humans in, and is bookended, as it were, by the surrounding ocean and dangerous shadow of Paxton Trenholm in the south and along its length to the northernmost end at Condon, located between the settlement of Port Headland and the pearling settlement of Broome (8).

---

2. Now referred to as the State Barrier Fence, it was built between 1901 and 1907 for the purpose of keeping the rabbit plague out of the State's pastoral areas; once completed, the No. 1 fence was the longest continuous fence in the world. As the invading rabbits advanced and broke through, the No. 2 and No. 3 fences were also constructed in the hope of continuing to protect agricultural areas of the State's south-west. See J. S. Crawford, *History of the State Vermin Barrier Fences, Formerly Known as Rabbit Proof Fences* (Perth: Department of Agriculture and Food, Western Australia, 1969).

Trenholm as "the bushranger" is also transfigured by the fence as pirate with his black beard and "folding brass telescope" (3–4), eluding capture as he travels the fence-line between its port-ends. In this, the dominating tropes of Australia are brought together, and the inhospitable outback is met by the continental boundary of the endless sea. The vast emptiness of the Australian interior creates a suitable corollary, enhanced by Trenholm's band of "camel-riding Malay murderers" (3) and his collusions with Aboriginal Australians to "have stormed the wire [and a]ttacked a stagecoach" (27). Not only does Rud make deft work of the adventure-story conventions of land and sea, but in this conflation of settings he enriches the narrative as believably Australian. The sea and the desert pervade Australia's literature and cultural sense of itself, in Rud's time and now, and I see "Bunyips in the Mulga" tapping into this ever-present yet uneasy understanding held by Australian reader.

Despite a certain level of textural references that draw on a more generic *idea* of Australia and which are, in some cases, not of flora and fauna endemic to Western Australia, Rud still manages to create something more than the generic that is then used as a device in service of a quick grab for an exotic location in which familiar action takes place. After the locus of the fence, he does so through a strategic use of the term "Yanks," which in my own lifetime continued to be a disparaging reference to people from the United States of America. Rud wields the term from within the Australian idiolect to set Americans apart as a different kind of immigrant to the Antipodes and distinct from Australians who were typically British or more broadly European, and yet he maintains a sense at the end that it is also only the adventuring "Yank" who can "'scare away the bunyips!'" (35).

Of the deeper and more problematic issues of racial representation contained within this story and which prevailed more broadly at the time of its writing, much could be said and is, indeed, well handled elsewhere by others more adept at such discussion than I. It is fair to say that when Rud's language choices fall back into some fairly historical standards of stereotyping and pejorative terminology, such as referring to Aboriginal Australians as "gins" and "bucks" (17–18) and Malaysians as "chinks" (6), he makes use of conventions that existed within society more broadly at the time. The reader, then and now, encounters and therefore understands non-white characters in consequence as stereotypes that facilitate the creation of an adversary against which civilized characters are pitted. It remains important to keep sight of the historic context in which "Bunyips in the Mulga" emerged, for at the time of this story's publication Rud's narrative did not overreach itself in terms of prevailing, though by no means universal, attitudes in Australia when the character Goelitz is framed as "[l]ike most Australians, he felt that the sooner the aborigines were exterminated, the better" (17).

Contemporary problematics regarding issues of race representation notwithstanding, the measured balance Rud achieves between genre convention, his contemporaneous societal stereotyping, and specifically Western Australian referents creates a satisfying read. His characters are drawn in such a manner that I find they correlate well with my sense of pioneering West Australians who were, in my view, very different from pioneering Tasmanians in a State where the landscape, climate, and motivations for colonization were very different. Rud's narrative implicitly acknowledges this historic difference, which only serves to heighten the sense of an authentic context in which the eponymous noble quest is immersed.

Enhancing this are the illustrations published with "Bunyips in the Mulga" in 1938, and consideration of these beyond the pulp convention of their inclusion is worthwhile. They evoke nostalgia for the kinds of stories and books I read as a child and had been found on the bookshelves of grandparents, uncles, and aunts; stories consumed on languishing summer holidays or when tucked up warm on cold winter's nights and seeking adventure in far-off lands. The illustrations are a delight in themselves and locate the publication of Rud's story to a period in time when such images and such stories were more widespread.

The illustrator was Jay Jackson (1905–1954), an African American whose work renders Aboriginal Australians as both instantly recognizable to an Australian reader in their studied mirroring of depictions from domestic publications of all kinds, and simultaneously disturbing as visual representations of the stereotypical "blackfellow." Jackson introduces the Aboriginal Australian as tall and strong (2–3), until the venturing hero, Sam Varney, unleashes his plan to dissuade their destruction of the fence. In this moment, Jackson draws the Aboriginal men as cartoonish and terrified by a simple trick (19), rather than as the formidable men he previously offered.

The illustrated human portrayals throughout the original publication work in complement to the narrative, providing visual cues for the actions, heroes, and villains of a world peopled nearly exclusively by men and of women shrieking in fear in a carriage (2) or hanging like a rag doll over the villain's arm before rescue by the hero (33). Having ventured out myself into the landscape Rud's narrative travels, I can feel on my skin the dirt and degradation of Tom Varney's life in hiding (21); I have encountered histories of men in hard and itinerant living, backlit by campfires at night (5). I feel a sense of northern warmth with the addition of a palm tree in the background and shadows of men on camels to denote the subtropical end of the fence at Eighty Mile Beach (9). For a sense of Western Australia, Jackson's illuminated subjects hold up well.

The inclusion of some standard Australian animals in the illustrations is fascinating in itself for what this implies about the *idea* of Australia in the early twentieth century. These images provide a certain kind of exotic familiarity and yet, curiously, the first illustrated animal of the story I encountered was the rabbit, framed by its caption as "The Villain" (11). It is vermin to be kept out, but it is also representative of the villain Paxton Trenholm and the villain Aboriginal "buck," both of whom are determined to breach the fence and must be deterred. Every other animal depicted takes its common name—the "Lyre Bird" (13), the "Koala" (17), "Kangaroos"

(23), the "Emu" (27), and the "Duck-billed platypus" (31)—and not all are endemic to Western Australia. The inclusion of these illustrations, accurately rendered overall, become devices for visually locating Australia as a real place for the reader *and* for enhancing a sense of the mysterious Antipodes filled with strange creatures. The lack of accuracy with respect to *where* in Australia these animals exist, when the narrative and action are so carefully located in Western Australia, tends to feed back into a lack of understanding about the continent more broadly that is not, to be fair, uncharacteristic of the times or, perhaps, even now.

It seems to me that with our modern proclivity in the West for cleanliness and order in the built environment, companioned by a data-driven need for metrics over everything and correlating societal politics, that we have been robbed of some of the magic of the unfamiliar that fuels our imagination and a sense of wonder about the world we occupy. Rud taps into Australia's own myths about itself as a place both exotic and hostile, a land with the capacity to swallow people whole. The memories and accompanying emotional responses I feel in reading "Bunyips in the Mulga" take me back to something older than myself to remind me that I live in a land that remains, even now, largely unknown beyond its cities and towns. It makes me wonder if our modern way of life is some part of what, in these early years of the twenty-first century, is fuelling the rediscovery of gems in the "pulp" of the past and the collective thirst we seem to have ignited for reimagining the adventure, the weird, and the fantastic. To be sure, Rud's story is outfitted with a certain level of formulaic plot construction, stereotyped characters, and elements of language that in the twenty-first century have become problematic; but where he genuinely triumphs, in my view, is in the presentation of a wholly believable depiction of the West Australian landscape that speaks of something grounded in more than just grabbing a few Australian-sounding words and images and stitching them together into an adventure pastiche. In my own weariness at the numbing demands of a world requiring me to measure and evidence everything for it to be deemed of value, "Bunyips in the Mulga" is, quite simply, a delight.

Lords of Halloween

K. A. Opperman

Though we sleep and though we slumber,
Buried in November graves,
We will rise in greater number
When again the cornstalk waves.

Though our masks and costumes crumple—
Pumpkin, burlap, purple leaves—
We will be the ones to trample
Down the furrows and the sheaves.

We will come like living torches,
We will come with smiles of flame;
Set a pumpkin on your porches,
Lest we come your souls to claim.

We will come with scythe and sickle
Glinting with a moonlit sheen;
We are fate, and fate is fickle—
We are lords of Halloween.

Beyond the Wall of Pain

Garrett Boatman

The object wrapped in the hand towel clinked softly as Krystof Kasparek placed it on the kitchen table. Krystof returned to the door and shot the deadbolt. For a summer's night, the neighborhood outside the Prague Lesser Town apartment was unusually quiet, for which he was thankful. The unairconditioned room was stifling, but he made no move to part the drapes or open the window.

A tall, thin man in his late sixties who looked older because of his stooped shoulders and gray hair, Krystof removed his jacket and hung it over the back of a chair. He ran the faucet till it cooled and poured himself a glass of water. He drank thirstily, set the glass upside down in the sink when it was empty, and turned his attention to his task.

A framed photograph sat on the table beside the bundle. The dark-eyed, intense young man in the black coat and tieless white shirt was Leos, his younger brother. Though a mere four years separated them growing up in the streets of Prague, decades distanced Krystof from the young man in the photo. No photo recorded an older Leos: less than a year after the snapshot his brother died under mysterious circumstances. Mysterious even for Prague with its centuries-old traditions and unequivocal acceptance of the supernatural. Though a man of science, Krystof was Czechia and not so ready to dismiss out of hand explanations his Western counterparts would consider unacceptable.

During the Prague Spring of 1968, Krystof and Leos had joined those youthful optimists who, chaffing under the old Soviet rule, rallied for a social-democratic Czechoslovakia. But during the difficult years that followed the arrival of Soviet tanks, dissention was dangerous work and didn't pay. As always, life happened. Little latitude was permitted an assistant professor, especially by the communist conservatives who viewed intellectuals with suspicion, and even less if you wanted advancement. So he had buckled down, kept his thoughts about the hardline communists to himself and his dinner table friends, fought for scraps of funding for his department, and published in his field of the transformative and information storage properties of metals, ceramics, and crystals.

Leos, too, had quit the profitless profession of radical dissident and thrown himself into his obsession, which had less to do with his job as university librarian than, for lack of a better word, his hobby. Leos, responding to an advertisement for test subjects in a psychic research project, had returned to their shared apartment bubbling with enthusiasm. A convert to his new religion of psychotronics, he was as zealous to spread the truth as he saw it as any man who has given up cigarettes or red meat. And Krystof, true to his Prague roots, having never divorced the science of chemistry from its hermetical origins (i.e., the alchemical quest of nothing less than the spiritual evolution of man), threw himself into the exploration of devices that might quicken the work of *homo faber* and accelerate the improvement of man and nature.

One day Leos came home quiet, not his usual exuberant self. Krystof asked him what was wrong but Leos answered "Nothing," so he figured his brother was coming down with something. As he was busy preparing for tomorrow's lecture, he thought no more of it until he put away his notes and, retiring, found Leos dead in the tub.

Leos had drawn a bath and slit his wrists with a paring knife. The water was red to his brother's pale chest.

He'd pulled the plug and laid Leos out on the white tiles and, knowing it was too late, tried to revive him. The ambulance came. The attendant confirmed what he already knew:

Leos was dead.

Despite the long, sleepless night of grief, Krystof pushed himself into action the next morning. He could not accept his brother's taking his own life. Leos had been fired by the quest of discovery. His was an eager intellect that seized on new ideas and burned to share them with others. His exuberance reverberated through the lives of those who knew him. To imagine him a defeatist, a suicide, was unthinkable.

From one of Leos's library coworkers Krystof learned of his brother's visits over the previous three days to a Dr. Grigorovich at the Biological Institute. Leos's friend said he had volunteered as a test subject in a project but couldn't talk about it yet. Krystof was surprised Leos had mentioned none of this to him, but thought perhaps he meant to surprise him. His heart beating in his throat, Krystof hurried to the Institute.

Dr. Grigorovich was present when he arrived. Workers were crating instruments under his direction. Apparently he had been visiting Charles University and was returning to the Institute of Physics and Technology, where he held tenure at the prestigious Lomonosov Moscow State University. The doctor expressed surprise and offered his condolences at the news of Leos's suicide. No, he hadn't noticed any despondency in any of his test subjects. Considering the circumstances, the doctor confided in Krystof that the nature of his investigation had to do with the latent bioplasmic field energy. From his own studies, Krystof knew he was talking about the controversial energy field surrounding and emanating from all living things.

Dr. Grigorovich expressed apologies for not being more helpful and shook his hand. Krystof thanked him and left.

Later, surfacing from his grief, Krystof realized he couldn't for the life of him recall the doctor's appearance—not accurately, anyway. A sensation of incongruity gnawed at him. It was as if he retained two conflicting memories of Grigorovich. On the one hand, he remembered the doctor being of average height, of unassuming posture and unarresting looks: brown eyes, brown hair, gray suit—nothing that stood out, nothing memorable. On the other—and this was like the mists of dissipating dream the mind clutches at after waking—he recalled a taller, blonder man. He hadn't marked it at the time—in fact, the whole interview had the quality of a fever dream that he attributed to his grief—but afterwards, at home seated at the table with a cup of warm tea in his hand, not remembering returning home or making the tea, he seemed to recall looking *up* at the professor, who was actually a couple inches shorter than himself. And then there was the persistent and perplexing discrepancy of the doctor's eyes. He seemed to recall a moment during the interview when, distraught and at his wits' end, he pressed Grigorovich for more information, and the doctor's brown eyes had flashed a pale and chilling blue.

And while the scathing blue transfixed him where he stood like a rat in a snake's cold stare, he'd gotten the distinct impression of blond Nordic hair superimposed over the limp, professorial brown.

The next morning he returned to the Institute only to learn Grigorovich had taken the train to Moscow the previous evening. Krystof followed.

A visit to the Institute of Physics and Technology proved fruitless: secretaries and researchers' eyes glazed over at the mention of Grigorovich's name. A personnel director informed him the doctor worked at the Moscow Institute of Physics and Technology's Biochemical Physics Laboratory. Krystof's heart sank when he learned the Institute was an OKB, an Experimental Design Bureau, one of many state-funded covert departments working on classified military projects in those pre-Glasnost days.

Lost in the frustrating labyrinth of Moscow's clandestine and close-lipped world of secret research and increasingly under disapproving eye of the KGB, Krystof returned to Prague. Despite the lack of evidence, he knew in his heart of hearts that Grigorovich was not what he seemed. The doctor had done something to Leos. Something that had driven him to suicide.

But how?

Brainwashed? Programmed?

Clichéd concepts, but after much consultation with experts from doctors of psychiatry at Charles University to a retired military intelligence officer in Virginia, he knew it could be done. But never so quickly. Reprogramming a human being took time. Negative reinforcement—shock, deprivation—was quicker, but even with the aid of drugs it took weeks, months, to coerce a strong-willed, intelligent mind such as he knew Leos to possess into destroying itself. He recalled no slackening of Leos's enthusiasm during their evening visits to the beer gardens, no quieting of his rapid-fire revelations of his latest discoveries.

Like a hawk with his eye fixed on the lone prey moving in the landscape below, Krystof's mind kept circling the singular figure of Dr. Grigorovich. Who was the man? Some mysterious Svengali capable of mesmerizing an intelligent mind into self-destruction? Some malignant, shape-shifting Wolf Messing figure capable of beguiling the eye into seeing what he wanted you to see?

A monster—of that he was certain.

Just as he was certain the brown-eyed, brown-haired, unremarkable professor was a masquerade.

Unable to resolve the *how*, his mind turned to *why?*

Why would anyone want Leos dead?

Why would a monster that came and vanished as mysteriously as a supernatural visitor in a ghost story mark his guileless brother for death?

And why was Grigorovich in Prague in the first place?

Prague's rich, esoteric history no doubt provided the answer to the latter question. Was Prague not the alchemical capital of the world? Where the English magus John Dee and his scryer Edward Kelley sought the *lapis philosophorum?* And where Tycho Brahe and Johannes Kepler, both secret alchemists, plotted their astronomical calculations? Surrounded by seven hills surmounted by seven churches with five sacred sites inside forming the "Rosy Cross," the city was a locus of sacred geometry emanating powerful numinous energy. It made sense that the Russian scientist's investigations into the latent bioplasmic energy field would prove all the more fruitful here.

Krystof himself had devoted decades of research into harnessing the elusive field. If properly channeled, the energy could supply a cheap and endlessly renewable source of low frequency electromagnetic energy. Composed of ions, free protons, and free electrons, the bioplasmic body or energy field was distinct from the four known states of solid, liquid, gas, and plasma. Some scientists considered it matter's fifth state. While the West was skeptical, research in the East had long been fruitful.

As a scientist, Krystof knew the Law of Conservation of Energy stated energy can change form but cannot be created or destroyed. Or as the poet had it:

> Nothing is ever really lost, or can be lost,
> No birth, identity, form—no object of the world.
> Nor life, nor force, nor any visible thing;
> Appearance must not foil, nor shifted sphere confuse thy brain.

Unable to solve the mystery of his brother's death and convinced that life was a force that did not, like a snuffed candle, simply vanish with death, Krystof tried communicating with him.

In his youth, one had only to go to a certain street in the outskirts of Prague, to a cozy house redolent of cats and lavender cachet, and pay a few rubles to talk with your dear deceased. But Fra Miller was long dead and the psychics he encountered in his search were charlatans or, worse, zealots self-deluded into believing their own hype. Still, he was a scientist and had pursued other ways to communicate across the veil.

He stepped into the next room and returned with his mother's Bible Kralická. He unwrapped the towel and placed the generator on the book's creased black-leather cover. Removing the chair from the head of the table, he stood and gazed on Leos. His brother had not always been so serious as he appeared in the photograph. He was a young man then, a university student, and perhaps thought it proper to wear the penetrating stare of the objective mind weighing the profundities of the universe. Oh, how full of philosophy and revolutionary ideals they had been! Nights in the beer gardens, he and Leo drinking with their circle of friends from Charles University. Leos, the youngster of the crowd, always trying to impress his older brother's friends and not really having to try because he was so brilliant.

No, not always was Leos's expression so serious. Krystof imagined Leos smiling over a mug of U Fleku's dark lager or a frothy glass of Old Gott. Oh, how they had thought themselves connoisseurs in the world's capital of breweries. How they built castles in the air and expounded on the golden renaissance about to dawn.

Before the Soviet tanks rolled in.

Ending his revelry, Krystof stood straighter. He focused on his brother's photograph a moment longer, on the dark, penetrating eyes. Then lowered his gaze to the device.

Shaped like a common seashell—an auger, to be precise—about eight inches long, pointed at one end and spiraling in smooth whorls to the other, the machine was anything but common. Its color was not that of any earthly shell, nor was its material. Glowing a pale, luminous green under the kitchen light, it sat like a thing from another world on his mother's Bible. A thing alive, waiting to heal.

Or to hurt.

Two snakes with a common tail crisscrossed each other and met face to face at the wider end. Ten small holes were drilled into the surface—four within the coils of the serpents, three on either side of their crossings. The ten holes formed the sephiroth, the Kabbalistic tree, linking the physical with the metaphysical.

As above, so below.

Each hole contained a small blue crystal. The sapphires alone were worth more than he made in a decade. He touched the raised serpent pattern, felt the silent thrum of latent energy under his finger, and again marveled at the complexity of the thing's composition and wondered at the ancient hand that had crafted it.

Krystof settled his mind for what he hoped would be a breakthrough. For a long time he stood gazing on the Caduceus pattern, allowing his eyes to run around the raised helix. Round and round and——

He felt a breeze. The temperature in the room plunged. He resisted looking at the window; he knew it was closed. Despite the sudden bone-piercing cold, he was sweating, his shirt clinging to his back. A pressure built in his head, as if the barometer had plunged as well.

He focused on the pattern. Round and round and—

The photo burst into flames. A single tendril of white smoke, and then Leos's smiling face was enveloped in licking yellow fire. Horrified to see the picture blackening and blistering beneath the glass, Krystof knocked the picture onto its back and beat at it with the towel.

Dismayed, he surveyed the damage. The white Formica tabletop was scorched. Worse, the photo—the only one he had of Leos as a grown man and, therefore, beyond price—was reduced to ashes.

He looked at the device sitting atop his mother's Bible. At the coiled serpents. A thing alive, waiting to heal. Or to hurt.

He felt feverish, drained. The loss of the photo was heartbreaking.

He left the kitchen, went into the bathroom, rested a shaking hand on the edge of the sink while he splashed water onto his face with the other. The temperature had returned to normal. He had recorded the device's effect on temperature before, but it had never set anything on fire. He raised his dripping face, met his tired eyes in the medicine cabinet mirror. His face had changed so much from his memory of himself, back when he and Leos raised glasses to the failed Renaissance. He wondered what Leos would look like now.

Like most siblings, they shared traits inherited from father and mother. He was four inches taller than Leos, his face longer, gaunter, his cheekbones angular, his jaw a deep V under thin lips resembling no one so much as his mother's father. Whereas Leos's face was broader, his chin less prominent, his eyes brown and more deeply set than his.

No, he and his brother shared only the most superficial resemblance. But his reflection . . .

Even as he stared . . . unable to take his gaze off the eyes of his mirror image, which even now appeared at once blue yet brown . . . his flesh crawled. Gripped by a sense of déjà vu that raised goosebumps on his arms, he realized he had seen this effect before . . . gazing into the eyes of the elusive Dr. Grigorovich in Prague a half-century ago.

Only it wasn't Grigorovich staring at him from the medicine cabinet mirror: it was Leos.

He stepped back from the mirror, dug the heels of his hands into his eyes.

His flesh crawled when he looked again. Now, Leos's face seemed to float in front of the mirror, as if his brother, bodiless, had stepped out of the looking glass. As he watched, the face drifted toward him.

Far from dead, Leos's eyes were animated, alive—not with the warmth and joy Krystof remembered, but flushed with an expression never borne upon his living brother's face. The coldly appraising gaze that infused this alien Leos's eyes, the cynical knowing smirk that distorted his almost feminine lips—these were the chilling features of a stranger's physiognomy and had no place in the vault of Kristof's memory.

Unaware he was backing up until he felt the towel rack press into his shoulder blade and heard the mute metallic thud of his heel striking the baseboard heater, Krystof opened his mouth to speak, but uttered only a thin and tremulous moan. Vaguely, as one is aware of being awake without consciously registering the fact, he recalled he had left the bathroom door open. The hall was to his left. His hand came to rest on the doorknob, but he made no move to retreat. Indeed, he found himself incapable of further movement.

The overhead fluorescent and the hall light went out. But rather than being plunged into darkness, the bathroom was bathed in an eerie bluish glow that seemed to emanate from the disembodied face floating like a 3-D hologram inches from his own.

Were an observer present, standing to the side with his back to the vinyl wallpaper, his flesh ghosted with goosebumps, he would see through unblinking eyes a tall elderly man pressed against the wall in a pose that mirrored his own: mouth open, lips stretched in a rictus of horror, eyes distended in a stare of mesmerized disbelief; the whole scene weirdly illuminated by some infernal bluish radiance that poured in gauzy tendrils from the disembodied face that bore a familial resemblance to Krystof but whose expression was unlike anything remotely human.

Krystof jumped as something grabbed his wrist. He looked down, made out an etheric hand, powerful luminous fingers encircling his thin wrist in a crushing grip. Then the face was retreating before him and he was pulled, stumbling, toward the mirror. He was peripherally aware of the pain welling in his chest, the needles and pins paralysis spreading up his left arm—as his arm was yanked into the mirror.

No hot pain of slicing glass. No spray of dark blood cascading into the white ceramic sink. No crash of mirror shards.

His hand and arm disappeared into whorling darkness.

Released, he staggered back across the room, blood spraying from the raw-meat stump of his arm, slammed into the wall, breaking the ceramic towel bar.

Only after he had slid to the floor and lay there gasping, clutching his chest, did he realize the origin of the spreading blood. And then the pins-and-needles pain of which he was hitherto only peripherally aware grew to gigantic proportions and slammed up his left arm and punched him in the heart.

Beyond the wall of pain, in the moments before he bled out and died, the scientist in Krystof Kasparek marveled at the fact that he had at last succeeded in reaching across the metaphysical veil.

Scabrous Oak

(Quercus scabrosus)

Steven Withrow

Lightning has blasted any number
of other oaks, and drought has thinned
a line of hemlocks, useless lumber
lost to the mill or the killing wind—

Yet *this* is not a blighted tree
infested, root to crown, with weevils,
but a totem of indecency
and stranger, more invasive evils.

An arborist, with different words
for the same plant without the need
to moralize, observes a bird's
approach but does not intercede

 when, like a whip, a limb goes slack
and then flicks up to catch the prize
a knocking blow and a twiggy thwack
that boggle human ears and eyes.

 Such motion, in a wizard's book,
might almost be explained away
by giving it a second look
through a magic lens. But who can say

what happens to the battered wren
after it hits the trunk? Do trees
grow scabrous lips and teeth like men?
There is no name for this disease.

The Manger

Michael Aronovitz

Interview Room #2

"For the record, what's your name?"

"Matti Gorberg. Sorry. Matthew William Gorberg."

"What was your business at the church?"

"Like I told the Sergeant, I was making a pickup."

"They need an armored vehicle for the collection plate?"

"You'd be surprised how steep the donations can get. It's an affluent neighborhood, and they'd had theft."

"What time was it?"

"Around seven-thirty, evening."

"Why so late?"

"It's an outdoor lockbox. Business hours don't matter."

"So it was dark."

"Pretty much. But there are lot-lights. And there are two outdoor security lamps on the front of the building by the main entrance."

"And you saw Gabe Cassidy?"

"Yeah, the church handyman. He had his pickup with the tail down, parked in the handicapped spot in front of the marquis board. He was almost done disassembling the nativity scene, with all the figurines scattered in the back bed of the truck. When I turned off my engine, he was bending into the makeshift plywood barn to scrape the hay out of it. He was using a tennis racket. I remember, because there was a cover on it that said, 'W' for 'Wilson.'"

"Interesting detail."

"Yeah, and I had to take a piss, and I was thinking that the church was locked up and I didn't want to bother this guy to open the door, so I might have to go off in the woods to the left. That's when I saw something. In the cab of the pickup truck through the back glass."

"What was it?"

"Human shapes sort of slouching toward the dashboard."

"Can you describe them?"

"Shawls."

"Pardon?"

"Veils or whatever. Shawls, they were wearing shawls."

"Like nuns?"

"Yeah, well, no, not quite. The one in the driver's seat was taller, way taller, especially considering most people are the same size sitting down. Thick and hulking. It was a guy, I'm sure of it."

"But you didn't see their faces."

"Don't matter. I saw their shapes. It was the shadow of a man and in his shadow was a woman."

Interview Room #4B

"Name?"

"Kasper. Like the friendly ghost, Dr. Louis Kasper."

"What kind of doctor?"

"I'm an obstetrician."

"What were you doing in Scutters Woods last night?"

"Jogging."

"Early evening? I would think that'd be a morning thing."

"I keep odd hours."

"It was cold last night. Weather lady on Channel Six said the nighttime windchill was going to make it feel like ten degrees."

"I bundled up: a hat, scarf, and a lot of layers."

"You always run in the woods at night?"

"Better than the street. I get shin splints. Soft ground makes it lower impact—you know, dirt and pine needles and such."

"It's dark back in there."

"Begging your pardon, Detective, but it's surprisingly well lit.

Moonlight splinters through the trees overhead just enough to provide you a picture, and down at the south end past the creek the church lights brighten the path as if you'd turned on a Broadway spotlight."

"So where exactly did you have the encounter?"

"On my side of the walking bridge."

"Which way were they headed?"

"It seemed they were about to cross over. Toward the church parking area. Then they heard me coming."

"What did they look like?"

"Hard to tell altogether."

"Why?"

"Well, first, the parking lot lights were so bright it made them silhouettes."

"Like shadows?"

"Yes. Black outlines."

"Did they speak to you?"

"Yes. The bigger one. He asked me where he and his fiancée could go to rent a room. He asked me about motels in the area."

"And your response?"

"I think I grunted acknowledgment."

"That's it?"

"They wouldn't have heard me if I'd said something anyway. There was the sudden rumbling of an engine and headlights sweeping across the forest. It was a truck of some kind, a big armored truck pulling into the church parking lot, and then the weird thing happened. The truck backfired, and almost like some sort of cosmic trigger-mechanism, the sky lit up, a bolt of lightning, then another right behind it making the air bristle and the leaves flash all around like stars. Everything was vivid, veiny, and overbright, and for a moment I could see their faces."

"The two at the foot of the walking bridge?"

"Yes."

"Can you describe them?"

"Yes, masks. They were wearing robes, shawls, and masks, the happy and sad drama faces with black holes for eyes. Oh, and the shorter one was robust."

"Come again?"

"Heavy. Portly. Fat. She had on the sad face, and she was pregnant."

Conference Room

"Gentlemen, this is Pastor McGillicutty. He manages the congregation at St. Mary's Church and teaches theology and English rhetoric at Immaculata University."

"I hope I can be a help to you, Detective. Such a shame about poor Gabriel, God rest his soul."

"What do you know about this?"

"Only what's been on the news. Gabe Cassidy, our groundskeeper, was found dead last night near the nativity scene he was dismantling."

"Pastor, his heart was removed."

"How awful."

"And rosary beads were stuffed in his mouth as if he was vomiting them, similar to two other apparent murders this month: Mark Brusco, a concrete contractor, and Benedict Scarfo, the janitor over at the middle school."

"Good Lord, is this the work of a serial killer?"

"Possibly."

"Am I a suspect?"

"Not at all. Pardon my abruptness, Padre, but you're barely four foot nine, and you're at least seventy years old."

"Eighty-three."

"A tender age, certainly."

"I might surprise you! I do ten pushups every morning and ten situps! However, I am afraid your assessment is more accurate than not. We don't use the second floor anymore, because I have trouble with stairs. Arthritis in the knees."

"Yeah, Padre, no worries. Gabe Cassidy's ribs were spread open by a powerful man, probably bigger and stronger than me. Besides, your alibi is air-tight, since you were in the presence of more than fifty others at the Country Squire Diner last night. I would assume that you were well into the podium speeches when Cassidy met his fate at around seven-thirty. We're just checking the box here when it comes to you as a 'person of interest.' More, we were hoping to benefit from your insights."

"Well, Gabe was non-religious as far as I knew. Quiet, almost to a fault."

"Can you think of anything, you know, spiritually that he would have had in common with the other two victims, maybe in terms of their professions as laborers?"

"Hmm, not offhand. Did all three have their hearts removed?"

"No, the killer took different trophies. Brusco's brain was extricated, and Scarfo got the worst of it."

"What was drawn forth?"

"His biceps. Also, his penis and testicles."

(Pause)

"Are there any other connections, Detective, maybe having nothing to do with religiosity?"

"Only one. Sorry to let you know this kind of thing about one of your employees, but they were all present at the Capital Riot in Washington D.C., January 6th, 2021, though none of them knew each other before that, at least we don't think they did. Scarfo was seen on video, breaking an unreinforced window on the Senate side with a stolen police riot shield. Brusco and Cassidy were in the crowd holding up the makeshift gallows, shouting 'Hang Mike Pence!' All three got suspended sentences." (Pause) "At first, we thought that maybe this was Antifa, you know, a political thing, but it doesn't seem so, wrong flavor, too much mystery. Ideological warfare is usually waged out in the great wide open."

"I agree. And I take it you don't have first-hand witnesses to the murders, correct?"

"We have two that were in the vicinity last night."

"Names, please."

"Matt Gorberg and Louis Kasper."

"Is Gorberg a tax collector, maybe working for the I.R.S.?"

"No. He drives an armored truck. Picks up the donations."

"How about Kasper?"

"Delivers babies. You all right, Pastor?"

"Can you get them? Now, I mean. Gorberg and Kasper. Do you have the legal right to apprehend them?"

"For why?"

"To bring to the hospital."

"For what purpose?"

"To pump their stomachs."

"Back so soon, Detective?"

"Neither of the targets were home."

"You should have taken me with you."

"Protocol, Padre. So what gives? I don't like running out of here like a bat out of hell on blind faith. No pun intended."

"No offense taken. For the sake of expediency, I thought the explanations could wait, but seeing that Gorberg and Kasper have already moved to the next level of this, I am afraid I must tell you some things you are not going to believe."

"Try me."

"You aren't going to like it."

"I already don't like it."

(Pause)

"Matt Gorberg and Dr. Louis Kasper are your murderers. It is possible that they were unaware of who they really were their whole lives and they blossomed simultaneously in what can only be thought of as a spiritual catastrophe. Or more likely, they noticed the similarities between their names and the biblical characters they are mirroring and invented foul purpose."

"What foul purpose? Who are they mirroring?"

"Matt Gorberg is the antithetic reflection of the Apostle Matthew, and Dr. Louis Kasper is the anti-image of the Disciple Luke."

"Weren't there twelve Apostles?"

"Doesn't matter. This is an adaptation, a bastardization, a debasement, pure blasphemy. They only need parts of gospel truths to form their anti-truths."

"Riddles, Padre. Get to the meat of it."

"An interesting metaphor, because Matthew Gorberg and Louis Kasper, Lou-K or 'Luke' for short, have both devoured the organs and body parts of the three victims."

"Eaten, you mean? Why?"

"A multitude of reasons. As I said this is ritualistic bastardization. They have combined things, conflating different texts."

"Explain."

"Well, first of all there is the nativity scene, taken down before the last murder. Jesus was born in a manger, a feeding trough, and it was believed that shepherds metaphorically feasted on the presence of the Messiah. Gorberg and Kasper represented this literally. *For I was hungry and you gave me something to eat, I was thirsty and you gave me something to drink, I was a stranger and you invited me in.*' That's Matthew 25:35. Then there is Luke 10:27, *'Love the Lord your God with all your heart and with all your soul and with all your strength and with all your mind.*' There, we have Cassidy's heart, Scarfo's penis and testicles representing the primal soul, his biceps to stand for strength, and Brusco's brain for the mind."

"But according to scripture, they feasted on Jesus. I don't see the three seditionists as anything near an equivalent."

"Agreed, but as I said, Gorberg and Kasper have conflated different texts. This latter, cannibalistic connection isn't with the Old or New Testament. It comes from literature, Dante's *Divine Comedy,* containing the first of three parts titled: *Inferno,* more precisely."

"Like the movie *Seven?*"

"Different section. Here the association is with the sight of the Devil himself, frozen to the chest in ice in the middle of hell. He has three heads, one European, one African, and one Asiatic, proving his influence over all races and simultaneously acting as a cruel parody of the Holy Trinity. Each mouth is busy chewing on a different man. One of them is Marcus Junius Brutus, your 'Mark Brusco.' Another is Gaius Cassius, 'Gabe Cassidy,' my groundskeeper, and the last being swallowed is Judas Iscariot, now Benedict Scarfo. Ironic that Caesar's reincarnated assassins were at the Capitol shouting 'Hang Mike Pence!' and this new incarnation of the world's greatest traitor was one of the first in through the broken glass, attacking the Constitution itself."

"So Jesus would have been a Democrat."

"Of course. And now the only piece missing is——"

"Excuse me, let me get this. Hey, Mar, I'm in the middle of something right now. What? Wait just a second, slow down. Where?"

"What is it, Detective?"

"My wife. My home. Someone is breaking in as we speak."

"Oh, my Lord, slow down. My arthritic knees, please, Detective."

"Officer Fetterman, send backup to 9 Saint Peter's Circle, three squad cars. Padre, you're coming with me, riding shotgun."

"So I live in a cul-de-sac. I've been there for years."

"How many?"

"Three and some change."

"Saint Peter denied Christ three times. You live at 9 Saint Peter's Circle. Dante showed us nine concentric circles of Hell, the ninth being the frozen lake holding Satan himself. The numbers are adding up, Detective."

"I'm Satan in this scenario?"

"I don't think so, but I believe it will matter more how Matthew Gorberg and Dr. Lou Kasper see it." (Pause) "No, don't turn off the headlights for the sake of stealth, Detective. They well know you're here."

Detective Bronson had his keys out and his firearm drawn, but the front door was open a crack. He shoved it with his shoulder and it rebounded with a hearty *clap* off the adjoining foyer wall, making him shove it away again with his elbow. The house was freezing cold; at the periphery, all the windows were open, some of the curtains pulsating with the night-wind. Mary was in the kitchen and like a pinned butterfly; she was affixed to the collapsed ironing board set at a rough forty-five-degree angle between the ceiling and the front of the oven. Her hands were over her head, bound at the wrists with zipties slung back over a wall hook. The bottom of the ironing board was secured behind the lip of a long, horizontal plank that was nailed multiple times through the top of the stove door. Fastened to the lumber at its two ends were steel bait buckets, and Mary's feet were thrust into them.

It was an upside-down cross.

It was also a birthing table. Matthew was standing next to Mary on Bronson's three-foot stepladder, pressing the twelve-inch butcher knife a bit harder against her throat, making the skin whiten.

"That's far enough," he said. "You shoot, I'll still have the strength to swipe this blade across. We don't really need her anymore, be smart."

"My God," Mary gasped. "It hurts so."

"You bastards," Bronson seethed. "She's not pregnant. What is this?"

Dr. Kasper looked back at him with calm disdain. He was sitting on one of Bronson's kitchen chairs positioned just below Mary's left foot. He was wearing a skull cap, scrubs, and rubber gloves.

"As Bruce Willis would suggest," he said, "she's as pregnant as a fucking cheerleader. And how would you have known anyway, hoss? Her wardrobe is all women's plus, all oversized, loose sweaters, big trenchcoats. You haven't touched her or wanted to for a decade, and we will bathe in the crimson blood of this birth, bearing witness to the entrance of our grand, new Messiah."

Bronson eyes were wide and dry. His wife was naked before him, helpless and bloated, and for the moment he could do nothing, couldn't believe this, couldn't seem to process anything. The harsh kitchen light treated her cruelly, age dots spattered across the top of her forehead just beneath the graying hairline, deep crow's feet at the edges of her eyes, parentheses at the corners of her lips, cracks in granite. She had jowls and turkey neck. There were patches of eczema on the points of her elbows and spider veins creeping around like ivy from the backs of her knees. She was fifty-seven years old.

She started to give birth, started weeping.

"But the masks are wrong," Bronson said, voice grit and sandpaper. "There was supposed to be the happy face of the father. You screwed it up. I'm not smiling, and my name isn't Joseph."

"But mine is," a voice said from behind him. "Joseph Virgil McGillicutty. *Father* Joseph Virgil McGillicutty, and I swear that I am smiling wide as the world."

Bronson didn't turn back, for the baby's head was crowning, his wife's vagina stretching, the tissue on the bottom splitting toward her anus like a midline episiotomy, and Kasper was playing catcher, and in a gush of blood and thick amniotic fluid the baby slid free. Mary slumped, arms strained overhead as Matthew hopped down and used the knife to cut the umbilical cord. The inverted cross dripped gore down the oven door-glass beneath it, dark arteries creeping like roads on the map of a new frontier built of sediment and grime, and Louis walked the baby to Bronson.

The detective shed his leather jacket to pool at his feet and cradled the child, hot from the womb, vapors in whispers. The infant was cooing, and he was all veins and translucent flesh. He opened slanted eyes, deep red ruby eyes, and Detective Bronson realized that it was the most beautiful thing he had ever seen in his life.

"But," he managed, "I'm not the real father."

"You're my foil," said McGillicutty, "and it is a time to celebrate those who have always paved a path for the success of the other . . . those who have consistently put their heads down and worked themselves to numbness . . . those who always knew that 'truth' was simply a point of view employed by liberals with agendas. This is your time for glory, Detective. The underdog has his day. The faceless gain features, and the common man once more has a purpose. You will make the world great again by loving this child desperately. Your soul will be filled and the rewards will be endless."

Detective Bronson saw his face reflected in the child's red eyes, mere prisms with sharp edges long dulled, and he thought about his life, about the modest pension he was stumbling toward, about his solid yet unremarkable conviction rate, the relationship with his father that had withered to small talk, the people he'd stood up to and those he'd run from, the hills he'd died on, the mountains he'd dreamed of yet never been able to move a damned inch. He thought of Mary and their first date at a U2 concert, the Philadelphia Spectrum, and the way she'd swayed into the aisle raising her hands above her head like some mystic belly dancer, and he saw the gravity of small disappointments accrue over time, weighing her down, dimming her sparkle. He saw his failed kitchen cabinet side-job and all the lumber scrap warped and age-spotted in the back corner of the garage. He saw the bathroom they both wanted remodeled but could never afford, the 2023 Harley CVO Road Glide he was never going to buy, the loving child they'd so been long denied.

There was a knock on the front door.

"Detective Bronson! Can you hear me? What is your status? Respond!"

He smiled gently. His status was that of a detective who would shield his son behind the blue line, protect him with the most powerful armed gang in the township, raise him to be a badge, a soldier, a general, king.

"There's nothing!" he called. "There's nothing here, false alarm, please go home!"

Revenants

Wade German

The ones you thought you could forget,
    Erased for they were fit to spurn—
But not before their curses set
    The time and place for their return:

The quiet, lonely ones who wait,
    For they have all of time to plot.
The ones with hearts that harbour hate
    Though long since gone the ways of rot.

The ones who hold the righteous grudge,
    The seed that flowers into wrath;
The ones impossible to nudge
    From off their predetermined path.

The ones who whisper evil mirth
    From six feet underneath your mind,
Evolving in subconscious earth,
    The worms within you, white and blind.

The ones who count your every breath.
    The ones who carry out the curse.
The ones who whistle at your death.
    The ones who drive your hellbound hearse.

C. L. Moore's "To What Dim Goal" and Its Progeny

Marcos Legaria

> But Anthony was very young,
>   And youth must sleep and dream,
> And what is murdered in the day
>   Will wake at night and scream.
>   —Frank Belknap Long, "Ballad of Saint Anthony"

> Your presence in Our brain as We meditated upon creation was strong enough to project your own thoughts upon the plasm from which We are molding worlds. When the figure of a girl flashed across Our mind, yours seized upon it and shaped it into your own interpretation of perfection. Unconsciously but surely, you created your own ideal, with all the features which seem to you capable of arousing love. Inevitably you felt that love when you gazed upon them.—C. L. Moore, "Greater Glories"

In the midst of America's Great Depression of the 1930s, Catherine Lucille Moore (1911–1987) reigned in the pages of *Weird Tales* magazine with her classic tales of science fiction and fantasy. Moore's iconic character Northwest Smith fought and resisted a gorgon-like entity with the aid of his trusty friend and partner in crime, Yarol the Venusian, in what is considered to be one of the best stories published in *Weird Tales* history, "Shambleau" (November 1933). An unknown Smith adventure did not fare as well: Moore could not sell it, so she relegated it to the trunk. She was inspired to salvage the story, extracting from it stories published in *Weird Tales* and its competitor, *Astounding Stories,* over the next two years. The stories Moore published in *Astounding* contained elements of supernatural fiction, as did most of her offerings to *Weird Tales,* even suggesting parallel themes. The history of the unknown

Northwest West story and these fugitive tales can now be put to the record from a reading of Moore's correspondence with R. H. Barlow and H. P. Lovecraft.

In the summer of 1934, Moore published four stories in *Weird Tales* and another for *Astounding Stories*, most of them written while Moore was a secretary at the Fletcher Trust Company, in her native town of Indianapolis, Indiana. R. H. Barlow, a young fan, wrote Moore praising her first published story, "Shambleau," but criticizing the interplanetary setting adhering to his mentor H. P. Lovecraft's philosophy of what a weird tale should and should not entail. Early in their correspondence, Barlow boldly advised Moore to revise her stories whenever these merited future republication in magazine or book form. Of course, Moore was not keen on the proposal, writing Barlow on 5 July 1934:

> Yes, I do much more revising that [*sic*] I care about. Have to, though it simply sickens me, and I hate everybody in sight while laboring away at the disgusting job. A story of mine which I've just sold to *Astounding* and which will appear in Oct. is really a third of one original N.W. Smith tale. I had that almost finished when I saw that it was two stories, and split it apart. Then the half I got to work on began to show amoeba-like tendencies toward division, and the third attempt resulted in "The Bright Illusion," which I've sold, to *Astounding*. The other two nuclei are still simmering gently in the back of my mind, and may emerge someday.

Moore's revelation that "The Bright Illusion" and the two other nuclei were birthed from this original Northwest Smith tale is intriguing. Moore's next letter to Barlow, of 21 August 1934, provides details about this mysterious Northwest Smith *uberlieferung*:

> Last night, reading *First and Last Men*,[1] I ran across the nucleus of a story which *Astounding* has been deliberating over for about three weeks now. Thank goodness it was already out of my hands when I read almost its counterpart in that book! It was the "race-mind" of the Eighteenth Men that so resembled the central idea

1. Olaf Stapledon's futuristic novel *Last and First Men* (1930).

of my own story—which by the way somehow got out of hand and rambled away into such theological fields that I may not be able to sell it. If not I want you to read it anyhow. I'll let you know later. Would like to have someone's opinion who understands what is good and what isn't. I never can tell, when I write a story, if it's a masterpiece or absolutely awful.

Moore referred to her latest Northwest Smith tale, completed in the past month. The tantalizing bits of information Moore provided Barlow, that it might not sell to *Astounding Stories* due to its daring concepts, make it apparent that editor Farnsworth Wright had a first perusal of the story and rejected it. For this submission to *Astounding,* Moore made sure to withhold the title character's name of "Northwest Smith."

Before returning to this unknown original Northwest Smith adventure, a closer inspection should be given to the first story it spawned, "The Bright Illusion." As to a date of composition, Moore told Barlow on 2 October 1934: "The great god IL in 'The Bright Illusion' was snatched out of the April on the calendar that stared me in the face when I looked for a good name." With this clue, the parent Northwest Smith tale can be dated to April 1934. Moore offers no evidence that "The Bright Illusion" was first offered to *Weird Tales.*

"The Bright Illusion" is basically supernatural fiction. Dixon, a Northwest Smith–like protagonist who is dying of thirst and hardship in the North African desert, is physically drawn to a huge glowing semi-ovate object he sees ahead of him. Once within it, he learns telepathically that he has been selected for a task by the godlike being who constitutes the glowing object. On another faraway planet, there is a rival god-being, whom the glowing light-being wishes to supplant. For this it needs Dixon, who can penetrate to the other god and discover its weakness. Since the alternative is death, Dixon agrees to do as the light-being wishes. He finds himself on a world with another dimensionality, incredible colors, and changing shapes, so alien that he would have gone mad had the light-being not encased him in a protective envelope that transforms the appearance of the outside world to his normality. The envelope also transforms his appearance to the natives, who are weird snake-like beings with a multiple sex system. Dixon meets what seems to be a beautiful young woman, a priestess who believes that he is a special emissary of the god IL. As they converse, love grows between them, although the young woman had not felt this emotion before. For this love, she is willing to help him destroy IL, who lives vampirically on his worshippers. Dixon and the princess, knowing that they cannot fulfill their love in their present forms, discuss death and the possibility of union after death. The princess fears that she will become a part of IL, whereas Dixon is torn between love, fear of death, and dismay as his protective envelope begins to weaken. He must act rapidly, using the information the princess has given him. He speaks the formula or invocation needed to admit the light-being, and the battle of gods take place. But the light-being does not win; it is IL who is victorious. IL, who is a passionless entity, is curious about the matter of love, which Dixon ultimately explains as a force that is part of the self. The lovers ask IL about death, and to their astonishment he replies that he does not know what happens after death, but he does not absorb those whose energies feed him. Something escapes. Thereupon the lovers ask for death, hoping to meet again, and IL obliges them.

The story had a powerful impact on readers at the time, a landmark story to this day with its theme of love that can surmount anything. Barlow sent Lovecraft the issue of *Astounding Stories* (October 1934) containing "The Bright Illusion." Lovecraft wrote Barlow on 16 March 1935 "Thanks very much for 'The Bright Illusion', which I had not seen before. There is splendid atmosphere in it, & the conception of a whole alien world with a hypnotic false front is really masterful. On the other hand, the mawkish, sticky, 1900-period sentimentality & love-through-the ages bull is wearily discouraging. Pulp & best-seller hooey" (*OFF* 218).

Lovecraft clearly identified the concepts and ideas Moore illuminated in "The Bright Illusion," pointing out the themes inherited from Moore's unknown original Northwest Smith adventure. After this evaluation, in a letter dated 20 March 1935, Moore gave Barlow an update on the story she submitted to *Astounding Stories* the previous summer:

> I've taken my courage in both hands and sent them another story on which I should have an answer the last of April. It's the same story, revamped, which they rejected last August with the suggestion that I rewrite the central theme and try again. I've been sweating out my life's blood over it ever since, devising at least a thousand different ends and beginnings to justify the middle and rejecting each one. When I finally got a fairly good idea all went well to the last few pages, and then the darn story kinda bucked under my hands and turned out so exactly like "The Bright Illusion" that I could have used the same paragraphs to close without even retyping them. Finally, it was tortured into a feeble ending which I sent off before I could lose my nerve.

"Greater Glories" was accepted—although in revised form—for the September 1935 issue of *Astounding Stories*. It is a detailed story, rich in its development, in which Moore continued to illustrate the odd sexual elements already found in her work for *Weird Tales,* and to this day it is an underrated tale from her classic period.

In "Greater Glories," the shipwrecked protagonist awakens on a desert island. Exploration brings him to a strange wall that draws him to it physically. Passing through it, he finds himself in an incredible building constructed to suit nonhuman requirements; it is also, as gradually becomes clear, a paraphrase of alien anatomy, with circulatory and nervous systems. After a time the protagonist becomes aware of a powerful entity around him; it is not unfriendly, but seemingly dispassionate. The godlike entity informs him that it is the creation and embodiment of an extinct race that constructed the building as a temple and abode for it. This being was intended to create a perfect world—a task that the being confesses is still beyond its powers. Nevertheless, it obviously has abilities that would be considered supernatural. Projecting its thought, the god-being creates before the protagonist an idyllic world, with mountains and meadows; in it is a human female, to whom the protagonist is attracted. As a creation or synthetic being, the woman is not really alive or conscious, but the protagonist succeeds in sharing with her some of his own life force, whereupon she awakens to a degree. But the result is tragic. She knows that she is not real, that she is a creation, and that she belongs to a world that does not exist. The god-being intervenes, informing the protagonist that his desire created her as his ideal, in response to one of the god's thoughts. She cannot become real or enter their real world. But the protagonist, if he wishes to chance the uncertainty, will be permitted to join the woman within the god-being. The protagonist is willing.

The daring concepts of love, sacrifice, and homage to a god that Moore first presented in "The Bright Illusion" continue in "Greater Glories."

As a result of Barlow instigating a correspondence between Lovecraft and Moore, she wrote Lovecraft on 11 December 1935 of her belief in the possibility of life after death—surviving in some form of energy, having explored the idea in her unpublished Northwest Smith story:

> I wrote a story once, which I don't believe you ever saw—starting out as my story "Greater Glories" started with a man lost in the interior of a giant body, being swept into its brain-chamber and finding himself in the presence of a god whose people have almost completed their race-goal. The people are of a peculiar structure which permits their amalgamation into one immense and rather horrid-looking mass, like a great vine budded with individuals who by now have sunk their individuality into the whole, being drawn together by a common race-love which through the milleniums [*sic*] of life has grown out of and taken the place of all other forms of attraction between individuals. The race has become a unit, but incomplete as the god is incomplete, because each lacks the essential attributes of the other. They are reaching their ultimate goal, which is the union of god and united people,

into a perfect whole which is to go on, perhaps, as no more than an atom at the bottom of some tremendous scale of unknown evolution—somewhere. I didn't sell the story, and finally cut it up into "Greater Glories" and "Bright Illusion" and another mass which I haven't tried to recast. (*CLM* 87–88)

Moore identified the mysterious Northwest Smith story in a letter to Barlow dated 12 December 1935:

It's so heartening to have something praised that I'm not sure of—and I'm never quite sure of anything I write. Did I ever show you that story I wrote called "To What Dim Goal?" I think I did. Anyhow, it wouldn't sell so I cut it up into gruesome little pieces and each piece grew into another story, "Greater Glories," "Bright Illusion" and another yet unfinished were portions of that dead tale, and I found ideas out of it cropping up in "Shape of Darkness." No doubt that murdered story will haunt everything I write for years to come, coloring with its dismembered theme all sorts of tales that have no connection with it whatever. Reminds me of that singularly apt sentence out of Goblin Tower—"Things that are murdered in the day Wake up at night and scream."[2] Not an exact quotation, but you see what I mean.

"To What Dim Goal" is the mystery Northwest Smith story that wouldn't sell, the ancestor of "The Bright Illusion," "Greater Glories," and others. From Moore's synopsis of "To What Dim Goal," the story's subject was ahead of its time, and the theme of "universal love through the ages" caused editor Farnsworth Wright of *Weird Tales* to reject it.

Moore revealed to Lovecraft "I've been writing a story about moon-dwellers lately, and at the start of it cast blankly around, as usual, for a name for the race" (9 December 1935, *CLM* 83). The story is the same one she just mentioned to Barlow as being unfinished. It ultimately took shape as the Northwest Smith adventure "Lost Paradise" (*Weird Tales*, July 1936). The story finds Smith back on Earth in New York City, where he and his friend Yarol do a favor for one

---

2. Frank Belknap Long's poem "The Ballad of St. Anthony."

of the Seles, a strange race from Asia who keep a fabulous secret. In turn they ask to be told the secret. The Selesian tells it, though he warns them that it may mean death to them. Through hypnosis he shows them the world his people lost, the moon, once full of happy people, but destroyed in a catastrophe. Smith learns the nature of this: the moon's atmosphere was kept through the power of an unholy trinity of gods, to whom at regular intervals young men and women would go to die of their own free will. The trinity fed on life's energy, but it had to be out of free will. Smith is in the mind of one of the men going to die, but afraid that he will die too. His mind rebels against the trinity, fights them, and so unwillingly causes the catastrophe in the past that left the moon without an atmosphere. When the Selenian learns that he himself carries the guilt of his world's destruction, he decides that they must die, as they can't live with the memory of the lost paradise. Yarol shoots the Selenian trying to kill the three of them, and Smith and his friend make their getaway in the crowd.

"Lost Paradise" resumed the theme of a vampiric sacrifice of sorts first seen in Moore's "The Bright Illusion" and "Greater Glories," but unlike the episodes in which the protagonists are willing participants in the name of love, Smith in "Lost Paradise" revolts against the trinity by the will of his mind.

A fourth story branched out from Moore's "To What Dim Goal," when she confessed to Barlow that she found ideas cropping out of it in "Shape of Darkness," an early draft of what later became "The Tree of Life" (*Weird Tales*, October 1936). By 31 May 1935, Moore wrote Barlow that she was tired of Northwest Smith, so she tried selling "Shape of Darkness" to *Weird Tales* without naming her space-faring rogue: "Well, have just received my first flat rejection from Wright. A harmless little tale about a sorcerer king of antediluvian times, his mysterious witch-queen and a time-traveler with a startling resemblance to a certain Mr. Smith whom I may have mentioned once or twice before, tho no names were named in the story." Three months later, Lovecraft read an advance copy of this early version of "Shape of Darkness" while vacationing in St. Augustine, Florida. He was not much impressed with the arboreal horror adventure, just as editor Farnsworth Wright of *Weird Tales* before him. Lovecraft wrote Barlow on 24 August:

> Well—anyhow, I've read the enclosed story, & think it distinctly good in places—though the rather conventional dialogue & general layout put it below "The Were-Woman." I presume the interepid [*sic*] & leather-clad time-traveller is none other than our old friend Northwest Smith. The other-worldly suggestions & descriptions of vague, non-human forms are excellently managed— despite a slight sense of disappointment in the climax. It beats most recent Mooreiana. [. . .] Most distinctly does it bear the impress of pulp influence. (*OFF* 286)

Moore revised "Shape of Darkness," and Wright published but only with two changes: first, the title had to be changed, and second, Moore must include Northwest Smith as the main character to make it more saleable.

"The Tree of Life" continued the themes of "sacrifice" first captured in "The Bright Illusion" and "Lost Paradise." Hiding from a patrol in the ruins of the Martian city of Illar, a helpless woman lures Smith down a well into another world. The woman is a priestess of Thag who has tempted Smith into a circular dimensional world from which there is no escape, and in which a primitive people live, in fear of Thag, an abomination from another time–space who reigns over this artificial dimension. The tree of life is Thag's gateway, through which he comes to feed. In the claws of the tree Smith fights for his life and mind against something that his mind refuses to see, as it is too dreadful to acknowledge. Firing his thermo gun into the essence of Thag, Smith is hurled back into the normal dimension by an explosion destroying Illar's ruins, but leaving him safe in the heart of the intra-dimensional explosion.

The story, though conventional in theme, manages to bring a feeling of primal fear to the reader, almost as if one really understands the potential evil of the soul, the fearful symmetry of Thag's being.

The final story extracted from "To What Dim Goal" deals with love transcending incredible obstacles on an unprecedented scale. This was a "Shape of Destiny," retitled by F. Orlin Tremaine as "A Tryst in Time" (*Astounding Stories,* December 1936). Moore had sent Barlow an early version of the story in the summer of 1935, during Lovecraft's second visit and stay at the Barlow household in DeLand, Florida. On 4 December 1935 Moore wrote Barlow:

> Spending a snow-stormy lunch hour reviewing the carbon of SHAPE OF DESTINY which I have down here at work with me, and a light as blinding as a Teril death has suddenly burst. Why not try it on ASTOUNDING? Probably not a very brilliant idea, because they're pretty sure to turn it down, but since they've taken a couple of HPL's and have already published two of mine scarcely less rambling and obscure than S of D, methinks it's worth a try.
>
> So, if you'll send back the original copy which you have I'll send it to ASTOUNDING. And if—and when—they refuse it I'll forward the carbon of the story to you with my blessing. I hate to tempt fate by putting both copies in the mail at the same time or would let you have the carbon now. Or—another incandescent light bursting—why not have you send it directly to A.S.? Do you think that would make it look so thoroughly rejected by everyone else that I had given up hope and was circulating it among my friends? Use your own judgment, which is better than mine in such matters. Either send it on from there or back home to mother for a fresh start from Indianapolis.

In "The Tree of Life," Eric Rosner, at age thirty, seems to have exhausted all the thrills of a violent life. He has encountered danger as a soldier of fortune, street brawl killer, cattle drover, leader of Tatar bandits, colonel of a Chinese regiment, and African explorer—in short, he was a veritable Conan of modern days. The older he grows the more he becomes aware that he is missing something, that he hasn't experienced something. Money, women, hardship—these mean nothing to him. Rosner becomes friendly with Walter Dow, a theoretical physicist who talks of the thrills of science. Dow specializes in inertia, and he mentions in passing that he has successfully harnessed the inertia of time. As Dow and Rosner recognize, standing still as time moves by would be the greatest adventure! Dow constructs a small backpack device that in effect will permit Rosner to move in time, though this is not Dow's theoretical concern, and Rosner departs on the first of a series of encounters. He visits ancient Rome, the paleolithic Basque country, Elizabethan England, medieval France, and other eras. Rosner then meets a beautiful woman with violet eyes. They are attracted to each other, but their encounters end with no possibility of fruition: she is dying, she is bound by religious vows, she is only a child, or there is some other impediment. On successive occasions, however, her recognition of Eric increases. In the Elizabethan period, when the woman is being burned alive as a witch, Eric is forced to shoot her in a mercy killing. When he activates his time mechanism, he finds himself in darkness. The woman comes to him with full recognition, and he learns what is behind it all. Because of some cosmic fault, he and the woman had been fated ever to miss each other; that fault has been expiated, and they can now step out together into life.

One wonders if Moore's manuscript of "To What Dim Goal" survives. Barlow was known to ask authors for manuscripts of their writings, and some ten years later Moore's husband, Henry Kuttner, wrote August Derleth the following curious bit of information on 1 May 1948: "Kat says thanks for sending along that script from Barlow; she'd forgotten its existence, and I doubt if she'll ever reread it. Somehow one's old stories always look so God-awful—at least mine do, and Kat says hers do too."

"The Bright Illusion," "Greater Glories," "Lost Paradise," "The Tree of Life," and "A Tryst in Time" are a testament to C. L. Moore's powers to draw five unique stories, from the ashes of a lost tale with the appropriate title "To What Dim Goal."

Works Cited

Kuttner, Henry. Letter to August Derleth (1 May 1948). Ms., August Derleth Papers, Wisconsin Historical Society.

Long, Frank Belknap. "Ballad of St. Anthony." In *The Goblin Tower*. Cassia, FL: Dragon-Fly Press, 1935.

Lovecraft, H. P. *Letters to C. L. Moore and Others*. Ed. David E. Schultz and S. T. Joshi New York, NY: Hippocampus Press, 2017. [Abbreviated in the text as *CLM*.]

———. *O Fortunate Floridian: H. P. Lovecraft's Letters to R, H. Barlow*. Ed. S. T. Joshi and David E. Schultz. Tampa, FL: University of Tampa Press, 2007. [Abbreviated in the text as *OFF*.]

Moore, C. L. *The Best of C. L. Moore*. Ed. Lester del Rey. Garden City NY: Nelson Doubleday, 1975.

———. "Greater Glories." *Astounding Stories* 16, No. 1 (September 1935): 111–29.

———. Letters to Robert H. Barlow. H. P. Lovecraft Papers, John Hay Library, Brown University.

———. *Northwest Smith*. New York: Ace, 1981.

Nightrider

Joe Pan

This happened over in Osceola County a few years back. I knew Davey's younger brother, Seth Harlison, maybe not too well but enough to share a beer with, and one night we found ourselves crowding the bar together at the Settle Down Saloon, popping vinegar eggs and swapping stories. He swears by everything I'm about to tell you, but all I can attest to is his swearing.

Seth's older brother Davey was a motorcycle collector—small-time, mind you—who ran a little bike repair shop over by the mall. Davey drove the fastest speedsters around, tricked out and built for racing. Cops couldn't catch him if they tried, and they tried. Folks hearing him grunt up behind them just slowed their cars and prayed for the best as he zipped by. But Davey, like his brother Seth, was a drinker. He had five shots of tequila in him at all times, and one rainy night he took a spill that nearly killed him, which also got his license suspended for a full year. After that Davey quit the hooch, poured all the cupboard whiskey down the sink, and put his mind to business. Two years later he'd grown that small repair shop into three small repair shops, opening a second over in Merritt Island and another up in Kissimmee, which helped him purchase a nice three-bedroom facing the Indian River and a few more hogs for his fancy bike collection.

So one night Seth gets a call from his brother. It's late, but Davey's voice is loud in the phone and it's clear he's in trouble. He asks Seth to meet him out by the Platte farms, deep in the country. So Seth gears up and rides out there. It's mostly dirt roads cut through farmland, with a stretch or two of asphalt splitting them. Seth tracks his brother down to one of these crossroads to find Davey drunk as a skunk and spinning out donuts. Davey was clearly out of his gourd, and Seth soon discovered why—Sara McCaw, Davey's girlfriend of ten years, was sending naked pictures of herself to another man. Seth slapped the stolen phone from Davey's hands before he could show him the evidence.

Davey said Sara was in the shower when her phone buzzed on the charger. It was a simple message, "Can't wait to see you again," but the previous messages up the chain were quite incriminating, and Davey took off out the front door before he let himself get violent. Hurting something awful, he cruised straight over to ABC Liquor before heading into the farm country, opening up his speedster to well over ninety along stretches entirely bereft of streetlights, just him and the deer eyes flaming out from the woods. At some point he couldn't see through the tears and pulled over by this cowpatch, he told Seth, and laid himself out in the middle of the road, staring at the stars and daring someone to run him over.

He was stretched out that way for about ten minutes before this stranger rolls up on him out of nowhere.

Davey said he didn't even hear the motorcycle pull round, just found himself suddenly encapsulated in a wall of light. He rolled over and struggled to stand as a shadow appeared on the other side. The figure was dressed in all black, boots to helmet, and didn't hesitate, marching straight toward Davey, who was not excited about being caught unarmed in the back country. But when the man spoke, it was like a voice from his childhood. Those were Davey's very words, according to Seth, "like a voice from childhood," but scratchy, as if it was being played through a busted speaker. The stranger never took off his helmet and without a word of introduction told Davey he could help him. Davey misunderstood, saying, "My bike's fine, I was just resting some." But the stranger made his intentions clear, saying he knew about the pictures. Not only the nudes, Davey said, but a lot of other things about Davey no person outside his family—and not even them—had a right to know. The stranger stood right there divulging Davey's deepest secrets to the night air as if he was reading them from a book.

At this point Seth thinks maybe it's not just alcohol that's swimming through his brother's system. It was also Seth's conclusion, which I shared upon hearing, that this nightrider was in fact the fella sleeping with Davey's girlfriend. Sara would have been mad about Davey stealing her phone, and for sure had access to some secrets Davey hoped wouldn't get out in the world. The more burning question for me was, why did this dude bother to hunt down Davey in the first place? And why the hell out there, with no one around?

At the bar Seth started getting a little gitchy, checking his watch, rubbing his eyes, probably wishing he hadn't started into this particular tale, so I lured the barkeep over with a twenty and ordered us another pitcher and that sufficed to keep his butt in the chair.

Long story short, this stranger, he promises to tell Davey the name of the guy sleeping with Sara, and Davey can go do with that information whatever he wants.

But maybe there's a more interesting option, the guys says. A more freeing option, something linked to darker wonders. Apparently he said the phrase "darker wonders," which right off the bat creeped me out. And right there, among the pastures and starry night, this stranger tells Davey he can help him live forever.

Now I know how this sounds. I sat in the bar and whistled myself, thinking the very same thing—we got ourselves a prime-A nutjob. Total weirdo. Watched too many vampire movies maybe. Had himself a god-complex. Whatever, something, so I ask Seth what else the guy said, and Seth quirked his face up and said, "Davey wouldn't say. I think he's just glad the prick didn't whip out a knife or pull down his pants."

According to Seth, his brother told the fella to go take a hike. And the guy did—just crawled back up onto his motorcycle and skedaddled.

I leaned back on my stool and wondered a bit. It wasn't a great story, but it was interesting, and I told him it was interesting, so's not to hurt his feelings. I thought it was going to end differently, knowing what I know about Davey.

But Seth wasn't finished, turns out—he was just reading my interest. I genuinely don't believe he wanted to continue, and I soon found out why.

Seth asked for the whiskey bottle in Davey's hand and Davey tossed it into the field instead. Davey wanted to keep doing donuts in the road, but Seth convinced him it was time to head home. He said Davey could crash at his place for a few weeks, get his head on straight, and maybe head over to the church gymnasium on Saturday and get back to earning those AA chips. After he said that, Davey got a real tired look about him and agreed that was probably the right thing to do, and the two brothers climbed onto their bikes and started back.

They were out in parts of Osceola that Seth wasn't familiar with— he didn't ride as much as Davey—so he couldn't say exactly where they were when the nightrider pulled up on them, only that it was at a red light.

There wasn't a car for miles, and they didn't intend to wait for green, but Seth heard the cycle grunting beside him and glanced over and there he was, the dude in black. Even his gloves were black. Seth sort of eyed his own reflection in the guy's shiny helmet, then turned back to his brother to crack a joke, but Davey was shaking. Seeing his older brother looking like that—it freaked him out. But then the light turned green and the devil cyclist took off, all gas no brakes, disappearing into the faltering darkness.

Weird, right? Well the exact same thing happened at the next light, and Seth swears by this too—there was no sound as the guy approached. The nightrider just coasted right up to the light and stopped, ten feet away. This time Davey gets angry and starts yelling at the guy, berating him, telling him he said no and to back the eff off or he'll get what's coming to him. The nightrider gives his engine a little rev, baiting Davey. Seth is one hundred percent convinced this guy is pissed 'cause his little blackmail scheme involving Sara and those illicit pics wasn't going as planned. Seth wants to brain the guy with a ratchet, or at least tell him where to shove a ratchet, but the light turns green and zip, off goes the stranger again.

Seth turned to his brother and dead-eye asks him what the hell was going on. What did he say no to, exactly? Davey was clearly holding back, and just shook his head and said, "We gotta get out of here. He wants me to race him. But if I race him and lose . . . well, I don't exactly believe what he said, but I don't want to find out." Seth pressed some more but Davey offered no more explanation beyond that.

There are plenty of places to hide a motorcycle out along those roads, so Seth kept his eyes peeled. The nightrider was obviously pulling into some corn rows or cloaking himself in some wooded area, waiting for them to pass so he could creep up on them later. But Davey wasn't interested in looking, pushing his speed up up up as Seth struggled to keep pace. Davey was on his best bike, his fastest, made for blowing out competition on the roads, and probably didn't even notice how fast he was going.

Now imagine this: the soft glow of the approaching town rises up in the distance. Seth doesn't even bother slowing down at the next light, which is of course red, and burns right through it. But Davey doesn't. Davey drops his feet to the ground and waits. Seth slows to a stop, turns around, and waves him forward. But Davey is waiting for the nightrider. And the nightrider appears.

Seth reminds me again these roads are full of sudden curves and long stretches of asphalt turning to dirt, which will put a motorcycle down quick. He watches his brother harangue the nightrider, shouting obscenities, talking smack, revving his engine and letting that back tire burn a bit. He's raring to go. But the nightrider pays him no mind. He's staring straight forward. But then he tilts his head slightly, as if to regard Seth across the way, and for no good reason Seth gets the impression that the stranger is chuckling behind his helmet, and this sends a chill right up his spine. Seth tells me it was as if death caught him in its eye.

When the light turns green, the two bikers gun it.

Seth waits for them to pass before peeling out a U-turn and chasing after them.

They're neck and neck the first hundred yards, but Davey's switching gears like a champ and ekes out a small lead. This is how Seth tells it, dreamily, with a wide smile, and it feels strange and makes me think maybe Seth isn't all there himself. He starts telling the story as if the race is between good and evil and gets this wondrous look in his eye, and now I'm beginning to regret that second pitcher myself.

Seth is going full speed, whipping past corn and pastures, trailing the two speedsters by a good amount, because their bikes are built for speed and his is built for puttering up and down a beach with a cocktail in hand. That's when he notices a sign fallen over in a ditch. It takes a second for the words to formulate in his mind properly: Road Work Ahead.

He blares his horn, but the two bikers don't hear it or don't care.

They pass another sign, this one with the words torn out by a shotgun.

There isn't a third sign, just the look of the newly paved beginnings of a bridge that doesn't yet exist. Seth watches as Davey rides over the cliffside and into the darkness.

You see, a month earlier the bridge that was supposed to be there had been struck by a semi, cracking two pylons, so they had to demolish it to rebuild it. The other side was only partially constructed, too, a mess of concrete and rebar.

Davey flew through the air and struck a long piece of rebar so hard his body split in half, torso going one way and legs the other.

But the nightrider—he continued on through the sky, traversing the arc clean to the other side, where he was lost to the night.

I finished my beer and poured another in quick succession. Seth said he took the off-ramp down and found Davey in a ditch, somehow still alive, a bloody torso attempting to claw its way back onto the highway. He died before the EMTs arrived. Seth said they shared some words before he left. They never did find his legs, apparently, probably carried off by coyotes. Which, to share such a thing, again made me question Seth's general mental well-being.

It's an odd tale, one I've had trouble wrapping my head around. It's odd for many reasons. I later discovered that it was Seth who was sleeping with his brother's girlfriend; whether or not Davey knew that detail, I have no idea. Nor do I know why Seth would even choose to tell me a story where he was the secret bad guy, but I guess that's guilt for you. Also, after his brother's death, Seth inherited three bike repair shops and a riverside home, and maybe that puts more spit on the spin. From what I hear he lost it all, though— to divorce and foreclosure and a drawn-out fight with nose powder. But you know how small-town talk is.

Do I believe Seth Harlison killed his brother out there in the country? I'm not sure I disbelieve it. Do I think Seth was telling me the truth about some demon biker looking for a showdown, betting a soul his bike was faster than Davey's? Sounds like standard horse manure to me.

But heck, I'll lived in this town for a long time, and I've seen some shit, so I just take it as a warning: people will steal your love; they will push you into misery and turn it into a game; and just when you think you've seen the worst of it, some animal will crawl off with your goddamned legs.

Those Kids Just Don't Listen

Katherine Kerestman

"It has to have a bottom—everything does!" Evan said derisively.

"No, it doesn't—it goes on and on forever! It must go all the way through the earth and out the other side!" insisted Frankie.

"I'll believe it when I see it," replied Evan, rubbing the toe of his sneaker in the dirt. He looked beyond the acres of ornamental shrubs that were squatting in somewhat straight rows in a field of his father's nursery, and beyond the plastic-covered greenhouses in the distance, toward a grove of trees. It was kind of dark in there, among those trees, and so far back from the road.

Frankie looked toward the trees, too. "I threw a rock in—and I never heard it hit bottom!"

"Maybe the bottom is just real far down."

"Come see. I'll show you, Evan. Then you'll believe me."

"It'll be dark soon. We'd better not. My dad says to stay out of the woods."

"I'll bet you're afraid." Frankie had a knack for reverse psychology.

"Am not!" answered Evan. "Geez, if it means so much to you, I'll go look at it. Let's get going, so we can be back by dark. We don't have flashlights or anything."

The boys started plodding through the shrubs, kicking up the soil with each step. It was already after seven o'clock when they started for the woods; they typically stayed outside later at this time of year, for school was out, the summer days were long, and the nights were warm.

The lower part of the sky was beginning to glow, an orange razor-edge giving notice that another summer day was drawing to a close. It had been over eighty-five degrees all day, and the boys' damp T-shirts smelled like it. Evan dragged his baseball bat, inscribing a wavering trail in the dry dirt behind them, while Frankie tossed his ball up into the air and caught it in his mitt in time with every other step he took. His attempts to dry his wet shirt by stretching its hem and waving it in the sun were ineffectual, and Evan remarked that the distant wood would probably be much cooler than the sizzling open field they were crossing.

"I wonder if we'll see a bear," replied Frankie. "Are we supposed to stand still or run if we see one?"

"There aren't any bears here," rebuked Evan. "But I do have my baseball bat—just in case."

"Just make sure you don't tease any bear cubs: the moms always get mad when you do."

"I'll be glad to get in the shade. We got some sunburns today."

Evan said that he felt cold. They were a quarter of a mile from the sylvan gloom, and the air temperature had dropped appreciably. "How come it's so cold, when we aren't even in the shade yet? Is a storm coming?"

"The sun is still out—no clouds. Not even wind. Maybe we just hit a cold spot."

"Weird."

"Evan, do you suppose anyone lives in the woods? In a cabin or a cave or something?"

"Not unless there's a bank robber on the loose."

"I haven't heard of any hold-ups lately."

They continued their march, arriving at the edge of the grove. "Here's the trail," said Frankie, pointing to the right, "where I was exploring when I found the hole. There's all kinds of cool stuff in the woods, if you know where to look."

"It's so dark," Evan said, nervously, when they had walked a few yards into the bower. "It's like day and night. Where'd the sun go? It's not even eight o'clock—we should have over an hour of daylight left."

"It's just the shade," answered Frankie. "Look, all these plants are dead! They're black and slimy."

"Oh, I hope it's not a plant disease. My dad's always afraid something'll kill the plants in the nursery. Bugs and things."

"Watch out: the ground's slick—the plants are oozing. Don't fall in that gross stuff."

"I still say it's too early to be so dark. Maybe we should go home."

"Are you afraid again?"

"Don't call me afraid."

"Then let's hurry up to see the hole and then run home after."

"We better hurry, though . . ."

"Evan—Evan—hey, did you hear that?"

Crouching, "What did you hear?"

Whispering, "Listen."

The friends held their breaths and listened to the voice of the dark forest. The wood was shadowy—few slivers of light were able to survive the death-defying journey through the fortress of branches—and the silence was overwhelming when they actually stopped talking and paid attention to it. There were neither voices, nor the rumbles and whooshes of cars on the road, nor bird calls, not even the sound of blowing wind—but there *was* a snapping, such as the sound a twig might make when trod upon by a foot, and there *was* a cracking noise, the sound a branch makes as it is being broken from a shrub. Frankie crouched down beside his friend. Instinct counseled silence.

When, after five minutes, they had heard no other sounds, Frankie's courage returned. "We're almost there—how about we hurry and get a look at it and then go home?" Not wishing to appear a coward, Evan agreed, especially after Frankie said they'd be out of the wood within ten minutes. Frankie leading the way, the boys trod as soundlessly as they knew how, not wishing to attract the notice of unseen mother bears in the gloom. They followed a rough trail that was overgrown with roots designed to catch boys' toes and trip them up and branches that stretched out to grasp their clothes. Pricker bushes snagged their shoelaces. A log required climbing over, and a great, slick mud puddle demanded stomping through.

"Here it is!" said Frankie, pointing to a hole in the ground, about six feet in diameter, that was illumined by a shaft of jaundiced light. The jagged rim of the hole was formed of soil-covered rock to which a hideous form of mildew clung somewhat desperately, as if in perpetual peril of losing its hold on this world. The inside of the hole was black—a void—for, although the solitary ray shone directly upon the prodigious hole, it fell short in its pains to illuminate its interior. The boys could not make out the plunging walls of a cavern; neither could they discern the slippery sides of an abandoned mine; nor could they see a pool of water at the bottom of an old well. There was only the abyss. "Wow," exhaled Evan.

"Throw something in—it won't hit bottom," said Frankie. Putting down his bat, Evan picked up a rock the size of his fist and tossed it in. Both boys leaned over to listen for a clunk or a splash. They waited. And they leaned in a little more, so as to hear better.

"You're right. There is no bottom," said Evan. The sound of the crunching of leaves in the deepening gloom causing him nearly to lose control of his bladder, he picked up his bat and held it as if it were a cudgel.

"It's just a deer—or—or a raccoon," Frankie said, trying to keep the uneasiness he was feeling from his voice. "It's okay. But it *is* getting dark now, and we'd better head home. We can come back another time. Next time we'll bring flashlights." He stepped onto the path and looked back over his shoulder. "Come on, Evan."

The loud crackling of splintering branches caused the friends to spin around in the direction of the sound. As Evan turned, he swung his bat—and the momentum of his swing carried him over the edge of the hole into the abyss. Evan's screams mingled with Frankie's frantic "Evan—no—Evan!" An owl hooted in three-part harmony, its music unnoticed by the boys.

When Frankie stopped screaming, he heard a sound: a high-pitched noise like a whistle, a soprano voice, or a woodwind instrument. He dropped the ball and glove, which he had been carrying all this time, and ran out of the wood as fast as his legs would carry him—fast enough to have earned a triple home run if he were playing baseball. He fell face forward several times, when gnarly roots snaked around his ankles; and he struggled to free himself from the clutches of the reaching branches that tore his T-shirt. Running—both to get help for Evan and to outrun the advance of a mounting guilt—he raced from the forest to Evan's family's nursery, hoping that his friend's father was still at work.

It was twilight, and Evan's dad, Mike, and the crew were locking up for the night when he arrived at the office door. Seeing the mud and the blood, and the tattered shirt his son's friend was wearing, Mike rushed to the doorway. "Frankie, where's Evan? What happened?"

Mindful of the desperate plight of his pal, Frankie struggled valiantly against the relentless pounding of his heart and the terror that threatened to overwhelm him, and he managed to answer, "He fell in a hole!"

Instructing his office manager to call 911, Mike and his crew jumped into a pickup truck. Frankie sat in the front seat next to Mike, showing him where to go, as Evan's father steered the truck over the lumpy furrows, filling the air with brown dust kicked up by the tires. At the edge of the wood, the men jumped from the truck and plunged into the murky grove, lighting the perditious footpath with their lanterns. Soon flashing red and blue lights surrounded the truck and uniformed men with dogs joined the searchers.

All night, and into the next day, they searched the woods. Evan's mother joined the search, sobbing as if the wringing of all the moisture from her body could wring the pain from her heart as well, and she called, "Evan, baby, it's all right. Mommy and Daddy are here to get bring you home."

They called off the search after a week. Not a trace of the boy had been found. Not even the hole—it, too, was never located. Frankie went into a deep depression, answering questions "yes" and "no" as appropriate, and mechanically repeating his story, insisting that Evan fell into a hole. People feared for his sanity. Mike and Evan's mom, Dorothy, were seen on television, pleading for someone to help them find their boy. Evan's sixth-grade class picture was on milk cartons and the evening news, as well as in the weekly county paper and the big city daily paper. A dull sadness settled upon the town. People stopped talking about it. Evan's mom and dad grew numb. No one could guess what Frankie was feeling. The old guys at the feed mill would repeat, from time to time, "It does no good to tell the young'uns to stay away from the woods. Those kids just don't listen."

Evan, meanwhile, was being sucked into the void, unsure if he were swallowing it or if it were swallowing him—for he and the void were one and the same. The blackness was not a color, but a thing in itself, and it was swirling, and he was swirling in it. Grotesque forms—and his baseball bat—were swirling, too, in the infernal void, visible in the utter blackness only because of their phosphorescence. He glimpsed a rhinoceros that had a snake where its horn should be, and a hideous head with two hands but no body. Other strange and loathsome forms danced in the gloom, twirling around like phantasmagoric ballerinas. Evan could not tell if there was a bottom to the grisly gulf, and he tried to look up and see out of the hole. He could not believe his eyes: around the top of the hole, where moon and stars ought to have been observable had there not been so many treetops blocking the sky, he saw a circle of prodigious teeth, sharp and pointed.

He had fallen into a mouth—an enormous mouth—and he was in its gullet: the never-ending esophagus of a nameless being that was all mouth and throat, no more and no less, and which waits in the forest for adventurous children to stumble into it.

Slayer of Suns

Scott J. Couturier

The plague came down on cosmic winds
weeping from stars of static dread.
It slew sunlight & struck seers blind,
animating anew those stricken dead.

The Gods: sacral shrines profaned,
blighted boils marring each idol's face.
Waters reeking & black-stained by
some insidious infection, the rot of space:

Symptoms progress from fever chills
to scabrous growths of splotchy hue.
Fungal follicles will chest cavities fill
as lungs a phlegm frothy & septic brew.

Ultimate wail of agony, incarnate pain:
the body falls still until it stirs to breed.
Bone-petals unfurl to expose its brain,
swollen with suppurant of diseased seed.

Slayer of suns, & of all crawling flesh;
contagion of nebulae, pox of the void.
Virulent virus of ether, eager to thresh
bodies infected, raised up, & deployed—

At last final blush of life is out-blown,
darkling world of thrall-corpses in bloom.
They root & loose astral bacilli full-grown—
cranial germs ascend, spread spores of doom
to further spheres ripe for pestilence sown.

Irish Cultural Hauntings in Dorothy Macardle's *Earth-Bound*

James Goho

Dorothy Macardle (1889–1958) was an Irish novelist, playwright, historian, feminist, and political activist. Her political and gender concerns infiltrate her fiction and nonfiction works. She is most remembered for *The Irish Republic* (1937), her history of the Irish revolutionary era. Her 1941 haunted house novel *Uneasy Freehold* was developed into the film *The Uninvited* (1944), which became the title of all subsequent editions. Siobhra Aiken, Irina Ruppo Malone, and others note that Macardle's work was virtually forgotten after her death which is true for other Irish female writers of the nineteenth and early twentieth centuries. In 2010, Abigail L. Palko observed that none of Macardle's novels were in print (10). Much has changed. Ireland's Tramp Press reissued *The Uninvited* in 2016, followed by Macardle's *The Unforeseen* (1946) in 2018 and *Dark Enchantment* (1953) in 2020. Macardle is also beginning to gain critical attention for her fiction, for example, by Leeann Lane and Jennifer Molidor. Writing in 2022, Elena Ogliari argues Macardle deserves to be recognized and considered alongside her more famous Irish male writers (8–9).

Macardle was active in many Irish republican causes throughout her life. During the Irish Civil War (1922–23), she supported the anti-treaty side and its leader and future Taoiseach, Éamon De Valera. Arrested at the Sinn Féin Dublin offices on 9 November 1922, she was imprisoned until 9 May 1923 at Mountjoy, Kilmainham, and North Dublin Union prisons. During her time in jail, Macardle wrote many stories; nine appeared in *Earth-Bound: Nine Stories of Ireland*, published by Harrigan Press in Worcester, Massachusetts, in 1924. Swan River Press in Ireland republished the original stories, along with others, in *Earth-Bound and Other Supernatural Stories* (2016) for the first time since the original publication. In these short stories, Macardle meshed her political and feminist concerns with a supernatural sensibility to express the trauma of Ireland's centuries-long history of colonization, rebellions, and suppressions.

The first story, "Earth-Bound" (written in Mountjoy prison), sets the stage for the collection with talk of the "companionship of the dead" that one feels in Ireland and the long "seven hundred years" of colonization by the British (*EB* 1–2). These two themes of hauntings and oppression sound throughout the collection. In "Earth-Bound," Michael O'Clery tells of his and Donal O'Donel's escape from Mountjoy Prison and their flight to and hiding in the Wicklow mountains and glens south of Dublin on the east coast of Ireland. The story combines Irish rebellion history with a supernatural appearance from the past. Set during the Irish War of Independence (1919–21), it spans hundreds of years of Irish history. Alerted to the nearing Black and Tans,[1] the two men flee into the moorlands and mountains during a bitterly cold winter. A spectral figure joins them. When the Black and Tans seem to be closing in on the two, that shadow leads the British away. A magical helper often appears in folktales at a critical time to help the hero as Vladimir Propp found in his study of the units of plot actions in quest folk narratives. It is also a common motif in ghost stories. Algernon Blackwood also chronicled many instances where an unidentifiable ghostly figure appears in a time of crisis for explorers during their real experiences (134–53).

That ghostly figure in "Earth-Bound" is *Aodh Ruadh Ó Domhnaill*, also known as Red Hugh O'Donnell, who led an Irish rebellion during the reign of Queen Elizabeth I. *Aodh Ruadh* was jailed in Dublin Castle for four years. In 1591, he escaped along with Henry and Art O'Neill and hid for two nights in the Wicklow

---

1. The Black and Tans were a British paramilitary force formed to suppress the Irish independence movement. They were present throughout most of Ireland and committed many atrocities against the Irish.

Mountains. Art O'Neill died from the cold, but Aodh Ruadh was rescued, almost frozen to death, by Fiach MacHugh O'Byrne. In Macardle's story, the escapees find safety with the O'Byrnes of Glendasan, as if history repeats itself. In Ireland, the past never dies. Here the spectral image is beneficent while the terror arises from the night-gaunt Black and Tans, a force that was a "potent symbol of British brutality during the revolutionary period" (Lane 147–48). The Black and Tans appear in other stories, for example, "The Brother" and "By God's Mercy." The Black and Tans represent a sustained cultural traumatic haunting in Macardle's collection—a terror that persists beyond the grave to haunt the Irish. But the return of dead Irish represents a recovery of the Irish past. Macardle's stories are a form of witnessing of Irish history—a witnessing of trauma but also a reclamation of cultural heritage through the spectral remembering of a genuine Irish past.

Macardle wrote the *Earth-Bound* stories while imprisoned with other women. Their cells seemed to be a living death. In her Jail Journal, Macardle wrote she felt that she had been "thrust living into a tomb [. . .] it was the chill underground smell [. . .] a sepulchre might smell like that" (quoted by Lane 51). Routinely mistreated by prison guards and suffering in cold, overcrowded, and unhealthy prison conditions, the women prisoners formed a communal bond, part of which was storytelling. That prison experience informed Macardle's stories, as she composed them in an oral environment. Molidor argues that Macardle invented and wrote them by listening to the stories of her cellmates (49–50). Aiken points out that current inmates invited new arrivals to tell their accounts (94). Macardle also read drafts of the stories to her fellow inmates. It is not clear how much she modified them through the oral process, but it seems that the reaction of the listeners affected the final state of the stories (Lane 79; Molidor 46). Developed in an oral surrounding, the stories' structure, flow, and narrative style reflect that origin. The book's structure recreates the oral nature of its composition with a narrator and an audience for each story. Recently exiled republicans from Ireland tell their stories in the Philadelphia home of Úna and Frank O'Carroll, exiles too. This use of a framing device for narrative embedding is an old tradition in ghost and gothic[2] tales. Each testimony carries a sense of the authority of an eyewitness.

The vivid presentation of these narratives is akin to first-hand testimonies, some of which come from the long departed. They seem like testimonies that attest to trauma. The straightforward, non-lyrical style of the stories reflects telling them to an audience in a dangerous environment. It is also part of their dark power and sensitivity. The stories in *Earth-Bound* are austere, reflecting prison conditions where lyrical phrases seem out of place. There is little poetic expression here, only the facts enlivened by supernatural elements that are often grim like prison walls. And the stories represent the communal solidarity of the prisoners because they unite with their ancestors through their storytelling. It is a form of exorcism of past possession by connecting with the Irish dead silenced by the British. Macardle's supernaturally charged stories express the trauma of colonization, internal Irish conflicts, and the effects of religion and power structures on women through testimonies from the living and the dead.

A specter of one recently bayoneted to death by the Black and Tans appears in "The Brother." The character, Larry O'Donovan, tells this story. His brother had planned the capture of Kilbride prison to free the Irish prisoners set to be hanged and then to blow up the prison. This tale was probably popular with those incarcerated. The Black and Tans waylaid Pierce O'Donovan and killed him before the design could be executed. But Larry and others kept at it. Larry's role was to hide out in an isolated barn and to provide details of the plan to a group who were going to assist in the assault. The ruined barn seems to represent Larry's descent into the underground because it had a "cold, damp, earthy smell," as if "you were in your grave" (*EB* 26). Larry's brother, Pierce, inhabits that grave. He aris-

---

2. In this essay, I follow George E. Haggerty's advice to use the proper noun "Gothic" for the classic literary tradition and the common noun "gothic" for the literary motif in its ongoing expressions.

es, "forgetting that he was dead," to alert Larry that the group of men are imposters (*EB* 30). This story and others depict specters from dead generations returning to assist the living in their struggle for freedom. In a sense, the story is a form of propaganda literature, but the narratives go beyond that simple characterization because they are part of a political gothic of trauma.

In *Inventing Ireland* (2001), Declan Kiberd writes that the Irish were the first modern people to decolonize. He argues that Ireland's centuries-long history of British colonization is unique with its long history of uprisings, brutal suppressions, and its unfinished work at decolonization, that is, the continuing inclusion of Northern Ireland in the United Kingdom. These conditions have fashioned a distinctive literature of the supernatural—a literature Edwina Keown argues centers on politics, resistance, and struggle. This has been central to Irish gothic writing, including what Keown calls the innovative "political Gothic" of such Anglo-Irish writers as Sheridan Le Fanu, Bram Stoker, Elizabeth Bowen, and others (1). Aoife Dempsey identifies a gothic propensity in Irish and Anglo-Irish writing, which she contends arises from the colonial experience in Ireland. She says the political gothic is a forum for the expression of trauma, resistance, and the supernatural. When expressed, it shows shades of darkness and terror, which were the experiences of those imprisoned with Macardle.

Resistance in a prison environment is challenging. One has virtually no power. "The Prisoner" focuses on the nature of imprisonment. In the story, Macardle describes the effects of a hunger strike: the delirium, the despair, the fatigue, and the feeling of being haunted. It captures the anguish of Liam Daly in a "punishment cell [. . .] dark always, and dead quiet" in Kilmainham prison during the War of Independence (*EB* 31). He is a hunger striker in a cell where the nature of time changes. It becomes a "whirlpool—time going round and round" (*EB* 32). Macardle described the mental torment of a hunger strike where you cannot "keep hold of your mind," where you think you are in a coffin, where the darkness is "thick and powerful," where you "race between madness and death" (*EB* 32–33). Liam Daly survives his ordeal partly through the appearance of a spectral young lad in his cell. The women prisoners seemed to share their cells with ghosts. These Irish ghosts embody trauma, symbolizing how the dead haunt the present. That sobbing, beaten, starved, and fettered young boy comes from the past. He tells Liam his story of imprisonment during the rebellion led by Lord Edward Fitzgerald (1763–1798), who died in Newgate Prison. The boy needs to speak, to tell his story, because he fears his mother will believe he betrayed his country as the guards taunted him will happen. And more than tell, "it must be written down," he cries (*EB* 34). Liam Daly survives his thirty-eight-day hunger strike and tells of the dead boy's heroism in 1798. The boy's history would probably be printed in the *Tri-Colour*, the republican newsletter that Úna and Frank edit.

Jodey Castricano suggests that "to be haunted is to be called upon" (16). Liam Daly was called upon by a ghost arising from a past rebellion. Here, instead of bringing help, the returning dead asks for assistance. Macardle ended this story with the inscription *"Mountjoy/Kilmainham"* (*EB* 38), which suggests that she worked on it during the time of her week-long hunger strike. Malone suggests the story may be a "survival-account of the author's own imprisonment" (100). Clearly, it was informed by her personal experience and that of others, who endured 219 hunger strikes (Aiken 91). Macardle dedicated this story to "E.C." (*EB* 31). This was Eithne Coyle, who was another hunger striker (Aiken 96). The brutal treatment of the ghost probably reflects the cruel treatment of the female prisoners at Kilmainham while being forcibly removed to the military prison at the North Dublin Union to crack the hunger strike of Mary MacSwiney and Kate O'Callaghan. Macardle documented this in "The Kilmainham Tortures: Experiences of a Prisoner" (1923). The emotional impact of "The Prisoner" arises from these personal experiences. The lack of food and starvation appears throughout the collection, for example, in "Samhain," "The Portrait of Róisin Dhu," and "De Profundis." Hunger seems a deadly ghost in these stores, akin to a Banshee that signals death. It is a trauma that reflects the actuality in Ireland over the centuries of British rule.

The ghost in "The Prisoner" needs to speak and be listened to because that specter is trying to overwrite unrememberings, misperceptions, and the falsification of the past. Threatened, erased, or fragmented Irish histories are recovered by the appearance of ghosts. The story reclaims republican memory of 1798 since it becomes "written down" (*EB* 35). Macardle emphasized the importance of reconstructing memory and overcoming "pathologies of memory" by writing the truth about the Irish past (Brogan 6).

In *Specters of Marx* (1993), Jacques Derrida argued that even though it may seem impossible, it is essential "to speak *to the* specter" and "to *let* a specter *speak*," which is what Daly lets the young boy do (11). The specter is at the heart of Macardle's narratives because her stories call forward or provide a space for the return of something that haunts. And that arises from the impossibility of ghosts, yet their presence is everywhere. These encounters are not a mystery to be solved, but as Colin Davis suggests they are calls for an openness to all those voices calling from the past—voices that speak about personal or social trauma. "The Prisoner" returns an ancestral voice, that is, the voice of one who was silenced when alive. His terror yet resonated in the place he suffered in and haunted. As the colonial trauma is passed from generation to generation, it clings to places. Jarlath Killeen suggests the past does not stay past in Ireland (10). He argues the cataclysmic nature of Irish history is part of the reason that gothic literature is so prevalent in its history (17).

Stories like "The Brother" and "The Prisoner" appear as male narratives. However, it is likely "The Prisoner" expresses the direct hunger strike experience of women. And the young boy's mother figures prominently in the story as a symbol of the expected role of women in Ireland's struggle for independence. Stories such as "By God's Mercy" and "A Story without an End" are female narratives that speak directly about women's experiences. These stories stress sacrifices made by women to Irish causes. Within Macardle's prison stories, you can hear the anguish of generations of Irish women, anguish for their fallen fathers and brothers, anguish for their mothers and sisters, and their diminished roles.

"By God's Mercy" addresses the complexity and anguish of females in Irish colonial times. This story reflects on the grief-stricken experience of women who supported the vision of a free Ireland, no matter the cost. Nannie Maher, a young woman, tells the story of her brother, Brian. Akin to the young boy's in "The Prisoner," her story must be remembered; "it should be written down" (*EB* 59). And akin to "The Brother" another recently dead returns to warn the living. Her tale recounts the escape of "the Chief" (that is, de Valera) from the "murder gang" (the Black and Tans, or the gothic night-gaunts) pursuing him (*EB* 60). Nannie's brother had been charged to bring the Chief safely late that night to the family's barn. Brian's mother is alarmed her son may dishonor Ireland if he fails in his task. She says, "better to see you slaughtered before my eyes" than that anything happens to the Chief (*EB* 61). The mother and Nannie worry out the night until terrified by gunshots. Nannie thinks she hears Brain outside at the window. In a voice that is "whispering, gasping and full of dread," he tells her to go to the nearby bridge (*EB* 65). On the way, she spots the Black and Tans and tricks them into ignoring her. She warns the Chief. But the Black and Tans burn down her and her mother's home and tell them to find Brian under the bridge, where his body is half submerged in the stream, riddled with bullets. His mother keeps saying, "he did his work well" (*EB* 61). But Macardle surfaces the mother's hidden trauma and anguish as she "died [. . .] before the month was out" (*EB* 61). The story expresses the role of sacrifice and honor that Irish women were expected to uphold in spite of their anguish. Yet it also expresses the trauma of that sacrifice. Macardle's gothic story shows the horror of Brian's mutilated body and the sounds of his dying voice at the window in contrast to the ideal of motherly glory in sacrificing her son. That trauma destroys Brian's mother. This story was dedicated to "A. M.," who was the teenage Annie Moore, one of Macardle's cellmates, whose brother, Brian, and fiancé were shot and killed (Molidor 50). "By God's Mercy" reads like the anguished personal testimony of a heroic young woman who witnessed terror and loss but experienced a supernatural mediation.

Traditionally, the Irish gothic engaged with political and ideological debates. Macardle continued that tradition by using gothic language and imagery to explore and expose the issues of her time such as war trauma, the need for witnessing, and gender issues. Irish women have a long history of writing in the gothic mode. Although largely forgotten today, Anne Burke (fl. 1780–1805) was an early author of Gothic novels, such as *Ela; or, The Delusions of the Heart* (1787) and *Emilia de St. Aubigne* (1788). Other early practitioners of the Irish Gothic include Regina Maria Roche (1764–1845), whose *Children of the Abbey* (1796) went through several editions. Roche also wrote *Clermont* (1798), which was noted in Jane Austen's *Northanger Abbey* (1817) as a notorious Gothic novel. Albert Power argues that Roche was Ireland's Ann Radcliffe, but Roche died almost forgotten (35). Another Anglo-Irish author, Charlotte Riddell (1832–1906), is remembered more than her predecessors and many of her successors. She published an early collection of supernatural tales in 1882, *Weird Tales*. Emma Liggins argues that Riddell covertly used gothic elements to highlight the struggles of women for recognition and their subjugated status in society. Many other female Irish writers who were widely known for their novels and other works have been overlooked for a long time. Some examples are Rosa Mulholland (1841–1921), L. T. Meade (1844–1914), Katherine Tynan (1859–1931), and Clotilde Graves (1863–1932), each of whom has had her gothic short stories recently republished in book form.

Gerardine Meaney argues that gothic fiction allowed Irish female writers covertly to question dominant patriarchal values. Macardle's "The Return of Niav" and "The Portrait of Róisín Dhu" examine relationships between women and demonstrate what Meaney calls "an acute awareness of the dangers of women's symbolic function in [Irish] nationalist ideology" (978). Both stories are narrated by Maeve. Maeve is the anglicized Irish name *Medb*. *Medb* is the name of the legendary warrior queen of Connacht, who is a heroine in *Táin Bó Cúailnge*, the most important tale in the Ulster cycle of stories about the Ulaid, a prehistoric people of Ireland (Carson xi). Macardle chose a name from the deep past of Ireland before English rule. "The Return of Niav" reclaims elements from Irish folklore, where the world of the *sidhe* intersects with the real world. This story was probably influenced by the Irish Cultural Revival movement when writers and artists looked back to traditional Irish literature and folklore for inspiration. Leaders of this revival included W. B. Yeats, Lady Gregory, George Russell (Æ), Lord Dunsany, Alice Milligan, Maud Gonne, and others. Gonne was imprisoned with Macardle, who dedicated "The Return of Niav" to Gonne's daughter Iseult Stuart, who was also imprisoned.

Macardle embedded this story in the reality of the Irish colonial experience and the Irish storytelling tradition. The Irish faerie world may be presented as fantastic in some children's books, but the *sidhe* do not bring wonder; they bring misery as did the colonization of Ireland. In the story, Maeve tells how she nearly lost her daughter, Neoineen, to the *sidhe*. Maeve and Neoineen play act as Oisín and Osgar in a forest, the "Druid's wood" (*EB* 41). Neoineen wanders into the forest to gather wood for their fire to lure the fairies. It is St. John's Eve, Midsummer's Eve. On that day in Celtic days, great bonfires were set to protect the crops from disease, misfortune, and the *sidhe*. The *sidhe* were most powerful at that time (Palko, "Queer Seductions" 291). Neoineen returns with flowers gifted by a girl named Niav from a place called *Tir-na-n-Óg*, which refers to the Otherworld, the country of the young in Irish mythology, or the home of the *sidhe*. Niav and Neoineen become playmates throughout the pleasant summer. But Neoineen begins to refuse to eat, perhaps as a tool to express her emerging captivity by the *sidhe*, akin to the prison hunger strikers. At the call of Hugo Blake, an artist, Maeve leaves her child for a time. When she returns Neoineen is changed, her "little face was terrible [. . .] shrunken and blue [. . .]

like a cunning old woman—dead" (*EB* 47). Neoineen was taken by the *sidhe* and replaced with a changeling. This is the experience of a child in the world of *sidhe*, which is a metaphor for a colonized country. To rescue her daughter, Maeve returns to the practices of Irish folklore before the British conquest. She performs an old pagan fertility rite to restore (rebirth) her daughter. She gathers wood of nine kinds and sets a fire on a druid's stone. She circles the stone nine times and flings fiery ashes over the changeling who is banished into the darkness. Neoineen is reborn completing the return of Irish history and the eviction of the *sidhe*, or the British.

Hugo Blake also appears in "The Portrait of Róisín Dhu." The title of this story probably refers to James Clarence Mangan's poem "Dark Rosaleen" (1847). Rosaleen is an anglicized Róisín, an Irish female name. Based on the Irish Róisín Dubh (a traditional song with Róisín as a metaphor for Ireland), Mangan camouflaged his patriotic poem as a love poem. It was a form of subversion when any nationalistic expression was banned in Ireland by Britain. Molidor suggests that Macardle may have modeled Hugo Blake on the Yeats family. W. B. Yeats lived in a tower, his brother, Jack, was a painter, and his father, John, was a portraitist (Molidor 51).

Blake asks Maeve to help him find a model for his great work. In the west of Ireland, she discovers Nuala, a young girl with beauty and radiance. But Nuala is sacrificed in the painting. Modeling in his dark tower, she falls pale and emaciated as the painting progresses. This is another image of starvation that pervades the collection, Irish memory, and the actuality of hunger strikes in prisons. Blake ignores her suffering and says, "I shall have done with her soon" (*EB* 73). She dies under a willow near the loch. This is the theme of Edgar Allan Poe's "The Oval Portrait" (1850), wherein while the husband's painting grows more lifelike, his wife, the model, ails and eventually dies. It is also similar to the theme of Clotilde Graves's "The Vanished Hand"[3] (1914), where an artist chooses artistic glory

---

3. "A vanish'd hand" is a phrase from Alfred, Lord Tennyson's poem "Break, Break, Break" (1842).

rather than life for a woman who was his muse. As with other stories in the collection, the dead do not stay dead. Nuala returns to haunt Blake. He writes to Maeve that Nuala "has never left him" (*EB* 75). She returns to lure him into the loch. His empty boat is found drifting there.

Macardle expressed the layers of meaning in the story early: "No woman in the world [. . .] had been Hugo's Roisin Dhu; no mortal face had troubled him when he painted that immortal dream [. . .] that wild, sweet holiness of Ireland for which men die" (*EB* 68). Blake had a model from whom he drained the life displayed in his painting. Macardle pointed out the danger of personifying a woman as Ireland for whom men will die while real women lose their rights. It is a story about a male artist misusing a woman and the danger in Ireland of idealizing specific roles for women. She questioned using women in venerated imagery, especially to stir patriotic passion, but then mistreating them in real life.

Another woman, Nesta McAllister, narrates "A Story without an End," the final tale in the collection. Akin to all the stories, she tells it in the studio of Úna and Frank O'Carroll. The evening was devoted to "recalling old prophecies, forebodings, and tales of bad omens and dreams" (*EB* 77). This might have happened often in prison among the prisoners. They were incarcerated in terrible conditions and subject to continual physical and psychological degradation (Lane 50–51, 77–78; Molidor 49; Ogliari 6). Storytelling reinforced prisoner solidarity in a cold, dark environment of fear, mistreatment, and dread. With "A Story without End," Macardle may have replicated an experience of storytelling in the prison environment, where women shared their hopes, fears, and dreams. Nesta tells of her dreams. She and her husband Roger were hiding in the mountains of County Cork during the War of Independence when martial law had been declared in parts of Ireland and drumhead courts were used routinely by the British. These were akin to battlefield courts with the right of summary conviction and execution if so deemed. In the first dream, four men carried a dead man into her cottage, a man with a long, thin face, a bandaged head, and deep eyes she had seen earlier staring at her from the fireplace. In the second dream, she sees her husband shot by a firing squad ordered by that dead man. The strange part of the second dream for her was that the soldiers wore green uniforms, the color of the Irish Republic Army. The first dream actualizes, as four men carry that man from the dream into the cottage, but he is alive. But Nesta discounts her second dream, as "a combination of hopes and fears" (*EB* 80). Listening to this story behind prison walls, republican women likely felt a sense of betrayal of their efforts during the Independence fight and despair at the Irish killing Irish. Throughout the Civil War, at least 681 women were imprisoned (Aiken 91) because republican women seemed to pose a threat to the Irish Free State created by the treaty (Lane 33). In this story, the reality of the Civil War is horror. Macardle suggests that the traumas of the Irish past may have bred a malevolent present. She documented the pain of the Civil War in *Tragedies of Kerry* (1924).

"De Profundis" is a less effective story, although the Irish dead keep resurrecting and the hauntings from starvation continue. It is more sentimental in tone and features a religious intervention. But it illustrates the devastating effects of famine and influenza on ordinary people in Ireland. Father Martin narrates. He and his eight siblings lived in severe poverty, especially after their father died. The story is set in Southwest Ireland when "the 'black Death' [. . .] swooped on Killerane" (*EB* 53). That black influenza infected his mother, who begged him to get a mass said for her. He sets off to find the parish priest who attended to many homes affected by the plague. Late at night, he stumbles upon an old crumbling chapel surrounded by a graveyard and a dark grove of trees. The eerie nature of the place panics him, but an unusual light shines from the chapel windows and the panic leaves him. Inside, he finds a priest preparing for a mass, and he serves as an altar boy. By doing so, he releases that specter from his sentence of saying mass eternally because of a minor sin. At the time of writing this story, Macardle had disavowed Catholicism and already identified as an atheist (Lane 70). Macardle also never married. These two things set her off from the norm in Ireland. A norm codified in the 1937 Irish constitution dictated that a woman's role was in the home and as a mother. This story, akin to the others, was composed in an oral environment. And it may have also evolved from tales told by prisoners. In prison, most of Macardle's cellmates were Catholics. The religious overtones and the sense of divine intervention may have been salutary for them. However, there is some irony in a divine punishment sentencing a priest to say mass forever. Yet the story's images of extreme poverty and hunger may haunt readers.

The trauma of Irish hunger also pervades "Samhain." Written in Mountjoy prison, the story may be set during *An Drochshaol*, the Great Hunger or Irish Famine of 1845–51. According to Declan Kiberd, nearly one million people died from starvation and associated diseases during the Famine, while one and a half million emigrated (21). This story was selected for inclusion in *The Best British Short Stories of 1925 with an Irish Supplement*. Alexander FitzGerald, a Celtic etymologist, narrates the tale. The story mixes Christian belief with pagan lore and a sense of the dark unknown. Fitzgerald describes a time in Kerry with his friend Father Patrick O'Rahilly during a season of "heart-breaking tragedy" for people who dwell in the "Valley of Shadow" when the "spectre of famine" comes (*EB* 14). It was another time of starvation when children fell "wizened and sickly" (*EB* 14), and the "grey, murderous sea" (*EB*16) gave up no fish, only drowned fishermen, eight in all. These two images appeared in Katharine Tynan's "The Sea's Dead" (1895), collected in *The Death Spancel and Others* (2020). The story rouses the looming, dreadful presence of the sea as if a god that gives and takes life, akin to the "famine that is always stalking ghost-like in Achill" (12).

With the "famine days" came "the scourge of the poor, typhoid" (*EB* 15, 17). Father O'Rahilly became ill. His crisis came on Samhain, the Irish Halloween. According to Irish mythology, the Otherworld opened on Samhain. It was an ancient Celtic festival of the dead. Fitzgerald said a pagan prayer for the priest. More effective was a host of the dead, who filled the priest's oratory and prayed for him. As the horde departed, one softly called to Fitzgerald to join the departing dead. He hears "long, wailing gusts of wind that seem to blow out of infinity" (*EB* 19). And an appalling eternity fell on him. It was a void, an abyss. Fitzgerald feels the infinite, uncaring darkness and the "mysteries of the dead (*EB* 11). The story illustrates the complex environment within which Macardle composed her stories. As stated earlier, most of her cellmates were religious; she was not. Macardle based this short story on a tale told to her in Mountjoy by Tessie O'Connell, to whom Macardle dedicated it. The story shows how she adapted stories told to her in prison to the needs of her audience, yet retained her view of the world. This perspective is found throughout the collection. Her judicious use of gothic elements illustrates the uncanny intersection of different worlds, times, and beliefs. And this story illustrates the Irish tradition of "friendship with the dead" (*EB* 11) while showing the long dark shadows of hunger and suffering that stalked the country.

The Irish gothic is riven with political issues. Macardle's nine stories are embedded within that Irish gothic tradition. Her collection arises from the complex traumatic background of Irish colonial history, the harsh condition of prison life, and the anguish of the Irish Civil War. Agnieszka Soltysik Monnet argues that supernatural horror fiction is not only about fear, monsters, or the unknown. Horror authors engage with contemporary philosophical, political, and social matters. Mario Praz maintained that an important function of the original Gothic was to reveal the despicable practices of political, social, and religious power structures. That tradition continues. The gothic often embodies the terrors of the real world, generally in disguised and deformed modes. And that is one reason why it continues to be an essential literature today. It explores questions about human or inhuman conditions in unusual and often terrifying modes to speak about critical aspects of life. *Earth-Bound* provides a spectral voice for those silenced by a dominant military, economic, and ideological power.

The nine Irish stories of *Earth-Bound* exhibit the scars of individual and communal trauma through supernatural and realistic images. Macardle merged politics with the gothic to illustrate the anguish of Irish colonial history. She wrote of terror and death, hunger and starvation, detention in prisons, resistance in dire circumstances (hunger strikes), and the struggle of women in Ireland. *Earth-Bound*'s ghosts embody Irish cultural traumas that Macardle reanimates to restore memories erased or distorted through centuries of colonization and suppression of Irish culture. The characters in her stories are not frightened because the ghosts are their ancestors. Listening to these ghosts and retelling their stories work to recover erased history, to revive a lost past. It was as if Macardle listened to the voices of her cellmates and the voices embedded in the walls of her prison cell. She wrote tales based on those voices of the dead and the living as a form of collective recovery of Irish history and identity. If trauma is a form of possession by past wounds, then Macardle's Irish ghosts perform their own exorcism.

Works Cited

Aiken, Siobhra. "'The Women's Weapon': Reclaiming the Hunger Strike in the Fiction of Dorothy Macardle, Máiréad Ní Ghráda, and Máirín Cregan." *Journal of War & Culture Studies* 14, No. 1 (2021): 89–109.

Blackwood, Algernon. *The Lure of the Unknown: Essays on the Strange.* Ed. Mike Ashley. Dublin: Swan River Press, 2022.

Brogan, Kathleen. *Cultural Haunting: Ghosts and Ethnicity in Recent American Literature.* Charlottesville: University Press of Virginia, 1998.

Carson, Ciaran. "Introduction." In *The Táin.* Tr. Ciaran Carson. London: Penguin Classics, 2008.

Castricano, Jodey. *Cryptomimesis: The Gothic and Jacques Derrida's Ghost Writing.* Montreal: McGill–Queen's University Press, 2001.

Davis, Colin. "Hauntology, Spectres and Phantoms." *French Studies* 59, No. 3 (2005): 373–79.

Dempsey, Aoife. "Hyphenated States: Joseph Sheridan Le Fanu and Settler Gothic Fiction." In Jarlath Killeen and Valeria Cavalli, ed. *Inspiring a Mysterious Terror: Years of Joseph Sheridan Le Fanu.* Oxford: Peter Lang, 2016. 117–37.

Derrida, Jacques. *Specters of Marx: The State of the Debt, the Work of Mourning, and the New International.* Tr. Peggy Kamuf. New York: Routledge, 1994.

Graves, Clotilde. *A Vanished Hand and Others.* Dublin: Swan River Press, 2021.

Haggerty, George E. *Queer Gothic.* Urbana: University of Illinois Press, 2006.

Keown, Edwina. "Exorcising Trauma: Uncanny Modernity and the Anglo-Irish War in Elizabeth Bowen's 'The Last September' (1929)." *Études irlandaises* 36 (2011): 131–46.

Kiberd, Declan. *Inventing Ireland: The Literature of the Modern Nation.* London: Jonathan Cape, 1995.

Killeen, Jarlath. *The Emergence of Irish Gothic Fiction: History, Origins, Theories.* Edinburgh: Edinburgh University Press, 2014

Lane, Leeann. *Dorothy Macardle.* Dublin: University College Dublin Press, 2019.

Liggins, Emma. "Introduction." In *Weird Tales* by Charlotte Riddell. Brighton, UK: Victorian Secrets, 2009.

Macardle, Dorothy. *Earth-Bound and Other Supernatural Tales.* 1924. Dublin: Swan River Press, 2020. [Abbreviated in the text as *EB.*]

———. "Kilmainham Tortures: Experiences of a Released Prisoner." Kilmainham Jail Archives. (Military Prison, North Dublin Union, 1 May 1923.)

———. *Tragedies of Kerry, 1922–23.* Dublin: Emton Press, 1924.

Malone, Irina Ruppo. "Spectral History: The Ghost Stories of Dorothy Macardle." *Partial Answers* 9, No. 1 (2011): 95–109.

Meaney, Gerardine. "Identity and Opposition: Women's Writing, 1890–1960." In *The Field Day Anthology of Irish Writing: Irish*

Women's Writings and Traditions. Vol. 5. Cork: Cork University Press, 2002. 976–81.

Molidor, Jennifer. "Dying for Ireland: Violence, Silence, and Sacrifice in Dorothy Macardle's *Earth-Bound: Nine Stories of Ireland* (1924)." *New Hibernia Review/Iris Éireannach Nua* 12, No. 4 (Geimhreadh/Winter 2008): 43–61.

Monnet, Agnieszka Soltysik. *The Poetics and Politics of the American Gothic: Gender and Slavery in Nineteenth-Century American Literature.* London: Routledge, 2017.

Ogliari, Elena. "Breaking the Silence: The Irish Civil War in the Short Stories by Dorothy Macardle." *University of Bucharest Review* 11, No. 2 (2022): 5–19.

Palko, Abigail L. "From The Uninvited to the Visitor: The Post-Independence Dilemma Faced by Irish Women Writers." *Frontiers* 31, No. 2 (2010): 1–34.

———. "Queer Seductions of the Maternal in Dorothy Macardle's *Earth Bound.*" *Irish University Review* 46, No. 2 (2016): 287–308.

Power, Albert. "Regina Maria Roche." *Green Book* 11 (Bealtaine 2008): 35–41.

Praz, Mario. "Introductory Essay." In Peter Fairclough, ed. *Three Gothic Novels.* London: Penguin, 1986. 7–34.

Propp, Vladimir. *The Morphology of the Folktale.* 1929. 2nd ed. Ed. Louis A. Wagner. Tr. Laurence Scott. Austin: University of Texas Press, 1968.

Scott, Bonnie Kime. "Macardle, Dorothy [Margaret Callan]." In Robert Hogan, ed. *Dictionary of Irish Literature.* Rev. and expanded ed., M–Z. Westport, CT: Greenwood Press, 1996. 736–37.

Tynan, Katherine. *The Death Spancel and Others.* Dublin: Swan River Press, 2020.

Ysella

Oliver Smith

As dusty winds shook the autumn flowers,
sad King Branok wept in his gilded hall.
Lords and legions and land held no delight.
They were as ghosts, as rust, as desert sand;
as dust, as rotting bones, as barren shore.

All Branok sought was to speak once more
with his dead betrothed, the sweet Ysella.
Ysella haunted, haunted, haunted him.
When wild November wind rocked his tower,
in his sleep he screamed, "I hear, I hear her!"

His faithful chancellor begged, "marry another."
Branok would be drowned in his own salt tears
rather than abandon his Ysella.
At midnight, into his silken chamber,
crept gaunt Jarn Maur, the necromancer.

A censor glowed; King Branok shivered.
Smoke rose, lush with morbid incense;
with musk, with myrrh, with Prester John's poppy,
and resinous dust of Egyptian mummy.
Smoke-eyed angels wept dark tears and darker

spectres, full of menace, muttered of spheres
of hellish cold, of endless, peaceful worlds,
of the most holy, heavenly flowers;
Jarn Maur conjured limbos, shadows-past
and strange apparitions of futures-after,

and in none of these dwelled dead Ysella.
Jarn Maur said "somehow, somewhere, Ysella lives."
King Branok beat with bloody fist upon her tomb;
cracked the mighty marble slab that sealed her,
and cursed at the foot of her empty bier.

His poor heart wept. In what horrid satire
of death had she been laid to rest within
her lonely crypt? and where now had she fled?
The King and his sorcerer enquired,
"Where now dwells the lovely, lost Ysella?"

The King left behind his grieving chancellor,
sat idle before an abandoned throne.
King Branok put aside his golden crown,
and with his wise and wily necromancer,
rode from his gates to reclaim Ysella.

King Branok rode on, led by gaunt Jarn Maur.
They followed omens over wide oceans;
crossed russet deserts in search of some sign;
at a portent, they descended canyons
unreached by noonday sun, so deep they were.

One day, in a far city of sunset spires,
they unwound some path of mystery and fear,
that coiled like serpents and slyly twisted,
until, on a mortuary ground, a ruin stood.
Born beneath the eye of unhallowed stars,

its tumbled walls were of black basalt carved.
Within, the corpse of an old witch mouldered
by the cold ashes of a long dead fire.
Jarn Maur set a spark to her empty sockets
and from her dead lips required an answer.

The witch stoked the ash and her cauldron, stirred.
"Your lost love will be found in lands of ice.
In the utter north lives Queen Ysella."
Her bones creaked and the undead thing grinned.
"She dwells in the Azure Fortress of Midwinter."

Northward; they walked a road through bone-bare
trees, crouched like a tribe of crooked goblins.
By a poisoned stream, horrid spectres writhed
serpentine in starlight, in the blue clouds
 of a storm corpse-lights burned, and the thunder

tore wild purple skies as they crossed sundered
lands. Yet, the King was beguiled, her portrait
shimmered for Branok in each frozen pool.
Jarn Maur begged "Oh King, go no further,
do not seek the cruel Fortress of Midwinter."

But sad King Branok swore that in the air
he heard Ysella's lonely whisper.
Her ghostly image danced; grace in the mist,
bewitching him among the long barrows
and grey grave-mounds of ancient warriors.

It seemed a flickering shadow ran. "Ysella?"
Called the King. Between the tombs, it slipped
away and reappeared by a stony tarn;
the king followed. It vanished by a stone gate
that arched like a dead man's frozen fingers.

Though Jarn Maur muttered many spells before
the door, it remained sealed. But Branok's touch
unclasped the bolts. Through the pass, beyond, stood
a palace carved from a living glacier;
the great Azure Fortress of Midwinter.

The King called, "I have come for my Ysella."
From ice and rime, a knight; half rotted corpse,
half frost, in rust and rags, rose up to lead
beyond the walls of bluest ice. Inside,
the palace echoed with Ysella's laughter.

Through putrid guards and decayed retainers,
King Branok rushed to find lost Ysella.
Though a necromancer, Jarn Maur recoiled
from the evil things his eyes unveiled
in the Azure Fortress of Midwinter.

Skeletons embraced waking cadavers
before a queen, exquisite, icicle crowned,
enthroned upon a thousand hollow skulls.
Green was the glitter of her rime-frost eyes.
Before her fires burned, yet the air was bitter.

At last, King Branok had found Ysella.
He told her how he loved and wondered why,
when resurrected, she had not returned
to his side, but fled to this horrid place
and made him journey so far to find her?

Ysella answered, "I lay alone before
the threshold, awaiting the new world
hereafter. I saw through that door ajar;
I was to be the meat of the old gods
feasting, in a burning world of fire.

As I crossed," she said, "I called the haunter
of nameless night under the white bone moon
and through the starless void, an ice-winged
angel fell and, in return, for my mortal soul
in sacrifice, she granted my desire."

At this, gaunt Jarn Maur, the necromancer,
begged King Branok to forsake her.
"Come quick, my king," he said, "let us leave
this place, your beloved is an enchantress,
an accursed, hell-bonded witch; a monster."

King Branok would not Jarn Maur hear.
The anger surged molten in Branok's veins,
before the entreaties of gaunt Jarn Maur.
Branok called Maur, "a grave-worm" and "spider"
and buried his sword in the necromancer.

King Branok's blade pierced Maur like a skewer.
Out, the wounded wizard's red blood gushed,
puddling on the flags like a crimson mirror,
reflecting mad King Branok on his knees
before a thing of incarnate horror,

a demon conjured from the void. Where fair
Ysella's face should be, mocked an alien
form, that never on the sweet Earth was born,
half-merged like some infernal twin, rooted now
in Ysella's mortal flesh. Sheer terror

unbound Branok from Ysella's glamour.
He raised his blade dripping with ichor;
the poison blood of the necromancer.
The demon Ysella unfurled great wings
and fell on Branok with vicious claws.

Torn and bloody, to his breast bone laid bare,
in her embrace; he struggled not for his life,
but against damnation. Branok pierced through
the heart, this devil fallen from the stars.
Yet as she bled, he lay down beside her.

At last, Branok held his lost Ysella.
With only the midnight dark to clothe her,
the King drew close her strange, cold flesh,
placed a pure kiss upon her icy lips,
and swore his soul away to keep her.

When Mount Pulag Awoke

Dmitri Akers

Part I. A Spanish March

"Padre, where's the town of gold again? I need something to entice this rabble of a host." Alcalde Don Manuel's voice betrayed avarice. "We've been marching for nearly a week from Manila for some tobacco expedition. Even if they're a mix of lowlanders, *mestizos,* and Spaniards, gold will rouse them. Not tobacco."

Padre Pedro Vivar scratched a gaunt face. The mix of altitude and humidity got to him; it was the kind only found in the tall climes deep within the heart of Luzon.

The two of them rode abreast on black stallions as they led a procession of foot soldiers through a thinning rainforest. The luscious trees eventually gave way to stony crags. In the cloudy heights above, the shadow of an immense mountain loomed amidst the dull halo of silver light.

"You soldiers need the directions of prayer, not the directions towards the next *El Dorado,* Alcalde," replied El Padre as he held up a wooden rosary.

"*Mierda!* You've been to Tonglo before. How much gold do they have?"

"Greed's a sin."

Don Manuel thought silently for a moment with a fiery lust in his dark eyes. To El Padre he seemed yet another holdover from the days of the *Conquistadores;* he even resembled Pizarro in his benighted nature.

Finally Don Manuel spoke with a certain wiliness: "What did the town look like then? At least tell me that."

"It's sparse, if I must say so," Padre Pedro said. "It lies in a gully formed by a steep mountain, where there is not even a stretch of level space."

"It sounds like a place with no sure footing." Don Manuel seemed to mull over something tactical before shooting the question. "Why'd you leave, Padre?"

"It's too hard to bring supplies there. Besides, the people are unwilling to hear the Good Word." The friar spoke with some newfound bitterness. "They follow their old gods, which are no real gods, since they're all evil spirits."

"*Infieles.*"

A moment of quiet came between them. A gale whistled within a hollow formed in the mountain's side. In the distance there was a bird's call. It was more like a ticking of a clock: *tik-tik-tik.*

El Padre clutched his rosary in his hands; he threaded the little wooden spheres like precious pearls through his finger and thumb, as he mumbled the Lord's Prayer.

"I cannot complain that you left," Don Manuel yelled out at El Padre. "Since you now lead me to Tonglo. How far is it?"

Padre Vivar finished his meditation and put the wooden rosary back around his neck.

"It's not far," the friar said. "We'd better take rest at the other side of the mountain. It may get dark by the time we get to the foot of the mountain."

"Very well." Don Manuel groaned. "But we go to Tonglo first thing in the morning!"

El Padre had no response for that. He swiveled his mount and stared back at the soldiers' march. In a line of four men abreast, they snaked along a meandering cliffside path.

A bird still called out in the faraway canopies as a cold wind blowed.

El Padre peered into the distant greenery that slightly shivered under an overcast sky. There was something there. Even his horse whinnied anxiously. What Padre Pedro Vivar saw was an otherworldly shadow, as if only paper-thin, that slowly enlarged into the shape of a woman; it walked out from the dark into the pale light.

This shadow was an oddly proportioned woman with not only thin, skeletal arms but also a distended belly as if in the latter stages of pregnancy; it had an animalistic face that resembled a carabao, the Philippine water buffalo. The eyes were wholly black.

El Padre was motionless. He could not breathe. Was he under the spell of some ancient sorcery? The thing beckoned him with slender talons that looked as if chicken feet.

When El Padre blinked, it disappeared. His heart coursed loudly inside his head. Still, he stood frozen. The sound of Don Manuel's voice woke him from a reverie.

"What is it, Padre?"

El Padre shook his head until he fully came to. He bent his head to listen. The wind howled. But the bird was silent. His horse neighed and snorted loudly.

"I think we draw nearer," El Padre said, trying to control his horse. "Make sure we keep account of every man. No one ought to be lost."

"I'll make the commands, Padre."

El Alcalde bellowed some orders across the path over the valley, something about keeping account of every man and never being left on one's own.

As the army behind El Padre re-formed, the friar's horse walked forward. The animal, afeared as it was, began to leap and gallop from an ambling pace. El Padre held the reins anxiously. It sped down the path. Rocks were hazardously strewn. The friar cried out and attempted to reign it in.

The horse sprinted up the path and careened around the corner. Suddenly it cried at something on the other side; it reared and threw El Padre off his saddle. Winded, El Padre must have also hit his head, which throbbed with pain. Painstakingly, he opened his eyes and saw the horse had fled. There was also a little boy on the path holding a spear—much too large for a child.

Padre Pedro tried to remember some phrases he learned from the people of Tonglo, as blood poured out of his head.

"Friend," El Padre said in Ibaloi.

What happened next astounded the friar, since the sable-haired boy held the spear aloft quite awkwardly, then sang: *"Gayumko gimangaman; gayumko gimangaman. Gaya, gaya, maykaga."*

These were not words that the priest had learned fully, but he knew some of it meant "spear" and another word close to what he understood as "sacrifice." *Dios mio,* El Padre thought, am I to be speared to death?

The tip of the spear pointed toward the friar. It was then lowered. The boy let out a gutful of laughter as his bronzed cheeks became rosy with glee. After the boy had enjoyed the joke to the fullest, he threw the spear aside. He helped pull the friar off the ground.

"Good boy," the friar said. "Are you an Igorot? Ibaloi?"

The boy's ears pricked up at the mention of it.

"I was going to the base of the mountain," El Padre explained. "For a mission."

The child scratched his head full of thick, black hair. He seemed a bit distracted by the strange wooden rosary around the friar's neck.

"This? You want to hear of Christ?" El Padre asked and held the crucifix on the rosary's end. "You want to hear the Word?"

Suddenly the sound of Don Manuel came from around the corner. His horse arrived at a hurried trot. El Alcalde's eyes smoldered at the sight of the boy and the nearby spear. Don Manuel unsheathed his cavalry sword before preparing to run down the boy.

"Don't!" El Padre yelped. "He aided me when my horse reared."

"Where's he from?" Don Manuel asked suspiciously. "Is he a scout?"

The sword reflected a ghostly aura from the gray sunbeams that filtered through the clouds.

"Would he help me if he was a scout?"

Don Manuel thought it over, harrumphed, then sheathed his sword. He spoke with some frustration, as if the prize of bloodshed had been robbed from him: "Ask him where he's from."

"You weren't at Tonglo?" the friar asked the boy. "We're going to Tonglo."

"Tonglo," the boy repeated.

"Does that mean he's from Tonglo?" Don Manuel queried.

"I'm not sure where he's from. I never saw him when I was in the area," El Padre said and caressed his sore head. "Many mountain people trade with one another. He could be from somewhere else. Perhaps he is lost. The locals say an *anito* can lead them astray."

El Alcalde snorted: "Well, whatever he is, we can keep him as a hostage."

"Look after this boy. He meant me no harm."

"We'll look after him, Padre, with a watchful eye." Don Manuel scanned about as he spoke. "Say, where's your horse?"

The friar's bleeding was reduced to a congealed trickle, but the aching still encompassed his skull.

"It ran off."

"Seems like you're on foot for the time being, Padre. Maybe you can extract some information from the boy as we trek down the mountain path."

Part II. A Dead Volcano Stirs

Once at the base of the mountain, the army began to set up camp as dusk gave way to pitch-dark night. Fires were started. Rations and cups of hard drink were divvied out.

El Padre sat in his tent with the boy, who was still bound. The boy spoke little, but that may have owed to the rope around his neck. El Padre knew so few Ibaloi words that no information could be extracted. In the distance, the faintest sound of a bird going *tik-tik-tik* was heard.

Outside, as they danced along the fires, the lowlanders drank a strange coconut liquor; its pungent aroma and stronger taste put off any European. The sound of greaves upon twigs and dirt came from outside the tent. Then El Padre saw someone put a gloved hand through the tent's opening; it held a dark glass bottle.

"Sherry is rare nowadays," Don Manuel's voice called from outside. "Due to so many wars with England. Jerez has fewer wine merchants now. But I got my hands on one."

"Come in, Alcalde," the friar said. "Pour yourself a glass."

Don Manuel crouched and entered the tent, sneered at the boy, then placed a wooden mug down to fill with golden sherry. He held it up as an offering to the friar.

"No," El Padre said. "Give it to the boy. He needs his energy."

El Alcalde gritted his teeth but obliged the boy, who sniffed at the cup and sipped, until he skolled it.

"The boy enjoys it," Don Manuel scoffed. "Little drunkards, these *infieles* are."

"It's not uncommon for the locals to drink," the friar said. "Though I've never seen a child drink. But it's customary in Europe for a boy his age to enjoy a bit of wine, is it not?"

Don Manuel shrugged, drank from the bottle, then wiped what sweet liquid clung to his lips. El Padre heard the soldiers outside grow rowdier, although not entirely from the drink; there was a disturbance of some kind.

"The soldiers have found something," Padre Pedro suggested.

"Imbéciles!" El Alcalde blurted, swigging as he left.

El Padre rose and peeked through the flap of the tent. In the glow of one of the firepits he saw the army of men stand back from a shady shape. Don Manuel approached with readied sword.

"Don't be scared of your own shadows," Don Manuel spat.

The friar leapt out of the tent. He ran toward the circle of soldiers.

"Don't, Alcalde!"

"Get back, Padre. I'm in charge here."

The shadow metamorphosed in front of the crowd. They gasped as a chorus. The thing had a new form—a beautiful woman, naked in the humid night. She possessed striking dark features: long hair down past her buttocks, a lithe figure, almond eyes of the deepest brown, and bronzed skin.

Don Manuel threw down his sword and approached her. The woman embraced him, kissing his neck and unbuttoning his blouse, as he smelled her long hair. El Padre looked at the soldiers around the fire; they stood motionless, stunned as he was before.

"Wake up! It's a witch like Circe."

Suddenly Don Manuel was no longer with a beautiful woman; it was the same big-bellied creature with bony arms and legs, as well as a bovid face. Even if El Padre saw the monstrosity's true form, El Alcalde still ran his fingers lovingly across its fetid skin covered in plaques and pustules.

A loaded musket stood against a crate in the radiance of the fire's light; El Padre dived at it, grabbed it, then aimed it at the witch.

Before he pulled the trigger, the thing's talons stabbed at El Alcalde's midsection. Simultaneously, something came out of its mouth toward Don Manuel's face. He screamed out in pain and fell to the dirt.

A shot rang out as a smoke plume wafted.

The creature screeched. It bolted into the darkness with impossible speed. Gathered around, the soldiers finally came to their senses and equipped their weapons. Others cried out in confusion. Some aided El Alcalde.

The friar threw the musket aside and ran to help too; however, he heard (before he saw it) the whistling of an arrow through the air. One Spaniard, who helped Don Manuel, was struck in the neck. They fell to the ground and cried in agony.

A cloud of arrows sailed through the dark sky. Scabbled from stone, hundreds of arrowheads pierced through skin and clothing, or damaged whatever armor had been haphazardly donned in that night of revelry cut short. El Padre hunkered down in the dirt.

Without any orders, the soldiers began to shoot blindly into the night. Still, hails of missiles came down, including even large spears. Soldiers fell like flies. But hundreds more reloaded and shot into the darkness with exasperated yells.

After what seemed like an eternity of shots and missiles, Don Manuel had miraculously been animated. Raised by two men, he bellowed, "Bring the cannons to the centre! Fire outward toward the forest, away from the tents and the mountain!"

Artillerymen hauled the twelve-pounders toward the fires, loaded and packed them, whilst fuses were lit. A cacophonous battery thundered into the night. After the first few volleys, the missiles from the forests died away.

Padre Vivar looked up. Don Manuel, with a bloody hole where his right eye used to be, held the wound with his right palm; he also put pressure on where his left kidney once was. The friar pushed himself up, walked toward the man, and asked, "Are you grievously wounded?"

"Alive," El Alcalde replied.

When the friar rushed to the tent, the boy was gone.

Come morning, the dead had to be counted. The friar gave an extensive service for the dead, but there were too many to name, if their names were all even recorded. But there were still a handful of Spaniards and *mestizos* left, as well as at least sixteen hundred lowlanders. Don Manuel told the remaining that survived, "We march on Tonglo today, to avenge our fallen and send these *infieles* back to hell."

It took until noon to find the right path in the valley. The men were especially on edge, to the point that they often fired into the trees at any sudden movement of animal or wind alike.

Don Manuel's eye had been covered in an eyepatch and his kidney had been bandaged. He ordered with a wince: "Save your bullets for Tonglo."

As the mossy trees, vines, and long grass died off to a bare land of odd elevation, Padre Pedro pointed toward an ancient track.

"There," the friar said. "That's the way to Tonglo."

"Artillerymen, keep a loaded cannon up here. Spaniards, keep a vanguard ready to defend it," Don Manuel ordered.

The procession went forward, like pilgrims toward a city not of holiness, but of riches. This hidden path also meandered, until the town of Tonglo appeared in the distance; natives leaned against their wooden houses, brought around baskets of yams and the like, whilst some pushed carts full of precious metals, including gold.

When El Alcalde brought up his looking glass to his remaining eye, he exclaimed: "These people wear gold on their teeth. My, what riches they have."

"I failed to mention it," the friar admitted. "The upper-class families wear gold on their teeth."

"Try not to blow their heads off fully," Don Manuel told the artillerymen around the loaded cannon. "Get ready to fire."

The men positioned the cannon as to hit the houses first, but it was never an exact science on such an uneven field.

"Fire!"

The lit fuse hissed like a serpent and the explosion came, deafeningly. El Padre noticed a house cave in as it was struck. Shocked natives jumped to the ground; ululations rose through the air.

"Now we've caused some confusion," El Alcalde told his men. "Go in, shoot everyone, burn everything. Keep the gold!"

The artillerymen set up a cannonade. More barrages screamed, as Tonglo disintegrated into fire and rubble. Whatever warriors that met the Spanish on the field died via shot or blade. Eventually, corpses piled in the center as more destruction and death filled the air.

Despite the loudness of it, El Padre heard some thunderous sound behind them. When he turned, the friar saw the mountain send out a jet of steam.

"*Dios mio,*" he said to Don Manuel. "Point your looking glass toward the mountain. It's alive!"

El Alcalde gave a bemused look. Once he studied the mountain, the looking glass fell from his hands.

"What is it?" the friar asked.

There was no response.

El Padre grabbed the looking glass and directed it toward the steam. But it was no steam, he soon realized. There were green wraiths: translucent, demonic things with large eyes like tarsiers, as well as fangs that protruded from wide maws. They held great nets from distorted monkey paws.

These spirits, whatever they were, glided along a current of wind until they hovered over Tonglo in their thousands. In some ancient tongue that could never be transliterated, the demons sang a dirge. El Padre whispered a prayer to God, but he could not block out this terrible elegy.

It became obvious the nets were dragged along the air, as some more transparent spirits of blues and greens rose from Tonglo, albeit these were in the shape of men, women, and children. The demons were collectors—they harvested the souls of the dead.

Part III. The Ancestral Caves

The day died off slowly as darkness swallowed the world once more. Gales howled and gnawed at the two men's bones. El Padre's muscles and joints ached as they hiked for hours. Goatlike, Don Manuel led the way as he found sure footing with each step.

Above a cliff, El Alcalde spotted the mouth of a cave. He pointed at it to the friar. It took a while to get there, but they were both relieved to be safe from the elements. Once inside, the two sat in the dank shadows where no light lingered.

"What is this place?" Don Manuel asked. "Demons attack you in the night and catch souls in the day."

No one had said anything since the abandonment of the siege on Tonglo. El Padre decided not to answer; instead, he took off his rosary and went through the Lord's Prayer and Miseries.

"Still praying," El Alcalde groaned. "After all we've seen and heard. Priests are stupid like that."

Once the friar finished, he put the rosary around his neck. The darkness stared back at him, it seemed. He said, "I believe the Lord God will reveal Himself in our time of need."

"Don't bet on it," Don Manuel hissed. "All I got was a company of dead or routed men. And a priest who won't stop praying."

"Did you keep a flint at least?"

"Yes. I've some kindling. But not any fuel for a proper fire. Outside, the wood and bracken are too wet. Too cold."

"Light it."

"Why?"

"I want to see."

"Very well," El Alcalde said. "Some warmth will do us good."

It took a moment for the kindling to light, but eventually there was a small glow within the darkness. The two held their hands over the tiny fire and their spirits rose slightly.

But then El Padre looked around the cave and became more disheartened than before. There were men about them, but no ordinary men. Their tattooed skin was long dried over into a crude hide, their bones were visible through the flaked flesh, and their faces revealed centuries past.

"*Jesu*," the friar muttered. "We're in a tomb."

Don Manuel looked around, aghast; he wailed: "What have these *infieles* done to their dead?"

The mummies were propped up in tiny wooden coffins, contorted into little balls of flesh and bone. Whatever decomposition would have turned them into dust had been halted by practices of some ancient art passed down through millennia. The hollow sockets even seemed to stare at the two Spaniards with righteous indignation. Had the Spaniards disturbed their ancestral resting place?

The boy's voice rang through the darkness: "*Gayumko gimangaman; gayumko gimangaman. Gaya, gaya, maykaga.*"

However, there was nothing in sight except the two Spaniards, the mummies, and the darkness.

"This place is hell!" Don Manuel cried as he ran out.

El Padre followed him. As the lunate light slowly revealed itself from the passing of clouds, the two men found themselves stuck in the density of some vine-covered trees on the mountainside. Even as they ran through the community of trees, the boy's song pierced their ears. They ran and ran, until they were almost sent off the perilous cliff before they grabbed at the last branches.

"Damn this land!" Don Manuel cursed.

"We have to turn back," the friar said.

As they both turned, they saw the boy in the trees, his face illumined by the hoary moonlight. The song lilted, although his lips remained unmoving. Something held his small hand; it was a talon of chicken skin. El Padre grabbed his rosary and held it up at the boy as he commanded the demon to retreat in Latin with the Lord's Prayer and Hail Mary.

From the darkness, the pregnant witch came in Hydra-like form; its many heads resembled some abortion made through the pairing of centipede and snake. There were many tongues that slithered out of its many mouths, but these all resembled even tinier snake-centipede heads, ad infinitum.

Don Manuel, mad at the sight of the thing that took his eye, raced forward with sword held high. The witch shot its talon through his chest and took out the heart through bone, organ, and sinew. It devoured the still pulsing heart as it must have devoured his eye and kidney.

El Alcalde fell to the ground in a heap as lifeblood poured onto the ground and shimmered ever so slightly in this lunacy. The boy and the witch drew closer to El Padre, whose feet were on at the precipice of the cliff. When the friar held up his rosary at the witch, it responded in some unknown tongue of arcane origin. The boy's face briefly morphed into the leathery, preserved face of a cave mummy.

In that moment of terror, the witch shot a centipedal tongue at El Padre's face, but he was able to hold up his hand in defense; the rosary was spattered in blood and fell to the ground, as the friar stumbled backwards.

It took only a few steps until he fell off the cliff. El Padre descended through the air; his stomach caved in as he felt the plummet's force. In the crazed moonlight, bluish spirits circled the sky; they were the souls of men, women, and children, who flew through the winds in ethereal form.

The last thing El Padre saw was an azure phantasm: a ghastly spirit of a boy. It was *the* boy. This child spirit sang until the world fell into darkness.

Notes on Contributors

Dmitri Akers is a poet and writer from Adelaide, South Australia. His poetry has appeared within *So It Goes, La Piccioletta Barca,* and *Spectral Realms,* while his nonfiction has appeared in the *Modernist Review* and the Undergraduate Library. In 2020, he was Highly Commended by the Global Undergraduate Awards in the Literature category.

Manuel Arenas is a writer of verse and prose in the Gothic horror tradition. His work has appeared in various anthologies and journals including *Spectral Realms* and *Penumbra.* In 2021 he released his first collection of poetry and prose, *Book of Shadows: Grim Tales and Gothic Fancies,* from Jackanapes Press. He currently resides in Phoenix, Arizona, where he pens his dark ditties sheltered behind heavy curtains, as he shuns the oppressive orb which glares down on him from the cloudless, dust-filled sky.

Michael Aronovitz is a horror author, college professor, and rock critic. He is the author of such works as *Alice Walks, The Sculptor,* and *Dancing with Tombstones.* His newest novel, *The Winslow Sisters,* will be released in January 2024. He lives with his wife Kim and their son Max in Wynnewood, Pennsylvania.

Leigh Blackmore is a Rhysling and Australian Shadows Awards–nominated poet. His fantastic poetry has been widely published in magazines and anthologies. Representative samples can be found in *Spores from Sharnoth and Other Madnesses* (2008) and its variant spinoff, *Sharnoth's Spores and Other Seeds* (2010). A third weird verse collection, *Azathoth and Other Horrors by Edward Pickman Derby,* along with a weird fiction collection, *Nightmare Logic,* are forthcoming from IFGW Publishing Australia.

Garrett Boatman is the author of *Stage Fright* (originally published by Onyx [1988] and reissued by Valancourt Books in 2020), *Floaters: A Victorian Zombie Adventure* (Crystal Lake Publishing, 2021), and *Night's Plutonian Shore* (Crossroads Press, 2023). Garrett's stories have appeared in *The Valancourt Book of Horror Stories, Savage Realms, Penumbra,* and *Weird House Magazine* among others. He is an active member of the HWA and SFWA.

Deborah Bridle has a Ph.D. in English and teaches at Université Côte d'Azur, France. Her research focuses on fantastic literature, specifically on short fiction and the subgenres of the weird and supernatural horror. She is interested in the expression of philosophical views such as pessimism and nihilism in horror and weird fiction, and in the representations of mysticism and esotericism in Decadent fantastic literature. Her latest publications are devoted to Thomas Ligotti, China Miéville, and Arthur Machen.

Scott J. Couturier is a Rhysling Award–nominated poet and prose writer of the weird, liminal, and darkly fantastic. His work has appeared in numerous venues, including *The Audient Void, Spectral Realms, Tales from the Magician's Skull, Space and Time, Cosmic Horror Monthly,* and *Weirdbook.* His collection of weird fiction, *The Box,* is available from Hybrid Sequence Media, while his collection of autumnal and folk horror verse, *I Awaken in October,* is available from Jackanapes Press.

Harris Coverley has more than ninety short stories published or forthcoming in *Hypnos, Penumbric Speculative Fiction Magazine, JOURN-E,* and *The Black Beacon Book of Horror,* among many others. A Rhysling Award nominee, he has also had more than 200 poems published in journals around the world. He lives in Manchester, England.

Livia E. De Souza lives in Connecticut, where she writes horror and speculative fiction. Her short stories have appeared in *Literally Stories, Tales to Terrify,* and *Bewildering Stories.*

Wade German's most recent full-length poetry collection is *Psalms and Sorceries* (Hippocampus Press, 2022). His first collection, *Dreams from a Black Nebula,* is available from the same publisher. Other titles include four slim volumes of his selected poems with Portuguese translation: *Incantations, Apparitions, Phantasmagorias,* and *Chapel of Celluloid* (Raphus Press).

James Goho is a researcher and writer with many publications on dark fiction. In 2014, Rowman & Littlefield published his *Journeys into Darkness: Critical Essays on Gothic Horror.* McFarland published his *Caitlín R. Kiernan: A Critical Study of Her Dark Fiction* in 2020. His higher education research is found in academic journals, and his infrequent short stories appear in literary magazines. He lives in Winnipeg, Canada.

Maxwell I. Gold is an author of weird fiction and dark fantasy. His work has been published in *Spectral Realms, The Audient Void, Hinnom Magazine,* and elsewhere. His short story "A Credible Fear" will be published in the literary journal *The Offbeat* from Michigan State University's Department of Creative Writing and Rhetoric. He studied philosophy and political science at the University of Toledo and is an active member of the Horror Writers Association.

Norbert Góra is a poet and writer from Poland. Many of his horror, science fiction, and romance short stories have been published in his home country. He is also the author of many poems in English-language poetry anthologies around the world.

Ellen J. Greenham is a Lecturer in Career Learning at Murdoch University in Perth, Australia, previously teaching in English and Comparative Literature, History, Sociology, and comparative General Humanities. She is the author of *After Engulfment: Cosmicism and Neocosmicism in H. P. Lovecraft, Philip K. Dick, Robert A. Heinlein, and Frank Herbert*, published by Hippocampus Press in 2022, and several papers on Jim Morrison, neocosmic apocalypse, and American and Russian science fiction.

S. T. Joshi is a widely published literary and cultural critic and the author of *The Weird Tale* (1990), *I Am Providence: The Life and Times of H. P. Lovecraft* (2010), *Unutterable Horror: A History of Supernatural Fiction* (2012), and many other volumes. He has edited the work of H. P. Lovecraft, Ambrose Bierce, Lord Dunsany, H. L. Mencken, Leslie Stephen, and other writers.

Katherine Kerestman is the author of *Lethal* (PsychoToxin Press, 2023) and *Creepy Cat's Macabre Travels* (WordCrafts Press, 2020), and the coeditor (with S. T. Joshi) of *The Weird Cat*, an anthology of weird cat stories by writers living and dead (forthcoming from WordCrafts Press). Her Lovecraftian and Gothic works have been featured in *Black Wings VII, Penumbra, Journ-E, Spectral Realms, Illumen, Retro-Fan,* and *The Little Book of Cursed Dolls* (Media Macabre, 2023).

Marcos Legaria is a scholar of H. P. Lovecraft, R. H. Barlow, Clark Ashton Smith, and related writers. He is a member of the Esoteric Order of Dagon and a contributor to *William Hope Hodgson: Voices from the Borderland* (Hippocampus Press, 2014), the first full-length study devoted to the life and work of Hodgson. His articles have appeared in *Crypt of Cthulhu, Lovecraft Annual,* and *Spectral Realms.* His full-length study *L'Affaire Barlow: The Feud between R. H. Barlow and Derleth-Wandrei-Loveman over Lovecraft's Literary Executorship* is forthcoming.

Ngo Binh Anh Khoa is a teacher of English in Ho Chi Minh City, Vietnam. In his free time he enjoys daydreaming, reading, and occasionally writing poetry for personal entertainment. His speculative poems have appeared in NewMyths.com, *Heroic Fantasy Quarterly*, *The Audient Void*, and other venues.

Duncan Norris is a native of Australia. He has written on numerous unusual topics, many of which concern the work of horror icon H. P. Lovecraft, and enjoys both literary and physical archaeology, having done both in his experiences with excavation of atypical—a.k.a. vampire—burials in Poland.

K. A. Opperman is a poet with a predilection for the strange, the Gothic, and the grotesque, continuing the macabre and fantastical tradition of such luminaries as Poe, Clark Ashton Smith, and H. P. Lovecraft. He has published four poetry collections to date: *The Crimson Tome*, *Past the Glad and Sunlit Season*, *October Ghosts and Autumn Dreams*, and *The Laughter of Ghouls*.

Joe Pan is the author of six books. His work has appeared in such venues as the *Boston Review*, *Bowery Gothic*, *Columbia Review*, *Denver Quarterly*, *Fuck You Next*, the *New York Times*, and the *Philadelphia Review of Books*.

Carl E. Reed is currently employed as a call center agent at a retail fixtures company just outside Chicago. Former jobs include: U.S. Marine, long-haul trucker, stage actor, cab driver, construction worker, and door-to-door encyclopedia salesman. His poetry has been published in *The Iconoclast*, *Spectral Realms*, *Black Petals*, and *Deathlehem: Holiday Horrors*; short stories in *Black Gate*, *newWitch*, *Sci-Fi Lampoon*, *Penumbra*, *Eldritch Tales*, and elsewhere. A collection of his short stories and poetry, *Dark Matter*, will be released by Hippocampus Press in early 2024.

Geoffrey Reiter is Associate Professor and Coordinator of Literature at Lancaster Bible College. He is also an Associate Editor at the website *Christ and Pop Culture*, where he frequently writes about weird horror and dark fantasy. As a scholar of weird fiction, Reiter has published academic articles on such authors as Arthur Machen, Bram Stoker, Clark Ashton Smith, and William Peter Blatty. His poetry has previously appeared in *Spectral Realms* and *Star*Line,* and his fiction has appeared in *Penumbra* and *The Mythic Circle.*

David Rose is an avid fan and reader of weird fiction. Along with being a self-proclaimed Brian McNaughton scholar, he is the author of such works as *Lovecraft's Iraq* and *The Scrolls of Sin.* His newest release is the collection *Forsaken, Fantastic!: Tales of the Future.* He lives in Orlando, Florida.

Ann K. Schwader lives and writes in Colorado. Her newest collection, Unquiet Stars, is now out from Weird House Press. Two of her earlier collections, *Wild Hunt of the Stars* (Sam's Dot, 2010) and *Dark Energies* (P'rea Press, 2015), were Bram Stoker Award Finalists. In 2018, she received the Science Fiction and Fantasy Poetry Association's Grand Master award. She is also a two-time Rhysling Award winner.

John Shirley is the winner of the Bram Stoker Award for his story collection *Black Butterflies: A Flock on the Dark Side.* He has been guest of honor at the World Horror Convention and a special guest at H. P. Lovecraft Film Festival. His novels include *Demons, Cellars, Wetbones,* and *Stormland.* His new story collection is *The Feverish Stars.* His first collection of weird poetry, *The Voice of the Burning House,* has been nominated for an Elgin Award.

Oliver Smith is a visual artist and writer from Cheltenham, England. His poetry has appeared in *Abyss & Apex, Ink, Sweat, and Tears, Strange Horizons, Spectral Realms,* and *Sylvia Magazine,* and has twice been nominated for the Pushcart Prize. He holds a Ph.D. in Literary and Critical Studies from the University of Gloucestershire.

Arthur Staaz is the alter ego of a retired government lawyer and writer, a spelunker of nightmares and collector of hallucinations. His publishing credits include *Pseudopod, Morpheus Tales, Tales to Terrify,* the *Coachella Review,* and several others. He is currently in exile from reality, having recently exchanged the dark woods and empty-windowed farmhouses of New England for the fairy-haunted hills and glens of Ireland, in all their terrible beauty.

John C. Tibbetts is Professor Emeritus at the University of Kansas in Film and Media Studies. His books include *The Furies of Marjorie Bowen* (McFarland, 2019), *The Gothic Worlds of Peter Straub* (McFarland, 2016), *Those Who Made It: Conversations with the Legends of Hollywood* (Palgrave Macmillan, 2015), *Peter Weir: Interviews* (University of Mississippi Press, 2014), and *The Gothic Imagination* (Palgrave Macmillan, 2012). He was awarded in 2008 the Kansas Governor's Arts in Education Award, presented by Governor Kathleen Sebelius.

DJ Tyrer is the person behind Atlantean Publishing and has been published in *The Rhysling Anthology,* issues of *Cyäegha, The Horrorzine, Scifaikuest, Sirens Call, Star*Line, Tigershark,* and *The Yellow Zine.* The e-chapbook *One Vision* is available from Tigershark Publishing. *SuperTrump* and *A Wuhan Whodunnit* are available for download from Atlantean Publishing.

Steven Withrow's poems appear in *Spectral Realms, Asimov's Science Fiction,* and *Dreams & Nightmares.* His poem "The Sun Ships," from an Elgin Award–nominated collection of the same title, was nominated for a 2016 Rhysling Award. His most recent solo collection is *The Bedlam Philharmonic.* His collection with Frank Coffman, *The Exorcised Lyric,* contains "Toward Solstice Station," a nominee for the 2022 Rhysling Award. His newest chapbook is titled *The Nothing Box.* He lives on Cape Cod.